The

Cul-lud Sch-oool Teach-ur

Also by Sandra E. Bowen

THIS DAY'S MADNESS

The

Cul-lud Sch-oool Teach-ur

SANDRA E. BOWEN

iUniverse, Inc.
New York   Bloomington

The Cul-lud Sch-oool Teach-ur

iUniverse books may be ordered through booksellers or by contacting:

iUniverse
1663 Liberty Drive
Bloomington, IN 47403
www.iuniverse.com
1-800-Authors (1-800-288-4677)

ISBN: 978-1-4502-3304-0 (pbk)
ISBN: 978-1-4502-3305-7 (ebk)

Printed in the United States of America

iUniverse rev. date: 6/2/2010

Acknowledgments

I am grateful to my agent, Dr. James Schiavone, for his patience and persistence.

Thank you Cozette Lagway, former ASU colleague, for your assistance with technical computer problems, typing, and checking MS form.

I shall never forget Dr. V. P. Franklin, Social Historian; Jeanne Hudgens, Educator; and Janice Montana, Philanthropist, Virtuosa; for reading the draft and making comments and suggestions.

Shirley Curtis, former ASU colleague and editor, thank you for your suggestions during the first stages of my writing, in addition to your recommendations regarding chapter headings.

To SciFi writer Terry Smith, thank you for your technical and psychological support during computer crises. In addition, my gratitude to you for assistance in preparing and submitting this manuscript for its second printing.

THE CUL-LUD SCH-OOOL TEACH-UR is strictly a work of fiction and does not represent African American life. Any resemblance whatsoever to persons or events is purely coincidental. For the sake of reality, the author placed the mythical city Granston geographically near actual cities and cited existing institutions. In order to enhance reality, the author referred to titles of books and authors, in addition to the names of selected celebrities.

NOTE: The terms colored and Negro are used as they were during relevant time periods.

To my Goddaughters:
Cassandra Lewis
Dina Lewis
Aleta Lewis

And in memory of my aunts:

Sarah Abigail "Abbie" Bowen Williams Smith

and

Mary Ellen Lewis Jones

Prologue

There was a time when colored school teachers were revered by practically everybody in their southern communities, white and colored. That day extended from its post-slavery beginning to World War I, for a period afterwards, certainly to World War II, and is said to exist in some remote places today. These respected mentors were predominantly female and taught in public elementary schools where the bulk of southern colored school attendance was concentrated. Traditionally these women were CCC– the "cream of the colored community," their character without public flaws; dedication to the classroom their faith and religion. They were choice ladies sought after and targeted maritally by a coterie of colored men, many who had not completed the elementary grades, and were low wage earners, whose "thang" was to marry one of these women distinguished by their roll books and having principals as immediate bosses. Most of these men were decent, and some loved the women who would elevate them to statures they would never attain otherwise.

As this trend continued, driving new or nice cars, well-dressed, a look of pride on their faces, and informing people "My wife she teach at Booker T. Washington Elementary School" or "My best friend he married a woman who teach at George Washington Carver School" defined who these men were. The distinction gave them prestige in the colored community and a modicum of respect from white filling station workers, bill collectors, and even bank tellers, who remarked, "Hey there, Boy. Heard you mar'red a tea-chur," and "How's that school tea-chur wife of your'n?"

Colored mothers were often accused of raising their daughters and loving their sons unconditionally. Families educated their daughters, the primary aim being to prevent their "working in white folks' kitchens." Men could always "work with their hands and make a living." Some of the men said the women "thank they better'n us." The irony of it, so did the men, which was the main reason they sought out these women. Despite dreams to marry them, a number of these husbands used and abused their wives, bossed and boasted, complained and complied, ridiculed their wives' bourgeois attitudes, and criticized them if they were lacking. These up-to-date women lied, supported their men, and endured.

Sporadically doctors, lawyers, educated preachers pastoring big churches, and undertakers married "light-skinned teachers with good hair." Teachers were victims of the traditional double standards, but, in addition, whatever white women suffer is squared with Negro women. The darker they were and the kinkier their hair, the more difficulty they had getting husbands, even uneducated low-wage workers. Men, no matter how dark, no matter that they had "cockleburs" for hair, were acceptable and were the most adamant critics of dark skinned women. Their rationalization about themselves was always "I'm a man." Dorothy Borden, daughter of Granston, North Carolina's first colored lawyer, who became a teacher during the mid 1940's and had observed earlier victims who taught her, recalled a college campus joke that black-skinned boys took seriously: They would ask, "What's any better than a pretty brown-skinned girl?" Their reply: "A knock-kneed, cock-eyed, snaggle tooth *yellow* one." Thus the standard of acceptance. This trend did not begin to diminish until the 1960's when the "Black Power" Civil Rights Movement popularized "Black Is Beautiful."

Engrossed in egotistical desirability, their availability, and knowledge that school mistresses had to settle for one of them or become old maids, (the term was still used in Granston), and the deep-rooted belief that marriage was the absolute remedy for all women's ills, teacher-possessed men were unsuspecting of anything foul. Besides, society pressured women into lifelong legal mating.

However, there was a silent and secret less than one percent of schoolmarms who took a different type advantage of the teacher-craze so apparent among the men. Helping to make up this minuscule unit was Johnnye Jamison. No one in Granston knew very much about Johnnye Jamison; that is, what they would relish knowing.

CHAPTER 1
Johnnye Jamison Appears in Granston

Johnnye Jamison appeared in Granston in September during the late 1940s, when the white Superintendent began summoning "his" colored elementary teachers for their meetings. She sat quietly chewing gum in the assembly of appointees, old and new, assigned to Booker T. Washington Elementary School. During the introductions, the teaching population, mostly female, ninety-nine per cent of them "dressed to kill", looking as if they stepped out of *Vogue,* attired in the first meeting finery, suddenly focused roving eyes on the new appointee. She sounded different, unlike one of them. And she was chewing gum slowly, picturesquely. The Superintendent's eyes were fixed on her also while she gave them what sounded like pertinent data they should know and not forget.

"I'm Johnnye Jamison. *Miss* Jamison." She paused after the announcement. Mr. Superintendent wanted to tell her to go on, but didn't. Before continuing, Miss Jamison inhaled and exhaled, as if her listeners needed time to deal with whom she was. "I'm from Shelby, Pennsylvania, a small–city–not far from Darby, and attended Shelby Community College before going to Columbia University, where I received a B.S. degree in Elementary Education.

1

And graduated with honor." Another Johnnye Jamison lull, "My assignment and Home Room are Third Grade, Section 2."

Johnnye gave this information in an affected northern brogue without a complete smile, just a pleasant impish look, impish in spite of her five feet nine inch, 150 pound body, which certainly did not appear that large. She sat down and continued to chew gum with dignity and defiance Granston teachers could not help but envy, even though they wouldn't dare chew gum in public, especially in the presence of the white superintendent. Chewing gum publicly was a major offense.

Firmly believing all Negroes liked to laugh, and because he could amuse himself, as well as white teachers and friends with the anecdotes, the white Superintendent required each teacher to include in the introduction something humorous or unusual about him or herself, if new, and something funny that happened during the summer if returning. Without his suspecting, the teachers laughed among themselves as they prepared anecdotes to amuse and often to ridicule their boss and the system. Johnnie Jamison had not.

The Superintendent addressed all his colored teachers by their given or nick names. He hesitated to be that informal with Johnnye Jamison. He adorned his colored-teacher smile and refused to recognize she had a name: "Tell us somethin' humorous about yo'sef. Somethin' to make us laff at you. Nothin' helps folks to know each other like somethin' funny." He let them know this was colored-fun time, and he could "git on they level and talk lack them."

The impish smile left Johnnye's face. She looked him in the face and shifted her chewing gum in order to speak clearly. "I came to Granston to teach, not to be a buffoon."

The white superintendent turned red. His teacher population nudged each other nervously. He avoided Johnnye thereafter by asking for volunteers. Nobody knew when or why, but jokes disappeared from his agenda.

Johnnye Jamison, head so high that she appeared to be looking upward, shoulders erect, chewing gum defiantly, left the school meeting as curious colleagues watched her get into the small used but shining car she had driven to Granston. The few men stared at her in disbelief mixed with admiration. A lively discussion broke out: Didn't she know that colored teachers in Granston, especially women, didn't drive or own cars! She's liable to get fired! Worse than that, colored and white teachers' salaries would never be equalized because the City and County would think coloreds were making too much money. –And they would never get a City or County bonus like white teachers. Above all, she had the *nerve* to say what she did to the Superintendent about her not being a buffoon! She better watch her step. The least little thing she does could get her fired! The women added that Johnnye had not talked to them before the meeting or after, and only smiled when they spoke to her.

Away from the superintendent, and the men, the female clique fell into their relaxed vernacular.

"She coulda at least offer somebody a ride. Two or three more can fit in that car."

"Wonder if she can teach. We don't want folks from around here ruining our reputation. Let-lone somebody from up North."

"Oughta be able to teach. From Pennsylvania. And a degree from *Columbia!* With honor too!"

"Heard where she lives?" A whisper drew them closer.

"Girl–I heard–"

"I didn't. Tell me–"

They gathered closer and whispered lower.

"She's staying with that woman folks say is 'funny.' Nobody who thinks anything of themselves'll stay there."

"She's new. Maybe she didn't know."

"She must be 'one of those thangs', and somebody sent her there. I'm gonna keep my distance. Glad she didn't ask me to ride."

"Me too. Folks'll put us in her class."

The assemblage watched Johnnye drive away. Then stared after the car disappeared.

CHAPTER 2

Johnnye Jamison's Record

Johnnye's academic record revealed that her name was once Sadie Mae Johnson, and she was twenty-three years old. She listed an aunt, Ruby Johnson, Shelby, Pennsylvania, as next of kin and to be notified in case of emergency, no home or work telephone. Later, based on rumors stemming from Johnnye's personnel record, colored folks continued to whisper.

"Folks saying that new teacher from Pennsylvania who came here talking so proper with her hind parts on her shoulder and chewing gum even in meetings with the Superintendent is a widow. It's on her record in both the Superintendent's and Principal's offices."

"A dead husband young as she is? Who said so?"

"Dee."

"Dee who?"

"De niggers."

And they laughed at their private joke.

"Did Dee see it?"

"Said they did. You know Dee can find out what's on just about any colored folks' records. Even hospital and doctors' files."

"Why is she–what's her name? –Jamison–keeping it secret?"

"It's no secret if it's on her application."

CHAPTER 3

Why Johnnye Jamison Came to Granston

Johnnye's record did not include her having taken a nursing course and meeting a fascinating experimental medical researcher. The two women were drawn to each other immediately, recognizing in each a rare and mysterious complement. She teamed up with this new companion, who called her Johnnye instead of Sadie Mae in such a way that she changed it on her records. This friend confided in Johnnye a "really master-plan" and emphasized that it would materialize successfully only if their affiliation remained a secret. No one should ever know if the friend is male or female, white or colored, old or young. If their association is even suspected, it must be vehemently denied and proven false. When away, Johnnye must think of this person only as The Associate in order to guard against a name or identity slip. "Call me TA if you like," The Associate suggested. Success in their venture depended totally on two factors: *The secrecy of their association and that the South still had uneducated colored men anxious to marry teachers and paid homage to them in spite of the WWII Bill that provided college tuition for many of these men.*

Johnnye smiled to herself, wondering if she had given off vibes that hinted she had a secret—and pondered over telling about the bit by bit rat poison she had put in her husband David Jamison's food and liquor, which is the reason she had him cremated. There was something entrancing about having power over life and death and watching yourself use that power. Maybe she'd tell TA later.

Johnnye was intrigued with what she learned from her alliance with TA, much of it sexual, far too "sophisticated" for most colored people and certainly for Granston; that is, "not a part of their sexual experiences" according to The Associate. Johnnye also became enlightened about and fascinated with scientific experiments. Disappearing at intervals, The Associate returned with stories shared with Johnnye after their sexual capers. TA told of transplanting cancer cells, some that "took" and some that did not, of drugs that produced heart attacks and strokes and drugs that affected the liver instantaneously or over a period of time. There were compounds that depressed the immune system as well as those that enhanced it. Everybody had potential invaders that the immune system controlled. When the system ceased to function properly, hidden health enemies, lying dormant, would take over, whether genetic or by transmission. And there were mind-altering medicaments, unlike anything the public knew about. Johnnye's friend breathed in her ear. "I've seen experiments that make Nazi Germany look tame and incipient." Johnnye envisioned scientists involved in all kinds of exciting provocative adventures.

The Associate prepared Johnnye for Granston and assured her their monetary profit would be abundant. "It's an investment. Just as white people buy stocks, bonds, shares, and real estate."

Observing Johnnye closely, TA continued. "You don't have to send for an application. I have some. Just fill one out and send it at once. They need elementary teachers."

"How do you know they'll hire me?" Johnnye asked.

"I don't know one hundred percent, but I know somebody there who'll give recommendations. List that name first under references. –And you're from the North. They like to hire new blood."

"Suppose it doesn't work out?"

"Oh, I'll get you in North Carolina somewhere."

"Why North Carolina?" Johnnye wanted to know.

"They pay colored teachers more than in other Southern states. And white folks a little less 'rebbish'. I keep up with the lynchings and all... Don't waste time. Colored men are using the GI Bill and going to college."

Johnnye, an excellent listener, absorbed additional advice: Marry as soon as feasible. But let the man do the pursuing. Johnnye must not be obvious, but always alert to the man most vulnerable. If he has a drinking problem, or any non-communicable disorder, good. *Plan.* Be ever prepared. After the death of the first Granston husband, and a respectable interlude, Johnnye must marry again and remain with this one longer than the first. When each husband becomes ill, she must care for him, especially during the beginning. The more care, the quicker his demise. During the "care" was the time to under medicate, or over medicate, or use placebos—and add immune depressing drugs to his food. The Associate would supply all necessities and set up meeting places and time. No contact via mail. Before the illness, to avoid suspicion, Johnnye must be especially devoted. Putting everybody at ease is conducive to success. Johnnye was ecstatic over the prospects of such an escapade. And for money!

"Oh yes," TA continued, "an important warning. Occasionally there is a man who'll take girls for rides and end up in the country, woods, or a cemetery and threaten to put them out of the car if they don't get in the back seat. You know what that means. Men who do that just *love* taking girls to old graveyards. Don't think these bozos won't put you out and leave you. They will! They like to try this on teachers since they'll be too embarrassed to report it—and scared of losing their jobs."

Johnnye exhaled in disgust.

"Don't worry. I'll prepare you for that. First, I'm going to teach you to drive, and if a bastard tries it, you'll drive yourself home—or to one of the women I want you to know. Remind me to give you their names and addresses. You can trust them—you could stay with them. Since you'll be after–well–men, you might not want to. Folk'll talk about you, and men'll stay away. If you leave, the ladies'll understand and still be your friends. Who you think is your friend can't always be trusted. –Don't want folks to call you 'hincty.' In Granston that means stuck-up–snobbish. Be friendly, but not too friendly. Folks scramble for city school jobs, and folks'll do you in for them. Some are like buzzards. They read obituaries to see if a teacher died. Colored teachers are just beginning to retire instead of dying on the job–Anyway, you'll have somewhere to go if a man plays his dirty tricks on you. Even put *him* out if you want to. You'll be in control. Remember— *Always be in control.* Don't *talk* about how you can take care of yourself. Makes you sound callous. Always be a lady."

"You mean put the man out of *his* car?"

"Yes. –You can use the needle. A shot that'll knock 'im' out. Or use the spray you'll carry in your purse like it's perfume. Does a real job on eyes. And handcuff' 'im. We even have that special tape to put over his mouth–the kind that Murder, Inc. used. Or get out the car and do judo or wrestling. We have a special instructor, but I'm just as good–almost. And you can beat the hell out of whoever needs it with brass knuckles that you can wear under gloves when going out with someone who acts suspicious. You'll be able to take on anybody–even somebody with a gun."

Johnnye was livid. "I'd like to kill the son-of-a-bitch who tries to pull a dirty trick on me."

"And I'd highly recommend it, but you'll drive *his* car back, and everything points to you. Times are changing. Colored women used to be able to kill colored men and get away with it. Can't take that chance, especially when you don't have to."

"What do you recommend?" Johnnye controlled her fury.

"Depends. Brass knuckles make a lotta blood. Got to be close up to use the needle, and you may not be able to get to it. *Judo.* Get out of the car and pretend to run. *Judo.* Nobody expects you to know it. And I'll teach you how to yank and twist his dick and send 'im into convulsions. But don't—unless you just have to. You want folks to be on your side. Even women seem to find it over killing."

"You are really serious."

TA nodded her head slowly. "I know a girl who had to get in the back seat because she couldn't defend herself. —Begged the man not to. Told him she was saving herself for a husband."

"What happened to her?"

"She left that night and never taught school again."

"What happened to the man?"

"Somewhere still proud of his 'manhood'."

"What about the girl?" Johnnye asked.

The Associate appeared not to hear. Johnnye asked again. Still no answer. They both were silent for a while.

"Don't start thinking about all the crap men do and throw your weight around." The Associate advised after the respite. "Be a 'nice' girl, and a weight-throwing bitch only when necessary."

During the Granston preparation, it was needless to tell Johnnye that having a child was definitely a no-no, but she was counseled. Should it happen, all connections with The Associate would terminate. Johnnye would have access to a competent gynecologist in Richmond. Since he's part of The Association, there will be no financial obligations.

"Soon as you 'miss'—I mean if you're a *day* late, start planning a trip to Richmond. Don't *ever* wait more than a week. I'll give you a telephone number. It won't be the doctor's, but the lady who answers will know what you want soon as you say, 'I just called to say hello and to keep in touch. Tell Aunt Mary'—everybody has an Aunt Mary—'I won't see her this weekend.' That means you *will* be in Richmond to see the doctor."

"How will I know where to go?" Johnnye asked.

"Oh, Uncle or Aunt somebody'll meet you. —Three strikes and you're out. That's the doctor's rule. —You'll be coming to Richmond weekends. We'll meet there."

"Our trysting place," Johnnye smiled.

"Yeap. Except when you see the doctor. You can drive there early Saturday or Sunday morning," TA continued to explain, "and go back to Granston the same day, or spend the night. Or I can meet you and drive you back."

"How will you get back to Richmond?" Johnnye asked, knowing The Associate had to disappear soon as possible.

"Get a taxi or an airport car to Greensboro or Winston-Salem and take a plane."

There was more. "Get a dog," The Associate suggested. "People see you buying dog food and hearing you talk about your dog or cat makes them think maybe you're not such a bad person. Some of' them will. And it'll keep you from wanting a baby. A small dog. Easier to get to a kennel and somebody will keep it in an emergency."

Johnnye liked animals and was too intelligent to become involved with anything as intrusive as a child of her own, she assured the advisor, telling her, "I've got more sense than let a low-income man pump me up and bring another something like him into the world for me to take care of, call me Mama and end up with a Nigger-job, or in jail, or trying to marry somebody like me."

"You'll do all right in Granston," The Associate assured her, but also knew she had to tell Johnnye more, especially how intrusive the white superintendent was in the private lives of "his colored teachers." Perhaps white ones, too, but that was kept secret. The community and principals played roles in usurpation also, especially regarding "their" female teachers' sex lives.

"Johnnye, the Association sent their first 'Representative' to Granston in the 30's." TA paused, then continued. "A married teacher had a miscarriage. It wasn't a secret. She took sick leave. Somebody told the Superintendent the woman had an abortion. The family doctor's name is listed on all applications, so Mr. Super called him…"

"What!" Johnnye interrupted.

"You haven't heard nothing yet. The doctor said he didn't

know his patient was pregnant, so Mr. Super sent for the woman and her husband and demanded to know *why* she and her husband had not seen their family doctor–"

Johnnye didn't want to believe what she was hearing. "If he did something like that to me, I'd catch him out by himself one night and give him one of the Treatments you're going to teach me."

"Nothing like that'll happen to you. Wait 'til you hear the rest."

Johnnye chewed gum angrily as she listened to the rest of the story:

A woman with inhibitions, the victim had to tearfully tell the Superintendent that she had irregular monthly periods, her doctor could verify, and neither she nor her husband knew she was pregnant. After much interrogation, the distraught couple convinced their superior no abortion had taken place, thus saving their jobs–and legal indictment. Some of her colleagues whispered that they knew the woman had an abortion and her family doctor knew, and that the grapevine had informed the Superintendent.

"Who's the grapevine?" Johnnye asked.

"Another teacher trying to ingratiate him or herself to the Superintendent. Get on his good side so he won't fire them when firing time comes. Had the woman and her husband lost their jobs, there would have been two slots–maybe for members of the informant's family."

"The more I hear, the more something tells me not go to Granston," Johnnye said, not because she was scared, but out of rage.

"Granston is America." The Associate was unruffled. "Even with all that's wrong, it is still the best place in the world."

Johnnye was silent, but The Associate continued. "A lot of Superintendents encourage tattling, and even call teachers in on a basis of anonymous calls and letters. Sometimes the informer uses parents as carrier pigeons." TA returned to her story. "Since colored teachers don't get maternity leave, they try to get pregnant

11

in early October or November, work until March or April, have the baby in June or July, and return to work in September. That woman's pregnancy was not on schedule."

Johnnye closed her eyes and breathed deeply with disgust.

"You'll be O.K.," The Associate was confident. "Just don't think because it's the 1940's, Granston is a 1940 big city. It's like every other place, small or large. Knowing the past helps you know what to expect. You can be prepared and in control."

In addition to intrusion, Johnnye was reminded of another negative about having children. There was no decent baby nursery for colored, which means she would have to hire someone to come to her house or take the baby to someone who kept children. Both were almost always undesirable.

"Colored people don't want to work for colored people. And most won't."

"That's what everybody says," Johnnye admitted.

"Employees and employers criticize and complain. Employees say colored teachers want to be treated like they're white and refuse to give services reserved for whites and even charge colored teachers more. The workers don't want to take Negro babies out for walks unless they are light-skinned. They can put caps on' em and hide their hair." The Associate laughed.

"I don't think it's funny," but Johnnye smiled anyway.

"Teachers say the workers make colored children stay inside and play quietly with something that won't make a mess. And workers eat and drink the children's food and fruit juice. –You know some colored women carry on over white children. They don't with colored ones, specially if they're dark with bad hair."

"Bet the ones who are so prejudiced are black and nappy headed themselves." Johnnye said.

"You know they are. Yellow folks don't dare act like that even if they want to."

The Associate informed further. "Some of the workers talk about it in hairdressing parlors. 'I ain't gonna take that black nappy headed young-un no where. One even called me by my name. Like they white. Told' em to put a handle on my name. Have' em thinkin' they good as white folks just 'cause they mammies teach.'" The Associate mimicked.

Colored teachers resented being "given the colored treatment." They heard all about it in hairdressing parlors, and even men talked about it in barber shops. Workers aired white babies daily unless the weather was inclement, did the children's laundry, and cleaned the house while their charges napped, and prepared dinner for "their white folks." It was not unusual for employees to wash dinner dishes and put children to bed before leaving. As for care in private homes, often a child was there with a cold or a childhood disease. Most working mothers could not afford to stay home with sick children.

Johnnye learned of other intrusions by the Superintendent and community. "But don't act scared or nervous. That makes you look guilty. Just be careful." The Associate cautioned and continued with advice regarding functioning in the school system day-to-day. "Join a church. A large one that Big Shots attend. Members too busy being Big Shots to bother you. They don't have a lotta problems with their children. If they do, they settle them. Little churches like to get into your business. Members invite teachers to visit and to Sunday dinner. If possible, refuse. *Politely*. And principals are big on the PTA. It gets the community on their side, and helps them keep their jobs. Attend. They don't meet often. Don't walk out. Sometimes they're too long. If you just have to leave, fake a cold. Start coughing and do it a while before leaving. –And suggest that parents hold as many PTA offices as possible. Saves you work. And makes parents feel important."

The Associate advised Johnnye to avoid confrontation with parents. "They can be deadly. Give their urchins benefit of the doubt. Tell parents of the really dumb ones –*never* use the word dumb no matter how dumb they are – that their children are still internalizing, and once they begin to externalize, they will become A and B students. Parents won't know what you're talking about, but it sounds good and will shut them up. In event they do know, smile, agree with them, and let them do the talking. Another escape or tactic is to steer the conversation to the child's good points. Have some stock answers. If at all possible, pass each student to the next grade. Social promotion is O.K . –in extreme cases. However, *teach*. If you are a fraud, *everybody* will know, including your students, even the stupid ones. More important, never forget we cul-lud, as they call us, teachers supposed to be superb. Remember, classes are monitored, observed, and evaluated. There are 'prescription lessons' to follow–no, to honor. See that your Lesson Plans are written accordingly, even if you want to re-teach, something a good teacher should not have to do according to the system. Never mind each child learns at a different pace, or the class just did not get it that day. Since most colored teachers ignore no re-teaching, pace your classes so that there is time for re-teaching and intensive review. Remember, students are questioned overtly and covertly, even by your colleagues."

Johnnye had a receptive memory, organized, rarely if ever clogged. While automatic categorizing took place, she listened for more.

The Associate told Johnnye slowly, "Remember elementary school teachers are hallowed. Don't let anything interfere with that concept when it comes to our classroom."

"Anything else?" Johnnye asked.

"Oh, yes," T.A. smiled. "Maybe most important of all. *Wear tasteful clothes.* Please–no plunging necklines, bustles, tight skirts, and spike heels like some, especially the ones less respected as good teachers. They try to compensate for being inadequate. Don't be frumpish either like white teachers. Poorly dressed colored women are not liked or respected as much as well-dressed women, in both the Negro and white communities. And–colored men are drawn to women who wear pretty clothes. You don't have to buy the most expensive things in Granston or wherever you shop, but stay away from cheap stores. Don't be caught looking in the windows. Where you shop enhances your reputation. Observe well-dressed conservative colleagues. Save your daring outfits for very private parties."

The impish smile returned to Johnnye's face and she listened for the final instruction.

"Last, but certainly not least. Pay your bills!"

CHAPTER 4

Johnnye's Agenda

Johnnye Jamison had arrived in Granston with her agenda, a docket disguised by her impish almost smile–and her northern brogue that commanded awe and veneration in the small southern town of Granston, North Carolina. Her disdain for children was secreted within layers and folds of shrouded arrogance, knowing that she possessed a command of subject matter and superior teaching skills, qualities that educators, who wrote books but did not teach, never had, nor ever would. She called them her "Hallmark of a Master Teacher." She had even more: conceit enough to employ her skills and make them viable, in addition to absolute certainty of her success.

After painting her portrait and seeing that students, principal, colleagues, and the community mounted it for all to admire, and for some to idolize, Johnnye made a mental list of all single uneducated men in Granston with acceptable incomes–who had not served time in jail. Her primary focus was John Henry Woodard. He was quiet, didn't have a family in Granston, and only a few close friends who were "on his level." He worked steadily and had a "good paying job" in a local mill. Johnnye discreetly stalked John Henry, and discovered where he shopped for food and where he took his clothes to be laundered and cleaned. She even knew where he had his shoes repaired. –And that he cashed his checks at the tiny Bank of Granston Colored Branch and had money saved there because she saw him standing in the savings account line.

Seeing John Henry was shy, Johnnye timidly initiated a conversation with him in the Super Market one Saturday morning. Her face glowing with concern, in her most pleasant Northern brogue, Johnnye cautioned him concerning selecting a container of milk without checking the expiration date.

"They put the oldest food in stores where we shop. They even change dates, especially on meats because they can stick another date on top of the old ones," she whispered. – "Oh, by the way, my name's Johnnye Jamison. I teach at Booker T. Washington Elementary School."

John Henry blushed and told her his name and thanked her for telling him about dates on food packages. He had never noticed.

"Mr. Woodard," Johnnye beamed benevolence, "I don't come here often. I go to a cleaner and larger market on the other side of town in a white neighborhood."

To his timid, "Do they act like they want to wait on colored people?" Johnnye assured him they did, and if they didn't, she would report them to the NAACP. And the next shopping day, she would come by his house and take him to the white A & P, or he could follow in his car.

She lowered her voice to a seductive whisper, "We Negroes should stick together. I'll help you select nice fresh bargains instead of the old stuff they have in stores where a lotta colored people shop."

John Henry smiled shyly and accepted.

The next Saturday morning in the cleaner and larger Market, John Henry in awe asked Johnnye if she drank. Even socially. Johnnye looked at him in astonishment, and lied, "No!"

Embarrassed, John Henry confessed in his slow monotone, "I might as well tell you 'cause somebody else will. I drink too much, but cuttin' down. I use to drive to South Carolina and Virginia to get sealed whiskey. They wet states. I try not drink that bad homemade stuff called 'white lightin'.'"

He waited for Johnnye to say she couldn't have anything to do with him, being a teacher, before adding. "I'm not rioty or noisy and don't use cuss words and never drive when I drink too much. Just go to sleep. And drinkin' never make me stay off my job. Never miss a day except the time I had pneumonia."

Johnnye knew all of that, but told him, "All that's past. You'll stop. I'll help you. If not, I'll take you to AA."

"I heard about AA, but too 'shame to go. One's in Greensboro and Winston-Salem. I tell myself I'll stop." He added bashfully, "It's past time for me to marry, and I got to get myself straight so a decent girl'll want me, and I won't be too shameface-ded to ax her to be my wife."

Johnnye selected a large beautiful T bone steak and a box of frozen lobsters and placed them in his cart. After they got to the check-out counter and he paid for them, she would exclaim, "Oh! I meant to put them in *my* basket." Of course he should not accept reimbursement. This was a test.

About his getting a wife, Johnnye assured John Henry, "You won't have a problem getting a nice girl, and flashed him a fully prepared smile.

"Hope you're right. I'm in my thirties, and it's pass time to settle down, save money, and buy a home—And join a church."

New information to Johnnye. As they waited in line, she smiled at John Henry. She knew they would become John and Johnnye—very soon.

God must be in on this, thought John Henry as he returned her smile. Their names even sounded alike, John and Johnnye. He would certainly join a church. Maybe hers.

CHAPTER 5

Johnnye and John Wed

Teachers were expected to "room" with reputable families and often share the accommodations with roommates, especially female teachers. Johnnye was among the first to live alone in one of the small two-family apartments white realtors began building especially for Negro teachers. Since the housing was constructed by white companies, criticism was almost nil. Johnnye invited John Henry to her apartment, served him fruit juice and slices of brown bread with a delicious spread. While they sipped and munched, Johnnye suggested he make out a budget and explained to him the advantages. John told her about his bank account and insurances with the Mill and the two colored companies, North Carolina Mutual and Winston Mutual. Johnnye kissed John everywhere she could without upsetting him, and shifted her chewing gum between her gums and cheek where it could be retrieved when this was over. She had sex with him, and found he performed just as he spoke: slowly, carefully, apologetically, monotonously. Afterwards Johnnye lay quietly on his chest as he asked her to marry him. She did.

John put a huge down payment on a modest five-room house, and thanked Johnnye for helping him get his life together. He stopped drinking "cold turkey," joined Johnnye's church, became a deacon, and gave generously to Christian causes. Less than two years later, John Henry Woodard was dead. Dee whispered that Johnnye "had done away with John Henry Woodard and split the insurance money with her doctor and the undertaker." Johnnye calmly chewed gum and stopped using his name. She liked the sound of Johnnye Jamison.

CHAPTER 6

Dorothy Borden Returns to Granston

In the meantime, Dorothy Borden, daughter of Granston's first colored lawyer, returned to Granston from the Bronx, New York, after her first marriage failed. She moved into her old childhood room in her parents' home, along with her young daughter, Frankie, who was installed in the extra upstairs bedroom next to Dorothy's. She accepted a position teaching freshman composition and literature at L.C.N. –Lexis College for Negroes, a four-year Land Grant college commuting distance from Granston. Dorothy, who did not drive, commuted with faculty members or students, and at times used Greyhound or Trailway buses.

Even though they would never meet, Dorothy Borden's and Johnnye Jamison's lives would cross. The parallelism began when Dorothy met Joe Cephus Divine, one of the first colored men selected to join "Granston's Grandest" as the Police Department was labeled. Jackie Sullivan, Dr. Sullivan's daughter, a high school teacher, and one of Dorothy's high school friends, introduced them. Jackie was "yellow" and had married a "yellow" Lutheran Pastor whose brother was also on the local police force, which is how Jackie met Joe Cephus. He paid homage to Jackie and her husband, Pastor Thadeus LeGrande, visited their church, and thought of joining but didn't feel comfortable in a church where most of people were "too light skin-ded." Joe Cephus didn't talk about his first marriage, and was not satisfied with any of his former girlfriends, all beauticians. He asked Jackie to introduce him to some of her eligible friends, which is the reason he began visiting the Lutheran church regularly, hoping they were all, like her, high school teachers. He classified women on the basis of the grade they taught. Hence those who taught in the upper elementary grades were superior to those who were assigned to lower grades. The first grade was reserved for women who had attended college less, perhaps not even finishing, or were not smart. Lower levels were never ascribed to men. Since there were so many more women than men, Joe Cephus felt he would never be forced to marry a woman below the fourth grade level.

Knowing Jackie Sullivan had upgraded Joe Cephus' fantasies. He began to see himself married to an adoring young woman whose assignment was grades eight to eleven, high school grade levels in Granston then. Dorothy Borden, a professor at Lexis College, far surpassed his goals, plans, and dreams. They soared. Marriage to her would crown his already successful life. His angelic silhouette in place, he showered Dorothy Borden with attention. Using his best grammar and enunciation, he spoke to her and around her in a genteel manner. Took her to his favorite spot–a North Carolina colored beach. He courted her Granston-Officer-Joe Cephus style. Dorothy, fatigued from a dull, uninteresting marriage, was restfully receptive and told herself she enjoyed it. Granston wasn't a prolific hunting ground for men. It didn't matter. She just wanted to be entertained and to entertain, not married. Joe Cephus begged her to marry him. If she did, Dorothy rationalized, she would stay in Granston near her parents, her daughter would grow up in the Borden home place as she had, under the influence of Dorothy's father whom she and her daughter adored and who worshipped them. Furthermore, although needing minor repairs, Dorothy's playhouse was still there. So were the swings and sliding board, sand pile, and a large yard for dogs. Dorothy would spend summers in New York attending graduate school–and in Europe. She thought about this unexpected change in her life only on the surface, daring not plunge into reasoning, logic, or cognition. – To Joe Cephus marriage to her told him he would live happily ever after.

CHAPTER 7

Joe Cephus Divine: Dorothy Borden's Second Husband

In spite of her parents' caution not to marry another uneducated man, Dorothy Borden married Joe Cephus Divine. In addition to detesting marriage personally, Dorothy was not in love with him. At least not in the way she was capable of loving. Neither had she been in love with Luther, her first husband. Dorothy even detected the same cryptic feeling of disdain for Joe Cephus that she had for Luther. She had left him before the feeling of possession enveloped her as it must for people who spend years, and even their entire lives, with mates they do not love, or even like, and for whom they have that mysterious feeling of disdain. Sometimes it became active malignancy.

Years later, Dorothy Borden would realize that had there been no Joe Cephus Divine, her second novel would have been vastly different. Not that he was inspiration in the positive interpretation of the word. She deemed Joe Cephus Divine, the most wicked person who ever became a part of her life. So evil that he unsheathed her baser nature as no one or anything else had.

Evil exists in famines, wars, disease, natural disasters. It is personified in human form as seen in antisocial behavior, sometimes so heinous that perpetrators are incarcerated and even executed. There are also evil people who attend churches and occupy positions in all avenues of work and compensation, sometimes enforcing laws of Deities and Populace. Joe Cephus Divine represented the latter. He had waited and watched for the woman who surely must be waiting and watching for him. Her vigil had been ordained the day he was permitted to join "Granston's Grandest," the Police Department. And she found him. A belief that all female teachers craved forever-and-ever marriages beyond anything that heaven and earth could offer had flowed down through the years and adorned Joe Cephus Divine as if he were a royal manikin. He thought about it until he became pleased to the point of perverted arrogance concerning his marrying Dorothy Borden.

Dorothy said Joe Cephus was the son of the devil and slime Satan designed especially to give birth to him. He wasn't:

Joe Cephus was the first child and son of Moses Noah (genesis: Moore), a self-named, self-ordained preacher and a wife he renamed Mary Rebecca. The Reverend Noah had managed to complete the first five grades in a one-room school for colored in Cottontown, Georgia. When he told people, many of them wondered how he could read and write so well. He always gave his teacher credit, who *made* him read and write. When he heard his preacher talking about a man name Noah, Moses Moore began to read about him. He admired Noah, and it rhymed with his family name Moore. Surely God wanted him to be like the man who saved mankind and animals during the flood, thus saving the world. He became Moses Noah and convinced his family they should call themselves Noah instead of Moore. They did.

The Reverend Noah named his first son Joe Cephus. Because he resembled a cherub, the father spelled it so that his angelic-looking child could have the same initials as Jesus Christ. After the Reverend Noah heard about Father Divine, the deified Harlem, New York, preacher and prophet, he changed his surname to

Divine and became The Reverend Moses Noah Divine. He left the hard, ill-paying Georgia farm life and uncertain church assignments that labeled him a "jack-leg preacher," and took his family to Winston-Salem, North Carolina. The Reverend Moses Divine got a job as janitor in R.J. Reynolds Tobacco Factory and worked himself up to stemming, a process in manufacturing cigarettes. His vocabulary amazed white bosses and made colored workers proud. They came to him with almost everything they couldn't read or write. He reminded them also that he never finished the elementary grades in the one-room school, but he had a good teacher. Between pregnancies, Mrs. Divine also worked in the tobacco factory. With even more pride, The Reverend Divine rented a building and established what people called a "store front church" because it had once been a small grocery store. Along with his wife and a small group of followers, he considered himself a bona fide Sanctified Holiness Minister.

The couple destined their handsome son Joe Cephus to follow in his father's footsteps. Joe Cephus had retained his celestial aura, and The Reverend Divine believed his son could become another Father Divine or Daddy Grace, also a Harlem, New York minister with a huge devoted congregation. To the contrary, Joe Cephus was ashamed of his parents. He saw his mother, "her arms full, house full, and belly full" and was glad when she had a miscarriage or when a baby died.

Mr. and Mrs. Divine raised their surviving five children according to the Bible that stated "spare the rod and spoil the child." Not one of three boys and two girls got in trouble at school, in the community, or with the police. The slightest indication of departure from Biblical teachings prompted The Reverend Divine to whip them back to the Christian path with his belt. Mrs. Divine used switches, school rulers, and a toy called rick rack that was a paddle with a small rubber ball attached by a rubber string. Mary Rebecca Divine feared the hell her husband preached about, and was determined no one in her family would go. Their children didn't know which was worse, going to hell or their parents' efforts to keep them from going. Parental discipline, they were taught, was a Commandment their parents quoted constantly, "Honor thy father and thy mother that thy days may be long upon the land God giveth thee." Any discussion or criticism would subtract from their earthly life which meant a longer existence in hell. The Divine children grew up believing fathers and mothers never made errors, especially where their children were concerned. Hence there was no need for apologies. They also learned a man's role was to be in charge, and destined by God to be honored for that role.

Joe Cephus, venerable because he was male, handsome, and oldest, was "boss" over his siblings and absolutely in charge when his mother worked. He perceived early that a man's admitting being wrong meant loss of respect and lessening of the male role. Hence his every action was righteous. That righteousness was etched on his face and became a part of his demeanor. When both parents were absent, and the neighbors heard screams coming from the Divine house, they told each other that the Divine boys were fighting their sisters, but Joe Cephus would make them stop. This belief was confirmed when they saw Joe Cephus' virtuous guise and he lowered innocent eyes. However, he had beaten his sisters. He had learned not to fight his brothers who battered him so badly one day that they became afraid he was really injured. Joe Cephus, too embarrassed to tell their parents, but more afraid his brothers would kill him if he told, invented a story of falling out a tree. He hated and avoided his brothers the rest of his life. He never ceased to console himself by abusing his sisters. His favorite was kicking, and telling them how he would do it. "I'll kick the shit outta you," and "I'll kick your black ugly ass 'till it ropes like okra." As he grew older and listened to boys at school talk about girls, he delighted in telling his sisters "girls so nasty they bleed every month, even their own Mama, and I'll kick you 'til yo' pussies bleed like hogs at hog killin'." The girls knew it was useless to tell their parents. Joe Cephus had only to register saintly surprise, and they would be whipped for lying.

Joe Cephus saw that his mother's life centered on pleasing her husband at any cost. He had handed her life's greatest triumph: becoming *his* wife. Joe Cephus thought something was radically wrong with any woman who did not want to become a man's wife, have children, cook, keep house, boast about how nice she washes and irons his shirts, and hangs up his clothes. And works and pays the bills when she's not in bed having a baby. Without knowing it, Joe Cephus had no respect for his mother or women. He never thought in terms of examining his concepts or of modifying them. For anyone to question his belief was a declaration of war—providing he could win physically. And he did, since he only engaged in combat with colored females who he thought would not fight back, colored children, and small animals. His arsenal, verbal and physical, was bare when confronting white people and colored men, traits he would maintain throughout his life, explaining "I don't talk much."

Attempting to enhance himself, over the years "dirty words" festered in his thoughts rather than surfaced for the public to hear. He listened politely to men telling off-color jokes, but did not tell them himself. He drank very little, sipping alcohol only at selected social gatherings. Each night he knelt at the foot of his bed and said the prayer his mother and father taught him as he learned to talk.: "Now I lay me down to sleep. I pray the Lord my soul to keep. If I should die before I wake, I pray the Lord my soul to take." The times he did not kneel were because he had temporarily forgotten, such as when a wife had needled and provoked him or had refused him sex, and he had to show her he was man of the house by slapping and kicking her until she was under control. When he remembered, he got out of bed, knelt and prayed before going to sleep. Prayer was a part of his life, and he demanded that it be respected. He knew his mother prayed every night, but it never occurred to him that she did not repeat the prayer she taught him when he was a baby. To enforce respect, he pushed or kicked wives from his bed to make them pray on their knees before sleeping in his bed. Rejecting his father's and mother's Holiness and Sanctified worshipping, he joined a small Methodist Church, took pride in attending each Sunday regardless of weather, and contributed a dollar each Sunday.

Prior to his adult and marrying years, Joe Cephus hearing his father "whooping and hollering and rearing and pitching each Sunday about God and the devil, saliva in the corners of his mouth, and Amens and preach it Reb'n Divine" from the tiny congregation mortified Joe Cephus more. He wanted something else– and better. He planned to finish high school and would have if he had not listened to a white man who came to Frederick Douglass High School recruiting colored boys to work in the local factory. The man promised him a job as Floor Boss—Foreman– over all the colored workers. The factory would permit him to return to high school later while holding the Foreman job for him. His parents tried to persuade him to complete high school even if he didn't get the job. But what did they know, he wanted to be Foreman, a Boss, and accepted the job that turned out to be Head Janitor. Joe Cephus was drafted, WWII, never returned to high school and remained angry, but not with the white man who had recruited him.

After Joe Cephus Divine was discharged from the army, he decided to leave home. Never mind Winston-Salem being a city, he wanted a change and thought about Charlotte, Greensboro, or even leaving the state of North Carolina and going maybe to Washington. But that was "too far away, and he didn't have no kin folks there." An army friend told him "they" were planning to hire Negro policemen in Granston. The colored population was smaller than it was in those other places, and colored men would have a better chance. That's where his army friend was going. He would stay with an aunt, and get a job in a knitting mill or furniture factory while waiting for the Policemen's Exam. J.C., as the friend called him, should come along. He did.

Joe Cephus Divine, considered extremely attractive by most people, clean and neat, was polite and genteel to be colored according to white people. His English, oral and written, was not bad for a Negro boy who almost finished high school. His interview with the Granston Police Department was positive. He stayed with the army friend and his aunt and worked in a mill until he was the first of three colored men selected to integrate the police force. The friend was not selected. Joe Cephus left and moved into a house where he could board and have a private room.

However, because he had not completed high school, the Police Department required him to take special courses to qualify. Joe Cephus considered the requirement a stigma, but controlled his rage, led people to believe he had completed four years at Douglass High School and never mentioned that he had not.

Joe Cephus wore his uniform with arrogance, vowing he would never rise so high he would ignore folks below him. Thus, at intervals, always in Department attire, he visited people he had met in the Mill. When invited, he went to their houses for dinners and to their parties, wearing his uniform with an air of regalia. He socialized at their parties sparingly, smiling not too broadly, answering questions, but asking none, talking little as possible. The more he saw of these people, the more disgusting he found them, especially the girls who would become like their mothers. Joe Cephus never got around to visiting the man who brought him to Granston or the man's aunt. When it was impossible to avoid them in a place the size of Granston, Joe Cephus explained, "Po-leecemen keep busy, specially me, the first cul-lud hired."

Dorothy Borden made the same mistake with Joe Cephus that she made with her first husband, Luther. She knew almost nothing about him. Joe Cephus knew Dorothy was "all right." Dorothy lived in a big house framed with trees, shrubbery, and flowers like white folks. And she was a professor at L.N.C.! She had attended Hampton, in Virginia, and New York University. It was in the paper when she got the job at L.C.N. Joe Cephus was pleased. By the time Dorothy would hear his story that she called "J.C. Divine's HIS-STO-RY," she had already said wedding vows for the second time and more ready to dissolve them than she was the first time. Dorothy wondered how she would have responded had she known the truth about Joe Cephus, especially his first marriage.

CHAPTER 8

More About The Real Joe Cephus Divine

Joe Cephus began to want to get married badly. To enhance himself further, he planned to buy a second hand car from one of the white officers, soon as he saved enough money. He'd keep it simonized to a blue sparkle and grin when the officer told him it would put the sky to shame. Joe Cephus visualized his wife, well dressed, coming home to him with papers and a roll book, but letting him know he was first in her life. Joe Cephus knew men married to women like that, and the men didn't have the position he had. They worked in the mill and would all their lives. Some were even chauffeurs and handy men for white folks. Joe Cephus, a man of his rank, wanted and deserved a woman he could brag about and who would cook, clean his house, wash and iron his clothes, and contribute her salary to running his house. She would be there to sleep with him every night and all day on Sunday after church, and he would "get all he wanted" without having to take her to a movie or buy her a hot dog and a coke, or use gas to ride her around. Besides, he was a po-leece and scared to "get it" in the back seat of his car. "White po-leece wuz always looking for colored fornicators, calling them folks who screwed without license."

Joe Cephus grew a black glossy mustache. He admired himself

and his mustache, inspected it daily, and began to plan how he would meet the woman he wanted and who without a doubt would want him. The opportunity came when Gerard LeGrande was permitted to join the Police Department. He was "high yellow," and Joe Cephus decided to keep a distance since he did not trust yellow colored folks–or colored folks who were too black. Something *had* to be wrong if they were too far one way. –That is until Joe Cephus found out Gerard was dating a teacher in Murfreesboro, a town not too far from Granston–if you want to use gas going to see a woman. Far more important, his brother, Thadeus LeGrande, a Lutheran minister, was married to a high school teacher. Joe Cephus began to grin at Gerard LeGrande, and soon as he knew Gerard better he planned to ask to meet his sister-in-law, who would introduce him, Joe Cephus, to some of her "teacher friends." However, there was to be an interruption of his dream plan. Dorothy did not discover the appalling details of this interruption until after her marriage to Joe Cephus.

Gerard LeGrande, along with his brother and the local NAACP, were bold enough to suggest to the Chief that he assign colored policemen instead of white ones to monitor colored high school football and basketball games–unless they assigned colored officers to the white high school. Joe Cephus and Gerard LeGrande got the duty immediately, alternating games. Only one officer was needed at colored games. Joe Cephus' assignment led to his attending high school games when he was not on duty. He began flirting with a pretty high school senior. She was flattered by the attention of this "good-looking old man" who was a policeman. An honor student, she was also the prize cheer leader. Joe Cephus followed Mildred, whom he called Millie, to night basketball games, fondled her whenever he could, and sneaked her into his room. When she became pregnant, he said, "Ah, hell!" and asked if she could do something about it. When she asked "What?" he got scared. Even the suggestion of anything like that in North Carolina was a felony. "They" emphasized that in Police Training. He didn't want Millie or her parents to contact the

Police Department, and tried to think of a way to keep Gerard LeGrande from finding out. Anyway, he would never let anyone know he "had to marry" a high school girl. Anger possessed Joe Cephus. Rage and indignation warped his speech patterns, even his walk. However, he controlled himself at work.

Joe Cephus told Personnel he had married. Considering Mildred beneath him, he never mentioned his wife again in the Department, and planned to divorce her soon as she had the baby. Her mother did domestic work by the day, her father an itinerant janitor, and they lived in a multiple dwelling called flats, a derogatory term in Granston. When his landlady told him she rented to single people only, Joe Cephus begrudgingly rented a tiny one bedroom Granston-style apartment.

Mildred was ill throughout her pregnancy. Her morning sickness lasted all day. When she went into labor during her seventh month and began hemorrhaging, neighbors rushed her to the colored wing of Granston's white hospital and sent for Joe Cephus. He became angry. What could he do? She was in the hospital. When Mildred failed to deliver, doctors performed an emergency Caesarean section, and told J.C., as they called him immediately, that he had a son and both his wife and son were very sick. Neighbors told him to get somebody to come and stay with his wife when she got out of the hospital. Joe Cephus asked Mildred's mother who told him she could come at night, she had just started a full-time job working for some real nice rich white folks, who expected her to work from seven to seven. Joe Cephus was livid. He hadn't told his mother and father he was married, but went to a pay phone and called the store where the owner, a white man, took messages for colored customers and left word for his mother to call him at the Police Department. He wished he had somewhere else for her to call.

"J.C., you didn't tell us you married!" She told him over the phone the next morning.

"I'm tellin' you now, Mama. Daddy can take care of things

for a week or so. I need you to help 'til Mildred is able to get
about."

"Who's Mildred?"

"My wife, Mama. She just had a baby and weak from
bleedin'."

"Well, you got to wait 'til Saturday when me and your Daddy
get paid. I'll get a Greyhound or Trailway, whichever is cheaper.
Give me your address in case you can't meet me."

Mrs. Divine came. Stopping to rest, alternating from one
hand to the other, she walked with her baggage to her son's house
and waited on the porch. Soon as he arrived, she cleaned the
three rooms and tiny bathroom, went to the neighborhood store
for food, and set out for the walk to the hospital and saw her
daughter-in-law for the first time. Her heart went out in pity to
the pretty little sick girl burdened down so young with her son
and a baby.

Joe Cephus saw his son for the first time when nurses handed
him to his mother to take home. Neighbors expected this young,
good-looking couple to have a pretty baby. As if whatever is
responsible had sneered, the baby was a flesh parody or caricature
of Joe Cephus. Its head was far too small, its maroon colored face
wrinkled and monkey-like, just as its tiny body. Its eyes darted
about too much for a young baby. It cried very little, making a
whining sound. Mildred named her son Joe Cephus, Jr. and told
herself she would call him Sonny Boy. Mrs. Divine said he would
outgrow the way he looked. Mildred had no milk to nurse her
son who also refused a bottle. Mrs. Divine prayed and used a
medicine dropper to get the hospital formula into its mouth which
she had to force open. She got a large jar of Vaseline and oiled her
grandson's wrinkled body constantly.

If his son's personal appearance shocked and dismayed Joe
Cephus, it was nothing compared to what he saw during a change
of diapers. His son's penis resembled a red pin stuck in a tiny
rumpled cushion. He whined and turned a deeper maroon when

he urinated. Joe Cephus never touched his son and avoided looking at him.

Mrs. Divine continued to pray and asked God if her son's seed had been cursed. She stayed almost two weeks and saw the telltale look of love escape Mildred's eyes when she looked at Joe Cephus or talked about him, and she prayed that Mildred would get well and leave Joe Cephus before too late. Mrs. Divine never saw her grandson again. Joe Cephus did not tell his mother when his son died, but she knew. She felt his death before it happened and was with him in spirit when he passed. A presence fell into her arms.

Even though Mildred continued to drop formula into her son's mouth and oil his tiny puckered body and talk to him about what they would do when he got bigger, after six months, the baby gave up trying to adjust to whatever it was that meant his survival. One morning Joe Cephus and Mildred woke up, but their son didn't. Joe Cephus, telling his wife "no need to have a funeral, spendin' a lotta money on a baby," got the cheapest coffin available and had his son buried quickly. He also told Mildred that now "her baby was dead there was no use for them to stay married." But it was too late. Mildred was pregnant again. Joe Cephus blamed her. She had a miscarriage. Neither knew why since Mildred didn't go to a doctor. During eighteen months, of her four or five pregnancies, neither she nor Joe Cephus was certain because she always seemed to be "big," there were no survivors. Joe Cephus was glad.

Joe Cephus began physically abusing Mildred. He fought her in the house, on the back porch, in the street. Neither knew exactly what he fought about. Neighbors heard him shout, "You got 'big' and tricked me into marryin' you. Now you holdin' me down stayin' 'big'. You oughta know how to letta man have some pleasure without gettin' 'big' every time. You keep getting 'big' so you won't haveta work and pay yo' hospital bill." To keep the P.D. Department from finding out his wife was pregnant before they married, Joe Cephus did not submit the bill for insurance coverage. His paying the hospital two or three dollars each week infuriated him more.

After a beating during her last pregnancy, Mildred had a miscarriage and did not conceive again. She felt listless all the time and became nauseous each time she tried to eat the canned food and cold cuts Joe Cephus brought. He warned if she didn't hurry up and get well, she'd have to go back home sick. She was probably just "playin' sick to keep from goin' home and gettin' a job when she could stay and let him take care of her." When he gave her a dollar or two for food or money to pay the rent, she began buying "bootleg likker." She became an alcoholic. Her beauty waned. Joe Cephus bellowed, "All you do is lay 'round and drink likker. So no good, you can't get 'big' no more. If you gonna stay here, get a job and help pay all these damn bills I got 'cause you here eatin' and sleepin' and usin' my lights and water. You holdin' me back. I'll never get ahead wif you! Wasn't fer you, I'd have a car by now. I'm still paying yo' hospital bill!"

Mildred had difficulty with even menial employment. When an employer showed interest and pity, Joe Cephus beat her and packed her things in an old cardboard valise and a box. "You going wif that white man.. That's the most low-life-ted thing a cul-lud woman can do." While they waited for a colored cab, Mildred begged him to give her another chance. She would stop drinking and get a job. She was *not* going with that white man and no man. Joe Cephus was the only man she ever went with. Please give her another chance. Her mother had told her "not to come home. A woman oughta stay with her husband." Joe Cephus had already put her things in the cab he hailed and told her to get in or she'd have to walk. The cab driver shook his head in sympathy with this colored policeman. Joe Cephus dumped Mildred's things in her parents' yard and left her crying .He left in the same taxi and never contacted Mildred again.

Before most Granstonians forgot about Joe Cephus' first marriage, completely ignoring that Mildred had been a teenager, many people felt sorry for him. After all he was a man *and* a policeman. And good-looking. And looked so good in his uniform. They told anyone who would listen, "That po' po-leece's wife didn't do nothin' but drank and go wit white men. He just had to put 'er out. Now he look so pitiful. She laid up wit 'im before he married her and got 'in the family way.' He was nice enuff to marry her, and she didn't 'preciate it." Women shook their heads in disgust. Men sympathized with Joe Cephus.

Not long after Joe Cephus removed Mildred from his life, one Sunday morning his father preached himself into a fatal heart attack. Joe Cephus' siblings and their mates came for the funeral. Mrs. Divine told them about their brother's marriage. After the funeral, the brothers went to Granston, met Mildred, saw her beauty and possibilities that could be restored, and offered to take her "up North." Unfortunately they also saw Mildred while she was on a "drinking spree" and she was unable to make a decision.

Joe Cephus began to pursue his on-hold dream. He had remained a staunch Christian and went to church every Sunday and put a dollar in the collection. Sometimes he wore his uniform to the service and explained to the minister and parishioners that he was just leaving all-night duty. During work lunch time, he began "confiding" in Gerald LeGrande, who ate in Miss Ware's Grand Blue Diner most days. Joe Cephus brought a cold cut sandwich from home, but sacrificed and bought a bowl of soup at the cafe in order to talk to Gerard. "I need somebody to talk to." Adorning his spiritual profile, Joe Cephus told his fellow officer all about how his wife had become alcoholic and walked out on him. He had begged her not to leave, to give their marriage another chance, and he would take her to a place where she could get treatment. He was in the process of buying them a brick house. But she – well–she had started drinking and fighting him. She drank so much that she lost a baby he wanted so badly. Now–he–just had to pull himself together and begin a new life. Joe Cephus suggested meeting Gerard at his brother's church one Sunday. He, Joe Cephus, had never been to a Lutheran church, and most of the members were "light-skin-ded," which he did not like. But he began attending the church because he wanted to meet the Reverend LeGrande and his wife Jackie. He did. "They" called him Pastor LeGrande. One Sunday Pastor LeGrande asked his brother and Joe Cephus to have dinner with them. They always had enough food for unexpected people. It would be no trouble. His wife wouldn't mind. He did most of the cooking anyway, and all she had to do was set the tables, clear it, and put dishes in the washer.

Joe Cephus wore his halo at the dinner table. The food was delicious, but he was not prepared to believe that a man would cook when he had a wife. And a preacher. He began visiting Pastor LeGrande's church, which led to his meeting Jackie LeGrande's friend Dorothy Borden.

Before meeting Dorothy Borden, Joe Cephus purchased a "nice looking" second hand green car, a later model than the blue one he couldn't get because Mildred "stayed drunk and didn't work." He kept it as glossy as he did his shoes and mustache. After delayed plans and promises, he drove to see his mother and saw how well she was getting along with a pension, how clean she kept the house, how good her cooking, and moved her to Granston into the house he had begun purchasing after putting Mildred out. Because he had not filed for a legal separation, Joe Cephus qualified for a GI Loan listing his wife, who was expecting a baby, as a dependent living with him. It was a nice small brick five-room house on a nice paved street, in a nice colored neighborhood, where colored people were tying to become middle-class. Soon as the paper work was completed, Joe Cephus filed for a divorce from Mildred.

Mary Rebecca Divine became housekeeper, cook, and washerwoman for her son. She hung up his clothes, replaced buttons, turned shirt collars, and kept the house spotless. She pleased her son more by using her pension to supplement this three dollar a week food allowance. Being diagnosed as high risk because of hypertension, she had retired a few years earlier with an additional modest compensation. Joe Cephus saw the Company envelope that was different from that of her pension and opened it. He explained to his mother that he did it accidentally. The next month he "came up short" and asked her to contribute to the mortgage payment. She contributed until she fell dead scrubbing floors on her hands and knees because Joe Cephus said mops did not clean his floors the way he wanted them.

Because he was so devoted to his mother and took such good care of her, people began referring to him as a "mama's boy." Joe Cephus had reminded himself often that his mother wouldn't live always and began seeking a replacement.

CHAPTER 9

The Marriage of Dorothy and Joe Cephus Divine

That replacement was Dorothy Borden, college professor and daughter of an attorney. Needless to say her family was not happy with her choice.

Mr. Borden lectured to his daughter:

"Your mother and I told you your next husband should be a professional colored man–if you decided to try it again. Under *no* condition should you marry a *divorced* man!"

"Daddy, I'm divorced!"

"That's different. It was Luther's fault. He was too old for you anyway. What do you think, Emma?" Mr. Borden asked his wife.

Mrs. Borden as usual said, "I'm not going to get involved in Dottie's personal business. As long as Frankie stays with us. I don't want her living with a stepfather."

Frankie was Dorothy's daughter, their first grandchild, both precocious and beautiful. And the grandparents were right. There was no room for Frankie where Dorothy went to live as Joe Cephus Divine's second wife. In fact, she would learn later that her daughter would have "cramped Joe Cephus' marital style."

Joe Cephus ran the household on his terms, Dorothy quickly found out. He began giving his mother five dollars a week food allowance instead of three. He immediately assigned Dorothy a dresser drawer for whatever could be kept in a narrow compartment and a small prefabricated closet for her clothes. She kept lingerie in a valise that Joe Cephus ordered her to keep under the bed since the room was small. He asked, "Do you mind using the same bed me and my first wife used?"

Dorothy knew he wanted her to buy a new bedroom suite. "No," she replied and didn't mind. "I'm going to use the– same *'everything else'*– you and your first wife used. " Joe Cephus was not pleased. Neither was Dorothy. She looked at him, around the room, at the prefabricated closet, and thought of night. Her mouth filled with fluid, the prelude to regurgitation. She hurried to the bathroom. Nothing came, but the fluid in her mouth would not let her leave for a while. She flushed the toilet, washed her hands and returned to the room with the sensation of vomiting still haunting her.

As Dorothy hung a few clothes in the closet, fearing it might topple, Joe Cephus asked, "What bills you gonna pay? You oughta pay all of them while you work. September to May. I pay them the months you don't work. June, July, and August."

Dorothy had been amused about the drawer, closet, valise under the bed for lingerie, and even about sleeping in the first wife's bed. The last remark regarding paying all the bills for nine months during the year sent a burning current racing through her body. She felt flames must be flaring from her face. But she remained silent, as usual, when she had a mind-set and felt conversation would be ridiculous. Joe Cephus was displeased with her silence which etched the beginning of an almost perpetual frown on his face.

Dorothy had an answer, but withheld it while her face burned: "You should turn upside down and talk out of your bottom part. Your mouth is spewing feces."

In retrospect, Dorothy knew she should not have married

Joe Cephus, and certainly should have moved out that night. Resorting to quarrels and physical fights, Dorothy would learn that her husband never discussed anything. Before they married, he told her that he had to learn to disagree. She discovered that his learning to disagree was only with colored women, his wives, and girlfriends. He was mute around men and white people, with his explanation, "I don't talk much" that Dorothy learned was his escape.

Dorothy even attempted to be amused rather than insulted over J.C.'s budget plan. Joe Cephus asked again, "Well, what bills you wanna pay?"

"I don't *want* to pay any." And added in a tone that even Joe Cephus suspected was derision, "Let me know how much you charge for the dresser drawer and cardboard closet. Oh, yes, how much rent do you want for the space under the bed? And for each meal. Sometimes I eat dinner in the college faculty dining room." This comment proclaimed Joe Cephus' frown becoming a fixed scowl except at work and when conversing with outsiders.

"We'll just deposit our checks and pay bills," Joe Cephus announced. "You got charge accounts?"

"Yes. And grad school tuition this summer, and I have to save for the student trip to Europe. I can deposit what's left."

Joe Cephus tossed his shoes in a corner, something he never does. He took care of his clothes. He really was displeased.

"Since we just married, cancel the trip and summer school."

"Certainly. If NYU topples into the Hudson River or the ocean dries up so ships can't sail, or the sky falls and planes can't fly."

Joe Cephus was irate.

Dorothy's marital woes began immediately after the honeymoon. Her regard for marriage was such that she didn't discuss them with Joe Cephus. But she aired them to almost anyone, even in context to strangers she met on planes, buses, or while shopping. One of her most admirable traits, loyalty, was on hold for the duration. Women told her "not to talk back to her

43

husband. Hold her tongue if she wanted the marriage to work." She vocalized more, resorting to, "I refuse to stifle myself just to have J.C. sleep with me. Everything was destroyed right after we married." But to herself, she admitted, she should have left him then, because "after he kicked me he unloosed something vile in me."

CHAPTER 10
Dorothy Borden, Abused Wife

Dorothy had been married to Joe Cephus and back in Granston less then two weeks after their honeymoon, a long weekend at a North Carolina colored beach, a favorite of his. Dorothy remembered it as the potato salad site, another episode of her ordeal with Joe Cephus she told to whoever would listen. The memory of Joe Cephus' kicking Dorothy formed mental scar tissue. She wore its cicatrix, feeling forever pox marked. Joe Cephus had rushed home enraged, shouting, "I heard you use to go wif [Granston's words for dated] Al Benson!" Joe Cephus was almost incoherent. Dorothy managed to decipher that the local man Al Benson had told Joe Cephus at sometime in the past that he, Al, knew a girl who would violate the biggest sexual taboo between colored men and women. Joe Cephus described the taboo in street language, and shouted, "Nobody want to kiss a person in the mouth who did something like that!" accompanied by an attack of kicking, slapping, and using his fists. For some reason he removed his watch, took off his coat, removed his tie, rolled up his shirt sleeves.

Dorothy was stunned. She managed to decipher that J.C. had seen Al that day, who said, "J.C., I heard you married Dottie

Borden. I know her. I used to take her to Greensboro to that All-You-Can-Eat seafood place."

Dorothy recalled that while visiting one summer, Al had been in a group that had eaten at the All-You-Can-Eat seafood restaurant in Greensboro. A popular place, the Manager had a large clean area for colored patrons and hired pleasant colored help. In the car pool, Dorothy had been assigned to Al Benson's car, and he sat next to her in the restaurant, the beginning and end of Dorothy Borden's association with him. She never got around to telling Joe Cephus. It would have made no difference. A man's word was gospel. Joe Cephus' reaction had mangled infinitely any positive emotions Dorothy had for her husband. The marriage ended then for Dorothy. Joe Cephus begged her not to leave, even had his minister talk to her. Dorothy told the minister, "It's easy for you to suggest staying and working it out. You'll be home. I'll be the one stuck with this mule!" Joe Cephus wept. It sickened Dorothy. She stayed, guarding her ulcer, exposing it each time she could in both amiable and hostile discourse.

Her experiences, involvement, and memories were unpleasant from Day One after moving into Joe Cephus' house, even the first meal. She never recalled what they ate. As he devoured food, she recalled how he protested her leaving the portion of potato salad she made at home in order for her daughter and friends to have a "picnic." Joe Cephus had asked her to make salad to take to the beach with them on their honeymoon; she had made more purposefully, and explained to him that it was far too much. Joe Cephus had insisted on taking all the salad. Dorothy made another batch for the children. After realizing they had brought far too much, Joe Cephus conscientiously tried to eat it all. He sampled it after breakfast, came in for a taste after returning from the beach, and snacked on it at nights. He even tried to sneak some into the garbage. The over abundance of potato salad had to be thrown away. Dorothy held on to the exhibition and began to dislike Joe Cephus and was certain she should not have married him.

Eating remained unpleasant. Dorothy began to have chronic indigestion. Even though Mrs. Divine was a good cook, Dorothy discovered she was dissatisfied with the lack of variety in the bill-of-fare, as well as the exclusion of what Joe Cephus considered "stuff cul-lud folks ate when they try to be white." Dorothy missed brown bread she and her family had eaten since she could remember. Joe Cephus had dinner with Dorothy's family a few times, once invited and at other times just dropping by. He refused vegetables, such as asparagus, Brussels sprouts, any green salads but lettuce and tomato, and ate only the inside of brown bread. Dorothy also missed exotic omelets her father prepared, as well as other dishes. She never mentioned it to anyone. She liked Mrs. Divine too much.

The answer regarding Dorothy's financial contribution had inflamed Joe Cephus. Dorothy sensed the heat. Felt it physically—the tingling stinging burning sensation like electric charges became commonplace. Dorothy knew powerful thoughts and potent feelings traveled on waves. However, seemingly Joe Cephus failed to perceive that Dorothy Borden detested married life and invested in it miserly. It was second on the list of things she did not want to do: (1) Die (2) Be married. She wondered why she did something she abhorred. It wasn't that she had to—like dying.

The financial arrangement Joe Cephus had with his mother disturbed Dorothy. In addition to the five dollars Joe Cephus gave his mother each week to purchase food, when necessary he bought staples like five pounds of sugar and flour. Mrs. Divine was responsible for meats, vegetables, and everything else they ate, which she purchased at a neighborhood store. Joe Cephus rejected Dorothy's advice to buy staples used frequently in quantities and to take his mother to an A & P or to spacious Granston Market, made up of a variety of concessions, where there were enormous selections and lower prices. Even rich white people went there, or sent their servants. Dorothy suspected Joe Cephus refused because of fear he would be expected to pay for the food since he would take his mother to these markets.

There was something about the Divine house that was so negatively charged that living in it even a few days left Dorothy unable to sleep. She lost weight, was tired most of the time, and felt herself aging. Joe Cephus had earned the reputation of being a mama's boy. He tried to enhance that reputation by defending his mother against the most minute difference of opinion, considering the difference criticism. Possibly fearing Dorothy would learn the truth, he created an atmosphere that made her uncomfortable. Dorothy perceived that Joe Cephus disliked his mother. In addition to exploiting her financially, he ignored her socially, and at times was verbally abusive, but secretly. Dorothy listened outside her door while Joe Cephus issued reprimands. Mrs. Divine told Dorothy, "If I hadda known J.C. was going to treat me the way he does, I woulda crossed my legs when he was coming out," the method it is said some women used to choke babies before the doctor or midwife arrived. Calling her affectionately Miss Mary-Bekki, Dorothy considered Mrs. Divine a model mother-in-law. She did all the cooking and cleaning and was easy to get along with. Joe Cephus had asked Dorothy's parents what he should call them. Their response was "Mr. and Mrs. Borden." He did.

Joe Cephus was an expert at creating an inimical atmosphere. And he would. He seemed most contented during hostility. He didn't always look angry during his tirades. Sometimes he had a facial expression that Dorothy labeled a "recuperating smile" or a "smile in intensive care." He never repeated the fury with the intensity of the first kicking scene when he accused Dorothy of "going with Al Benson." Never again did such rage beam from his face. At intervals, for no apparent reason, Joe Cephus would say, "You no better then nobody else. Just remindin' you." Or in a confidential tone, he would tell her, "Somebody told me something about you. A friend of yours," and even give a clue to the identity of the girlfriend who betrayed the secret. Dorothy's responses infuriated him, sometimes to the point of physical fights. To the first statement she might say, "No. I'm no better than anyone else, but *you* think so. You shun people on *your* level. Just reminding you." The second statement, would elicit, "Whatever it is, don't tell me. If it's the truth, I know more about it than anyone else and know who told you. If it's a lie, keep it and enjoy it."

Dorothy felt personal hate for the first time, and didn't like it. Joe Cephus also continued to drench her with two questions that were the essence of marriage, permeating his concept of their relationship: "How you gonna make up for the three months you don't work?" and "Are we gonna frig or fight tonight?" Only he used the F word because he knew it disgusted her. Dorothy felt her sexual desire for Joe Cephus turn to muck and watched herself refuse any attempt to permit purging. She felt personal disgust and hate for Joe Cephus continue to mount. She wondered why she had permitted somebody like Joe Cephus to invade her life and tried to understand why she remained with him, in a place she called Lucifer's Liar and Devil's Den when Joe Cephus would tell her, "Folks say you married me to get my house." An expert at creating negativity, antagonism occupied the Divine house like a diseased inmate. Dorothy did nothing to alleviate, cure, or treat the malady. It would have been in vain since Joe Cephus ended almost every outburst with his sick smile, sneering, "I can't help if you let me treat you this way."

As Joe Cephus begged Dorothy not to leave, neither apologizing or asking forgiveness, just stay, she saw total repugnance in everything that included him: listening to him speak, looking across the table at him, the sight of his driving, seeing how ridiculous he looked in his shorts, thoughts of his lying on top of her. He really looked ludicrous having sex. He folded himself in such a disgusting hump, the hump appearing before he began humping. Dorothy wondered if she looked asinine. Joe Cephus considered his penis the totality of his manhood. Showing no modesty, he paraded around nude. Dorothy realized he resembled his penis! They both looked like a turd: the same color, shape, and size. In all earnestness, Dorothy asked him how he happened to dress himself instead of his Manhood. They both looked so much alike. And when he flushed, how did he know which of the three to flush down? Himself, Manhood, or the turd? They were identical. Like triplets. Insults didn't seem to bother him. Sometimes he would respond quietly, "You too nice-sa-girl to say something like that."

One night when Joe Cephus was parading in his shorts, as he announced, "If a man don't use his Manhood, he'll lose it, and I show won't lose mine. We gonna fuck or fight tonight." Dorothy saw Manhood peeking through the opening in Joe Cephus' shorts, a perplexed look on its face. She pretended to have a camera and snapped its picture. The next day she placed the "camera shot" on the mirror. It was a crude drawing of Manhood with a Joe Cephus mustache and a vacuous Joe Cephus face. She began to truly know that Joe Cephus did not mind derision. He only said, "I thought you were too nice-sa-girl to draw nasty pictures." He was most loathsome when she was at her best, acting like a lady. Dorothy often thought about his pleased look the night he pinned her down on the floor slapping her and she bit him on his chest so hard that it bled. He got up, a peculiar smile on his face as he blotted the blood with a handkerchief. Later Dorothy would see him looking at the scar rather fondly. In retrospect Dorothy considered Joe Cephus' reaction frightening.

Joe Cephus' scowl began to register even more during sex. Dorothy wondered why he bothered and wished he wouldn't. There was no way he could enjoy the act as it was meant for normal people. Dorothy learned that rapists did not enjoy sex as normal people. It was power. Joe Cephus seemed to will an erection, regardless of the atmosphere. Dorothy knew when she saw the look on Joe Cephus' face as if he were seriously trying to combat a severe constipation problem, or if he looked as if he were on the verge of retching, after trying not to for an uncomfortable period of time, it was humping-pumping time. She closed her eyes so that she did not at least have to look at the sum total of sexual disgust.

Dorothy fought a war against healing, tearing into old and new wounds with supercilious placidity. No matter what happened, Joe Cephus was undaunted maritally, convinced he and Dorothy would and should remain together regardless of how much she indicated and told him that she detested him and that the union should be terminated. He would stare at her, his eyes and mouth widening in stark disbelief. As abuse became worse, insults more corrosive, and sex more distasteful, the more Joe Cephus begged Dorothy not to leave, and the more he seemed to consider the marriage a culmination of success. Joe Cephus was quite contented and determined to spend the rest of his life with Dorothy Borden. Sex became more and more his primary focus with an increase in I'm-gona-make-you-like-it harshness. In spite of it, all that mattered to Joe Cephus is that they remain man and wife–and forever. Dorothy had heard of such relationships, but never had the faintest idea they existed like this–and *she* would be involved.

Dorothy knew the marriage wasn't ever going to work and was glad. She was not as sick as Joe Cephus and wondered what she was waiting for as she dreamed and planned for freedom: Teaching in a college in NYC; Broadway and Off- Broadway plays; a diversity of friends with whom she shared similar pursuits and visions; summer travel to faraway continents that left her breathless with awe, even a bit frightened. There would be a man who held her hand gently but securely and walked with her in splendid and magnificent places, treasuring sights and sounds, and who sat with her in romantic cafes and gardens, and talked about wonderful magical things a man talks to a woman about. And they pleased, respected and satisfied each other–And marveled at each other. And together they sought Shangri-La.

Dorothy became profane. Her impiety was not traditional. She was too creative and Joe Cephus too unique. She was poetic at times. She never called him curse-word names that people use in anger to classify each other. Instead she gave him titles befitting only him, like Officer Joe Feces and Officer Joe Fester or Joe

Festus. Joe Cyphilis was her favorite. She even sent him a card through the mail and spelled syphilis with a C. She never told him to go to hell. Instead she would suggest or advise that he return to his great great –a series of greats– all the way to his Rhesus monkey stage—to his grandfather's semen and start all over. Dorothy began to realize that Joe Cephus thought men were endowed with magic power, without a doubt he himself. This enchantment flowed through his Manhood into a woman, and banished, eradicated, erased, annihilated all things noisome in a marriage. That same wonder-working was all he needed to keep him out of hell and ensure him a special place in heaven. To keep this power flowing, he must use the magic instrument often. Very often. In his language, a wife could be frigged into contentment, without recognizing her contentment, which was Dorothy's case.

Joe Cephus did not understand why a man should be nice or kind to his *wife*. Or even civil. Common courtesy and ordinary politeness were for company, most colored men, and white people when he had to be around them. He and a wife were *married*! And that was all it took. Everything else fell in place. That's why a man married–to be himself. Dorothy knew Joe Cephus would never know he was entirely out of her consortium, and she certainly would not socialize him.

Almost daily Dorothy fantasized killing her husband, devising unique methods. Her favorite was putting a poisoned tack in his shoe. Rat poison was easy to get. Joe Cephus was so stingy he wouldn't go to a doctor until it was too late. The poison would have entered his foot and gotten into his blood stream. Better than his dying, his foot, the one he used for kicking, would first have to be amputated. Dorothy saw herself at his funeral. Her pointed breasts, tiny waist, and model hips outlined in a white princess style dress. A white pill box hat with a veil and white pumps would defy the customary window's black. She would walk slowly behind the casket, drying her tears. She, of course, would weep. Crying was not a problem. She cried at funerals, even those in movies. Never asking, but looking, Dorothy saw a container of rat poison in a hardware store. There was the skeleton on the label. The purchase could be traced, even if she got it in New York. Dorothy knew and accepted that she had to be contented with her fantasy. Dorothy was certain of discovery if she killed J.C. or hurt him seriously, and she was afraid *not* to kill him if she hurt him. He would be more deadly than a wounded animal. And Dorothy had too many dreams to do anything to rupture her life, such as paying a price for murdering somebody like Joe Cephus Divine. She knew the marriage would end before too long, and waited for Joe Cephus to do something to end it that he was so certain would not. And he did.

In the meantime, Dorothy continued to console herself with her work, visualizing teaching in a college or university in New York and searching for Shangri-La during summers. Thus she occupied herself as much as possible during her husband's humping-pumping sessions.

Although Dorothy had been married to Joe Cephus only a year, it seemed a lifetime. It was beach time again. Joe Cephus didn't mind her coming along since she brought lots of good food. Good food was expensive at the beach, even hot dogs and dry tasteless hamburgers. Dorothy didn't mind going with him. He didn't fuss and fight at the beach, just silent and ghoulish, and his Manhood took on Joe Cephus' mood and was easier to endure. Dorothy observed that Manhood's facial expression changed along with Joe Cephus'. However, this time he would not take Dorothy. She didn't ask to go either. She acted sick. Throwing up every morning. Pleased, he continued selecting beach clothes.

Dorothy's last monthly cycle did not come around, and this one was late. Joe Cephus told himself now was the time to show this woman who was boss. She was pregnant! Finally he had her where he wanted her. If she did anything about it, she could go to jail, and she was married to a po-leece who could report her. The first cul-lud hired. She'd be scared. And the Bible said a woman would go to hell because it was self-murder. Dorothy Borden wasn't crazy enough to do something that would land her both in jail and hell.

The look of triumph on Joe Cephus' face became an I-gotcha-now grin. He didn't want children, and disliked them intensely. He thought of the consequences: Children meant years and years of trouble. That's why he was glad those Mildred said were his didn't live. –Joe Cephus put the wrong pair of shorts in his valise. –Suppose Dorothy left and got a divorce? Colored women were beginning to ask for child support legally. Not like it used to be. Being a teacher and a lawyer's daughter, Dorothy would be too ashamed and proud to ask for more money than he wanted to contribute, if any. Her parents would take care of their grandchild. They should. They had more than he had. –He found the right shorts—his favorite.

Joe Cephus continued to analyze: If Dorothy had a baby, she wouldn't be so quick to leave a second husband with another child. The bad part about it, he'd have to use *his* money while she took time off from her job. When she worked she'd have to use her money to take care of it, and he'd have to take up that slack. Another possibility: Dorothy would have to pay his mother to take care of the baby, and he wouldn't have to give her the five dollars weekly for food. –Suppose Dorothy got *her* mother to take care of it?

–He certainly didn't want a baby crying all night and peeing all day. –Using more lights and water. Too late now. Dorothy is going to have a baby. He was glad since she didn't want one. Said so before they married. In fact they both said definitely *no*. They were too old. –Now she'd have to get another house with another bedroom. She'd buy a bed now! She wouldn't when they got married. Slept in the bed he and Mildred used. He never thought Dorothy Borden would do that. He asked her about it, and she said she had no intention of buying any furniture for his house, and what could have been bedroom suite money she added to her NYU tuition. He was so angry he slapped her. Well, she'd buy a bedroom suite and a house to put it in because there was nowhere to put it in his house. Joe Cephus was delighted. —Suppose she decided to stay home and not work? Hell, he'd give her the first three F's Fuss, Fight, and Frig until she would be glad to get back to work, and even take a night job. Be a– what did they call it–ad–something–adjunk. No point in marrying a woman with a good job and she not working. No matter what, he wouldn't use the money he had saved in that bank in High Point. She didn't know about that. Joe Cephus slung his valise in his car and drove away making plans, not even suspecting that while he cast taunting looks, Dorothy had already made plan A, and B if A failed, and C if B failed–and praying for him to leave.

Joe Cephus was shocked when he returned to find Dorothy Borden still had control of her life, so astonished that he did not fuss and apparently forgot about kicking. He decided to shame her. Adorning his celestial visage, summoning his halo, he asked with Joe-Cephus pathos, "What happened to the po' lil' baby, Dottie?"

Silence.

"God sent that baby, Dottie." His eyes half closed with piety that also enveloped his words.

Mimicking him softly, she replied, "And I sent it back, J.C."

He would scare her. "You know you're going to hell, Dorothy Lee Borden."

Unconcerned: "On my own terms, calling the shots, Joe Cephus Divine."

There must be something he could say—to make her feel bad. "Dottie, that po' lil' baby would have made our marriage work. I would have something that is really a part of you."

It was working! She looked at him so touched. So genuinely sad. He waited for her to cry.

She replied as if on the verge of tears, attempting to control herself. "I'm so terribly sorry. –I'll make it up to you and give you something that is a part of me—*really* mine. The next time I have a victorious bout with peristalsis, I'll see that you get the results."

Joe Cephus looked puzzled before replying, "I thought you were too nice-sa-girl to know anything about doing what you did to a po' lil' baby."

"I'm just the type to know—and do it, Joe Cephus."

Later, one night during a rare civil session between the two, Joe Cephus asked, "Dottie, tell me in plain words what you meant when I came home from the beach and thought you were still going to have a baby. Remember?" If Dorothy had a baby, he, Officer Joe Cephus Divine, the first cul-lud hired and married to a college per-fesser, would look even greater in the Police Department. —And he and Dorothy would be together forever.

"Oh, yes, I said the next time I have a bout with peristalsis—"

"Yes. That's it. Explain what you really meant." Maybe she meant she'd have a baby later.

"I really meant if you want something that is a part of me and comes out of my ass, I'll shit you a turd."

Joe Cephus stared at this wife before telling her, "You too nice-sa-girl to talk nasty talk like that."

"Don't insult me, Joe Cephus. Men like you call girls and women nice and good if they can make fools of them. And I'd be a fool to have a baby I don't want by a man I don't want."

Joe Cephus was in one of his rare moods. "I still say you're too nice-sa-girl to say things like that to her husband."

"You didn't think I was too nice-sa-girl for you to kick, slap, and try to sell yourself to. A *man* doesn't do those things to a too-nice-sa-girl," Dorothy mimicked again. "Of course that eliminates you."

Joe Cephus adjusted his halo. "Bible says folks oughta forgive over and over. You too nice-sa-girl not to forgive her husband for things he did when he was mad."

Fantasies soothed Dorothy somewhat: She pictured Joe Cephus ill, and sending for her. After Jackie—along with her husband Rev—kept saying it was the Christian thing at least to go see a dying man, Dorothy would go and stand at the foot of his bed. She would look at Joe Cephus resembling a Rhesus monkey even more after weight loss. While others said Joe Cephus was good-looking, she didn't think so even when she liked him. Like most people, he wasn't ugly. Dorothy thought all monkeys were adorably cute, but not people who looked like them. In her daydream, she would move to the head of the bed and say like a good Christian, "I understand you're on your way to hell." Dorothy didn't relish being that sick, and continued to wonder why she was unwell, weak, or whatever it was, enough to stay with him. Perhaps, she told herself, it would be time already served in event she went to hell.

This was Joe Cephus' parade. She had made it possible by permitting her life to enter this void. Something was vacuous about her, beyond that which she considered inane in him. *He had what he wanted in life and wanted to keep forever—and on his terms. She had what she wanted least and hesitated to rid herself of it despite wanting to shed it forever.* Dorothy felt disgust climbing mountains, and didn't like it.

Dorothy felt Joe Cephus' eyes on her one night as she sat in the living room reading. She looked up. He was staring at her, shaking his head. As usual in conversation involving Dorothy, he made an effort to be what he conceived as "cul-lud as possible," showing her he didn't have to put on airs or act white because she was a college teacher. "You sure must be mighty *dumb*. Always readin'. You must don't know nothin'. You never see me readin' no books, and I pass the po-leecemens tess-es. The first cul-lud they hired. You always got to be readin', and call yourself a teach-ur. A *college* teach-ur at that. You even got two or three dictionaries. One's not enough. You must don't know many words. Whatcha need wif a dictionary? Didn't you learn nothin' in college? At least words." Joe Cephus picked up a *Thesaurus*. Glanced through its pages. Tossed it aside. "Nothin' but words. No readin'. I never had no dictionary in my house, and no books either, 'til you come.

Now book shelves in my livin' room makin' mo' for Mama to dust. Book shelves in my bedroom. Wouldn't be surprised if you put one in my kitchen. All you do is read and use my baf tub. Run up my water bill. As much as you bav and as much water you use, you must be mighty nasty. I hear my water runnin' at night and again in the mornin'. Just hog my baf room."

Then he added his favorite theory: "If a woman's not sleepin' wif but one man why she have to bav every night? Not unless she's stoppin' wif men before she get home. Water rust iron, and it'll rust me. I get in the tub twice a week. Wins-dey and Sad-dey night. And I don't stink."

Somewhat amused–Dorothy wondered how Joe Cephus managed to appear so well-bathed. He didn't have an odor, and he looked clean all the time. She had noticed how immaculate he was before they married. It never occurred to her that he did it with two baths a week in a little over a quarter tub of water. At times he showed her the amount he used. And he took the shortest baths. It always took her such a long time. He commented, argued, and theorized before she began, while she was bathing and after she finished.

Joe Cephus had not accomplished his goal, had not shown his real power. "And you always correctin' papers. Puttin' red marks on 'em. Every night, even on weekends you correctin' papers. Must don't teach the students nothin'. Got to always correct they papers. And they call here as-ting about they papers. Tyin' up my phone. I heard you tell 'em when they go to New York to work doin' the summer, go to some cul-lud li-berry in Harlum, 125th St. Charm-burger. You'll meet 'em there. If you so gooda teach-ur, why you have so many papers? Why you send 'em to li-berries—and way up in New York? Can't you tell 'what you want 'em to know you so gooda teach-ur?"

"They go to libraries to do research. I correct papers because I have three freshman composition classes. Thirty students in each class. And a lit class." Dorothy explained as usual. "The lit class is listed in the catalog as focusing on reading and writing about literature. I encourage research–and a lot of students enjoy it."

Angry because either he didn't understand his wife's answer or didn't like it, pretending it was an accident, Joe Cephus pushed a stack of student assignments on the floor. If Dorothy protested, he'd have a good reason to slap her. All he did was accidentally knock some papers on the floor. Acting as if he didn't see them, he scattered the papers as he walked aimlessly across the room. Silently Dorothy picked them up. This wasn't working. Joe Cephus had to do something else.

"I been thinkin'," Joe Cephus began, "A woman not sleepin' round with a ganga men don't have to wash herself as much as you do. How many men you screwin'?"

"Not even *one*," Dorothy responded softly. "And that is the truth if I never tell the truth again."

"Better be true."

"It is and will be as long as I sleep with you."

Joe Cephus was pleased. He reached for his billy stick, once the only weapon allowed colored policemen. He caressed it. "They teach us how to hit somebody wif one of these and almost kill 'em. They show us how to beat a person wif somethin' wet like a sheet and almost beat 'em to death and not leave a scar. Folks respect us. No matter what I do to you, you got to report it to where I work, and they believe *me* over you."

Dorothy went to the book shelf, which gave Joe Cephus a chance to brush against her, maybe even knock her down. He almost succeeded. Dorothy took the blame and politely said, "Pardon me." Joe Cephus was disappointed. He'd make up for it in bed tonight. He felt his crouch and considered making her go to bed now, but had a feeling Manhood might fail. A couple of nights he had lain awake wondering why Manhood was lying in such a dormant heap.

Dorothy thought how she'd love to *almost* kill him, or have somebody do it. She would want him to live to know about it. Dorothy knew she had to get out.

As much as she considered Joe Cephus a liability, and finding him more repulsive each night, Dorothy still waited for that inevitable departure day. It was so bizarre and unreal. So was Joe Cephus. He never forgave her for being right, and taunted her when she was not. Attempting to fathom what happened, Dorothy admitted hearing while on their honeymoon, warning sounds of a rattler, sounds that became more piercing each day. There had been no tenderness, no sweet surprises that weren't, but were. Even before: During their courtship she heard subdued hissing. It never occurred to Dorothy that the rattling and hissing would magnify to such monstrous proportions. Joe Cephus appeared to be on another plane committing acts to chase a person away whom he genuinely wanted to stay. As with a slave-master acting out, I need you to make me master, and your being my slave, gives me powerful prerogative to maim you, destroy, harness you, lest you rise up and I lose my kingdom.

One night after Joe Cephus worked the extra shift, Dorothy heard him slam the car door, then the back door. Their bedroom door was open, so he slammed it against the wall. Realizing what he had done, he inspected the mark it made. Joe Cephus really did not want to harm his house, car, or clothes. "Don't needle me. I'm tired." He began undressing, threw his clothes on the floor, and ordered her to pick them up. She did.

"Don't you go near that toilet. I'm gonna use it."

"I've had my bath. Don't take an extra shift it if makes you that tired," Dorothy suggested.

"I didn't ast if you took a baf. I said don't go near that toilet. And don't tell me what to do on MY job. I ast you not to needle me and you doin' it anyhow."

The next thing she realized, Joe Cephus had torn her bathrobe off and pushed her out the front door naked. She heard him laugh as she rushed back in.

Without knocking, he went into his mother's room. Dorothy heard Miss Mary-Bekki say, "Joe Cephus I told you 'bout comin' in here without knockin'. I know it's yo' house, but I live in this room." When Dorothy heard Miss Mary-Bekki ask, "Joe Cephus, have you gone asylum crazy?" Dorothy knew he went for the small gun he said was for her protection.

"Mind ya business, Mama! I'm tired and can't stand no needlin'." Joe Cephus rushed back into their bedroom. "I don't need no po-leece gun." He aimed it at Dorothy. She just looked at him, while he waved the gun looking like a Rhesus monkey in his shorts. Not the least bit frightened, Dorothy told herself to dare him to fire it, or grab his hand, aim it upward, and pull the trigger. Dorothy did not believe the gun was loaded. Joe Cephus was too much of a coward, the type of bully who made faces at babies to scare them, and licked their daddies' boots to prove he was innocent.

Miss Mary Bekki banged on the door. "Boy, if you don't brang that gun back in here, I'm goin' to report you to the po-leece myself. You'll sho' lose your job!"

Joe Cephus took advantage of the excuse to return the gun, but not before aiming it at Dorothy again. What became one of his morning delights, early the next morning Joe Cephus toyed with the light switch, turning it off and on so Dorothy couldn't sleep, hoping to get a response. He rushed into the bathroom and prolonged his stay, knowing she had to commute over thirty miles to make an eight o'clock class. When Dorothy reminded him, which was just what he wanted, he reminded her, shouting, "This is MY house, MY toilet, MY water. I told you last night not to needle me," and watched her dodge his fists and feet. He would think about it all day. He had beaten and annoyed his wife, a college per-fesser. Nobody on the po-leece force in Granston, white or colored, maybe in the whole state of North Carolina, could say that.

CHAPTER 11

Dorothy Borden's First Husband

Taking inventory of her life deepened creases in Dorothy's brow. Marriage was not first with her, nor second, or third. It was not even on her list–as much as she considered men a necessary element in her life. Dorothy knew deep inside before each of her two marriages that she was doing what she did not want to do. She was paying for it.

Under threats of annihilation of her family if she didn't make a choice, Dorothy would be forced to choose Luther, her first husband. He was woefully dull and uninteresting, but he had deep compassion for children, old people, and animals. Joe Cephus actively disliked anything or anybody that he could not beat, have sex with, and order to pay his bills.

Dorothy wondered how much of a compromise white women made. Although much better off, she had heard that many white women didn't have it too good either. However, just as other positive elements in society, white women had more of the legal system on their side and used it far, far more than colored women. There was something so wrong with the social and psychological structure of colored women and relationships, according to Dorothy's experiences, personal and vicarious. Marriage benefited the man. Other than legitimizing a woman's children, Dorothy could not determine its asset. Marriage was an impediment. A psychological, sociological, sexual, growth and developmental intrusion even with Luther, despite his positive traits. This inventory began to remove a veil. Dorothy began to realize that she had completely missed her partnership role: *she should have been a man's mistress.* She felt like crying. What a delightful mistress she would have made. She and the man both had been cheated.

Dorothy recognized that she had not acted wisely. Luther had been a stranger. Dorothy did not even know his correct age or that he had been married previously and had a son until she accidentally found his army discharge papers after they married. He had not indicated a previous marriage on their license. According to his discharge papers, the son was an adult when WWII ended. Dorothy remembered how Luther entered her life.

Immediately after completing a B.S. degree, at Hampton Institute, A Negro college in Virginia, Dorothy went to seek her fortune in New York City. Jobs were plentiful during the World War II era, and she had passed the New York City teaching exam, and was hired immediately. She met Luther at an USO in Hackensack, New Jersey where she went out of curiosity with friends, one who had a brother in the service. Luther went to the South Pacific, they corresponded, and when he returned to New York she had her first sexual experience and married him. She wasn't in love, or particularly fond of him, and the sexual experience left her wishing she had not. Disgusted with herself, Dorothy had marred the beautiful picture she had of matrimony. She had no hopes (only foolish dreams) of marrying the man she loved, who had chosen a wife while she was still in undergrad school and he in the Army, WWII. This man she wanted to be her first, but now he would not want her, even if he were not married. Now that she had had sex with someone else.

Dorothy and Luther both fell into the "for-a-whiles." Luther, soft-spoken, kind and gentle, appeared to be deeply interested in her pursuit of a Master's degree—for a while. He even got his first library card in order to get books she needed. Dorothy settled down to acting wifely–for a while. She made the error Nella Larsen cautioned about in her novel *Quicksand*: Dorothy stopped thinking. Fortunately, for a while.

Before they married, Luther came to Granston and met Dorothy's parents, even went to church with the family. He visited Dorothy's grandparents. Dorothy never met Luther's family except his brother, his wife, and his brother's in-laws.

Not that Dorothy regretted divorcing Luther, who also genuflected to her profession, he at least read at times. He liked Zane Grey novels and talked about them. He also mentioned scenes that sounded like James Fenimore Cooper. He went with Dorothy to Broadway plays, where they sat in the balcony for less than two dollars at that time. He liked movies and Burgess Meredith as an actor, and discussed the first King Kong movie. He read *Leave Her to Heaven*, saw the film, and compared them. Luther knew New York subway history, when each was built, how long it took, and the number of people injured or killed during construction. He tried to establish conversation between Dorothy and himself, and wanted her to be happy, but asked a question that destroyed any possibility: "What else do you want? You have a husband and a baby!" Dorothy was not marriage material. She detested being someone's housekeeper, cook, and as she saw it, fuckee. In his Luther way, he was a good father and worshiped their daughter. The child soon learned to dress herself, attend to most of her personal needs, put away toys, and even set the table. Luther insisted these were Dorothy's duties, and demanded, "What you think I got you here fur." On his day off, Luther smiled broadly, as he talked with his little girl. He bathed and dressed her, combed her hair, and took her to parks, sometimes all the way to his job in Queens, showing her off. Luther's income was not sufficient, but he was generous with it. At times Dorothy would think he would make a different girl a good Luther-husband, a girl who considered her role to be a cook, housekeeper, and an incubator, or one who did not realize she was donating services as an overworked cook, housekeeper, and nanny, whose compensation was systematic nightly and days-off incursions she accepted as love-making.

Another one of Luther's traits that Dorothy found most annoying was his attitude toward sex, which she later learned was a much much milder version of Joe Cephus who also thought sex eradicated all that was wrong or undesirable in marriage. Luther wanted Dorothy to enjoy sex, to find it irresistible with him. Joe Cephus didn't care. Sex to him was something to *have* because you were man and wife. Having was the enjoyment to Joe Cephus. Dorothy wanted Luther to offer something or at least dream of or consider something that wrought permanent gratifying change, such as his getting a higher paying job. More income could bring about an entire new lifestyle and a more rewarding sense of self. Sex was O.K., and most times enjoyable, but afterwards there was no enduring desirable transformation. Same Bronx apartment, same not enough money to pay bills, same wondering if the "birth control" will work. When she attempted a discussion, Luther's answer was always the same: "You not satisfied wid me?" or "Who been here?" He made Dorothy feel as if she were incapable of criticizing her situation, and. above all, void of aspirations–and dreams. Like Joe Cephus, he appeared not to be curious about a vast world that even people like them could edge into–challenge–and even conquer a bit of it. His marriage to a school teacher was the culmination of his dreams. He did not realize that Dorothy Borden could not be frigged into contentment.

CHAPTER 12

Back to Joe Cephus

How Joe Cephus boasted about his wife, yet resented her role, such as Dorothy's attending conferences, being asked to make speeches, or students calling to clarify assignments, and meeting them in libraries to supervise special research. After conferences, he spent nights making coitus distasteful. Its failure to be consensual was ammunition. The act became abusive. Looking back, analyzing, Dorothy described Joe Cephus as a neophyte pathetically searching to validate himself.

The summer Dorothy went to Europe, a program sponsored by her graduate school, Joe Cephus boasted that his "wife–a college per-fesser–was going to school in Europe and his money was short." He withheld the dollar he put in his church's Sunday collection. Upon Dorothy's return, he seemed to have prepared an armory stockpiled with humiliation, stating, "she been to Europe with all them white folks. White men made love but colored men fuck." He stressed women preferred the latter. His demonstration was enough to turn a woman against sex. Dorothy told herself and friends it was fortunate she had a positive experience before marriage to Joe Cephus and was looking forward to another one. Joe Cephus acted as if he were truly psychologically flawed.

Dorothy's opinion that J.C.'s thinking was seriously blemished solidified when he came home one night seeking sympathy: "Dot, me and Officer Peters had some words today. He's that white po-leece who can't stand cul-lud folks, especially cul-lud po-leecemen. I told him I was a po-leece just like he was, the first cul-lud they hired, and walked away. He followed me and pushed me. It didn't hurt, but he had no business puttin' his hands on me."

"He *pushed* you? What did you do?"

"Reported 'im to the Chief and the Union."

Dorothy felt the familiar heat rush to her face and through her body. She closed her eyes and wished so hard Joe Cephus had not told her. Disgust for her husband was squared, and if any respect lay dormant, it vanished forever. Here was a man who kicked and beat his colored wives, and intimidated and threatened an old colored woman with arrest who he said was gossiping about his having an extra marital affair, which he was. He had the woman terrified. Here was a man who put his colored wife out of the house unclothed and chased his first wife in the streets, who delighted in brandishing his gun at the women he married—and *reports a white man, a fellow officer, to a union for assaulting him. Physical contact in anger is interpreted in Granston as ASSAULT. He says pushing him did not hurt.* Words continued to bellow inside Dorothy's head: *You stupid cowardly fool, you should be able to leave your foot up that Cracker's ass. The same foot you used to kick me. It did not hurt? What kind of colored man are you? NIGGER, it should be your greatest pain—and shame. You helped elevate a common white man to the status of conqueror, a man who has no stature except that which he derived from showing his disdain for a fellow policeman because he is colored.—The man committed an unprovoked assault.* —Somewhere in the dark soundless yet deafening void, Dorothy heard Joe Cephus add, "They made him apologize—."

Dorothy could understand a colored man's hesitating to strike back at a white man, but could not accept the colored man's cowardly "bravado" toward his colored wives, his boasting about his temper, and that "he didn't take shit off nobody." Her thoughts were so loud, had he been listening, he would have heard. It must have been a prayer as Dorothy's silence shrieked, *GOD, DON'T LET THIS SLIMY EXCUSE FOR MAN CLIMB ON TOP OF ME AGAIN. He wants me to be his cook, housekeeper, and supplement his income –*

She had to say something aloud, and did so quietly, hoping Joe Cephus would feel the depth of her words: "You say you have a high temper and can't help it, and you don't take anything off *anybody*–and you reported a white officer to the Union for *ASSAULTING* you–"

Joe Cephus shouted, "THE MAN SAID HE WAS SORRY! NOW FORGET IT! OUGHTA NOT TOLD YOU. YOU ALWAYS TRY TO STIR THINGS UP. MAKE 'EM MORE THEN THEY ARE. KEEP SOMETHIN' GOIN' WHEN IT'S ALL OVER WIF!"

Over with? Dorothy thought, *IT IS ANOTHER BEGINNING of the continuation of white men's disrespect and contempt for you. His pushing you is a vestige of the slave and master syndrome. Every white and colored officer will know that.* Dorothy did not know what Joe Cephus should have done. *–But at least RETURN THE CRACKER'S PUSH.* –She knew the scene would remain with her forever, further corroding the image of Joe Cephus Divine. It was his greatest abuse of her.

Later, one night Joe Cephus looked up from his daily reading the obituaries, "Dot, Chief Spry ast how me and Officer Peters wuz getting' along. I told 'im all right and that I was just as good as Officer Peters and anybody else. Even if he call me J.C. and I have to call him Officer Peters, God made me, too. I got the same initials as Jesus Christ. There's a church on Blues Street wif a picture of the Lord painted on the window. About my color. I told the Chief I look like that picture. Like the Lord."

Dorothy smiled in amusement and pity. She observed Joe Cephus, and closed her eyes to see him better. *If God made Joe Cephus, God must have run out of clay and used sh–offal.* Dorothy used to imagine how God looked. He changed from the huge bearded giant in elementary school to looking like the white man

Western artists painted. At some time he became the colored Master Artist, power emulating from his Omnipresence. Never in her stormy turbulent imagination had she thought in terms of God resembling a Rhesus monkey-looking cheap, stingy, woman abuser. She'd have to change her prayers to honor Joe Cephus. "Now I lay me down to sleep, I pray to Joe Cephus my soul *not* to keep. If I should die before I wake, I pray Joe Cephus my soul *not* to take." She'd end with "What a man" instead of "a men." – And *she* must save her soul—*soon*–.

Their marriage ended one night after a "we gonna fuck or fight tonight" round. Joe Cephus had "carried on" until he lost his erection. When Dorothy breathed a sigh of relief, and Joe Cephus questioned her, instead of feigning sorrow, or acting innocent, she truthfully told him that it was the most enjoyable part of having sex with him. He slapped Dorothy repeatedly, and hissed his customary remark, "I'm not hittin' you that hard. I can't help 'caused you bruise easy," followed by caustic laughter. He ridiculed her natural sensuous body warmth he had once praised, and according to her first husband Luther many women would give half their lives to have. Before their marriage, during intimacy, Dorothy had revealed that Luther had been her first sexual lover. Joe Cephus remembered and jeered, "You the only girl I know who couldn't get at least one soldier to lay her doin' war time. Shoulda wore a sign 'Free Red Hot Tail.' His customary kick missed its mark as Dorothy threw whatever was in her reach at him.

She heard his mother knock on the door. Joe Cephus opened it wide enough to shout, "This MY house MY wife and MY business, Mama. KEEP OUTTA MY BUSINESS!" He slammed the door.

"Boy, open this door. I wanna talk to you."

He opened the door, stood in it.

Rarely showing anger, Miss Mary-Bekki did not conceal it when she said, "I told your Daddy you didn't have good sense when you was a baby. Told 'im when you was growin' up you was a devil. Just foolin' folks. But not me. Somebody's gonna find out how mean you are, and, Boy, the devil's gonna charge you. You mistreated two wives. The first one nothin' but a child. Yo' next wife's gonna make you pay. Mark my words!"

"Puttin' bad mouth on me. My own Mama puttin' bad mouth on me. Much as I do for you."

"I ain't no fool, Boy. *I do for you*! Don't think I don't know. Boy, you gonna catch it one of these days."

"This woman's gonna catch it NOW. Mama, you don't know this woman. Throwin' things at me."

"You fightin' her. Kickin' and carryin' on. I know now how you treated yo' sisters."

"How I treated my sisters got nothin' to do wif it. –And she got no business throwin' things. This woman even got rid of my baby. Flushed it down the toilet!"

"That's what happened to all your seed. Your seed's cussed. As many women you had, everythang you put in 'em went down the toilet. 'Cept that po' lil thang the Lord let live awhile to show you how you sinned by messin' up that child you had to marry."

"This woman can go down the toilet. I'M PUTTIN' HER OUT THIS NIGHT WHAT'S HERE." And he did.

Joe Cephus dragged Dorothy's valise from under the bed, stuffed what clothes he could in it, emptied contents of her dresser drawer in the valise, forced it to close by standing on it, tossed whatever he found that belonged to her in his car, and told her to get in. He drove to the Borden home and dumped everything on the porch. As he left, Dorothy Borden told him with relief, "This is the end of our marriage, you know." And it was.

Joe Cephus sped away.

Dorothy knew this was what she had been waiting for–the act Joe Cephus was destined to commit. Relief mounted. She knew with all certainty that this was marriage-death. And there would be no resurrection. She also knew what would happen next with Joe Cephus. And it happened.

Before it happened, using the key she always kept, Dorothy let herself in her parents' house, hers again now.

"That you, Dorothy?"

"Yes, Daddy. You don't need to get up."

Neither one of her parents was surprised that she returned. First, she went to the kitchen for ice. A cold pack would reduce her swollen face. She didn't want her father and mother to see. Daddy would certainly beat the hell out of Joe Cephus before having him arrested. Not that she cared, but she didn't want her father involved in a low Joe Cephus brawl.

Careful not to waken her daughter, Dorothy closed the child's room door, went to her own room, lay across her childhood bed, applying ice to her swollen face, planning. Early the next morning she would call the car pool driver and tell him not to pick her up and the College Department secretary to request sick leave. After her father left for his office, she would put on sun glasses, avoid her daughter and mother, but explain hurriedly that she left Joe Cephus and had to attend to personal business immediately. She would go to the bank and have her name removed from the joint account, withdraw her last deposit, open a new account at another branch, go to the post office and have her mail re-routed to her house, the Borden house. *Permanently.*

It began to happen as Dorothy predicted. Joe Cephus certain that he had solidified his control, and Dorothy was anxiously waiting for him to ask her to return, haughtily called later that morning and left word for her to call him at home in ten or fifteen minutes, or at work after that time. Dorothy knew she would never call Joe Cephus again. And she didn't. That evening, he waited on a corner for Dorothy to come home from work, but she hadn't gone. He was hot with resentment thinking she spent the night with one of her colleagues. He called late that night and hung up when Mr. Borden answered. Joe Cephus decided the best thing to do was to go to Dorothy's office. He'd take half-day leave. He didn't know her class schedule, but would try about lunch time. She always acted like a lady at work. He didn't want to keep her waiting too long for him to tell her she could come back. He'd wear his uniform. Make her proud. He inspected his mustache again.

After a class session, Dorothy found Joe Cephus sitting at her desk in her shared office. Grinning as if nothing had happened, he asked, "Hey. Hungry? Let's go get a sa'-mich. Hot dog or something."

"Office hours. I can't leave," Dorothy lied.

"I didn't come to take you to eat," Joe Cephus grinned broader.

I know you didn't, Dorothy thought. *You're too cheap and stingy.*

"Ain't you gonna ast me what I come for?" He asked still grinning.

Ignoring him, Dorothy looked through students' papers.

"Came to tell you, you can come on back. I'll come get you and yo' things tonight."

She continued to examine papers.

An office mate entered, "Hey, Dottie. This must be your husband. Heard he was a policeman."

Joe Cephus grinned, and waited for an introduction. He introduced himself, and left out "first cul-lud hired." Progress, Dorothy thought.

"I didn't check my mail box," she told her office mate. "We're supposed to check soon as possible when we get here and before leaving." Dorothy rushed out. She did not know when Joe Cephus left because she had lunch in the faculty dining room and went from there to her next class.

Joe Cephus even ventured to her house at a time when he figured Mr. Borden was at work. Mrs. Borden answered the door her fashion, her face placid. She did not respond to Joe Cephus' grin. He waited while Dorothy completed reading what she had planned and came into the living room, sober faced. There he was. Tears rolled down his cheeks, entered his mustache. "Dottie, you know I don't mean things I do. Come on back. Please. They won't happen no more." He wiped the tears.

Dorothy had been wondering what she could do to get back at Joe Cephus. It had to be subtle, without public ignominy. He was stupid enough to think she wanted him–Dorothy looked at him compassionately, and with sympathy and understanding she told him, "Joe Cephus, you are making me see that a lot of what happened is my fault. But if you ever hit me or put me out again for any reason, we're through for good. Understand."

"Yes."

"And, Joe Cephus, I'll give us a year, and if things are all right, we should have a baby."

Joe Cephus could hardly believe what he was hearing. He grabbed her hand, began thanking her profusely for giving him a chance to prove to himself and Granston that he knows how to treat a wife and children.

"I'll come and get you–tonight," he gushed, assuming his most pharisaic look. "You too nice-sa-girl not to be married. Trashy women don't stay wif they husbands."

"I know." Dorothy dropped her head. "Let me come back myself. This week end." She led him to the door.

He dried his eyes. "I learned my lessen. I'm gonna change. I'll give you another dresser drawer. Find somewhere else to put my things. And get another closet. That one's getting shaky."

"Another drawer will be helpful–and a stronger closet. I'm going to change, too. Pay more bills. Even all of them from September to June just as you want me to."

"Dottie, let me kiss you–"

She controlled the urge to regurgitate. "Let's save everything for the weekend."

"O.K. We'll spend all day Sunday in the bed."

Dorothy swallowed the rising sensation to heave.

She watched Joe Cephus don his innocent "work and outside" face. He paused to admire his uniformed image in the foyer mirror and opened the door for himself. "See you this weekend. You come back. I really want you to."

"Thanks," Dorothy told him quietly, and watched him strut down the walk. As he got into his car, he lowered his eyes in obeisance to something in his world that told him it was appropriate.

Two days later, Friday, Dorothy's classes ended earlier. Joe Cephus was still at work. He had called each night telling Dorothy how glad he was that she coming back like the nice girl she was. Not wanting her father accused of aiding and abetting, Dorothy did everything herself, including hiring the colored man who owned "WMAA–We Move Anybody Anywhere" business to transport her books, shelves and other left behind things back to the Borden house. She said good-bye to Miss Mary-Bekki, thanked and hugged her for being so nice, and left the Divine house forever.

CHAPTER 13

Joe Cephus' Awaking

Dorothy was pleased, calculating that Joe Cephus sincerely had no idea his action would cause such an ending. Later, when he called, she explained: "Joe Fester, your putting me out was throwing a rabbit into the briar patch. You thought I'd come back and you'd begin where you left off, kicking, humping and pumping, using me as a receptacle for pus from your pumping–and looking forward to a future housekeeper and a bill-payer, a washerwoman and a bill-payer, a cook and a bill-payer. It won't be me. And nobody like me. You are where you're going. Five, ten, fifteen years from now, if you're not dead, you'll be here in Granston peddling your pumper. I'll be teaching in a college in New York City, traveling in the summer, and being made love to, not pumped." She hung up.

Nothing halted Joe Cephus' begging-back campaign. Not even her duplicity. Joe Cephus did not regard her deception as deliberate, but a change wrought by jealous outsiders: He continued to call. He wrote letters that she corrected with a red pencil. He begged to come to her house and to take her riding. He resorted to threats:

"I'll report you for getting rid of my baby." And pulled his rank. "Folks'll believe me 'cause I'm a po-leece. And I'll tell them that's why I put you out".

"And I'll say you put me out because I wouldn't let you perform phallasia with me. In case you don't know what that means, it's what you accused me of doing with Al Benson and kicked me about. I'll have him subpoenaed and prove you lied about him and me."

Dorothy knew there was not need to say anything else. Joe Cephus would not risk being accused of committing the most disgraceful act in his sexual world. Beyond that, he would not risk a confrontation with Al Benson. A colored man can be a formidable foe when battling another colored man. Sometimes worse than a white man who didn't have to prove as much. Joe Cephus fell silent. Dorothy hung up and left the receiver off the hook.

Dorothy didn't mention she would also tell he owned and brandished an illegal gun. She just might really report that, and to mention it would alert Joe Cephus. He would get rid of the gun. Dorothy remained seated at the telephone table. For a moment she felt sorry for Joe Cephus. He had so much to prove–or thought he had. And he had no idea how, but thought he did. –Her father– whatever he had to prove, he did, or he controlled it, leaving himself undiminished to regard his family with tenderness and bestow on them the acme of protection–even if it was necessary to use the word *colored to describe the aegis.*

Joe Cephus called and played the trick on her that he boasted about playing on other girls: He would lay the receiver down, go away, and leave them talking. Dorothy retaliated, adding her tricks, "Hold on. I want to go upstairs where I can talk privately," or "Hold on. Someone's at the door," never returning to the phone until she knew he had hung up.

No insult overtly frustrated Joe Cephus. The more he insisted that he wanted and needed her, the more determined she was not to be involved in Joe Cephus' needs and wants. However, she began to enjoy taking advantage of his persistence. During one of his telephone weeping sessions, he begged fervently and sincerely, "Dottie, I'll do ANYTHING if you come back. ANYTHING I wanna be married like anybody else. I'm just as sorry as I can be about anything I did you think I should-na done."

Dorothy smiled, telling herself she would put on an act that would give her an Academy Award nomination. She'd get an Oscar.

Dorothy sighed as if fatigued and ready to give in. "Joe Cephus, are you telling the truth?"

"Dottie, you KNOW I am. You too nice-sa-girl not to forget all them bad things."

"I can, Joe Cephus, and we can start anew. –IF–" –*In drama was this the McCready pause?* –Dorothy smiled–

Joe Cephus waited.

Then – "Dottie, *please* let's start over *please.*"

Dorothy Borden hesitated again. "All right. I'll give you another chance," she responded with quiet sincerity, passion, and even more fatigue. So real this time. "We're too old to carry on like this and should try to make this marriage work. And it will. On three conditions. This absolutely my final offer."

"Just name them. I'll do them." Joe Cephus told himself he had won! He knew he would if he kept begging. Dorothy Borden was nobody but a woman like other women who wanted to be married. Quickly he began making plans: While they were on good terms, he'd do everything possible to see that Dorothy became pregnant again. She could not go to New York and travel in the summer with a baby.

Dorothy waited for Joe Cephus to grasp her faked sincerity and clutch it to whatever represented his heart and soul.

"Now listen carefully. Wish you could record it so there won't be a misunderstanding."

"It won't!" Joe Cephus was jubilant. "Just tell me the three conditions!"

Another Dorothy Borden interlude. –"Your buttocks will have to solidify and become a gold nugget. Your testicles will have to ossify and become twin jewels. And your penis will have to ejaculate liquid silver. –So it is stated, so let it be done." She quietly placed the receiver on its hook.

Joe Cephus began "dating" and called one night warning Dottie he'd better not catch her dating. She hung up. Christmas came. Joe Cephus called sounding as if things between them were patched and pleasant. "Let's go to the CPCF–Cul-lud Po-leece Christmas Formal. Let me know the color of your dress, so I'll know what kinda car-sarge to get you. I'm gonna rent a tux instead of wearing my uniform."

"I'm going to spend Christmas in New York."

"Stay for this dance. Go later. It's cold up there."

"Already made plans and got plane reservations. It won't be cold where I'll be." Dorothy did not add that she wouldn't go with him anywhere under any circumstances, including heaven.

Furious, but desperately hoping to prove it wasn't true by persuading her to stay in Granston, Joe Cephus accused her of the unforgivable. "You must be going to see white men."

Quietly, she responded: "*Man!* Understand me? *Man!* I don't need but one." She placed the receiver quietly on the hook, smiling, knowing that a man prizes denial in a woman even as he begs for truth.

While Joe Cephus continued to call at intervals, without telling him, Dorothy made plans to leave Granston. She filed job applications in New York, went for interviews, and placed her name on the lists for an apartment. While Joe Cephus searched for a male connection Dorothy might have in Granston, she spent long weekends in New York, Connecticut, and Rhode Island establishing, activating, and continuing friendships and bonds.

Joe Cephus filed for a divorce based on two years separation and received it uncontested. Two years had not passed according to their actual separation date, and Dorothy was surprised that he had the nerve to tamper with legal terms, especially being a "po-leece—the first cul-lud hired." She concluded that either he had really forgotten or wanted her to contest the divorce. He would be so proud to say, "She didn't want me to divorce her. Tried to stop it." She was finished with Joe Cephus forever and didn't care how he obtained a divorce as long as he paid for it. He did. Dorothy Borden sighed with relief. And felt the returning of her self she liked.

Joe Cephus, adorned in his immaculate uniform, badge gleaming, night stick polished, grinned at Dorothy's friends, offered to take them for rides in his recently simonized car, and even smiled and flirted with wives. Dorothy listened to their amusement, and accepted a position in a four-year college in Brooklyn that had a large colored student enrollment and was under pressure to enlarge its colored faculty. She left Granston, promising her daughter she would bring her to New York soon as she got an apartment. She visited Granston often. In a little over two hours she could be in her house in Granston from New York for less than one hundred dollars round trip. During these visits, friends and people who wanted her to know said Joe Cephus was "peddling his peter" as she had predicted. He dated a beautician briefly, a teacher in near by High Point, and still sought Dorothy's eligible friends. But never one of his former before-Dottie girlfriends. The last she heard of him, he was "tight with Johnnye Jamison."

CHAPTER 14
Dorothy's New Life

Dorothy Borden certainly had no intentions of ever marrying again. But she did. She didn't announce it via the paper in Granston, as required of colored middle-class marriages. She told her mother, but since her father's heart was "acting up," resulting in two heart attacks, they decided not "to tell him just yet." He had expressed so adamantly that if she married again, it should be to "a professional colored man." It would certainly set an example for her daughter if nothing else. Lawyer Borden, as he was known in Granston, died without knowing of his daughter's third husband.

In retrospect, Dorothy called her third and last marriage to Magdar Zelard, a Hungarian, rehabilitation after Joe Cephus. Magdar admired her and her métier, but in a different way. He delighted in discussing academia and wanted Dorothy to help him perfect his English. But she liked the way he spoke. Example: Instead of saying "whisper," he said "tell it to my ear." They met in Washington Square Park after an NYU anthropology class taught by Ethel Alpenfels, their favorite teacher. Dorothy and Zelard began going to the library together. They debated theories, criticized each other's responses to assignments, explored Greenwich Village and searched for health food stores and restaurants. They sat in Washington Square Park where Magdar told some of his WWII experiences in Hungary. Dorothy related some of her experiences in the South, personal and vicarious.

Dorothy did something she never thought she could do hygienically. Without a toothbrush, deodorant, or douche paraphernalia, she spent the night in Magdar's apartment on Barrow Street in Greenwich Village. The next morning they showered together. Dorothy had felt she would never get or feel clean in the same water with another person. Dorothy and Magdar had such a good time, they found themselves married. She left her daughter's godparents' Bronx apartment and moved to The Village.

Magdar was kind and gentle, and didn't care what she did or did not do as long as she remained black, kinky haired, and intelligent. He liked running his fingers through her hair, and begged her not to straighten it, which was a contrast to Joe Cephus' and even Luther's saying her hair on the back of her neck was like a sheep's ass. Magdar wanted her to stay in the sun as much as possible and become darker, adding that if he wanted a white girl he would get one. This was *before* it was popular or acceptable for a black woman to show off her black skin and "nappy" hair, especially a middle-class Black woman. Dorothy recalled hearing how Dee "lorated" them. "Lorate" was a term Dee used to really put a person, especially a woman, way down. "She call herself a schoo-oo-l teach-ur wid that nappy head!"

Magdar adjusted Dorothy's bed pillows, covered her with a blanket if the apartment was chilly, wiped her face with cold towels and brought her ice water and chilled fruit juices when it was hot. He wanted Dorothy to be happy—and to enjoy sex, always making certain it was consensual. They both liked that. They became careless. Magdar saw the distressful look on Dorothy's face that became terror when the test was positive. He knew she was ready to fly away, and he didn't want any part of her to leave. He also suspected she had spent all her motherhood on one child. He gathered she had been a doting mother, almost too much so, an excellent caregiver, but no more. She now heaped it on students, animals, and him, where demands had strict limitations. She could give within those limitations, but not outside or beyond. Magdar took her back to his Hungarian doctor. Afterwards, Dorothy closed her eyes to the sad look in Magdar's eyes, as they both lay embracing each other, Magdar thinking what a beautiful baby it would have been. He saw himself walking a tousled haired boy in Washington Square Park, or a little girl with enough African that curled her would-have-been straight hair and brought a rosy tan to her would-have-been fair skin. Dorothy and Magdar silently decided they would not talk about it, and it would never happen again. Dorothy hugged him tighter and braced herself for causing Magdar this trauma and for being relieved that it was better his than hers.

Dorothy hated housekeeping. Magdar didn't seem to notice or mind if the apartment was in disarray, or that she kept lost and stray dogs and cats until they could be placed in suitable homes, spent lots of money on veterinarian bills and pet food, and called or left notes for him to feed and give fresh water to the menagerie when she would be delayed or had night classes. He appeared not to care that she rarely cooked unless it was a spur of the moment exotic dish, an ethnic treat, or a sudden craving. He brought ready or almost ready prepared food from health stores and served it.

Sometimes they walked around in the Village holding hands, pausing to buy what looked exotic and tempting, or they went to health food restaurants, especially on weekends or after a play or poetry reading. It sounded so right: both health food enthusiasts who read far into the night noshing on health goodies in bed, either with or without each other. They both took lots of vitamins. They could go for days without sex and not feel neglected or unmarried, both enjoying it to the utmost when they did, not because they hadn't, and it was time, but merely because they really wanted to. Magdar's tucking her in bed and adjusting her pillow usually was an indication he would sleep on the couch. He spent hours at night in a Village gym or SPA or bowling while

Dorothy went to classes at NYU, wrote, corrected papers, read, or just enjoyed being alone. They both liked allowing space.

Dorothy would be glued to themes and term reports when Magdar returned to the apartment quietly. Sometimes she would be enclosing checks to Animal Rights organizations and signing petitions. He would place a container of food on the desk or table beside whatever she was doing. She would look up and smile, maybe offer a kiss. Sometimes he just petted a dog or cat, or sneaked a peek at her papers and found every sentence had been scrutinized. He knew because he had inspected enough documents to detect even the slightest pen or pencil traces. She had made comments consistently, corrected grammar, dotted i's crossed t's, made suggestions, reacted to content. He could see and hear her smiles, shudders, her pleasure, and hope written in words, such as "WHAT! GREAT! WISH I HAD WRITTEN THIS! CONFERENCE?"

Sometimes students came to the tiny apartment for conferences. They had stopped by Chock-Full-of-Nuts and brought her favorites: cream cheese with walnuts on rye and hot chocolate. Once when they came before she returned home, Magdar asked, "How do students like Professor Borden?" They responded, "Serious students like her. Others complain." Magdar wished she had been his teacher, and remembered she often said, "I learn so much from my students. Hope they get half as much from me." He saw her schedule and discovered she observed far more than required office hours. She also spent time with students on the College Campus, in Washington Square Park, Chock-Full-of-Nuts, and quaint restaurants in The Village that featured large frosted glasses of fruit juices. Magdar didn't mind. There was enough of her left for him. Potency does not have to come in huge quantities, nor is it necessary to possess all of it.

Dorothy and Magdar delighted in personal hygiene and showered, bathed, and massaged each other with health store soaps and lotions. Both shunned alcohol and tobacco. They never quarreled; instead they had fun "psychoanalyzing" each other.

One of Magdar's friends, a psychology doctoral candidate, gave them the Rorschach test, but despite their begging refused to give them his analysis. The information was for his dissertation and confidential. They devised their own Borden-Zelard test, and had fun anyway.

Neither Dorothy nor Magdar said or did anything to hurt each other. Nor did they use profanity or say anything off-color. Dorothy felt corruption from Joe Cephus drain from her.

Dorothy and Magdar liked being seen together. He was very fair and didn't tan. In contrast, Dorothy looked black, but according to colored people she was "medium brown." It sounded so right. However, both were relieved when almost two years later they verbalized that it was not as right as it seemed. This was not the way they wanted to spend the rest of their lives. They wanted something else, something hidden and elusive. Dorothy began acting out discontentment in small ways. Magdar was first to mention it, "telling it to her ear" in his sensuous accent, as they lay beside each other.

"We should not lose the taste of what was so—delicious. Let it go, but stay in our hearts and take it with us along all ways. We will not forget forever."

Dorothy feeling weepy repeated to herself "take it with us along all ways." He might have meant "take it with us always," but she liked "take it with us along all ways" much better and knew she "would not forget him forever."

So they replaced sentiment with common good, common cause, and common sense.

Magdar informed Dorothy that he had money for a divorce. She never knew exactly his job description on Wall Street except he had the command of four languages and did a lot of translating and interpreting, and was in a large office with other personnel, but had a private phone. She had met him at his work site for lunch and dinner. His desk was piled high with papers, his shelves stacked with folders, surrounded by file cabinets. His brief case was heavy and always filled with papers he read sometimes at night.

He consistently had money for their needs and never asked her to contribute, rejecting direct offers with "as you say in America, hold on to that for a while" or "put it away –how you say it?—for a day when rain falls."

Since they had never taken a trip together and neither had been to Nevada, Magdar suggested they go to Reno for a quick divorce. Dorothy was delighted and offered to help sponsor a trip to Las Vegas. The two had such a good time they both sort of wanted to put the divorce off, but had come this far and used up most of the money they brought.

Afterwards, Magdar helped Dorothy get an apartment in The Village, an almost impossible feat for a colored woman unless she was a celebrity. Walking distance from him, on Christopher Street, they visited each other, but not for sex alone. They liked being together at times. Magdar suggested Dorothy keep the key to his apartment, but she demurred since she didn't want him to have a key to hers. With plans to bring her daughter to New York, she might as well begin establishing house rules: Dorothy never let her daughter "see or hear her do anything that suggested sexual intimacy."

Sometimes they had such a good time discussing so many things and strolling in the Village. And she was enjoying dating, and the theatre, the opera, and planned to do lots of traveling during summers. In addition, there was an older Asian business man who wanted to establish a relationship. One of her friends, white, was dating his partner. Dorothy was interested in this "dating frontier." Magdar suggested they give marriage another try. But Dorothy knew with certainty that she did not have the personality for matrimony. Some years later, she did not know how many, Magdar married a white girl. Dorothy heard no more from him, but saw a front page article about him, along with his picture in *The Village Voice*. The article was one of a series tracking World War II refugees and their lives in The Village years later.

She smiled and told herself she had been rehabilitated after her bout with Joe Cephus. She began a relationship with the

Asian man that lasted after her daughter finished college, after both he and Dorothy retired, and until he died. The association was different. He did not talk much, but said a lot. He did not pay her flowery poetic compliments, but his tributes were filled with sturdy blooming foliage. A business man, he was not rich, but gave her guidance and advice concerning the reality of her future financial needs. Dorothy considered her relationship with him the most satisfactory intimacy she ever had: no marriage, no living together, just bonding. It was also the most lasting. Oh, yes, Mr. Asian respected her job. The status made her more acceptable to his close-knit family. After a while, they actually liked her and considered her a part of the family. –Some of the waiters in his restaurant questioned her job since she did not work every day and all day like public school teachers. This association increased Dorothy's curiosity about and attraction for Mainland China, launching future trips that added opulence to her memory bank.

CHAPTER 15

Joe Cephus Marries Johnnye

During a visit to Granston, Dorothy learned that Joe Cephus had married Johnnye Jamison. When Dorothy expressed concern over another woman's becoming his victim, she was assured by "Dee" that *"Should Johnny Jamison need help, everybody knew she had women friends who would come to her rescue"*

Joe Cephus was ripe for Johnnye. And she was ready for him. Johnnye had chewed gum and watched him grin from one eligible schoolmarm to another. While a few ignored him, some returned his grin. Johnnye, retaining her impish smile as Joe Cephus turned away, knew the marms had cases of the too's: "Too old, too young, too fat, too bony, too ugly, too nice looking [Joe Cephus never thought in terms of women being pretty or beautiful], too un-teacher like, too uppity, too dark, too light skinded, too short nappy hair, too much booze, too goody-goody, too bad breath, too little deodorant, too silly, too much sense." Joe Cephus added another "too," Dorothy found out while married to him: "too low life-ted."

At the Beauticians' Annual Christmas Dance, which Johnnye attended because she heard Joe Cephus would be there, she "accidentally" spilled her drink on his trousers and shoes. Apologizing profusely, "I'm so sorry. I'm really sorry," she stooped

87

and wiped them with a napkin. "I'll have your suit cleaned. At that white place. Ace Cleaners. They're expensive, but good and take out all spots."

Joe Cephus watched her stoop and liked it. He smiled slightly as she stood before him. "Thank you. What about my shoes?"

"They'll be all right. If not I can take them to a place uptown. Swain's. Jews. They're the best in town. Their customers are mostly white."

He is good-looking, Johnnye observed Joe Cephus close-up in festive party lights. —"My name's Johnnye Jamison. I teach at Booker T. Washington Elementary School."

Johnnye saw his pretty mouth stretch under his just-enough mustache, shoving his gorgeous cheeks toward his glowing eyes enhanced by heavy black lashes and eye brows. His thick, glossy-black colored-folks-good hair was brushed to a sensuous Negro curl. Johnnye's glands began their usual dance when she saw a man who looked like he'd be great in bed, and told him sadly, "I'm a widow. My husband died two years ago. Heart attack. You probably heard of him. John Henry Woodard." She bowed her head in reverence.

"No." Joe Cephus told her quickly. He raised himself to his full height, attempting to look down on her, he tilted his head back, and announced, "I'm a po-leeceman. The first cul-lud they hired. I use to be married to Dorothy Borden. Lawyer Borden's daughter. A college per-fesser. Worked at Lexis College 'fore she went to New York after I divorced her. Folks say she's working in a college there."

"By the way, you didn't tell me your name," Johnnye reminded, amused that he told her about Dorothy Borden, and far more than necessary.

Joe Cephus frowned. Didn't she know? He told her he was a po-leece, first cul-lud hired. "Guess."

"Oh, I can't," Johnnye lied. "I keep to myself and don't know many people."

"Joe Cephus Divine," he announced and waited for her to

acknowledge his identity. When she didn't he added, "I live by myself in that brick house over on Applegate Avenue, near Plum Street. Know where Lawyer Borden's house is?"

"I'm not sure," Johnnye evaded the truth again, and asked a question she already knew. "You say you live alone?"

"Yeah. Ever since my mama died." Matter-of-factly, he explained in his best talking-to-a teacher voice and English. "I came home from work and found her dead, laying next to the bucket she was using to scrub my kitchen flo'–floor. I don't like my floors mopped. Mama did it the old-timey way. On her knees. Doctor said she had a heart attack, and her blood pressure wuz– was too high. She spent a lotta money on medicine. I spent a lot on her funeral, too. Used most of her in-shunce. She hadda policy where she use-ta work and kept paying on it after they made her retire."

Johnnye Jamison began serious preparation for Joe Cephus Divine to be her next husband. She dropped her head to show she shared his pain and verbalized sympathetically. "I live alone too. We can cry on each other's shoulders. One weekend I'll come to your house and make you a home cooked meal."

And she did. The next Friday night, she came via white taxi "to keep Dee outta her business." Teachers weren't supposed to even set foot in a man's place if he lived alone, and with caution if he lived with his family. Neighbors wouldn't see her second or third hand car parked at his house. She planned to stay the entire weekend, and arrived with bags of goodies: T-bone steak, fresh vegetables and mushrooms, rice, greens for salad, dessert: apple pie a friend baked for her to say she made and serve a la mode.

Joe Cephus swaggered to the table, grinned inwardly and outwardly, telling himself, "Now here is my kinda woman. One who spends her money when she wants a man." To make conversation, Joe Cephus smiled and asked, "Did you say you teach at Booker T. Washington or Carver? I use to know somebody at both." He spoke carefully, the way he did around white people and teachers.

"Booker T." Johnnye smiled, and put the largest steak on his plate, remembering TA advised establishing from the very beginning that the man's servings are special.

To solidify the impression, Johnnye made certain he saw the grocery bill. The next morning, she got up early and drove Joe Cephus' car to the A & P for breakfast food, prepared it, and served him in bed. She smiled at him while he drank coffee and juice and ate French toast and sausage with an air of arrogance as if she were doing exactly what she should, and it happened to him frequently. Johnnye smiled broader, poured more coffee, as she planned pancakes and bacon for Sunday morning. She spent the weekend as planned, and surmised he must be healthy since he was a policeman. The insurance company would require a medical examination for a large policy.

The sex part of the weekend was "nothing to write home about," Johnnye told her friends, "but Joe Cephus thought it was, and that's what counts." She had become such an expert at faking orgasms she "could fool herself" she added, and "Joe Cephus couldn't stop grinning. He strutted from the bedroom to the bathroom, saying, 'This is the way I like to spend my weekends. In a man's heaven,'" Johnnye mimicked.

Johnnye did not rush Joe Cephus into marriage. They dated for over a year. She wanted people to see that *he* was pursuing *her*. And he was. But she was in control. Tantalizing him, her own pursuit was subtle. She would slip away on weekends, at times secretly. Occasionally she'd be hiding away in a girlfriend's house, or even secluded in her apartment, listening as he rang the phone frantically. To keep in touch Johnnye called her girlfriends, and they used a two-ring-hang-up signal to reach her. Once Joe Cephus called and the line was busy. She told him the phone had been accidentally knocked off the hook. Another time Joe Cephus had an operator to check the line, who said there was a conversation in progress. Upon confrontation, Johnnye was offended that he believed "an inexperience, low-paid white operator" who had obviously made an error. The busy line had to be her old party line that she had gotten rid of. Maybe she should take her phone off the hook to avoid confusion. Joe Cephus begged her not to go that far.

For a while, Johnnye became silent and elusive, then sultry and amorous, as if there were no man on earth like him in bed, the role she found least palatable. As if on an impulse, she called him after midnight, "J.C., I'm so lonesome I could cry." They talked for over an hour about significant trivia, until Johnnye told him almost inaudibly, "I can go to sleep now, J.C. Good night." Only once did she make such a call. It was the type of thing a woman must do only once. It becomes to the man a tantalizing memory, so bewitching that it doesn't matter if it never happens again. Afterwards, Johnnye smiled, got up, mixed a drink to lull her in order to get a few hours sleep before morning. She sipped Bourbon and ginger ale slowly, thinking she must not permit Joe Cephus' quest to run its course.

Joe Cephus assessed his situation seriously. Folks were around for a reason. Johnnye came into his life for a reason. A purpose. A man *had* to have a wife. If not, all of his power and manhood would be wasted. A woman had to have a man to love, honor, and obey like the Bible said. And he tried to do things according to the Bible.

"No use putting it off," Joe Cephus began to tell Johnnye more often. He did not want her to get away, and he was tired of uncertain meals, paying for his shirts to be laundered, coming home to an unmade bed and dusty house, and being responsible for all his bills. "We might as well get married. We spenden all our time wif each other." He added grinning, glancing at his crouch.

To continue controlling Joe Cephus' thinking, Johnnye feigned concern. "My husband died," she waited to gather strength to continue, "but your last wife is alive and comes back to Granston to see her parents–" and hesitated in pretended pain – "you sure you two don't want to go back together? People do remarry."

Joe Cephus would rather have Dorothy because of her professional and family status, but she wasn't coming back. In consolation, he reminded himself that she didn't spend money on him and she never stopped telling him he was a coward and reminding him he took a white man to the union for pushing him, but kicked and beat his colored wives. She held things instead of forgetting about them. And she stopped wanting to have sex. The main thing a woman is for. And she said such nasty things he knew Johnnye would never say. He'd better let Johnnye know he wanted her and not Dorothy Borden.

"Don't know about her, but I'm sure about me. Folks say she's going wif a white man in New York, or some man who's not cul-lud." Joe Cephus stalled in order to harness his rage and impotence– "Nothing but a trashy low-life-ted cul-lud woman would go wif a man outta her race. 'Specially when she could get a good cul-lud man. No decent cul-lud man would have a woman that stoop that low. You too nice-sa girl to wallow in the gutter like that."

Johnnye kissed him to control her snigger, before consoling, "Not as long as I can get a good colored man like you." She could hardly wait until the weekend to tell TA. Joe Cephus told himself he was happy. He had finally found Miss Right.

On August 17, after the famous May 17, 1954, Supreme Court Decision, when Granston's colored teachers were facing uncertain residuals and the aftermath of that Decision, Johnnye told Joe Cephus at their wedding reception, "The Supreme court made its Decision, and we made our Supreme Decision exactly a year and three months later."

Joe Cephus grinned, then cleared his face for a serious statement: "You said cul-lud teachers won't lose they jobs like some folks say when schools start being mix. You keep saying integration's not bad for cul-lud teachers."

Amused, Johnnye kissed him, "Whatever happens, we'll have

each other." She held her glass for a toast, "Until death do us part."

As their glasses touched, hoping Johnnye knew what she was talking about when she said the NAACP, CORE, and Martin Luther King, Jr. wouldn't let colored teachers lose their jobs as some people predicted, Joe Cephus barely heard Johnnye repeat "Until death do us part."

CHAPTER 16

Joe Cephus Ignores Warning Signs

Johnnye and Joe Cephus had married both "hearing things about each other." Johnnye heard via Dee that Joe Cephus was "mean as a rattle snake and just as ornery" and had abused both his wives, even steady girlfriends. Dorothy Borden had been no exception, and she was Lawyer Borden's daughter. Kicking and brandishing a gun were his trademarks. Dee told Johnnye how cheap and stingy Joe Cephus was and looking for a teacher to pay his bills and be his housekeeper. And he relied on teachers sticking by their husbands with loyalty that was conspiratorial. Johnnye shrugged her shoulders and chewed gum. The more she heard, the more certain she was that Joe Cephus Divine deserved to be her husband. The others were sacrificial.

Dee told Joe Cephus–and his Cousin Daisy–"things about Johnnye." He berated the women. "You just jealous. All women do is set 'round and gossip. Glad I'ma man. You women folks don't have nothin' to do wif me and Johnnye business. You oughta mind yours if you got any. If not, get some. "Proud of his deep thinking, Joe Cephus grinned and continued, "Folks talked about Jesus Christ and lied on *Him*. You know they gonna talk and lie on Johnnye."

Joe Cephus discussed his situation with the wisest person in his life, the one he praised for being smart enough to rise so high: himself. He heard that it was Johnnye Jamison, not Dorothy Borden, Al Benson was referring to as the girl who would violate the biggest sexual taboo between colored men and women. Even though that error had cost Dorothy her first encounter with Joe Cephus' foot, he now said it couldn't be true about Johnnye because colored men didn't do nasty things like that. Because they didn't, neither did Johnnye. It just didn't make sense.

Some folks even had the nerve to say Johnnye "liked women," that she went "both ways." Joe Cephus knew that was a lie. How could it be true when she had been married and married to him now? Gossipers substantiated their reports by telling him she lived with some "funny" women when she first came to Granston. Joe Cephus reminded them that she moved out soon as she found out they were "funny." Dee wasn't ready to let go until they told him something most folks didn't talk about and denied hearing: *Johnnye "did something" to her last husband—John Henry Woodard.*

Joe Cephus laughed. "Everybody know John Henry drunk too much. Just drunk hisself to death. Johnnye couldn't stop 'im. You don't die befo' yo' time, and it was just his time."

The most important report to reach Joe Cephus was that one of Johnnye's suitors had given her a beating that left her so bruised she had taken sick leave and disappeared for a while. Joe Cephus smiled and tucked the savory story carefully away in his most treasured storage. It meant that Johnnye had experience with learning a man was boss. Joe Cephus was pleased.

Joe Cephus weighed his situation further: Johnnye was better looking than Dorothy and wore prettier clothes. —And she was just the right color, not "a egg plant," too dark; or "a squash, too light skin-ded she might thank she better then me." Johnnye kept her hair straightened. Sometimes Dorothy waited too long and her hair got nappy 'round the edges and on the back of her neck.

Best of all, Johnnye was working long enough in the same

place to get a good pension. Dorothy Borden didn't stay in one place long. –And the paper said colored and white teachers in Granston were now making the same salaries–just like white and colored policemen. Johnnye would pay a lotta bills. He would save a lotta money to add to his bank account in High Point.

Joe Cephus grinned, felt his crouch, and boasted to himself, "I'm the only po-leeceman in Granston, white or colored, who married a college per-fesser, a lawyer's daughter, divorced her, and married a better deal the second time."

Joe Cephus' Cousin Daisy wondered and questioned. Some folks said he got what he deserved. Nobody who knew Joe Cephus understood how Johnnye had persuaded him to sell the house he so proudly owned. Cousin Daisy had cautiously advised, "Keep your house and rent it. You don't know how this marriage gonna turn out. Don't get yourself where you won't have a place to stay."

Joe Cephus defended his actions. "It'll turn out all right. I wanna be married like other folks, and I'm gettin' too old to be shoppin' 'round."

"A man's never too old–"

"I'll be too old to get who I want. Johnnye want to start from scratch. She sold her house too. She want everythang *new*. We'll put the money on *our* house."

"What you gonna do with your mother's nice things? Her table cloths, china, and all?"

"They *my* thangs now. We'll sell what we don't want. You can have what you want. Sell it to you cheap. Gonna sell some to my good neighbor–you know where I use to eat after Mama died. Gave her a dollar every time I ate there."

"Still say you oughta keep your house," Daisy said sadly. "Wish I wuz able to buy it. I'd rent it if I could afford the rent."

"No. Like I said, Johnnye wanna sell the house and put the money on a new house. *Our* house."

"Still think you're doin' wrong. Everybody I talk to say the same thing. Folks say all kinda things about that woman. They surprise you married her."

"She's the best one for me. Not too old not too young. Cousin Daisy, I found Miss Right. —Folks also say she one of the best elementary teachers in Granston, white or colored. Ever hear that?"

"That ain't got nothin' to do wit what I'm talkin' 'bout, Joe Cephus."

"You talk like I'm the only one who wanted to get married. She did much as I did. Maybe more. She wuz always at my house cookin' and straightenin' up the house and always astin' me to meet her friends and takin' me to they houses for parties. More then I took her to meet mine."

"Humph. Wait and see how much cookin' and cleanin' she gonna do now. Talkin' 'bout friends—you ain't got none, Joe Cephus. After your Mama died, you don't have nobody but me."

"I got all I need: I got Johnnye, and I'm gonna keep her. And folks jealous. Like I always say, nobody's got nothin' to do wif me and Johnnye business." Joe Cephus stopped grinning. "Cousin Daisy, if I lissen to folks, I'll end up by myself. And I don't wanna spend the rest of my life wif out a wife." He knew now he never should have kicked Dorothy Borden about something he heard, and he was glad he had sense enough to marry Johnnye and not listen to something he heard. As if to assure himself, he added, "Johnnye say we gonna be together 'til death do us part—just like the preacher said."

Cousin Daisy looked at him, hoping he'd see the warning in her eyes since his ears couldn't hear.

CHAPTER 17

Warnings begin to surface

Joe Cephus didn't know, but Johnnye had a bid on a house. Using some of the money from the sale of their houses, they made a sizable down payment on this larger place in a colored middle-class neighborhood. The house was to collect secrets so bizarre that many Granstonians simply refused to believe them, ignored them, or carried them along as Granston colored folks lore.

Not too expensive, the initial payment gave them a fifteen year monthly payment plan. Johnnye was *determined* not to be stuck with a mortgage during her retirement. Since it would be expedient for them to be married for a while and *stay together*. Johnny had to make Joe Cephus' leaving difficult should he become too discontented. He would be too stingy to buy his share–if he had the money, which he would not. After the down payment, she invested most of what was left in expensive furniture, accessories, and linen, huge tropical indoor plants, extravagant chandeliers and chimes, including many lavish items salesmen suggested. Of course, there must be landscaping, especially the front– the back later. They would have cookouts, which were becoming a Colored middle-class form of entertainment in Granston. Joe Cephus discovered there was nothing left for him to bank.

Next, Johnnye suggested they take out a substantial policy on each other. In event something happened to one of them, God forbid, there would be some security for the survivor. They should get mortgage insurance that would pay any balance. Johnnye knew she would. When Joe Cephus found out the sum he'd have to contribute each week, month, quarter or year, he hesitated, but she could get insurance if she wanted to pay out that much money for nothing. He planned to live a long time. Besides, he had his pension and Social Security. So did she.

Johnnye acted as if she lost interest. When they went to bed, she called him J.C. softly, fondled and kissed him all over his face, neck, chest, and belly, making him feel quite uncomfortable. She kissed him so one night and not sticking to his mouth that to escape, J. C. whispered he was going to the doctor and have the examination so she could get the insurance she wanted. Johnnye did not respond and even shrugged her shoulders the next morning when Joe Cephus told her he would make an appointment with the doctor that day. The policy materialized, and it was J.C. who suggested she "up" the amount. Johnnye demurred, but really "upped" the amount and took out smaller Life Insurance policies with two local colored companies.

CHAPTER 18
Joe Cephus in Trouble

No matter how he tried to feign unconcern, there was something about Johnnye that disturbed Joe Cephus. She was so much larger than he. Taller. Weighed more. He knew before they married, but didn't really notice. She began to look bigger after they married and started acting "like her ass weighed a ton, and she was better then me," Joe Cephus admitted to himself. She didn't say it. "She bet not," he heard himself thinking angrily, but the way she acted. "Just chewing gum and shrugging her big old shoulders when I talk to her She got so much to say when her girlfriends come by or call. And she just walks out without telling me where she's going. A man's supposed to do that. She need bringing down a peg or two. All wives need it at times, so they won't forget who's in charge." He knew he should have let her know earlier. For instance, the time she left dirty dishes in the sink not only over night, bur all the next day. He let her get away with it. Of course, he was older and folks said the older you get the less you need to fight. Not like it was when he and a wife were younger and he had to keep her in line.

Joe Cephus heard that Johnnye fought a jealous lover and beat him so badly she had to drive him home. He was too ashamed to go to a doctor. The man never dated her again and eventually left Granston. Joe Cephus saw Johnnye's hefty arms and huge hands and didn't doubt she could hold her own. Her hands were wide, and just plain big, with more than one shade of pigment in smooth thick palms. But they were not unattractive. There was nothing unattractive about Johnnye. She was like she was supposed to be. He was fascinated as well as apprehensive. In bed, he saw Johnnye's huge solid thighs that almost hid her private parts. Her feet were thick and much larger than his and solid like her upper legs, as if made of Johnnye Jamison pig iron. If she ever kicked anybody, she'd be like that mule Dorothy called him. –Joe Cephus grinned as he remembered hearing that one of Johnnye's boyfriends had beaten her. Joe Cephus relaxed. People said the man left her face looking like hamburger. Joe Cephus was encouraged.

Joe Cephus discovered Johnny's reaction to his "bringing her down a peg or two" about six weeks after school opened. He waited for Johnnye to return from a PTA meeting. They had not had sex for three nights, and people just married should have it every night for at least the first year, or almost every night. Joe Cephus looked out the window, then the door. Turned on the TV, but didn't watch the program, whatever it was.

Johnnye eventually arrived. Those meetings were long. One of these nights he would follow her. –He got into bed and waited. She seemed to have to do so many things: check books and papers and arrange them on the dining room table for tomorrow. Put something in her pocket book. Pick out something to wear. Change her mind. Select something else. Go into the kitchen for a drink of water. Use the bathroom. Joe Cephus remembered how he would have actually thrown Dorothy in bed. Mildred? She would have jumped soon as she saw him in his shorts.

Johnnye finally got into bed. He began his customary reaching, reminding her that they had not for three nights and it was time. Johnnye shifted her gum for the night, jerked his hand from under her night gown, yawned and told him, "I'm tired. I worked all day and went to a meeting."

"You always say that after a meeting. What y'all do to make you so tired?"

"Work." She sighed with boredom.

In his sexiest voice he proposed, "That tired is different. A woman's not supposed to be too tired to do what she supposed to do. Just a li'l bit. It won't take long." What he oughta do is make her. She's his wife. Johnnye let him mount her and announced, "You had a 'li'l bit.' Now get offa me." She mimicked.

"Johnnye, you must be kiddin'!"

She turned her body using a shoving motion, and had Joe Cephus not caught himself, he would have landed on the floor.

He got up and turned on the light. "Don't you NEVER do that! You my WIFE!"

Johnnye got up. "Your wife because I married you. But MY ass! Don't you EVER forget that!"

"A wife BELONGS to her husband–"

"In that case, so do my frigging fists. You try to pile on top of me when I say no, I'll SHOW you."

A woman had never said anything like that to him. He oughta tell her what he used to tell Dorothy, "We gonna fuck or fight tonight" and show her. He looked at Johnnye. If he didn't start off right, things would never be right. And this marriage was forever. He just had to begin on the right foot.

"We ain' been married long, Johnnye. Now git in the bed," he ordered.

"For what?" She looked at the fly on his sunken shorts. "I'm not going to play with you, and you're not going to dig around in me with your filthy hands while you play with yourself."

She had made him lose his Manhood! Joe Cephus' jaws filled with air as he rushed towards her. He met her fist–right in his face. He threw one of his punches that landed somewhere near Johnnye's chest. Then he was on the floor without knowing how it happened. He attempted to get up, "You caught me off guard, Woman."

Something suddenly seemed to possess Johnnye. Like she had

gone mad. She must have hit him because his nose was bleeding. He aimed at her face, but she grabbed his fist and began twisting it.

"Woman, you bet not break my goddamn hand."

Johnnye twisted harder. "I heard about how you beat your other two wives. Mother Fucker, I'm going to do the beating now. Not only will I beat your ass, I'll KILL IT!" She dragged him across the floor to the door, and pushed him all the way out with her foot. He heard the lock click.

"Don't lock me outta my own room! My work clothes for tomorrow in my closet in there. You act like a trashy street woman–"

"You oughta know. I act like your mammy."

"Don't you play no dozens wif me."

"I'm acting the way you understand. A piece of ignorant shit like you don't know how to react to a lady."

"Johnnye, gimme my clothes for tomorrow 'fore I break down this door!"

"Break it, and I'll call the police, YOUR department, and act like a LADY around them and have you arrested. Tell 'em to bring a strait jacket – you're going crazy." Her voice took on a ladylike quality. She returned to her Northern brogue. "If you try to come in this room, I swear I'll embarrass you."

Johnny knew he would not break down the door. Too stingy. He'd have to pay to have it repaired. But she turned the key quietly and opened the door wide enough to toss something out. Joe Cephus didn't try to enter. It was his uniform. He picked it up, hung it in the bathroom. Blood from his nose had dropped on it. He wiped the stain with wet tissues. Then examined his face in the mirror and washed it. He had seen Dorothy put ice on her face. He sat at the kitchen table holding ice cubes to his jaw and nose, thinking of an explanation for his fellow officers if the swelling was not gone by morning.

CHAPTER 19
Joe Cephus' Problems

Johnnye and Joe Cephus stopped speaking for three days. Johnnye popped chewing gum so loud he could hear it no matter where he went. Loudest of all was in bed. She sat on her side of the bed, cutting or filing her finger and toe nails. She placed the file and scissors under her pillow. He tried to whistle, but wasn't good at it. He thought about sleeping in the other room or going upstairs, but this was *his* house, too, and "no woman was gonna run him outta *his* bedroom."

Joe Cephus began to ponder over more effective methods of dealing with a woman like Johnnye. He slammed his right fist into his left palm, trying to come to grips with the unexpected course his marriage was taking. He began to wonder how he looked with a woman larger than he, and he a policeman. But Joe Cephus could no longer pretend it was just Johnnye's size. There was something different about her—like *she* was the man. Sometimes, just glancing at the side view of her face, not seeing the outline of her bust which was so large she slept in her brassiere, far larger than any he had seen naked, *she looked like a man.* He wondered if people noticed and were laughing at him. Would they also know she actually would fight him back, and he couldn't make her do anything? But "like he always say, nobody's got nothin' to do wif his business." Too late now anyway. He and Johnnye were married and would spend the rest of their lives together.

No matter how Johnnye boasted in public that she was drawn to J's and they were J.C. and Johnnye, Joe Cephus knew that "something just wasn't right." He couldn't treat Johnnye Jamison the way he treated his other two wives. He was unable to decode whatever it was about her–a presence, a mien he had never associated with colored women but knew quite well since he felt it around almost all colored men and all white people. There was an invasive intrusive something, an endowment, that kept him from saying what he really wanted to say, or to say it differently. The same thing was true about something he wanted to do, but certainly would not do. It was an annoyance he knew he would have to accept forever in white people and most colored men –and now in a colored woman: *Johnnye*. Joe Cephus felt a lump forming in his throat as if he might cry, but "he was a man and a po-leece." He began to know he had to stop telling himself it was Johnnye's size. He knew it was more– and more than that one incident he let her win because she had caught him off guard. Joe Cephus promised himself it would never happen again. "A CUL-LUD woman, not only talkin' about his mama, but hittin' him back. She must be crazy, school-oo-l teach-ur or not. He would catch her off guard."

In addition, Johnnye's all-out changing accelerated, changes that Joe Cephus had controlled in his other marriages: The man was supposed to let the woman know that the honeymoon was over forever. He felt like slapping Johnny for beating him to it, and would have created a reason to do so, if she did not have that formidable aura he couldn't decipher. The differences in her public and private identities became greater. Her ignoring him at home was reduced to barely speaking and avoiding conversation. *He* had also controlled those segments in his other marriages. Furthermore, her Northern accent and classy "airs" had become as if they had never been, especially when they were alone. He had been listening to her and trying to sound more like her. Classy. He never said AX for ASK like most cul-lud folks. He pronounced the word right: AST.

Incidents kept happening until he just had to begin telling her about them, before they pile up and get worse:

"Johnnye, you keep forgettin' something every morning—"

She shrugged her shoulders and popped chewing gum.

"You gonna ast me what it is?"

"No. I don't forget what's important."

"Makin' up a bed not important?" Joe Cephus controlled his temper.

"What bed?"

"The one we sleep in." He would have slapped Dorothy long before now and kicked the hell outta Mildred.

"We means at least two people. You act like I'm the only one who sleeps in the damn bed. Use the other room and keep it the way you want it."

Joe Cephus felt fire leap to his face. He just could not let a woman talk to him like that. Not even his mother. He would sneak up on Johnnye, so she wouldn't catch him off guard like she did the last time. She wouldn't win this time. He looked around for something to hit her with. There were shoes, one of her large books, and oh, yes, the door stopper. It was small but heavy. Iron.

Joe Cephus spoke quietly. "Johnnye, I'm astin' you nice. Make up that bed 'fore you leave."

She chewed rapidly between words. "I heard you ordered your other wives around and you put them out. I give orders in *THIS* house and do the putting out."

"I heard things bout you, too." Joe Cephus retorted.

She had that Johnnye half smile on her face. "And everything you heard is true. *Every goddamn thing.* –Including *that.*" She boasted.

Joe Cephus' face was flaming. What was the *THAT* she was

bragging about? He wouldn't ask. Why did women have to tell the truth a man didn't want to know! He kept his eye on the door stopper.

Johnnye continued. "I heard you kick women. Dorothy Borden spread it all over town that you kick colored women and took a Cracker to the union who pushed you. If you ever kick me, you'd better kill me. If you don't you'll wish you had, you mother-fucking cowardly Nigger."

"Don't call me names like that. A wife supposed to respect her husband."

Johnnye was still calm. "Too good to frig your own Mama?" She made a loud noise with her chewing gum.

He could stand it no longer. Playing the dozens with him like a street woman. He'd treat her like one. He'd pretend to leave the room and catch her off guard. Joe Cephus turned to leave, but reached for the door stopper. As he bent over, without consciously aiming, Johnnye kicked him, a bull's eye in the rectum. Joe Cephus was too shocked to utter a sound. Besides he never realized a kick could hurt that bad. So bad that he lay on his stomach hoping the pain wouldn't last long.

But Johnnye hadn't finished. "This is what you'll get if you ever kick me, only I'll break your stinking foot." She grabbed his foot and began twisting it.

Joe Cephus screamed. "TURN MY FOOT LOOSE! WOMAN, TURN MY GODDAMN FOOT LOOSE. I TOLD YOU ABOUT TWISTING MY HAND. I DON'T TWIST YOU."

The more he screamed, the harder she twisted. "You better not. If you ever try, I'll wring your turkey neck the same way."

"YOU GONNA BREAK MY FOOT. I DIDN'T KICK YOU. YOU SAID YOU'D BREAK IT IF I KICKED YOU."

Johnnye dropped Joe Cephus' foot. "This is a Sunday School lesson. Wait till you see what I'll do to that stick-of-shit nobody wants but you. "

"You oughta be 'shame of yourself acting and talking like a street woman. Trashy women fight they husbands."

"If you mention the words 'street' and 'trashy' to me again, so help me God, when I finish with you, you'll never smile, shave, shit, or screw again. As if you can do the last one. An old wife-beater cracker-ass kisser like you got the nerve to criticize a woman for protecting herself." Johnnye stood over him breathing dragon-like, her eyes glued to him. "I oughta spit in your shriveled face."

Fearing she would, Joe Cephus struggled to get up and hobbled out of the room. He went into the bathroom to rub his foot in alcohol, maybe liniment. He heard the front door slam and Johnnye drive away. Tears rolled down the face folks had told him was so pretty. He looked in the mirror. The image told him his wife-beating days were ending unless he killed Johnnye, and he knew too much about prisons, especially for colored men, to ever do anything to go there—As he rubbed his foot, he wondered why he made such a fuss over Johnnye's making a bed. It really wasn't that important. He could ignore it or make it up himself.

Joe Cephus reported to the Department that he had tripped on the stairs. He took a taxi to work where the P.D. doctor treated him for a sprained ankle. Joe Cephus was too ashamed to tell him about the dreadful pain in his rectum. That pain never entirely left, returning at times, depending on the way he sat or walked. Sometimes it acted up when he was having sex. His ankle became a weather vane, warning him to expect rainy or humid weather.

While soaking his ankle that night as the doctor directed, Joe Cephus heard Johnnye come in. She saw that the bed had been made army fashion and vowed she would never make it again except to change linen. Johnnye decided that she'd always keep clothes in the upstairs bedroom in order to have a choice. She slept in the upstairs bedroom that night. But it was more fun to sleep with J.C. She could lull him to sleep chewing gum and even passing gas pretending to be asleep.

The next morning Joe Cephus acted as if nothing eventful had happened, offered Johnnye coffee and toast, which she refused, and hoped so hard she would join him in bed that night. She did. And popped gum so loud he wished she had gone back upstairs.

Most disturbing of all, Joe Cephus could not control Johnnye's money. Besides, periodically she would disappear early Saturday or Sunday mornings and stay away all day, returning after midnight or just before daybreak, sometimes just in time to report for work Monday morning. She never told him her plans. He knew when he got up and found her dog Darwin gone. His face hot with rage, he consoled himself with mental pictures "of beatin' her big black ass so bad she would be scared to do it again." One Saturday morning he woke up and asked where she was going, to which she replied, "To hell if I don't pray, people say." He wanted to check the odometer, but he never rode in her car, and she kept it locked. One day he saw a map of Virginia on the front seat, but couldn't see the city circled in red because of the way the map was folded. He could follow her, but she might find out, and thought of hiring a detective, but it would cost too much. Five years later, lying in bed, listening as Death slowly turned the door knob, bits of blunted wisdom attempting to pierce his petrified mind, Joe Cephus would wonder what difference it might have made had he hired a detective to follow Johnnye.

Each month when she received her check, Joe Cephus told himself that there had to be drastic changes. He had no intentions of supporting a woman whose salary was as much as his, maybe more. He never knew the exact amount. She bought something new almost every payday, and already had downstairs and upstairs closets filled with clothes. Some she didn't wear. –And now a brand new car! She drove a used one before they married. While undressing for bed that night, Joe Cephus calmly opened the financial discussion, speaking carefully, slowly, some words clearer than others. "Johnnye, I been thinkin'—nothin' was wrong wif the car you had. We just goin' deeper and deeper in debt. If we plan, we can make out wif one car. I could take you to work, pick you up, or you could get a ride wif somebody. A lotta husbands and wives do that. Folks who got more then we got. Even white people. I hear'em talkin' 'bout it at the po-leece Station."

Johnnye looked at him dumbfounded. "Have your forgotten I'm spending *my* money. You say we can get along with one car, sell *yours*, and do what you did before you got that third-hand sardine can. I certainly don't have time to take you. I have meetings and can't come and get you. I married to *better* my condition, and I had my own car *before* I married." She popped chewing gum angrily.

Johnnye, what I'm saying is I'm payin' all the bills, and hardly have nothin' left on payday," and wanted to add he certainly had not bettered himself. The way things were going, he'd use all the money he had saved before they married. But she didn't know about that.

"Didn't you pay all the bills before you married?"

"Yes, but I didn't have a mortgage. My house was paid for. Gas, water, and electric bills weren't as high. And I didn't have a furniture bill. Our food bill is higher. I buy groceries every week that we don't eat 'cause you don't cook nothin' unless it's steak. We could eat chicken, chops, or ground beef. Mama used to get pot roasts and ham we could slice off and turn into other dishes."

"I don't know how to cook roast or ham, even if I had time. Why don't *you* cook? You get home before I do most of the time." Johnnye sounded bored.

Real men don't COOK, Joe Cephus thought. That was a WOMAN'S job, and he a PO-LEECE, but he said "You could use a cook book–" Johnnye was getting angry, and he wanted to talk about the main issue before she got too mad. He asked calmly, "What I want to know is when you goin' to start helpin' pay some of the bills?"

Brushing her well-kept, hairdresser straight hair, Johnnye replied equally as composed, "When are you going to start paying me? For my services."

Puzzled, Joe Cephus frowned, stopped removing his shoes, waiting for her to let him know it was a joke, laugh, then list water bill, light bill, but Johnnye continued brushing her hair. And he had to ask, "What you talkin' about?"

"You men marry for a freebie. When you date, you pay. If you go to a prostitute, you pay. You marry and become freeloaders." Johnnye pulled a black lace net over her hair.

"You mean you're not goin' to pay no bills?"

"You mean you're not going to pay me?" She blew a large bubble. It burst on her face.

Joe Cephus stared at her as she expertly removed the gum. "You must take me for a fool."

"W-ell–." Johnnye brushed hair from her red satin negligee.

Not knowing how to respond, he said the first thing that came to his mind. "Woman, go straight to hell!"

Johnnye adjusted her hair net, popped chewing gum, and responded impassively. "O.K. When I get there and see your mother blowing the devil, want me to tell'er to save 'im for you?"

Joe Cephus rushed toward her. "I told you about playin' the dozens wif me!"

She picked up a huge nail file, and stood staring at him. She had gotten bigger. Now Joe Cephus was certain she was not that big and tall before they married and right afterwards. She had grown, and he had shrunk. He didn't have to beat her big black ass. He'd get her another way. Trying to control his voice, he threatened, "I'm not payin' another bill–light, water, gas, mortgage. Noth-thin'!"

Johnnye shrugged her shoulders and gave her chewing gum a loud pop. He slept on the couch that night. She locked the bedroom door.

CHAPTER 20

Joe Cephus Attempts Reconciliation

The next morning, Johnnye packed a valise with clothes she'd need for work, put personal articles in a case, led Darwin to her car, and disappeared. Even if Joe Cephus had somewhere to go, he would be too ashamed. After three days, he went to Johnnye's school near closing time. He parked close to the entrance and sat until children began leaving the building, running, skipping, calling each other. Why can't they walk and be quiet, he thought. Acting like they don't have good sense. He walked cautiously up the cement walk to the main entrance. Children were using a side door. Good. They'd knock him down acting so wild. –Best not to look for Johnnye's car. She could be parked anywhere, and he might miss her. Better go to her room.

Where was Johnnye's room? Better go to the office and ask. He hoped the principal wasn't in. Joe Cephus could handle women better. They thought he was good-looking. He was glad he was not in uniform. Didn't want folks to think he was on official duty especially if he had to deal with a man. Lucky. No principal. The smiling Secretary told him Mrs. Divine was in Room 606 and had not checked out. Joe Cephus walked slowly, looking carefully at the number on each room door so he wouldn't enter the wrong room–604, 605. The next one must be 606. The door was open. He heard children's voices.

"Mis' Dee-vine! Mis' Dee-vine, look what I did! Look!"

Johnnye was sitting on the floor, a large colorful smock covered her dress, children huddled around her. "Put the fire station HERE," one shouted.

Must be the model community he saw her drawing, constructing, and spreading out on the dining room table that she ordered him not to move, touch, or spill anything on. What a waste of time he thought when she could have been doing something for him, her husband.

"A hospital here," an alert little girl advised, imitating Johnnye, "so it will be cen-tral-ly loca-ted but not too near a lotta–lot of traffic."

"Gotta have room to park cars," a boy reminded.

"We'll finish tomorrow," Joe Cephus heard Johnnye say in a voice he barely recognized.

"Ah-ah–kin we stay justa while longer?"

"May we stay," Johnnye corrected.

"If she say may, kin we stay?" A tiny boy, much smaller than the rest asked.

Peeking, Joe Cephus saw his wife smile and pat the child on his shoulder. "Wish you could, but you have to leave while the patrol is on duty."

"We know how to cross streets. We go to the sto'–store–all the time."

"School regulations say you must leave before the assigned patrol leaves. Besides, your mommies and daddies will worry if you're late."

"They at work. Key in the mail box."

"What have I told you about omitting–?"

"Verbs!" They interrupted.

"Yeah, verbs," a smiling little girl repeated. "Say 'they *are* at work' and 'the key *is* in the mail box.'"

Another third grader added, "You can also use the contraction '*they're* at work'"

"Correct. –Now run along," Johnnye urged.

Children shouted in unison and then one after the other. "Let us hug you good-bye."

"Let me hug first!"

"No, me first this time. You first yes-diddy—yesterday," the child corrected her pronunciation, imitating Johnny. .

They squeezed Johnnye's neck as she appeared to genuflect for them to do so.

"We glad we in yo' room, Mis' Divine."

"Yeah. Lotta children want to be in *yo'* room. Not Mis' Davenport's. Last year in the second grade, she wouldn't let us hug her goodbye. No other time either. She mean–*is* mean. Not good like you, Mis' Divine."

"And not pretty like you and smell good like you," a plain-faced little girl held Johnnye's hand tighter.

"She say our hands and noses nasty–"

"And we git her pretty clothes dirty, and they can't be wash. Got to be clean, and cost a lot."

Johnnye stood erect, but did not appear to be looking down at her students. "Perhaps that was Mrs. Davenports way of telling you about–?

"Personal hygiene!" Most of them shouted.

"And what should you do?" Johnnye asked.

"Wash our hands a lot, especially 'fore–before we eat. Wash and change our clothes, and keep our noses wiped. To help kill germs."

"And wash our own clothes if nobody else will, even if we can't ion—i-ron them."

"Now scoot–look both ways before crossing." She led them to the door. "See you tomorrow."

As she turned to watch the children scamper down the hall, she saw Joe Cephus who had stepped behind the door. He grinned, relieved, glad she got rid of them. After he and Johnnye made up, he'd tell her she shouldn't spend extra time after school closed. She could spend that time with him—in the bed. He'd tell her she wastin' time with stinkin' children. He smelled them. She not gettin' over time pay. Got to even tell 'em to wipe they nasty noses. They no-good mamas and daddies ought do that, if they got daddies. Joe Cephus rescued his grin in order to woo his wife:

"Hey, Johnnye. Let me take you to Miss Ware's Grand Blue Diner on Blues Street to get somethin' to eat. They been there since I can remember, and the food is good. Same as it was when she was livin'."

"Why? –Sure you got the money. You complain about spending."

"I wanna talk to you."

"O.K. I'll follow you."

Joe Cephus didn't trust her to follow. "Let me take you. I'll bring you back to yo' car."

Johnnye silently got into Joe Cephus' car. He took her to the best colored cafe in Granston, where he did most of the talking as they waited for and then began eating fried porgies with French fries, turnip greens, and corn bread.

"Look, we can work something out. All married folks have ups and downs. Johnnye, you know yo-sef when two people work, they bof pay bills.

Johnnye acting, talking, eating as if bored, sighed, "I was doing all right by myself. Now I've a lot to pay also. Car payments, things on layaway, and the insurance you took that examination for. It's expensive."

"What about you pay the mortgage every other month–and the phone bill. You use it more then I do." Joe Cephus suggested.

"Yeah, but you had a phone before we married, and you paid the bill."

"Johnnye, we tryin' to work things out. We married now, and we want to be happy as possible."

"My paying your bills will make us happy." Johnnye's voice was toneless.

Joe Cephus couldn't tell what the statement meant, so he ignored it. "All I'm sayin' you pay the mortgage every other month and the phone bill."

"All right," Johnnye agreed, "*If* you pay it the alternate months, and the gas, water, and electric–and buy food. You eat at home more than I do."

This predicament was the opposite of the illusion Joe Cephus had of marriage. Gone were those secret bank accounts he planned to have in Greensboro and Winston-Salem., in addition to the one in High Point. But he had made some progress, and gradually he would ease Johnnye into paying more. Joe Cephus had an unpleasant feeling in his throat and eyes, as if he were going to cry. Johnnye smiled inwardly. How innocent and pathetic he looked. His public guise.

As much as he ate, Joe Cephus had never considered the cost of food. He considered the five dollars he had given his mother each week for him and Dorothy sufficient. After his mother died, he gave his next door neighbor, Della, a dollar telling her to buy something for their dinner. He praised his generosity and told anyone who listened how he helped his neighbor, who was divorced with two children, which was the reason he didn't mind giving her a dollar to help her out. She worked all day, had to shop and didn't have a car, had to come home, cook the food and wash dishes afterwards. Of course she would have to do those things if he didn't eat there. But she deserved the dollar. She was such a good old girl. And cooked such good food–like his mother.

Now Joe Cephus faced Johnnye's spasmodic preparing precisely what he bought. She emptied cans of corn, beans, or peas in too small or too large pots for him to heat. Unlike his mother Johnnye did not supplement the menu. Joe Cephus did not buy meats other than cold cuts, and he ate cold cuts he took from the refrigerator himself that often had turned green. He felt his eyes becoming watery as he removed the discoloration.

Now his lips trembled as Johnnye informed him that she did not know how to make bread from scratch so he might as well stop buying corn meal and flour—unless he planned to bake. She had no time or desire to learn at her age and was far too busy. Johnnye reminded him again that she had been much better off before she married him. Joe Cephus, learning to show patience by using words, while his fists and feet remained eager to perform, reminded, "Johnnye, married folks suppose to sit down and eat together."

"Sitting down eating together going to make us happily married. Shit," Johnnye responded, no trace of her Northern brogue, toying with her food, mixing it in heaps she wasn't going to eat.

He ignored her response, thinking she was wasting his money. Joe Cephus took his wife back to her school, where she told him she would be home later. Third grade teachers were having a meeting.

Night came while Joe Cephus sat in a living room chair waiting, recalling other eating incidents. Johnnye rarely ate when she cooked. Once Joe Cephus had asked, "Why you not eating?"

"That is a stupid question. I'm not hungry."

"Why?"

"I ate a big lunch in the school cafeteria."

"Johnnye, we can't get ahead like that. Buying food to eat at home, and not eating it."

"Stop buying it. I'm using *my* money I worked for and went to school to earn."

Joe Cephus had swallowed the food alone and in silence as Johnnye filled the tub with water. A bath this early meant she was going out. She'd leave the dishes. Well, so would he.

Joe Cephus lost his appetite. Contrary to the way his mother had prepared tasty meals, always supplementing his purchases, he now had canned food without aroma and seasoning that enticed him to sit, eat, and be delighted.—Even on Sundays. There was no fried chicken or baked ham and string beans or greens simmering in tasty "pot likker." No rice and hot rolls to eat with chicken or ham gravy. Johnnye went to a 11 A.M. church service and rarely returned before 10:00 P.M.

Joe Cephus bought breakfast food, and realized more the cost of food. He and Mildred had not eaten properly. She was usually pregnant or drunk and saying she didn't feel well. His mother always had what she called hot breakfasts. Dorothy would eat on weekends sometimes, but would be satisfied with that stuff she bought called yogurt. Joe Cephus remembered she put bananas or some kind of fruit in it. He tasted it once and wondered how she could eat it.

Joe Cephus thought of the morning he had said as nice as he could, "Johnnye, Mama fix me eggs, bacon or sausage, hominy grits and toast for breakfast. Before we married, you made pancakes. –There's plenty stuff in the ice box. We both can eat. It's a waste of money and food if we don't eat it."

"Mama didn't get up and go to work. I made pancakes *one* weekend before we married. I don't fix breakfast for myself. Just have juice or cereal."

"A man can't make it off that. 'Specially a po-leece. We work hard."

"A man can fix his own breakfast, 'specially a po-leece," she mimicked, "or do what he did before he married. I realize how heavy your night stick is and that gun you can't use. I should say billy-club. Your 'night stick' is light." She was too annoyed to pop gum, and really pissed-off because he didn't seem to be insulted by her reference to his "night stick ".

"Other women cook breakfast for they husbands and work same as you. You don't even wash and i'on. I send everythang to the laundry."

"You shoulda married one of them women. Joe Cephus, I didn't wash shitty drawers, snotty handkerchiefs, and funky sheets and towels before I married and ain't starting now. I'm through talking about it."

But Joe Cephus wasn't. "O.K. I can either put the thangs in the washin' machine myself or send them to the laundry. O.K.?"

"I don't give-va damn what you do."

A vision of how he used to keep wives in line flashed before him. He closed his mental eyes, and returned to Johnnye. "Suppose I get up and cook for you."

"No thanks. I didn't marry to get a cook."

"Johnnye, just why did you marry me?" Joe Cephus was serious.

She regarded him silently, without even chewing gum, thinking you'll never know, but one day you'll wonder like hell.

Joe Cephus relaxed. She must have married him because she just wanted to be married to him. Like he wanted to be married to her. Folks said he was good-looking. And looked so good in his uniform. Johnnye really dressed and looked good too. They belonged together.

Joe Cephus saw himself walk over to his wife, put his arms around her, and would have kissed her, but she was chewing too fast. "We not gonna fall out 'bout no breakfast. Let's eat together on weekends when you don't have to work."

Johnnye shrugged and popped gum.

Johnnye continued to sleep late on Saturdays and Sundays, or get up early and disappear all day, or she went shopping and returned hours later. Sometimes she told him she was having breakfast with colleagues to discuss school business. She rarely got around to under or over frying bacon or sausage and heating stale coffee. When she cooked, she left burned pots of grits and sticky plates in the sink. Again Joe Cephus felt a lump in his throat as he cleaned the mess or prepared food she had an excuse not to eat.

Returning to the present, Joe Cephus noticed that the living room was dark and he was still waiting for his wife to come home as she promised after he took her back to work from Miss Ware's restaurant. It would be time to go to bed before long. He went to bed early, rarely staying up after nine, and before then during winter. Dorothy could stay up for hours reading and correcting papers. Frequently Johnnye came home late and spent time preparing for bed. Mildred had been ready when he was. Eating and sleeping were the two main things husband and wives did together. What else was there to do? If those two things didn't work out, there was no real marriage. After another interval of waiting, Joe Cephus went to bed, lying in the dark alone, until finally he heard Johnny's car.—But she went to the bedroom upstairs. He was afraid to go there and kick her back downstairs as he would have Dorothy. He fought the lump in his throat. The next morning, as Johnnye acted the way she always did, he still battled the lump in his throat.

Knowing that Joe Cephus was anxious to solve their eating together problem, Johnnye insisted that J.C., as she called him publicly, take her out to eat frequently, even to drive-in places. There were a couple of nice colored restaurants in nearby Greensboro. Since food was his responsibility, Joe Cephus paid the bills. The piteous look on his face amused Johnnye. Joe Cephus proposed that they take turns paying. She agreed. When Johnnye's time came, they went to a really nice place. Royal Oasis, on Market Street in Greensboro. Because she would pay this time, Joe Cephus ordered smothered steak with mushrooms and all the trimmings, including desert, instead of the cheapest item on the menu. Steak was the first meal she had prepared for him. Joe Cephus hoped she remembered. Johnnye ate Creole shrimp and asked for three orders of southern fried chicken to take home, instructing the waitress that she would pick them up on their way out.

While the waitress prepared the check, Johnnye went to the restroom. Joe Cephus surmised the orders would be for their dinner tomorrow, but why three? Maybe in case they wanted seconds or a snack. Joe Cephus had learned not to question his wife. When she did not return, he asked the waitress to look in the ladies' room. Johnnye wasn't there. Johnnye had to come back. She left her sweater on the chair. They came in his car, he checked, and it was still parked near the restaurant. He waited almost an hour, even went to the phone booth and called home before going to the desk and asking about the three take-home orders of fried chicken. He was told a lady had picked them up nearly an hour ago. He got Johnny's sweater and returned to the cashier. Fortunately, Joe Cephus had enough money to pay the enormous bill. He hoped there was enough gas in the car to get home. He'd have to get an advance from his next pay. It was embarrassing. The Paymaster would automatically get the forms when he saw Joe Cephus entering the office.

Driving home, Joe Cephus tried to ignore the swelling in his throat. He walked carefully into the dark house lest Johnnye be there. She wasn't, and did not show up the next morning to dress for work. Joe Cephus called his job for emergency leave, saying there was a "busted water pipe" –and waited. Finally he called Johnnye's job. The principal's secretary informed him that Mrs. Divine was at home ill.

After work the next day, Joe Cephus found Johnnye lounging on the couch in the living room sipping Bourbon. It would have been such a simple matter with his other wives. He would have just "beaten the hell out of them and poured the likker on them." Of course, they would not have pulled such a trick.

"Johnnye," he began, hoping she didn't notice how his voice trembled, "what happened last night? I don't treat you like that." He remembered Dorothy Borden's saying the same thing, one night when he slapped her for a minor infraction he couldn't recall. His reply had been, "I can't help if you let me treat you this way." He hoped Johnnye wouldn't say that. She didn't. She shrugged her shoulders, shook the glass until the ice tinkled, and sipped Bourbon.

"We're married now–let's try to make it work–let's treat each other right." But Johnnye didn't seem to be listening. Was she humming "I'll Be Glad When You Dead, You Rascal You"? That song was popular when he was in elementary school.

CHAPTER 21

Joe Cephus Learns/Joe Cephus Weeps

One day Johnnye was performing her version of house cleaning when Joe Cephus asked, "Why didn't you hang up my clothes?"

Johnnye picked up the suit, shirt, socks, and undergarments he had left on a chair, opened the window, and tossed them out Johnnye fashion, carefully, methodically, one garment at a time.

Joe Cephus immediately regretted asking Johnnye to hang up his clothes. But he remembered leaving his clothes for his mother, Mildred, and then Dorothy to pick up. No point in letting Johnnye get away with this. He might as well put a stop to it. *NOW!* Even if he had to hurt her seriously. Joe Cephus rushed toward his wife, fists drawn. This time he didn't miss. His fist landed on Johnnye's face. Right below her eye–Now Johnny was on top of him, her elbow on his neck, she pounded his face with her fists. Her voice smooth as velvet, as in sex, unwanted and wanted, as in almost every word she spoke. *"Son of a bitch, don't you ever hit me again. Hear Me. Stupid bastard."* Joe Cephus didn't move. "I'll turn you into a eunuch. Maybe you'll learn to do something else."

Joe Cephus wondered if she knew judo and wondered what a "you-nook" was and what it had to do with him learning to do something else–and what something else? How he hoped his face wouldn't swell this time. He'd have to take a day off. He was never absent before marrying Johnnye.

She went into the closet that held her and Joe Cephus' clothes. She took every piece of clothing within her reach that belonged to him and began scattering them about as she talked. "Now hang 'em up, your ignorant cheap stingy self."

She watched Joe Cephus struggle to get up from the floor. She kept her eye on the door stopper. He might throw it at her. She would dodge and the stopper would hit the window or mirror and break it. Joe Cephus didn't want to break or destroy anything he'd have to replace.

Johnnye continued talking. "–And if you even *touch* a thing that belongs to me, so God is my witness, I'll get rid of *everything* you own. And say you moved them out. I'll make things so hot you'll have to get out. And take a protection petition against you. I'll subpoena both of your wives. Dorothy Borden did enough talking in beauty parlors for me to call them. I sold *my* house to get this one. Money from your house got the furniture and shrubbery in the front yard. This is *my* house, and I'm going to stay in it and do the beating if there's any." Johnnye decided to let up after this. She needed him a while longer.

Johnnye stared at Joe Cephus, knowing that staring disconcerted him. He went into the bathroom, washed his face, then into the kitchen where Johnnye was emptying ice into a glass. She dumped excess ice into the sink instead of the receptacle. She poured Bourbon in the glass, her eyes on Joe Cephus as she waited for the ice to take effect. Joe Cephus glanced at her. He used to be the one who stared. She observed his every move until he went into the bathroom and locked the door. He didn't stay long, remembering he had locked the door once before and instead of going upstairs, Johnnye had made urine in a pail and left it on his side of the bed, got her dog, a few clothes, and didn't return until the weekend. When he asked her about the pail, she reminded him it was another Sunday School lesson. Next time what she left in the pail would look like something he had and thought was so great, same color, size, smell, and shape.

Joe Cephus stopped trying not to cry. He wanted to leave, but where would he go? What would people say? He certainly couldn't buy his share of the house, and he had used almost every cent he had saved. There had been times when it was Johnnye's month to pay the mortgage, and she asked him to pay it for her and promised to make up for it. She never did. She didn't try to cut down on bills he had to pay, keeping lights on all night, leaving them on while she was at work during the day, and just letting water run while doing something else. She'd fill the sink with water to wash one glass, or a cup and a spoon. When he suggested waiting for dishes to collect, they piled in the sink so high that many of them toppled and broke. Even some of his mother's good china he told Johnnye to use for special occasions. Sometimes he washed dishes himself while uncontrolled tears formed paths down his trembling cheeks. He never washed dishes or did anything women were supposed to do when he was married to Mildred or Dorothy and while his mother was alive.

Joe Cephus decided to see a lawyer about his predicament. Maybe there was something he could do about getting money from his share of the house and moving out. Cousin Daisy was right. He should not have sold his house. Joe Cephus went to see the new, young colored lawyer Wayne Davidson, who immediately took Joe Cephus to get copies of the Deed and the Agreement Johnnye had drawn up. Mr. Davidson explained: The house belonged to Johnnye and Joe Cephus jointly and would remain thus as long as both parties lived. In the event of the demise of one, the house, land, all possessions, and all insurance policies will go to the survivor. The Agreement they both signed stipulated that in the event of divorce or separation, legal or otherwise, the party filing or vacating the premises will purchase his or her share or relinquish it. The party who does not file or vacate the premises is not obligated to provide monetary compensation and will retain all rights to said property.

Mr. Davidson added that Joe Cephus might ask his wife to provide monetary compensation. Joe Cephus was afraid Johnnye might refuse, and it would make his predicament worse. He told himself that Mr. Davidson might not know what he was talking about. He was young–and cul-lud. Joe Cephus gave him two ten dollar bills and told him he'd bring the thirty dollar balance the next pay day. Joe Cephus left Davidson's office angry that he charged him fifty dollars for nothing, and made an appointment to see J.J. Tyler, the white lawyer who handled his divorce from Dorothy Borden.

Between telephone calls, his secretary did not place on HOLD, J.J. Tyler grinned as he listened to Joe Cephus' grievance, and remarked jokingly in what the lawyer considered cul-lud folks talk, " Boy, you sho' have trouble wid them school-oo-l teach-urs." Tyler did not accept the Deed and Agreement Joe Cephus brought, and told him to stop by the secretary's desk. She would make another appointment after getting their own copies of the Papers. During the second appointment, Tyler explained the terms of the Deed and Agreement *precisely* as Wayne Davidson had, using copies of the same documents even adding as Davidson that Joe Cephus could ask Johnnye to provide monetary compensation. But go home and think about it, Tyler suggested. The third appointment, Tyler smiled and said, "Boy, them school teachers making you spend money," and gave him an itemized bill for $210.00: Consultation $50.00; Research for Deed, $50.00; Copy of Deed, $35.00; Second appointment, $40.00; Third appointment, $35.00.

Joe Cephus, a heavy lump in his throat, explained he did not expect the bill to be that much, and he could not write a check because they had a joint checking account, and he didn't want his wife to know, and please don't send a bill to his house. He would leave $35.00 and bring the rest to the office tomorrow. Joe Cephus rushed to a bank in High Point, withdrew $175.00, and felt tears forming as he looked at the balance of $137.16.

Joe Cephus wondered if he were trying too hard to make things work. Every thing was against him. He would sit down again with Johnnye, talk about it, and work something out. He'd make out with the food and washing and ironing. They weren't the most important things in a marriage. As for bills, he would cut down. He tried not to use much water. The bill was far too high. Johnnye at least didn't use as much water bathing every night as Dorothy had. Sometimes he wished Johnnye would, especially certain times of the month. He held his breath when she turned over in bed, and had the feeling she did it on purpose. –Johnnye stopped cuddling after their first fight. But she would snuggle close when she was having her period. Finally he would have to breathe and remembered he never had to hold his breath when he was married to Dorothy—or Mildred.

Joe Cephus remembered older people talking about "time flying." He knew now what they meant. Time was now another year. Joe Cephus became more "uneasy" as he had also heard old folks describe their feelings. Was he getting old and scared? When Dorothy's mother died, he did not pay the respects Granston demanded, such as going to the funeral home or sending flowers. Johnnye might not like it. Joe Cephus began to want to do something awful to her, and thought of poisoning her dog, or taking it for a walk and losing it, or letting a car hit it, but was terrified of the consequences. He hated that dog. And was angry with himself for not making Johnnye get rid of it at the beginning. He should have told her she had to choose between him and that dog. She even had him buying beef and having it ground for the bitch. A girl dog name Darwin. Joe Cephus felt "jittery" almost all the time. He didn't remember ever hearing men where he worked talk about being nervous. If the Chief knew, Joe Cephus would be called in, sent to the Department's doctor, and dismissed.

Joe Cephus sighed, hearing himself admit "Somethin' must be wrong with women I pick out. Johnnye pay more 'tention to them snotty nose children and that dog then to me." He remembered telling Dorothy that she "didn't love nobody but her daughter and her daddy." She didn't even say no like she was supposed to. A woman's husband came first. It's in the Bible. Dottie just said, "That is the only correct evaluation you have ever made of me—" or something like that.

Joe Cephus wanted both of his wives to love him so badly that at times he imagined, or thought, they did. Maybe they did, and just acted crazy. It didn't matter that he didn't love them or even particularly like them. He was a man. A woman is supposed to want and love a man and be more determined than the man to stay together and make a marriage work.

Johnnye's and Joe Cephus' sex life was almost nil. A man can take just so much. Paying all the bills and not getting anything at all! He recalled how he strutted about when he was married to Dorothy Borden, making sex compulsory, forcing, heralding the act with his classic question, sometimes modifying it with the reminder that he was master of the three F's: Fussing, Fighting, and Frigging. Now he had gone so long and really wanted sex. He was afraid to get a girlfriend, and he dared not touch Johnnye unless she wanted him to, and she never did. Even if he wasn't scared, girls he would have didn't pay him any attention since he married Johnnye. Even the ones who would go around with married men. He reminded himself that a man would lose his manhood if he didn't use it.

Joe Cephus went so long until one night he grinned and asked in his most polished, politest, playful tone, "Miz Divine, DIVINE Miz Divine, please may I petition you for a piece of poon-tang tonight?" He hoped so hard she would smile.

Johnnye shrugged her shoulders. –While Joe Cephus tried so hard, Johnnye chewed gum, popping it at intervals until he gave up and lay on top of her disgusted. Johnnye continued to chew and pop so loud that he rolled over on his pillow. J.C. wept.

While he wept, Johnnye decided she wanted Bourbon on the rocks. She turned on the light. Joe Cephus was lying naked on the bed. Johnnye laughed aloud. His genitals resembled two prunes and a shriveled, very over-ripe banana. She just had to tell him—and her cohorts. It was too good to keep.

Days, weeks, and seasons added another year at mercurial pace that baffled Joe Cephus. People noticed that he appeared confused—and much older unnaturally. "Boy, yo' hair is turnin' turn gray over night," his Cousin Daisy told him: Johnnye didn't seem to notice. In public, she continued linking arms with her J.C., calling him "darling," sipping from his drink and using her fingers to put tasty tidbits in his mouth, wiping it gently with her napkin. The moment they got in the car, heading for home, she chewed gum, popping it so that it sounded to Joe Cephus like subdued, taunting thunder. Knowing he would be with Johnnye "until death do us part," he wondered when she was going to die, and hoped he would be the "longest liver," as Granstonians described it. He longed for some peace before he died.

One balmy spring night Joe Cephus heard a car stop in front of their house. It was his wife, who had pooled a ride with colleagues attending a PTA meeting. He turned the porch light on so that she could see. Wanting her to know he was glad she was home, he stood on the porch smiling. —Joe Cephus' smile became an open-mouth stare. By the illumination of the street lamp and the inside car light, he saw Johnnye kiss the woman driver—in the mouth! A lingering kiss—the way she kissed him before they married and right after. This is what people said about Johnnye before they married and hinted about even now. Joe Cephus walked slowly back into the house and sat down in the living room, pretending to watch television so he wouldn't have to say anything but hello and something about TV reception. He stared at the screen for a while before going to bed. Their backs to each other, his face felt hot. He lay thinking how he would have beaten his other wives, and even a girlfriend. He would have almost killed them, and put his wives out. Now he was scared to admit what he saw.

The next morning, Johnnye smiled at Joe Cephus as she poured coffee in a large HER cup. He stood in the doorway watching. She smiled, "Good-morning, Darling," and asked pleasantly, "Have a good night? I did." She reached for the HIS cup. "Want some coffee?" The sound of her popping gum was like a gun shot.

There was just so much he could take.

"You goddamned bulldagger!" bellowed Joe Cephus pointing his police revolver at Johnnye. Without hesitation, she slung the pot of coffee at him. As the pot bounced off his chest, the hot liquid splashed on his face followed by a gun shot. The bullet lodged in the ceiling. Joe Cephus dropped the gun. She was on top of him, her thumbs gorging his neck in a way that made him want to tell her if she didn't stop she'd kill him, but couldn't speak. Johnnye must have heard what he wanted to say because she stopped.

As he lay on the floor, she grabbed the revolver, towering over him, she hissed, Northern enunciation gone. "This is *mine* now. Tell anybody I have it, and I'll tell 'em you shot at me and show 'em the bullet in the ceiling. They'll throw you off the Force, and put your stupid ignorant ass in the asylum. I'll tell the police you're crazy, and I'm scared of you." Johnnye looked at Joe Cephus on the floor. "I'm going to tell folks what happened and show them the bullet hole, and let my friends keep your gun and say you got scared and threw it away after you tried to kill me. If you ever *try* to do anything to me, your ass will be in trouble."

As J.C. wept on the floor, Johnnye advised him to report that someone attacked him in the driveway, took his gun, and tried to break his neck. Better go to the P.D. doctor so he'll see the bruises. Johnnye took sick leave because her husband had a terrible accident. She spent the day shopping in Charlotte where there were more and larger clothing stores.

The J.C. grin was permanently replaced by a fallen angel look. His mustache was one-sided. He couldn't remember the last time he had an erection. He sat in the bath tub looking at his has-been and held it pathetically when he made urine. He was too young for this to happen. There were men who had children long after his age. Ashamed, he was glad Johnnye was not interested. Once or twice he allowed himself to ask when was she ever interested. He felt like crying a lot. The P.D. finally replaced the revolver after protracted and embarrassing questioning and docked Joe Cephus' pay for the replacement. The incident also docked his standing in the Police Department. All the officers knew and Peters the officer who had pushed him stared at him with a pleased expression. Joe Cephus perceived that there was something missing, but failed to realize that he had no friend, chum, or buddy who would be in his corner no matter what. The Captain placed a written account in Joe Cephus' file that he was ordered to sign. Never having done much reading, he was not certain what the Captain had written. There was nothing more embarrassing than for an Officer to have someone *take his gun*, the Captain reminded him.

Joe Cephus wept.

CHAPTER 22

Joe Cephus' Illness

Just when Dee was beginning to say maybe Joe Cephus would live
out his days, one night Johnnye saw him lying in bed apparently
at the boundary of Dreamland. Commodities that had served
their purpose and no longer of value should not be permitted
to become clutter. Johnnye took the waiting-to-be used syringe
from a hidden compartment inside her handbag. In the event it
was ever discovered, the container bore the label CAUTION:
USE AS DIRECTED FOR DIABETIC COMA. Johnnye had
been told during a routine physical examination that based on
her family history and present lab tests, she had a tendency to
become diabetic. Johnnye took advantage of her assets as well
as her liabilities, and felt certain she would have no problem
explaining the syringe should the occasion arise. She looked at
J.C. His face was serene, his closed eyes moving slightly. In the
twilight zone there was something angelic about him. He is good-
looking. Johnnye smiled. His head is kinda small, and his legs
sorta bowed, but he is handsome. She called him Peahead, but it
was large enough. He didn't need a regular size head for what he
had to store in it. There was enough space for his teacher-craze,
his saying he was the first colored hired, and his penis pride.
Johnnye opened the snaps on J.C.'s pajamas and turned him over.

As the needle pierced his buttocks, he opened his eyes and asked sleepily, "Whatcha doin' to me, Baby?"—his question when sex was especially enjoyable to him.

The next morning, J.C. told Johnnye he didn't "feel right" and called in sick, and the next day, and the next. It would take almost a year for the compound to search through his body and find the lurking health enemy to which Joe Cephus was most vulnerable, and team up with it. Johnnye's doctor, who had become J.C.'s, told him his pressure was too high and watch his diet. And avoid stress. Pleased with the stress she had caused, Johnnye became quite solicitous, giving J.C. bland food, snacking with him, lacing his portions with medicaments that raised blood pressure, and making certain he had tiny doses of palliatives that depressed the immune system.

Because he was taking so much sick leave, a physician in the Police Department examined him and announced "the lab had found something in his blood. It was so minute don't worry about it." The doctor even joked—the way some white men joke with colored men like Joe Cephus: "That schoo-oo-l teach-ur taking too good care of you, J.C. Givin' you too much good stuff." Joe Cephus grinned, but continued to tell Johnnye something wasn't right.

Her face drawn at work and around her J. C., Johnnye prepared skim milk drinks and tasty juices that they sipped in their huge HIS and HER cups and glasses before going to bed, where she fondled and kissed him as she once did. He wished she wouldn't. Breathing heavily, Johnnye inched her bottom up too close to his head. Dottie and other women he knew didn't do that. They just did it the ordinary way—Missionary Way, folks called it. If Johnnye wanted to do something "funny," he wouldn't know how. He couldn't do anything at all. He felt too sick. Soothed by Johnnye's amenities, Joe Cephus decided to forget the unpleasant things that had happened. After all, nobody was perfect. Maybe he didn't see Johnnye kiss that woman. Even if he did, nobody's got nothing to do with it. It was they business, he told himself.

Joe Cephus' blood pressure began to soar. He could no longer work. The P.D. doctor told him he could retire with disability status and to apply at once. Protesting feebly, Joe Cephus retired. Leaving his checks untouched, Johnnye paid all the bills. After collecting them a while, she showed him the checks and massaged him into giving her Power of Attorney. If not white folks would take over. Colored folks should handle their own business. J.C. felt secure. His wife would take care of his business.

As Johnnye paraded a face that no longer had its perpetual half-smile, she paid less attention to her clothes, eliciting colleagues' sympathy. They commented on how worried she looked–and she must not give up. She must pray. God would not permit her to become a widow again unless it is His Will.

Joe Cephus had a series of minor strokes. Then a massive attack after sipping an entire glass of Johnnye's brew. His thinking faculties remained the same, but he began to soil himself. It sickened Johnnye. Nothing disgusted her like human excrement, or waste coming from men. Like babies, men had no habits of cleanliness she thought. They didn't wash their hands after peeing, just shook their things and went on eating, cooking, shaking hands. Maybe some did wash after doing their real stinky if a woman kept reminding them. Then they just rinsed their hands. No soap.

One morning when Johnnye was on her way to work, Joe Cephus soiled himself. As the odor reached her nostrils, she saw shamefaced Joe Cephus. Johnnye pretended not to notice, closed the room door, vowed he had to get out of her house, took her dog Darwin to a retired friend's house, went to work, and did not return until midnight. Joe Cephus had to tidy himself–and thereafter. Johnnye moved him to the upstairs bedroom. She began to ignore him more. She laughed along with her friends at her tolerance of Darwin's accidents, only shaking her head and saying "No—ooo– bad little doggie."

Joe Cephus wept.

His retired Cousin Daisy was his main visitor. Finally, he

admitted to her what she could see; Johnnye was neglecting him, and listened to Daisy remind, "I said you'd be sorry you married that woman." But he wasn't.

Cousin Daisy knew Johnnye left early and returned late, and that Joe Cephus ate lots of can soup and saltines.. "Can soup's nothing but salt and water," Daisy told him. "Worse thing for high blood pressure and that woman's givin' it to you on purpose. And you don't even add the can of water like you oughta." Daisy came almost every day while Johnnye was at work, and prepared J.C. "something decent to eat." He gave Daisy his key since he was upstairs and sometimes asleep or just could not make it to the door. She cleaned his bedroom and bathroom, changed and laundered his bed linen and pajamas.

Daisy dropped by on Sundays after church, and ran into Johnnye, who smiled sadly, hugged, welcomed and thanked her softly, offering pay, and explaining, "I leave so early and have so many meetings to attend. Integration has taken its toll. I don't have but two white students. But the superintendent is breathing down my back just as if I had a room full," Johnnye lied. "Let me pay you whatever you charge. J.C.'s insurance helps some."

"No. Glad to come. Joe Cephus is my closest livin' kin. I helped raise that boy."

"You certainly did a good job." Johnnye wondered if the woman was stupid enough to believe her.

"Did my best, with the Lord's help. He made the most of his life. Wish he hada gone to college. He'd been president of it by now." She wiped a tear.

Third Vice President of Janitors, Johnnye planned to add when she told her friends. Knowing she couldn't coax a tear, Johnnye gave Daisy what was planned to be a sad hug, smiling to herself. She had seen that Joe Cephus did not will Daisy—or anybody one cent. Power of Attorney meant lots of power.

Joe Cephus tried to look at the tiny TV Daisy put in his room, but the picture was too small, nothing much was on, and he didn't feel like getting up to change channels so he spent lots of time thinking. Dorothy Borden used to tell him people pay for the way they are, but he hadn't done anything real bad to women. And none of them had been sick. Mildred hadn't been really sick. She just had miscarriages like women do, and bled so much she had to go to the hospital to have blood transfusions. The hospital asked him to donate blood or ask some of his friends to donate. He asked two or three and they did. And he didn't have to let them take his blood. He'd never treat a sick person, even a woman, the way Johnnye was treating him. She slapped him for spitting up his food. Said he did it on purpose. He did, but she didn't know. She even beat him with a belt for throwing something at her. He was just feeling real bad that day.

One night before she moved him upstairs, he wet the bed. Just couldn't help it. Johnnye kicked him out. With her feet. He never kicked her. She made him change the sheets and put them in the washing machine that night. He slept in the other room anyway. He begged her to let him come back to their room. She told him, "Piss on me again, I'll amputate that turd-looking thing you piss through." He'd never tell nobody some of the things Johnnye did. He had never done anything that bad to her or nobody.

True, he used to laugh about giving women the Five F's: Find 'em, Fix 'em, Frig 'em, Fight 'em, and Forget 'em. Like he said "he couldn't help if they let him treat them that way. It was *their* fault." He certainly had not given Johnnye the Five F's. He had been nice to her. His first wife hadn't been on his level and didn't count. As for Dorothy, she got the first Four, but there were times when things were all right. The first Valentine's Day they were married, he gave her a heart-shaped box of chocolates. He couldn't help it if she didn't eat candy. That's why he gave her a small box that didn't cost much. And that first Christmas, he had given her two pairs of panties, not just one pair. He couldn't help it if they were too large. He took them back, but just didn't get around to getting some more, especially after Dorothy told him "those cheap drawers are so large you must have my butt confused with somebody else's." Oh yes, one time he and Dottie went to the beach and had a really good time. A man didn't have to be a goodie-goodie all the time. A woman wouldn't respect him. –And sometimes he just didn't know what Dorothy was talking about. So he just slapped her.

Trying to understand what had happened to him, what had gone wrong, Joe Cephus lay in bed frowning. He would never perceive that interred in his soul's grave were love and compassion. And understanding. Sprouting, growing, blooming on that fertilized mound were *his* want and need. He wanted and needed his mother to do what was assigned to a woman to do for a man until he found the woman he *wanted* to be his wife, The Symbol of His Success and Achievement. He *needed* that wife to complete his investment in life. Joe Cephus did not know the application of a simple law of physics to human relationships. He had no perception of it. He met his Symbol of Success in Johnnye Jamison. She wanted, needed a man to complete *her* investment in life. Alike charges repel.

Lying in bed, dying, Joe Cephus would not relent. Not even as hints and suspicion hovered over him that there was a possibility Johnnye "made him sick like folks said she did John Woodard." Joe Cephus saw the film of his life. He had attained his deserved elevation when he married Dorothy Borden, and he deserved to maintain that loftiness. His fellow officers, white and colored, would know that only a special kind of woman served as his wife. He would topple and plunge into something unbecoming, unworthy, if he married, for example, one of those young beauticians, who smiled at him and invited him to parties. He gave them up as marriage partners after learning he could do better. He certainly wouldn't have a maid who wore a uniform and worked in a store, no matter how exclusive the store, or operated an elevator and announced floors in "a educated voice."

Nurses at Frank Raymond were off-limit. They wanted doctors, and were not nearly so numerous as women who flashed roll books—and nurses didn't make as much money. He had never heard "nothin' 'bout they pension." He wouldn't share his pension and Social Security with a woman. No matter that she did all the housework and cooking. All women are supposed to do that, even most white women.

Joe Cephus continued his inventory. A domestic or factory worker was definitely out. "What would folks think, 'specially white policemen where he worked, if he couldn't do no better than that!"

Neither did it matter that there were girls, virgins, or almost virgins, and non- virgins, who would make serious and faithful wives, dedicated mothers, who would work along with a man. They would take the children to the woman who kept them and pick them up after work, without a car, and see that they went to Sunday School and behaved in church, and believed in Santa Claus and got Easter outfits, and later see that they got to school on time and had money to pay for costumes so they could be in school plays. Serving husbands they never stopped serving, these wives would work all day and come home to cooking, washing dishes, bathing children, putting them to bed, and still be ready to do their main duty–lie with their husbands, believing that they, the wives, believed that their husbands believed they were getting the best poon-tang, or whatever name they had for it, to be found. Without realizing it, these women would bolster what men like Joe Cephus believed: that magic power flowed through his wonder-working wand that enchanted his wife, and left God with no alternative but to admit him, Joe Cephus Divine, to heaven since he had served his earthly purpose and made the devil look the other way.

These women would be the first up every morning, preparing hearty breakfasts. On Sundays, holidays, and when friends came to dinner, the dining room would look and smell like a banquet hall. These women would lose their beauty, youth, and figures before their time. Some would defiantly hang on to some vestiges of them. And if they heard of their husbands' infidelities, they would feign disbelief, and if they did not, they would say there is some dog in every man, and remain dedicated to making their husbands happy. Usually the husband died first, and these wives would say "I had a good husband," still faithful and honoring them after death. And the women would not marry again because they could never get another man as good as the one who passed. Besides, another man might not be nice to the children, or be "too nice" to the girls, or run the boys away from home.

The only truly negative thing about those other women is that they didn't bring children's papers home to correct at nights and report to a boss known as their principal. Joe Cephus justified his rejection. The self that guided him bellowed: "But I didn't LOVE none of them—other women. A man's got to at least LOVE a woman he doesn't want. I MARRIED WHO I WANTED. A MAN DOESN'T HAVE TO LOVE WHAT HE WANTS!"

Now Joe Cephus lay in bed helpless. He had given Johnnye Power of Attorney: He had given her *power* over his life. She already had more than he thought any woman would have over him. Again he lamented that Dorothy Borden got away. He certainly didn't like her all that much. Johnnye was much better looking, her hair longer, and she dressed better, but he'd rather be married to Dorothy. Love was just some stuff in the movies that white people made pictures about to make money and get rich.

Joe Cephus let his thoughts remain unharnessed. Folks talk about Johnnye Jamison, but Dorothy Borden certainly was no angel, especially in New York where people in Granston couldn't see her. But folks found out anyhow. To show how good he is, he would have taken her back after divorcing her. *He* paid the lawyer. It would have been perfect after his mother died. Dorothy could have stepped right in to do the cooking and housekeeping. He would have told folks he didn't believe she went with white men, and "nobody had nothin' to do wif they business." He would have even changed from asking her to pay all the bills when she worked from September to May. He would have worked something out— like he did with Johnnye.—

Joe Cephus paused—what had he worked out with Johnnye? Something. He just couldn't remember what.

Oh, yes, had Dottie Borden come back after his mother died, things would have worked out the way they were supposed to. People would have believed they didn't get along because of his mother. Dorothy didn't even call him when she came to visit her parents. She was so trashy she rushed back to New York to white men. He heard about it. International dating, Johnnye called it. He wondered if Dorothy heard about what was happening with him and Johnnye.

J.C. began talking to himself. "A man's got to beat a woman to keep her in line, especially cul-lud women like Dorothy Borden and Johnnye Jamison. Let 'em know they're not better then nobody else. Men in the army said you didn't have to beat white women as much. Or as bad. Could just slap 'em and scare hell outta 'em. They not as tough as black women. And not as evil. That's why it's best not to bother wif women too dark. Blacker they are, evil-ler they are. Had to stop foolin' 'round wif that lil' teacher in High Point, the one whose picture was in the paper about her bein' The Teacher of the Year, white or cul-lud. She was just too dark! Evil, too. I could tell when she said I had to take her places like the movies and not just in the back seat of my car."

Realizing he was talking aloud, Joe Cephus put his hand over his lips so words couldn't come out. Those that didn't come out shouted how he should have started with Johnnye from the beginning. He should have just beat the hell outta her that first week. Because he had not, because he simple could not, J.C. wept.

CHAPTER 23
Joe Cephus Dies

Certain that Joe Cephus was going to die before long, with his written consent, Johnnye sent him to the veterans' hospital in Durham. J.C. wept. Johnnye tried to, but was still was no good at crying. Johnnye would have visited J.C. if she had not been too depressed and could bear seeing him in such a condition, she told colleagues and her principal in a choked voice. He advised her to take sick leave and go. Johnnye thanked him, took her dog Darwin to the local kennel, and contacted The Associate. They met in Richmond, Virginia, and had a delightful rendezvous in a little house that smelled like a hospital.

As Joe Cephus lay in bed helpless, VVAPs (Volunteers for Veterans Assistance Program, an organization for terminally ill veterans) smiled at him from his door, entered his room, stood around the bed, held his hand, and talked quietly as if he were already dead, the way people did in undertakers' parlors and at funerals. The volunteers talking as if he were already dead were white. Joe Cephus wondered if there were any colored volunteers, but he asked the white ones anyway to contact Johnnye and tell her to please come to see him. He thought she'd come because they were white. But she didn't. Pleasant white voices explained how distraught his wife was, how hard she worked to keep from

141

going to pieces, and that she would visit him soon as she had the spiritual strength.

Joe Cephus felt himself beginning to die. He didn't believe it for a while. He was actually going to die, do the thing that other people did. His cousin Daisy solicited people in her church Missionary Circle to drive her to Durham. Each time she came, Joe Cephus wept and asked her what had he done "to make his life end up like this."

Daisy replied, "Dyin' is a debt we all got to pay, Boy. Regardless of what we do or don't do. Christ died on the cross. Thank God you in a bed in a hospital. Pray so you can go to heaven and be wit your Savior."

Joe Cephus wiped his tears. "I haven't done nothin' NOT to go. Never stole anything. Never went to jail. Or kill nobody. And I'm a po-leece. Don't that count?"

"Everythang count one way or another. Pray anyway, Joe Cephus. We born in sin. And we sin just bein' human."

"I wanna go to heaven," Joe Cephus sobbed. "I haven't committed hell-going sins."

"If you have, God'll forgive you," she consoled. "You heaven bound. Just goin' sooner then I thought. Expected you to outlive me old as I am. Folks told you what happened to that woman's first husband–and that she went both ways. Them kinda women don't care about a man like she suppose to. We told you not to marry her."

Childlike, Joe Cephus dried his tears with his pajama sleeves. "Folks say Johnnye did somethin' to John Henry Woodard. They don't say what. I don't believe in that conjure stuff and women puttin' somethin' in a man's food. That slavery-time stuff." Joe Cephus sighed. Why couldn't his cousin understand. "Cousin Daisy, she HAD to care something about me. She MARRIED me–."

"You married three times. How much did you care about them women? You married that li'l girl 'cause you messed her up. Married Dottie Borden for who she was. Tied up with the last one

'cause you married the second one and thought yoursef too good
for somebody on your level. How come you think women marry
you 'cause they love you? Maybe Mildred did. She didn't know
no better. I'm tellin' you like it is as old-time folks say."

"Cousin Daisy, women DIFFERENT. They marry because
they SUPPOSE to—they WANT to—" Joe Cephus raised his
voice as much he could.

"Boy, you don't know *nothin'* 'bout women. And less 'bout
bein' a man. All you know is what's between a woman's and a
man's legs, and a man and woman is far more then those thangs
'tween they legs. Too late now, but what make you think your wife
cared 'bout you? What she do to let you know—besides marryin'
you as you say?"

"I'm a MAN, Aunt Daisy! A nice lookin' man with a decent
job! The first cul-lud they hired! Came out in the paper. Still got
the article ina pic-chur frame. Used to be on my livin' room wall.
I seen a lotta men who don't look half as good as me, and don't
have as gooda job, but they marry and stay married and have nice
homes and children—" His voice faded as it mixed with disbelief
that Johnnye had not married him because she loved him.

"Joe Cephus, them things you talkin' about important to you.
And maybe to some women you think you too good to go 'round
wit. You went around wit the wrong women, J.C. You married
the wrong woman—all three times."

"I know I did the first time, but who you think I shoulda
married the other times, Cousin Daisy?"

"Nobody till you got more sense in yo' head. Then you
wouldn't have married the ones you married. There were lots of
women out there who woulda made you a good wife if you treat
'em right."

"What did I do that wasn't right?"

"You didn't learn about bein' a man. Manhood sho' ain't
your fists and that thang you think women so crazy 'bout. You
thought mo' of it then any woman you used it on. Johnnye had
what she want right under your nose. She waited long enough

143

for it to look all right to get what she married you for, got it, and now *you* doin' the goin'. She got thangs fixed so when you pass, she'll be, like us colored folks say, Nigger rich. The truth is the truth, Joe Cephus."

Joe Cephus tried to control his trembling lips. He believed Cousin Daisy about his being heaven-bound. However, he didn't need her or nobody to tell him about manhood. Not his. He knew he had once been a man. A true real man. It was gone now, but once he had it. With a faint Joe Cephus grin, he remembered when it was smooth and brown, and could readily inflate into what he told girls was parlor size. Just right. Joe Cephus knew he once had true Manhood.

The phone was ringing when Johnnye came home. It was VVAP in Durham. Maybe they called to tell her Joe Cephus was dead. That would simplify things.

A pleasant white southern voice greeted her: "How yew, Mis' Dee-vine?"

Shit, Johnnye thought, *hurry and tell me he's dead.* "Trying to hold on. Tired from working hard, and–depressed. How are you?"

"Fine. Hope our news makes you feel better in some way. Mr. Dee-vine is asking to come home. We'll be responsible for getting him to Granston since the VVAP has its own ambulance, donated for situations such as yours. We'll also provide house service for the hours you're at work to assist you in granting your husband's final request as his devoted wife. There's no charge for this service, but our organization will accept a donation. And if it is within your beliefs, we'll accept contributions from friends and relatives who donate instead of sending flowers. –And you still there, Mis' Dee-vine?"

Johnnye wanted to hang up. "Yes. What is his final request?" Johnnye hoped she wasn't sounding mad as hell.

"To die in his and your home with you holding his hand."

AH, SHIT! A thought so loud Johnnye wondered if the woman heard.

Are you still there, Mis' Dee-vine?"

HELL, YES. Johnnye wanted to hang up. She was silent.

"Mis' Dee-vine, I know this is a trying time for you. All you have to do is see that his room is ready. We'll do the rest. You can expect us tomorrow—or if it's too soon, the day after. We'll arrive after you get home from work. Which day do you prefer?"

"Doesn't matter," Johnnye responded quietly.

"See you tomorrow. Mr. Dee-vine'll be so happy. He's fortunate to have you. Some of our veterans are entirely alone."

Johnnye's "I'll be dipped in holy shit" was a prelude followed by vituperation, expletive, obscenity, calumny. She swallowed her chewing gum. Later, when her favorite cohorts asked what she said after learning that Joe Cephus would be brought home to die, Johnnye was able to laugh and tell them, "I hung up quietly and did the gamut. It rattled the windows in hell. The devil got scared, slammed the gates and locked them because he didn't want me to bust a vessel, die, and he'd have to let me in."

Joe Cephus died of a massive stroke, but not before "hanging on" for almost two weeks. Johnnye avoided him, feigning unbearable grief. Disappearing when his passing became inevitable, Johnnye was determined there would be no hand-holding. She won.

Johnnye had Joe Cephus' written consent that he wanted to be cremated and everything was to be as inexpensive as possible. Cousin Daisy notified Joe Cephus' brothers and sisters to come and stop Johnnye from "having their brother burned up." Upon finding out he had left everything to his beloved and devoted wife, their concern cooled.

After carefully searching the most exclusive stores in Granston that didn't act funny when colored people want to try on clothes, Johnnye went to the most elegant store in Richmond, Virginia, and purchased a gorgeous black suit with all black accessories, the traditional funeral apparel for a widow. Secluded in her room, grieving while Joe Cephus' folks argued over cremation, Johnnye made plans. The suit would make an excellent traveling outfit, which is the reason she selected it. She would wear it to the rendezvous with The Associate. —Johnnye would stay out of school another week—Bereavement Leave.

After school closed, she and her friend in Granston would take a long trip—out of the country—on their own. Johnnye would make kennel reservations for Darwin at once. She had read in the local paper that Dorothy Borden did not take packaged tours. It was time for Johnnye to have a real adventure like that. She had borne Joe Cephus longer than she had her other two husbands combined. Johnnye could hardly believe the years had gone by that fast—almost six. The insurance would cover the remaining mortgage payments. Joe Cephus could have died years earlier, and the mortgage would have still been paid. He seemed to just hold on. However, his holding on had its merits. She was able to save a lot of her income since he was responsible for most of the expenses. Furthermore, she didn't want to overdo things. If he had decided to go back to the Police Department's doctor, he would have blood tests. Something that needed explaining would eventually show up. It was best this way. It eased if not entirely erased Dee's gossip.

Johnnye knew that Joe Cephus was her final escapade of that sort even if she married again, which she probably wouldn't. She remembered: moderation. Time now to reap and enjoy the harvest. She was just old enough and just young enough.

CHAPTER 24

Johnnye's New Life

As time passed, Johnnye Jamison resembled a steel structure, her voice like refined silky granite, with a tantalizing sultry tone, fascinating and strangely scary. Her body was firm and rigid like her aura. Although she began to gain weight, there was nothing out of place, nothing that should not be there, no mounds except those that defined Johnnye as if she should be defined that way.

Most Granstonians who knew Johnnye were united in eerie silence, lowering their whispery voices reserved for acknowledging she had finally killed her second husband, third if you count the one before she came to Granston. No one took issue, not even insurance companies. Some Granstonians continued to say there was no doubt Johnnye was "funny" but "went both ways." Most Granstonians could deal with Johnnye's being "one of those thangs" as long as she kept quiet and didn't bother children that way. No one had ever heard that any of the "funny" people in Granston, male or female, ever approached a child. However, being bisexual was more than they could decipher. So colored Granston whispered. Furthermore, Johnnye was said to be man-crazy—and the *only woman they knew who had defied colored people's greatest sexual taboo.** Never mind they were not certain with whom. Except maybe Al Benson. Wives covered their smiles with their

147

hands and teased each other: "She might be doing what colored folks don't do with *your* husband."* Men grinned sheepishly.

Still chewing gum —with dignity in public—, Johnnye retired from the Granston Public School system, her record spotless as an angel's wings. Principals had never called her into their offices except for commendation, parents did not complain about her, and children adored her. No matter how intoxicated she got at parties, it didn't reach the community moral-keepers, or the Superintendent's office. No matter how much she flirted with husbands, seduced, or dated them, or how much they fell in love with her, no wife accosted her.

Johnnye had an encounter with a furious admirer who had a hang-up on her too monetarily pleasing for Johnnye to refuse, and who trailed her to a Lovers' Lane as she nestled with his rival. The furious admirer escaped with his life after Johnnye and the rival finally threw him in his car and ordered him to leave before they broke his arms and he couldn't drive. However, the rival caught Johnnye unprepared after her teamwork. She displayed her swollen face and lips a few days later to a public that sympathized with her being in a car accident.

Johnnye was safe. White people weren't ready to believe that a colored woman could be so designing. Colored people were not ready to accept that one of them, especially a teacher, "did things like that." Colored men often died of diseases such as heart attacks, high blood pressure, and strokes that plagued colored men. Johnnye was safe. Hers was another type of story people in Granston knew happened but did not believe.

*Not until after the White House scandal in the 1990's would some Granstonians say the actual word.

PART II

CHAPTER I

Dorothy Borden Goes Home Again

Year 2000. Twenty-first century. Dorothy Borden, now in her seventies, returned to Granston embarking on an adventure to recapture fragments of days when she and her best friend Thomasena*, as teenagers, had sneaked into corners and crevices in search of secrets. And found them. *Some* of them. They were intriguing, belonging to grownup white and colored people, another generation. Another century. Dorothy had written about them, milestones and millstones so shocking that even people who knew they happened, chose not to believe. Along with nostalgia, Dorothy was engrossed in recent cabal and intrigue. She stood in the once white-only Hampton-Calhoun Hotel lobby, renamed Granston Grandest Caravansary, waiting for a high school friend, Jacquelyn Sullivan, a retired high school teacher. They had remained Dottie Borden and Jackie Sullivan to each other. Dorothy, never letting go of the past, used her maiden name in Granston and still thought of her childhood friends by their maiden names. Jackie had married Pastor Thadeus LeGrande, a Lutheran minister. Dorothy wished Jackie were more talkative, and had additional information about Joe Cephus Divine's marriage to Johnnye Jamison, his death, and its aftermath. Jackie had not known Joe Cephus, only met him through her brother-in-law, a member of the Police Department also. She had introduced him to Dorothy and even stood a wistful witness to the simple Sunday ceremony that had joined Dorothy with Joe Cephus, granting him, as she found out, kicking, humping, and freeloading privileges.

Despite Granston's being one of North Carolina's smaller cities, Jackie had not known Johnnye Jamison, the wife Joe Cephus was with when he died, except that she taught in the Granston Public School System, Booker T. Washington Elementary School, before integration. Dorothy did not consciously notice the way colored public school teachers socialized when she herself taught at Lexis College, a land-grant, all colored institution at that time, commuting distance from Granston. After scrutinizing her hometown and its role in the lives of characters in her forthcoming novel, Dorothy realized that elementary and high school teachers were rarely close friends. They attended the same dances and functions, but fellowship and camaraderie ended there. Elementary teachers organized clubs and played cards together, as did some high school teachers. There was only one colored high school at the time. College instructors were rare in Granston, since most of them lived and worked in college cities like Winston-Salem and Greensboro and socialized among themselves. Dorothy had retained her high school friends, regardless of their "teaching rank" or non-teaching status, and made new friends in Granston the same way.

Jackie promised to show the new Granston to the new Dottie Borden. New, since she had finally published the novel that she dreamed of over sixty-five years ago while attending Granston's colored Frederick Douglass High School, grades eight to eleven. She was in the eighth grade and knew she would write a great book that Boston would ban. In those days Boston's banning a book meant almost everybody read it, even some Catholics, and the writer became famous.

Like Pompeii, Dorothy's thoughts lay under a blanket of once searing ashes from the eruption of a Vesuvius. Acting as her own mental archeologist, she dug into preserving ashes to reveal what had been. While waiting for her friend, Dorothy closed her eyes so that she could see her mind's calendar: summer, 1939.

They had entered their teens, Dorothy and Thomasena. Dorothy's father, Lawyer Borden, as he was known to colored people out of respect and to some white people who didn't call him George and to whom Mister was out of the question, drove them to Winston-Salem to visit Grandma and Dorothy's favorite cousin, Bea, on Mama's side. Winston-Salem still smelled like tobacco in the late thirties and was the site of Dorothy's biggest secret of all, even bigger than the one about Merry Widows, the "rubbers" she had found in her mother's chest of drawers. Dorothy had taken a condom (She did not know the word then.) from its cellophane pack, hid it in the attic, and had shown it to no one but Thomasena. Feeling old and experienced, Dorothy had explained how it worked. Surely it happened just a few years ago, not over sixty. Memories were so vivid, so real that they were scary–like time had inverted and was *then* instead of *now*. The two teenagers blew their secret up like a balloon, filled it with water and were shocked at the amount of air and water it could hold. Teenage Dottie had another secret now, even bigger. Year 2000 Dottie closed her eyes again in order to see. And she did. And she heard the 1939 Dottie whispering:

"Thomasena, if I tell you something, you won't tell *nobody?*"

"You know I won't tell, Dottie."

"This is my *biggest* secret! If Daddy and Mama found out, they would *never* let me stay in Winston-Salem no more."

"Tell me! I tell you my secrets."

"You don't have one like this!"

"I might. Tell me!"

Dorothy looked around to be sure no one was listening, and lowered her voice anyway, "Bea's husband's brother is *nasty.*"

"What does he do?" Thomasena asked.

"Don't tell *nobody*! Daddy would *shoot* him!"

"Why?" Thomasena's eyes widened.

"Thomasena, this is *terrible*! One night Roger, that's his name, was here, everybody was downstairs, and I went upstairs to the bathroom, and he followed and tried to kiss me and feel me here." Dorothy indicated her pointed bust.

"Oh, Dottie! How old is he?"

"Too old to be feeling me! Way up in his twenties, maybe even thirties!"

"What did you do?"

"I told 'im I didn't let old men do bad things to me and that I had a boyfriend to feel me if I wanted to be felt and I'd tell my Daddy."

"What did he do then?"

"Girl, he got scared and wanted to give me five dollars!"

"Did you take it?" Thomasena's eyes were wider.

"No! Mama said *never* take money from a man."

"Mine says the same thing. How did you get away?"

Dorothy responded with sophistication: "I was movie star-ish about it. And acted like a grown girl in a book and told 'im I didn't want his nasty old money and my Daddy gave me money. Roger begged me not to tell his brother, Daddy, Grandma, or Bea, and left. –And Thomasena, this is worse of all—"

"What?"

Dorothy hesitated, whispered lower. "His old Thing was sticking up. I saw it through his pants! –Haven't I had some experience, but it's so bad I can't put it in a story."

"Yeah. You have really lived! I hope he doesn't come back." Thomasena looked around to see if he were hiding somewhere.

"If he does, don't go upstairs by yourself. If he catches you on the porch at night and says anything, tell him you'll tell me and I'll tell my Daddy. Everybody's scared of my Daddy."

Dorothy placed a protective arm around Thomasena's shoulders. "Know what–it was kinda exciting to be approached by an elderly man." That was Granston of the past–Dorothy's collecting past secrets–.

She heard echoes of teenage laughter that faded with thoughts

153

of the mystery regarding Joe Cephus Divine's death. What was Johnnye (Sadie Mae Johnson) Jamison Woodard Divine doing? Was she, as Black people jested, Nigger rich? Retired from Granston's City School System, she had a pension, Social Security, and did she have financial gains from Joe Cephus' death? Getting information depended on Dee. Did Black Granstonians still refer to gossip as news from "Dee–De Niggers?"

Hairdressing parlors and barber shops had been the best places to get news, and probably still were. Dorothy must find out if her former beautician Carrie Lee Pickens was still alive. Dorothy had been one of her prized customers, and the hairdresser had shared secrets and told Dorothy about Joe Cephus' association with a good-looking older woman, divorced with three adult children. Before his marriage to Dorothy, Joe Cephus accepted beauticians as friends, and boasted to a beautician friend who conveyed the news to the grapevine that the woman tried to trick him into marriage, pretending to be pregnant. He had avoided marriage, reminding her that a woman her age was "on the change and sometimes missed periods, so they had better wait and see." Joe Cephus proudly let it be known that the woman called him a few weeks later saying she had a miscarriage. He went to see her, and found her in bed.

The woman had inflated Joe Cephus' ego, which probably was one reason he thought that she, Dorothy Borden, would seal their marriage with motherhood, which would be sealing her fate, stepping into quicksand. It would have been beyond stupidity to have a child neither of them wanted–and by an abusive, parsimonious man she did not want. Dorothy knew the entire care of a child, financially as well as emotionally, would be left entirely to her. She told herself then and now, because she married Joe Cephus was no reason to let him continue to pollute her life, which was the reason she refused to put her life on hold and lose control of it. Not in any of the plans that she built around dreams to joust and revel with the world, were there any traces of Joe Cephus Divine, or any resemblance to him. And she had jousted and reveled—on five continents. All on her own, Dottie Borden style. She considered living in the Far East, Middle East, Near East, and *Africa*. And had checked them out. —Because she was determined to remain in control of her life. If Joe Cephus were alive, she'd tell him that acts to retain control should be retroactive where he was concerned. Perhaps they were—Johnnye Jamison style—.

A car stopped in front of the hotel entrance. Seeing it wasn't Jackie, Dorothy returned to her mental bout with Joe Cephus. She sighed, realizing she had behaved unwisely also, perhaps more so. She had married knowing she did not like that type of bonding. Joe Cephus had *wanted* to be married—regardless of his flawed reasons—and the cost. Considering what she observed, Dorothy concluded Joe Cephus did not think in terms of warped reasons and cost. He considered himself a winner. Perhaps he was. He married teachers. He got what he wanted. Twice. Marriage to women of his choice, women he considered worthy of a man like him. And he broke the racial barrier in the Police Department. Dorothy wondered what percentage of people can boast of getting precisely what they want, both in their professional and domestic lives. The words "How vain is learning, how useless art, lest it guides the spirit and mends the heart" sprang from a long-ago wellspring. Dorothy couldn't recall who wrote the quote nor why it came to her mind.

But Dorothy must get back to her mission. She reflected briefly whether her pursuit of details about Joe Cephus' death was a will-o'-the wisp, but began mentally listing people who might have information. Her former beautician, Carrie Lee Pickens, remained tops. They had never been on a first name basis, but Mrs. Pickens had confided in Dorothy, something not unusual in African American relationships. Remembering conversations they had when she, Dorothy, was married to Joe Cephus, Dorothy hoped the beautician was still alive. She recalled the one that labeled her a very special customer:

"Mis' Divine, I didn't know you are a teacher. Somebody told me you're Dorothy Borden whose name I see in the paper about making speeches at the Y and in churches. I recognize you now from the pic-churs. Just didn't make the connection at first."

Dorothy didn't know what to say other than, "I use my maiden name a lot."

"Yeah. Lawyer Borden's daughter. I got him to go over some papers when I bought my house and open my shop. –The first thing most teachers do is let me know who they are. They come in dressed to kill even on Saturdays, waving they roll books, or saying they late because the principal held them up, or they saw one of they students' parents and had to stop and talk. If other customers here, the teachers really carry on: 'My principal took my parking place' if they have a car; 'I had to send a boy to the office today who just won't behave in my classroom', and 'I forgot my roll book.' You never mention your roll book."

Yes, if this lady were alive, Dorothy would get information from her. Dorothy had made an impression, not purposefully, that the lady liked. Dorothy wondered if some teachers still advertised themselves the way Mrs. Perkins said they did.

Dorothy heard a car and looked from the lobby window again. It was Jackie, a little late, and Dorothy as usual was a little ahead of time. Jackie's once almost too much "good" dark brown glossy hair was thin, gray, and in a tiny ball near the top of her head. Her once creamy "white-folks skin" was darker and lined. A scarf concealed her neck. Dorothy wondered if she looked as old to Jackie as Jackie did to her. Dorothy had noticed that when she met people who had not seen her for years, they stared for a while as if to associate this shrunken, underweight woman with the used-to-be wholesome-looking, brown-skinned, WWII sweater and Pin-Up girl, who had once been Dorothy Borden.

Dorothy got into the sparkling car with her friend, telling her that people at the hotel–or should she say caravansary (They both smiled.) appeared not to mind serving Black people. Even the Black employees were polite to her. Dorothy could have stayed with Jackie and Pastor LeGrande, but preferred the privacy and convenience of a hotel, freedom from tidying responsibilities, chores a female guest was not expected to leave for a hostess. Dorothy had bargained with her former, high school friend: Take her to see how much Granston has changed. Jackie agreed, and to take her anywhere else she wanted to go. Yes, even to get information about Johnnye Jamison Divine if Dorothy knew where to go. Jackie didn't. Never having learned to drive, Dorothy couldn't use rental agencies. Dorothy knew she would be shown around in a year 2000 car (She didn't remember the model) since Rev, the name Jackie called her husband, insisted on using the '96 because she should show her celebrity friend around in the best. Dorothy also knew she was expected to admire the car, and tried to see what model it was. The model was usually on the dashboard somewhere, but Dorothy couldn't find it and told Jackie it was a pretty color, an "elegant silvery gray." Dorothy hoped she got the color technically correct, and quickly added that it was the first time she had ridden in a 21st Century car. Jackie released one of her rare smiles. Dorothy hoped she was acting thrilled over riding so royally in a 2000 whatever it was a retired, educated minister provided for his retired, school teacher wife, daughter of one of Granston's late prominent doctors. –Who was driving her novelist friend around, the daughter of Granston's first Black lawyer. Dorothy wondered if she were sufficiently elated and tried to think of something else to say about the car, but was tunneled and programmed for research about Joe Cephus and Johnnye.

No use asking Jackie about a beautician. She had "good hair," and colored women in Granston with "good hair" didn't dare go near a beauty parlor. A status symbol, Dorothy remembered. They were proud to wash their hair themselves. If you want to insult a colored woman, especially a teacher, who had naturally straight, curly, or wavy hair, ask "Who does your hair?" Dorothy smiled. Nowadays it had changed somewhat, even in Granston. Almost everybody was going, regardless of hair texture. (Except Jackie. Dorothy had called one day and Jackie said she'd return the call; Rev was helping wash her hair.) "Good-hair" had to be washed, set, or permed. Colored women were getting manicures! Even pedicures! And some brave souls were jogging, especially after reading that a famous Black woman writer–what's her name? –jogged in Winston-Salem. Oh, yes, Maya Angelou. Dorothy recalled with amusement how neighbors had stared and laughed when she first began walking her dogs, taking them to the mail box, or just strolling. According to Dee, one of Joe Cephus' duties was to walk Johnnye's dog and take her, the dog, for rides. On visits to Granston, before the death of her parents, and even afterwards, Dorothy was informed of Dee's observations.

Being in Granston disturbed images and voices, and Dorothy looked and listened to what no one heard or saw but her. Jackie was by nature not talkative and rarely spoke unless spoken to or pointing out something unfamiliar to Dorothy, so she was free to look and remember.

*Protagonist in *This Day's Madness*

CHAPTER 2
Dorothy Remembers

When her father died, Joe Cephus brought a small, potted plant, along with Johnnye's dog in the back seat of his car. That was before he and Johnnye married. Dorothy knew he wanted her to know he was dating Johnnye, Al Benson's ex, and she Dorothy could find out by inquiring about the dog's owner, typical of Joe Cephus' puerile unsophisticated tactics. Dorothy already knew via a close friend, Robert Barber, in Alexandria, Virginia, a confidant since their college days. Joe Cephus accepted her friendship with Robert Barber. Even though a robust, former formidable college football star, Bob was soft spoken, with an air of humility that pleased Joe Cephus. He called Bob and introduced him to Johnnye over the phone (Dorothy had never known Joe Cephus to make a long distance call, even though she paid the telephone bill.) He also invited Bob to visit Granston as he had when they, Dorothy and Joe Cephus, were married. Bob could spend the weekend at his house and meet Johnnye in person before they married. Dorothy was working in New York, and she and Bob kept in close touch. They both were amused, knowing Joe Cephus wanted Bob to relay the news to her. Dorothy encouraged Bob to go. He'd be near his family in Salisbury, North Carolina, a short trip via bus, and could visit them also. Joe Cephus could even drive him there.

The visit was a conversation piece. Bob arrived with candy and flowers for Johnnye and two fifths of Joe Cephus' favorite Bourbon. Being a moderate party drinker, the two bottles would last Joe Cephus almost forever. Bob took them to breakfast at Mrs. Ware's Grand Blue Diner Friday morning and to a drive-in "sausage, biscuits and egg place" the other two mornings, then to dinners in Greensboro at the popular colored Royal Oasis and All You Can Eat Seafood restaurant. In addition he purchased food and snacks for the three of them to have at night while sipping bourbon and Scotch, Bob's preference. Most of the food and drinks they did not consume Joe Cephus carefully stored.

Even though Dorothy had told Bob how parsimonious Joe Cephus was, Bob was still unprepared. Hearing him running water for a bath, Joe Cephus remarked in one of his more relaxed manner, "Man, you jest got here and washin' ya'sef a-ready? Whatcha been doing to need a baf? Don't drown ya'sef. If you not nasty, you don't need a lotta water." After Bob's next bath, Joe Cephus told him, "Man, you not sleepin' wif nobody. That's YOUR dirt on ya. Remind me of somebody else we both know. Can't stand your own dirt."

Bob told Dorothy he was too amused to reply, and just laughed. He told her about a call to Salisbury to let his family know when the bus would arrive so they could meet him. Joe Cephus suggested Bob reverse the charges since he would not be there when the bill came. A three minute call to Salisbury even during day hours was about 45 cents. Bob suggested calling the operator, getting the charges, and leaving the money. Joe Cephus became agitated. "Man, it's best to call collect. The bill might be more then the operator say, and she might forget to add tax. If you figger your folks don't think enough of you to 'cept the charges, I can use my gas and take you to a pay phone. You don't haveta call 'em no way. They'll be home. Cul-lud folks don't go no where. 'Specially in Salisbury. You can call 'em from the bus station after you get there." Joe Cephus stood and listened to be sure Bob reversed the charges.

Bob left that Sunday noon after arriving Friday morning. Joe Cephus didn't have to work, but made no offer to take Bob the twenty-five miles to Salisbury, which Johnnye said she would enjoy. Joe Cephus complained of tire problems, something she reminded him he had not mentioned previously. Daring to be facetious, Bob asked Joe Cephus how much he charged to take him to the bus station, which was not far in a small place like Granston. Joe Cephus told him, "I invited you here and won't charge a thing. If you want to buy some gas for the car, that's different." And added, "Just one or two open on Sunday. Don't want you to miss the bus so we better leave earlier to get gas." They did. Joe Cephus filled the almost empty tank with the twenty dollar bill Bob had given him. He carefully explained the change. Just to see what would happen, Bob told him to keep the change. He did.

Dorothy smiled to herself thinking how she and Bob had quite a laugh; however, he said he'd never visit Joe Cephus again nor invite him to Alexandria. Joe Cephus' effort to ensure that Dorothy found out he was dating Johnnye Jamison was unnecessary. Dorothy had petted the tiny dog and asked her name. When Joe Cephus said Darwin, Dorothy smiled and responded, "She was named after me," which was the last contact Dorothy Borden had with Joe Cephus Divine. The Funeral Home or Parlor (as it was called in Granston) and a family friend Lora sent notes acknowledging all expressions of sympathy, including one to Joe Cephus. The Funeral Home Receptionist informed Dorothy that Joe Cephus had come there daily and spent two entire days waiting for her. She and her family had made arrangements early and avoided going to the Funeral Parlor as much as possible. The Receptionist also informed Dorothy that Joe Cephus wanted "them to go back together, and said she should come back to Granston to be with her mother." In spite of her intense grief over her father, Dorothy never thought of returning to Granston.

And never once considered exchanging her present life to be a housekeeper, financial supporter, and fuckee for Joe Cephus. Her mother did not complain about joining other widowed ladies who lived alone. They called each other and talked about daytime TV series. Churches had by that time purchased buses for transportation and took non-drivers to services. So did church members. Neighbors, Lodge, and Masonic members took non-driving widows grocery shopping. And there were buses and cabs for uptown personal shopping. Most widowed ladies adopted one or two dogs for inside and outside protection. Mrs. Borden had three, adding another to the two that had belonged to her husband.

Joe Cephus married Johnnye Jamison afterwards. A picture of her announcing the nuptials appeared in the local paper that Dorothy did not see, but was told by a male friend that Johnnye "looked like a truck driver in drag." Later, Dorothy heard that Johnnye was quite attractive and the picture was unflattering.

Dorothy became aware that Jackie was driving extremely slowly. Dorothy also had not initiated a conversation, and she became more wrapped in her own constellation of phantom sounds, sights, and smells of growing up in Granston and becoming. It enveloped her like skin. There could be cessation in growing up, but becoming was perpetual. Even in the Year 2000 Dorothy was not certain if she held the tradition, or if it had grasped her in a forever embrace. Dorothy Borden had not shed Granston. All down through the years she had observed the Southern New Year tradition that colored people held almost sacred: On New Year's Day, no woman would dare enter a colored person's house until she was certain a man had entered first and walked all through the house, a ritual that ensured Good Luck. Every colored family Dorothy knew and those she did not, regardless of status, observed the traditional meal that also ensured Good Luck and Prosperity: collard greens cooked with hog jowl symbolized green money, black eye peas for small change and Good Luck, and rice to help usher Luck. Dorothy could hear her mother's voice raised just enough for a neighbor to hear next door or across the street. The Bordens and Dorothy's elementary school teacher Mrs. Hobson who adopted Thomasena were the only families on Plum Street that had telephones then. Dorothy smiled, remembering the tall black phones that stood on round bottoms, mouth pieces on top like heads, and the receivers on hooks at the side. Although she didn't think about it then, phones were heavy. And they lasted forever. Her mother's in-the-past voice interrupted the vision. Every New Year's Eve:

"Mrs. Brown, don't forget to send Mr. Brown over here first thing tomorrow morning. I'll send Mr. Borden to your house." They did.

Eidola. 1930's. Saturday morning. Time for "Let's Pretend," the radio show directed by Nila Mack in which boys and girls dramatized fairytale classics and their own original stories. In elementary school, a little colored girl, fired up after receiving a cowboy suit as a prize for writing a winning letter to Dear Don in a movie magazine, was going to send a story to Nila Mack and ask her to present it. Nila Mack wouldn't know she was colored, just as those magazine people had not known, and she had won a prize! "Let's Pretend" would dramatize Dorothy's story. She still remembered some of the players' names. Maybe they weren't spelled correctly. Amy Sedell, Miriam Wolfe (She played the witch), Betty Jane Blalock. Were they still alive?

–And Saturday afternoons– time for colored programs. The Reverend Elder Lightfoot Solomon Michaux and his Happy Am I Choir. How they sang. Dorothy still heard booming base voices responding to sopranos. And all colored.—

Saturday nights: Most of the food cooked for Sunday, except fried chicken. As usual, Daddy polished all shoes, church and everyday shoes, and lined them up. All you have to do was get yours and put them in your room. Baths taken. Mama inspected Dorothy's and George Jr.'s Sunday clothes and hung them separately, so they wouldn't get wrinkled. There was Sunday everything, even socks and underwear. Dorothy could hear her protests: "I want to take my bath on Sunday morning. White folks say colored folks bathe on Saturday." Her mother's habitual answer: "Too much rush to get you and George, Jr. ready for Sunday School if you wait until Sunday morning. Slow as you are. You bathe when you want to other times. Your Daddy and I have to get ready for church and be there before somebody takes our seats." The Borden pew: fourth row from the front, first four places from the aisle. Daddy on the outside, Mama next, then Dorothy and George, Jr. The two men always on the outside, as if protecting their ladies.

–Still Saturday night and something to munch on while listening to the Philco radio clearly saying "Round and round she goes, and where she stops nobody knows." Major Bowles Amateur Hour. One day this colored pre-teen will appear on Major Bowles reciting her own poems.

–Sunday morning and Sunday breakfast. Dorothy's memory bank overflows and she sees, smells, and hears: "Daddy's beautiful, delicious omelets and Mama's English muffins made from scratch that George, Jr. and I had to earn by eating cereal, oatmeal in the winter and corn flakes and bananas in summer." Getting ready for church while listening to "This is The Reverend Glenn T. Settle bringing to its last Sunday morning's audience 'Wings Over Jordan.'" Another colored program. –Daddy driving her and Junior to Sunday School, the largest African Methodist Episcopal Church in Granston. –Dorothy listening and talking about Biblical characters that seeped into composites helping to create story people. –After Sunday school, the best time of all. Never put the entire nickel or dime in the collection. Always keep something for the tiny store nearby that had the sweetest penny candy, even sweeter on Sunday mornings. The colored owner wouldn't tell. Sometimes they saw him in church. He always sat in the back and acted as if he didn't know the children who spent part of their Sunday School allowance on penny chocolate candy dolls, Baby Ruths, Butterfingers, and BB Bats–Back from the store in time for Junior Church. Sometimes Dorothy would be in charge. She liked talking about Biblical times. They were so romantic.

Daddy and Mama arrived with George, Jr., who went to a small Baptist Sunday School with his buddies. Sometimes she sat with them and sometimes with girlfriends while sugar and flavored residuals haunted their throats and mouths and colored their tongues throughout the main service. Dorothy both daydreamed and listened to the choir sing anthems and to the college educated minister who conducted short services. Not like that almost-all-day kind where uneducated ministers in smaller churches preached for hours and people sometimes stayed all day.

Home. Dorothy must take off her church clothes and put on after church clothes. Sunday dinner. A real biggie in the life of middle-class colored people. Baked ham or fried chicken. Both when company came. Potato salad. baked macaroni and cheese, string beans seasoned with pork. (Not too much grease. It gave Daddy dyspepsia.) Tiny white potatoes in the beans instead of potato salad. Spinach garnished with hard boiled eggs. Candied yams with pineapple and marshmallows. Tiny green peas instead of spinach, sometimes. Salad with crisp lettuce, cucumbers, and tomatoes. Pickled beets. Brown bread and hot brown rolls. Apple or potato pie. Ice cream for the pie. Lemonade or ice tea with mint that Mama grew herself. Cake if not pie. All food fresh and made from scratch except Sunday rolls and bread. Spinach tasted so different then. Everything did—and so much better. People said it was because food was fresh, but Dorothy knew it was more than that. She got fresh food from health stores and farmers' markets, and green vegetables she and her daughter grew in a small plot and also gathered from fields in Harmony, AZ where they lived. She had stopped eating meats at home. Besides being pro animal, meat was almost tasteless to her now.

Nostalgia would not release Dorothy: Sunday night, the biggest night of all except Christmas and Election. Especially during wintertime. She, Mama, and George, Jr. sitting in the living room around the radio. They munched on leftover Sunday dinner goodies. This room usually reserved for grownup company was theirs now, and they would be careful about crumbs and grease, even Junior. Daddy in his den or room reading and answering mail The radio beckoning: "We want Cantor! We want Cantor!" "WHO?" "The Mayor of Texaco Town." The Eddie Cantor show. He sang "Ida, Sweet as Apple Cider" and had five daughters. –Then "J-E-L-L-O!" Jack Benny with Rochester–his colored valet–Eddie Anderson. If she were to write about Granston, she could not shed it. Dorothy closed her eyes so that she could see the present. "Jackie, do you remember Sundays and Sunday nights when we were growing up?"

"Guess so. Why?"

"What were they like?" Dorothy asked.

"I don't remember them that way–what they were like. They were just–quiet. Like they are now."

"They were *different*, Jackie. There was so much of everything," Dorothy mused, "family, food, radio programs–. I was thinking that Sundays were subconscious confirmation that we, colored people, were no longer slaves. Churches, Sunday clothes, plenty of food, along with large family radios and small ones for bedrooms, and cars validated that we were masters and keepers. Am I making sense, Jackie? I'm going to write about all this, and want to know how it sounds."

Jackie sighed. "Just write about it, Dottie. It'll sound different to everybody who reads it."

"Like all sounds, people hear what they listen for." Dorothy accepted.

"Something like that."

CHAPTER 3

Learning to Read

Jackie could be a valuable source for more information about Johnnye and Joe Cephus, but apparently had almost none of substance. Dorothy needed additional information to develop and enhance her novel. If Dorothy could just get Jackie to really talk. Dorothy decided she might as well begin trying. "Jackie, how much do you think the material public schools used to teach colored children to read effected and affected them?"

"What do you mean?"

"Colored children learned to read from white books. I mean they all had white characters. –Remember in the 1950's and 60's, educators began saying 'Johnnye can't read.' and I began replying, 'If Johnnye can't read, Sammy can't find the book,' and white and colored educators explained *why*: The material is unrelated to colored children's experiences. Characters are all white."

Jackie was silent for a moment. "Come to think about it, just about everything I read was not related to my experiences. Sometimes teachers pointed out–how what we were reading was relevant or related: Material in math books made us think. Just about everything in our everyday life was based on physics.

You had already learned to read then. What about those learning-to-read years? How did they effect you? We were 'middle-class' colored people. Did the material have a more adverse effect on children who were not?"

Jackie inhaled, held it, exhaled audibly. She did not respond. Determined to elicit information, Dorothy continued. "My first reader was *Baby Ray.* He was a little blond boy. George, Jr. had *Tom and Betty,* two blond children. I read both of them over and over. Daddy and Mama got us, me especially, Robert Louis Stevenson's *A Child's Garden of Verses*, poems by Christina Rossetti, *Aesop's Fables, Black Beauty, 365 Bedtime Stories.* By the way, I saw the Bedtime Story Book printed in Chinese in a book store in Chengdu, China, in 1999. I got *Goody Two Shoes* from the school library. And fairy stories! They made me want to read forever. There were no colored characters. Oh, yes, there was a story in the daily paper about a delightful rabbit family. Uncle Wiggly and his little girl Baby Bunny were my favorite characters. Daddy read it to me every night.—Did you read the *Camp Fire Girls Series?* I loved those books. The girls had red or blond hair. I saw it, but it didn't–erase my fantasies of having adventures like Camp Fire Girls. –And I still do. I still have dreams and yearnings that beginning reading years sharpened. That is one of the reasons I traveled so much, propelled by books along with Daddy. Shangri-La replaced camp fire adventures and fairyland. *The Little Lame Prince.* I felt so sorry for him. Jackie, the only book with anything black in it was *Black Beauty.* The only book distributed then with a black character was *Little Black Sambo,* and Daddy and Mama wouldn't buy that. I read it either in the school or public library, or at somebody's house. They got me lots of stories by Charles Dickens."

Jackie responded, "I don't remember my first reader. I do remember sitting on Daddy's lap while he helped me with my lessons. And Mama helped when he had to be out. When I learned to read well enough I sneaked and read what I called Daddy's doctors' books, especially the ones about having babies. They were 'off limit.' "

"I remember," Dorothy smiled. "*True Story* and *True Romance* magazines were also 'off limit' to you. You read them at my house. I didn't like them long because they all sounded alike. I wanted to send stories, and heard they accepted them from colored girls. All they had to do was describe the characters as having blond or red hair and blue eyes."

"I remember the *Big Little Books,*" Jackie offered. "They were small in size, but very thick."

"Oh, yes. I had stacks of them. They would be worth a fortune now, but mine disappeared years ago. They were great and about everything and everybody, Joe Louis included. George, Jr. liked them and Comic magazines he called Funny Books. We used to exchange, especially *Big Little Books.*"

Dorothy wanted specific comments from Jackie, and Dorothy knew she would have to keep the dialogue going. "Because of those Black-Children-Are-Not-Reading and Can't-Read years, educators and writers began including minorities in reading material, especially Black or African American and Hispanic or Chicano characters. Did that reach Granston?"

"Yes, I remember the controversy about the story of a little black rabbit and a little white rabbit falling in love, or something like that. And there was the removal of *Little Black Sambo* and modifying his appearance to a cute little colored boy and calling him *Little Brave Sambo.*"

Both women were more amused than impressed. "Jackie, I had been teaching for years before I saw African Americans represented positively in books supplied and required by the State for children on preschool and elementary levels. In high school we had Carter G. Woodson's *Negro in Our History.* The course was required in our high school and an elective in the white high school. Do you remember the required American History text for Blacks and Whites?"

"Sort of—"

"I don't remember the title, but I'll never forget the picture of two pickaninnies, as they were labeled, eating watermelon while an old gray slave played a mouth harp and younger slaves danced.

That representation was in the chapter 'Slavery in America.' I'm wondering how much text books contributed to colored children wanting to be white. Did you ever want to be white? Or do you now?"

Jackie smiled. "Now is out. Too late. I don't remember if I ever did. Being light-skinned was enough. Or so I felt. What about you?"

"For a while," Dorothy admitted, "that I was conscious of. Especially in college where there was so much emphasis on hair and color. I wanted to be 'light-skinned with good hair' in order to be accepted by colored people—and 'pass' to fool white people who would be nonplussed when they found out. I'd laugh —I *gotcha*."

CHAPTER 4

Wanting to be White

As the two women continued their leisurely drive through the streets of their hometown, which like them, had matured and gone through a metamorphosis, Dorothy saw those bygone years and heard them. She conveyed some of the sights and sounds to her friend. Some of the mutations only she, Dorothy Borden, would see, hear, and understand. Time was when they were in elementary school. During the process of becoming, Dorothy and her classmates had no doubts they were *COLORED*. It didn't make them bleed or cause festering sores. If they wanted to be white, they didn't know it, even when they boasted about having white blood. Dorothy had listened, but never mentioned people in her family who had "crossed over and passed." One of the children's unflagging statements was "The darkest [Black was a dirty word then.] person in the United States got some white blood." Listeners would smile with pride, and show the lightest skin on their bodies to prove it, which was on the underside of their arms near their arm pits. Dorothy somehow knew, even then as a child, that white children did not talk about having colored blood, and displayed the darkest skin on their bodies to prove it.

Dorothy recalled hearing her father say white people admitted having American Indian blood, another source of pride for colored people. There was always somebody in a colored family who looked like a Squaw (now considered offensive), Chief, or Brave. But white people felt superior to Indians. Dorothy's father said the majority of white people felt superior to everybody. She was to have his statement confirmed unrelentingly in a New York City College. He added that this egotism and self-love permeated every race but colored people in America. Other races thought they were the Chosen of the Universe.

Dorothy was to spend over forty years trying to get Colored, Negro, Black, Afro-American, African American students to refrain from reaching for affirmation by simply saying "I'm good as you." Despite the early clamoring to be white and the mimicking years that followed, Dorothy was to hear from students "that's white folks' stuff" when referring to serious education and correct grammatical usage and "they give white students A's and B's" when white students indulged in "white folks stuff." She felt cheated, retiring with the knowledge that some Black teachers often gave up and white ones just didn't bother. Black resistance often elicited "It's just not worth it." Hopefully, she would be able to discuss this problem with Jackie later.

Dorothy wondered how much Black people had damaged their children in the process of helping them deal with identity. Parents and teachers used to whip children severely who referred to another person as black, reinforcing the negative connotation of the word. Dorothy was ahead of her time in terms of the positive use of Black in reference to skin tone.

Closing her eyes, Dorothy saw her elementary school classmates during recess, these children who displayed the underside of their arms, would put water on their hair to prove it "took water" like white folks' hair and didn't get nappy like colored folks' hair. These classmates would poke fun at hair that got nappy, and tell their mothers and daddies, too, if they listened, and even laugh and talk about it the next day and the next. These children would play the dozens with anyone who called them black and beat their asses because there was nothing wrong with being dark brown. They shouted they were proud of their color. Just don't call it black. It's dark brown skin no matter how black. When they were angry with them, these darker children called their light-skin playmates "ole yeller pumpkins" and said they thought they were cute and better than dark skin people. These children who did not know they wanted to be white, when they were not angry, hugged and kissed the fair-skinned playmates with good hair, told them how cute they were and had them for play-children. Dorothy never found out if white children had play-children and play mothers and play sisters. Dorothy had them all. Jackie never did, nor did Thomasena. Dorothy must write about this affirmation of family love.

Dorothy knew her parents tried to combat preoccupation with whiteness by having Santa Claus bring her colored dolls that Daddy said Santa Claus had to order special. Dorothy never saw colored dolls like hers in stores. Dorothy remembered that she loved her colored and white dolls and made clothes for all of them, but knew the colored ones were special. She took colored ones to school because teachers wanted the class to see pretty colored dolls that looked like colored people rather than caricatures. Dorothy also recalled her mother, in her sternest voice, ordered her daughter and playmates to stop saying they were marrying Clark Gable, Ramon Navarro, and Dick Powell when they played movie stars. Dorothy began to play marrying Joe Louis, Langston Hughes, Paul Robeson, Todd Duncan, and Herb Jeffries.

CHAPTER 5
Then and Now Years

Although at intervals Dorothy had verbalized her thoughts to Jackie, there was now a period of silence.

"Lots of places closed." Jackie brought Dorothy back to the present as they passed the boarded up Kress Five and Dime Store where they had shopped for ten cent fingernail polish and sweet smelling perfumes for a dime also. Disappeared, too, were the Bargain Basement and Fire Sale House, where they could get almost anything for five cents that smelled like smoke or damaged by water. –Now they were nearing the old abandoned colored Baxter & Associates Drug Store that had filled prescriptions for colored doctors before integration. If teenagers saved enough nickels, they sat at one of three tables and had a banana split for fifteen cents. A lot of money then.

Dorothy relished seeing and feeling Granston, touching, smelling, and tasting it. Segregation had been banished over thirty years–at least on paper–in public institutions, such as libraries and schools. (Thirty years? Dorothy realized again that her own birth had been only twice thirty years and three after Emancipation!). As Jackie Sullivan continued to steer the car snail-pace, silently showing Dorothy the New Granston, she thought of her hallowed, colored-only Phillis Wheatley Branch Library. She and Thomasena* had owned it. Authors had talked to them there, tuning their ears and minds forever. As segregation vanished, so did their colored-only library, Blues Street, Mrs. Ware's Grand Blue Diner, the colored pool room and adjacent barber shop, the two colored-only movie theaters, hot dog and soda stands, the colored paper and magazine rack, shoeshine stands, and colored men standing on corners, harmless, flirting respectfully.

While waiting for a business or a white family to offer them employment, even if just for a day or a few hours, the men joked about working for Standaleania Company: stand on the corner and lean against the building. The wooden two-story structure, the Williams Building erected by T.J. Williams, Granston's first colored doctor, that had housed Dorothy's father's law office and all colored doctors' offices, had perished with integration. Dorothy felt a tug at her heart thinking that the hallowed building should have been spared as an historical edifice. Even Colored people were Black now or African American. What was left of their refuge were barren parking lots erasing beloved corporeal Granston, their region of assurance. There were God, the devil, heaven, and hell, and at one time Santa Claus. All that was colored and had belonged to them was no more, like Granston's lightening bugs, June bugs, and butterflies that progress had devoured.

Dorothy inhaled and closed her eyes so she could see this gone-forever portion of her life and hometown, incorporeal and corporeal. It had been their Harlem, New York, during the 40's, 50's and before for some, and during the Civil-Rights 60's. Like Harlem's 135th Street and Lenox, Granstonians said if you stood on uptown Blues Street long enough, you would see anybody colored in Granston you wanted or did not want to see. Mainstream residents had consigned colored people to this habitat, and they had grown into it, and it into them, becoming their topography. It had become their locus, their trysting place, the depot where they met friends, proscribed and accepted. During World War II, girls went there, heads held high, shoulders erect, appearing to look straight ahead, with half-hidden shy smiles, to show they were married and pregnant and waiting for their husbands to return from overseas. And after the birth of their babies, these war brides brought them to this sanctuary to show them off. When the war ended, boys, men now, gathered there to prove they were still alive, to exchange war stories, eyes growing misty, throats constricted, remembering comrades who did not return, and wondering about girls they left in Europe and the South Pacific with and without brown babies.

Dorothy recalled talking to ex-service men and to her first husband Luther, and knew agonizing speculation invaded their mixed-up minds. These boys-now-men wondered if they were smart enough to take advantage of the GI Bill and go to college or learn a trade, puzzled over where they would work, and what they would do with their lives. They wondered if the GI Bill of Rights really would provide college tuition and home loans for colored men.

Combating tears, Dorothy closed her eyes. Her brother George, Jr. did not get a chance to join the Post War group. He had enlisted while a student in Howard University Law School, a volunteer for the paratrooper division. He was reported Missing in Action in 1944 and remained forever missing. Dorothy and her mother had been so grief-stricken that long after the War ended, they looked for him to return. It was just too awful to be true. Mr. Borden had believed it from the beginning and was raging angry—his only son killed in a "goddamned war he had absolute nothing to do with, and would never profit from, dead or alive, and neither would any of his descendants." Dorothy's mother telling her husband to pray, that he himself had risked his life in World War I, and that George, Jr. had volunteered, enraged her husband more. Dorothy thought of her only brother more in Granston, remembering that he left just when their poking fun days at each other had passed, and they had just begun to know and realize they loved each other.

Dorothy harnessed her thoughts, aiming them at research for her novel about Joe Cephus and Johnnye, and wondered how much the GI Bill had reduced the number of women like Johnnye Jamison who snared men like John Henry Woodard and Joe Cephus Divine. Researching widowed teachers would hardly be an indication. Men usually died first.

Dorothy asked Jackie to stop the car when they passed Frederick Douglass High School, where they both had graduated sixty and sixty-one years ago and where Jackie Sullivan had taught her first class. There it was, the school from which the classes of 1940 and 41 had voted Dorothy Borden "The Most Creative" and Jackie Sullivan "The Girl Most Likely to Succeed." Both Dorothy and Thomasena* had wanted so badly to have the title "Most Likely to Succeed" bestowed upon them. Jackie had won over Thomasena, who was voted The Most Talented. Dorothy wondered what the girl was doing now who got the title she herself had wanted so much. – And Dorothy still dreaming of fame and recognition as a writer. This–the "nowness"–was the most unbelievable of all that is unbelievable.

Life for Dorothy was almost over chronologically. She closed her eyes remembering herself: The little girl, a buoyant teenager, that young woman, maturing woman, matron, was now really old. She thought of Hawthorne's "The Ambitious Guest," a story in *The American Mind*, their high school literature series. It was one of her favorite stories. The dreamer in it had been a young man who yearned to leave his mark in life, but destined not to. Dorothy hoped her fate would be different. She also recalled Tennyson's *Enoch Arden*. Enoch went to sea promising to return. Like Annie Lee, Dorothy never saw her Enoch again. He had remained in life's sea. Unlike Annie Lee, she Dorothy Borden had no Phillip Ray. Then she was far from being an Annie Lee.

Thinking of one of her favorite high school literary selections, Dorothy began to smile, then laugh. Far too late, Dorothy knew the role in which she would have given her best performance, what she had been "cut out to be," as older people say.

"What's funny?" Jackie asked.

"I was just thinking—what a charming, delightful, and satisfactory mistress I would have made."

Jackie blushed. Dorothy returned to her thoughts.

Dorothy still thought there was no high school class like the one that graduated from "Doug-Hi" in 1940. Many of them had gone to college. Nine-nine per cent entered the classroom, teaching, the sweet profession for African Americans then, the only one really open. Most became elementary school teachers. Dorothy did not feel capable of functioning on that level. To her it was far too difficult, and she would not be comfortable with children so young and vulnerable—making them into what they would be for life. It was like God in a way—or an After God. The irony of it, Dorothy Borden did not want to be a teacher. Even in college, she vividly saw herself on the stage, an actress, in plays she wrote herself. She would become a novelist also. During World War II, the demand for teachers was so great that principals and superintendents actually went hunting for them in North Carolina. Dorothy permitted herself to be recruited and liked it all right, saying it would be just for a while. That for a while became part of her always. A Dean in a private secondary school, where she survived for a year, advised her to prepare for higher education. She was more geared to that level. And she was. As a college instructor, Dorothy was most contented, so contented that it began to reply to her needs. However, she never forgot her beginnings as a secondary school teacher. She was more than what principals described as normally dedicated and active in the classroom and extra curricular life, including withdrawn and ignored very black-skinned students, especially girls, in plays, dance recitals, guiding them to write skits from stories, presenting them in assemblies—and winning awards in North Carolina and Virginia high school drama tournaments for colored. On both conscious and subconscious levels, Dorothy Borden combated the trend and tendency to target lighter skinned and more attractive students as teachers were accused of doing when she as a student.

She certainly did not ignore "light skin students with good hair." Everybody had a fair chance.

"Douglass is a middle school now." Jackie woke Dorothy from her reverie. "Something you and I missed. It's supposed to be integrated, but there's always a way of keeping whites from coming into black neighborhoods."

Dorothy smiled, but not about Jackie's statements. Dorothy was thinking of their teenage years at Douglass. "Jackie, do you remember our club The Peppy Debs and how silly we used to be?"

"Oh, yes–"

"Remember the crazy things we used to do –like taking our mother's largest pocket books to school? Wearing silk hose–" Dorothy laughed.

"And lipstick–and using lots of perfume–We scented up halls and classrooms." Jackie recalled.

"Those were wild, mad things in those days. –But the wildest thing of all was Kate Crawford's suggesting we do something really awful–like go to school without our bloomers," Dorothy reminded.

Both women laughed so hard that for a moment they were teenagers again.

"I remember," Dorothy said laughing still, "the day we were supposed to do it, I came to breakfast without mine. Daddy, Mama, and Junior were sitting at the table waiting for me so Daddy could say the Blessing, and they could start eating. All three looked at me so funny. I told them my hands needed washing again, and hurried to my room and put on my bloomers, planning to take them off at school. Even got a paper bag to put them in. When I cam back, Daddy looked relieved as if he knew I had put on my drawers." Both women had not laughed so in years. "What about you, Jackie. What did you do?"

"I wore mine. I didn't have as much nerve as you all had."

"We called them bloomers then. And brassieres. I didn't say

panties and bra until I went to college. Started saying Grace then instead of Blessing. Daddy, Mama, and Junior never changed."

"Kate was a character. She's dead." Jackie told her softly.

"I heard. She died young. It was hard for me to believe a person like Kate would–die." Dorothy remembered Kate was the Daredevil Deb. She not only would go to school without bloomers, but she would sass teachers, take fruit and flowers from people's trees and yards while they were looking, even white people. And call white people "white crackers" to their faces, grown white people.

CHAPTER 6
Dorothy Examines Relationships

Dorothy let the innocent part of her past flow over her like a miniature waterfall. It was good to talk to Jackie, not having to use academic exactness. They could talk about trivia. Teachers who were friends could do that. They could make minor errors in grammar for effect without explaining. Even major ones. Dorothy remembered the task of conversing with Joe Cephus, and examples of Alexander Pope's "a little learning is a dangerous thing." Some people, especially men like Joe Cephus, expected perfection they would not recognize if it occurred, and expected teachers to have all the answers.

"You ah teach-ur an' don' know THAT?" "That" could refer to anything: "What time of day or night did Adam and Eve leave the Garden?" Attempting to be facetious, Joe Cephus had asked Dorothy. Her answer had been: "Dey lef 'bout seb-um 'clock one Sad-dey night 'cause dey had to go home and take dey bafs to be ready for Sunday service next mo'ning. Didn't wanna be late. Adam wuz a deacon and Eve wuz ah ush-ur."

Dorothy lamented that most of these critics were her Black men to whom she had stretched her arms, and who unfolded theirs, but failed to reach each other. Dorothy sighed. Another fragment of her life had been triggered. She had had no extended positive intimate relationship with African American men, and she had known them forever, even before they were colored, negroes, Negroes, Black, Afro-Americans, African-Americans, or African Americans. Many of them had been her closest friends and confidants whom she retained all their lives, and even after for they remained a portion of her self. There had been no lasting intimate relationship with White men either, but that was different. They had not been a part of her always, forever, and before. –But there had been the gratifying relationship with Mr. Asian that lasted about twenty-five years. How she wished he could have lived longer and longer, but without becoming ill, and they could have been as they were during the blooming years of their adventure. Dorothy knew that the bond had remained intact because they did not marry or live together.—Had she been a mistress or a shadow or silhouette of one?

One thing just triggered another, Dorothy thought. She and Jackie didn't talk about any one thing long. That was O.K. Kept them from getting bored and allowed for diverse information. There was so much she wanted and needed to talk with Jackie about in such a short time. Dorothy wanted to discuss marriage and relationships with someone who had real life-experience answers. In the past, she had learned almost nothing. Women only gave noncommittal stock answers: "Marriage is give and take." Give and take what? "Yes, I'm glad I married. What else would I being doing?" You're glad you married because you don't know what else you would be doing! Do you have any dreams— or *self*? "Marriage has its ups and downs." –*up* where and *down* where? You can have that without being a housekeeper, a cook, and washing his back and drawers. –"You just have to put your foot down." Down where, Dorothy wanted to know? Men usually gave the same answer about marriage: "It's up to the woman. She's the one who's got to make a marriage work–and make a man happy." What about the woman, Dorothy asked, isn't she supposed to be happy, too? Men usually looked a bit surprised that she didn't know a woman is happy when she makes her husband happy. –Perhaps that was the answer: Dorothy didn't think of making marriage work, *forcing* it to be what it was not. Something as ludicrous as her being happy because a man is happy struck her as pure insanity. And she didn't consider herself selfish: Look how dedicated she was to students! Look how she spent time with and money on godchildren–and animals! –The thought came to her again with all probity: *She should have been a concubine or mistress.* Dorothy glanced at the woman beside her: Not now, but Dorothy would get her talking about her own communion with Rev.

Since she was seriously writing, Dorothy searched for answers among her friends –and even acquaintances and strangers she met on airplanes and trains and while waiting for buses. Almost all of her female Black friends were contentedly married, and were in academe, and most of the women had not united with men in that arena. The women had married high school graduates, almost high school graduates, men who had "taken courses," and some who had not. There was her dear friend from Sunday School days Lora, living in Danielsville, Connecticut–Lora had introduced her to Jerome Speight! Dorothy thought of him at intervals. He once told her that a person's most treasured memories were not always the most pleasant ones as Dorothy discovered through him.

She led her straying thoughts away from Jerome Speight–and wondered if she would be happier if she were more like Lora: serene, no regrets, fulfilled, contentedly married to her second husband after the death of the first. Mr. Second One contentedly married to her, possessed with just enough ego to have a flair for perpetual courtship: flowers, perfume, never forgetting her birthday, Mother's Day, and oh, Christmas, still the really big holiday for Blacks. (Dorothy had read and also was told that its being the most celebrated holiday had nothing to do with religion, but that it's a relic from slavery when slaves were permitted an entire a day off from toiling and were even given an orange or apple.) Never letting Lora forget she was special–and so was he, divorced, Bill Prince, Mr. Second One, was not a college graduate either, but had taken courses under the G.I. Bill of Rights after World War II, and now retired from a position with Social Security. Lora had not wanted to become a widow, as Dorothy had told her she herself did. Lora with Husband Number One, willingly had four children–three boys and then tried-just-one-more time for a girl–and hit the jack-pot. She and Ronald, Number One, had raised them successfully in Danielsville. All four had college degrees: Ronald, Jr., Dean in a New York City community college; Keith, consultant in a New Haven law firm; Chad, a high school football coach and physical education teacher in Norwalk. Lora preferred to call her youngest son a lady's man instead of a womanizer. The daughter Veronica–Ronnie–married an Air Force captain, and spends most of her domestic life where the Air Force sends them. She teaches French in schools wherever her Captain is stationed. Two boys married well; one divorced. Now Lora has five grandchildren who flatter her by calling her Granny because she's so unlike the legendary granny.

After finishing A & T College in Greensboro, North Carolina, Lora left Granston for Danielsville, Connecticut, New York being too much of a city she told Dorothy. Lora began as a high school social science teacher; later, she became a counselor, then Director of the Guidance Department. Two M.A. degrees, one in Administration, propelled her into a principal's seat that led to her appointment as Assistant Superintendent. Lora retired as District Superintendent in Danielsville with a handsome pension. Her first husband held two jobs all during their married life: on the assembly line in a manufacturing company and night watchman. They had a palatial home purchased from a wealthy white owner and all that went with it– swimming pool, cabana, landscaped property with huge rocks, lights, trees, shrubbery, fauna and flora. Without lights, Dorothy thought of it as a miniature rain forest. The couple added two of the latest model cars to grace their elaborate garage.

Lora and Ronald were work-addicted, with hallowed work

ethics; they imbued their sons and daughter with the same values, and still managed to smile a lot and entertain lavishly. They were surrounded by couples who smiled a lot also, not as affluent in appearance as Lora and Ronald Height, but who appeared to be just as contented. In this set, although men earned what Black economy considered decent incomes, Connecticut being generous with its wages in comparison, their wives were usually the ones with college education and involved in formal education: nursery, day care, preschool, early childhood, elementary. High schools were practically off-limits for colored teachers at that time in many places in Connecticut. Differences in formal education in the couples didn't seem to matter. As far as Dorothy had observed, these women did not parade their roll books. Job discussions were in context just as discussions involving race relations, voting, morality, euthanasia, women's issues. Dorothy perceived there was mutual respect between these husbands and wives.

Dorothy always knew that Ronald, husband number one, was genuinely proud of Lora and her accomplishments. Dorothy called this spacious much-more-than-he could-afford abode his Taj Mahal to Lora. Dorothy never mentioned it, but the weight of it all might have contributed to Ronald's fatal heart attack. Lora's son Chad and his family lived in the showplace home now. All three boys wanted to keep it in the family as a memorial to their father who had worked so hard and wanted their mother to have it so badly. It had been beyond his means, the boys now knew, but not beyond his dreams. Lora and Number Two had purchased a smaller and less spectacular place on the outskirts of Danielsville. The house was stately with more rooms than they needed, even to accommodate two sets of grandchildren.

Dorothy glanced at Jacquelyn Sullivan LeGrande. She looked serene like Lora and her social set. Dorothy didn't question the depth of the serenity she herself did not have. —She had searched and searched and was still searching. All along she knew what she was looking for. At almost the end of her life, she still sought immortality in the world of prose.

Dorothy's friends and associates, male and female, who wanted only each other and home life seemed genuinely contented. Happy even. She detected no pretense, nor any irritating restlessness. However, Dorothy knew that domestic life such as theirs would create more turbulence in hers, and remembered telling her parents that "she'd end up a raving maniac if she stayed married to whom she had married, men who had done what she considered minimum with their lives, and who wanted to direct the course of hers." Was her domestic evaluation based on her measuring Black men by the dimensions of her father? Did her husbands perceive she deeply did not care if the relationship went awry and were desperately, ineptly attempting to make her care?

Dorothy had not escaped heartbreak however, the greatest one being the barb placed in her heart by a man who had reeked destruction upon her heart equal to a nuclear bomb. Something she could not write about, this man she thought so godly. She never had sex with him. She was very young then, in the throes of virginity and youth, her last year in college. The act itself was unnecessary to know that everything with him would be perfection–And Dorothy knew now she was at that time going through her first adult and perhaps only Lapsarian interval.— Dorothy could hardly believe that the man she loved more than any other, the greatest love of her life, she did not know sexually. Were there other women who had the same experience? She could not tell the story. It did not sound right in words, nor look on paper the way it happened. Her Enoch Arden disappeared into a matrimonial sea. Now in her seventies, Dorothy knew the liaison would not have been positive maritally either. Nor marriage to a man the replica of her father. The bond itself was as powerful a deterrent to her search for Shangri-La as the man.

Dorothy found safety in that tiny fold of the white world she was allowed to enter. Expectations from each other, white male and black female, had been just what each was willing to give without stress. There were no high stakes, consequently no heartbreaks. Dorothy frowned. A pleasant frown followed by a smile. No heartbreaks. No one asking her to marry in order to gain a servant-wife with whom he could also have a mistress he could sponsor with his extra money. No one wanting a wife to become pregnant to prove his manhood and have an unwanted child that would forever be a wife's sole responsibility, an anchor preventing her from pursuing Elysian pastures. No one settling for marital control in a world that controlled him. In the diminutive fragment of the white world Dorothy was permitted to enter, there were no trespasses against her. No threat of a nightmare invading her dream. Even with Magdar whom she had wed, divorced, and remembered with smiles. It was just a Good-Time time.

CHAPTER 7

Dorothy and Potential Scandal

Dorothy Borden's life had not been without intrigue. Even potential scandal. There had been a liaison that caused the greatest embarrassment of her life. The man, Jerome Speight, she met via Lora. The relationship had been short-lived, but long enough to fill memory-cups she could still sip from down through the years. Paraphrasing one of her favorite poets, Edna St. Vincent Millay, Dorothy's candle had "burned at both ends and made a glorious light." A telephone call. His voice seductive. "Dottie, meet me at the Hotel Sta-t-ler." And she would. Anticipation at his pronunciation of Sta-t-ler. Arriving via plane at his expense. Messages waiting. "Oh, yes, Mrs. Speight, we're expecting you. Mr. Speight called. You are to shop or visit friends." She would. The nearer they were to each other, the more she enjoyed doing what he asked. "Mr. Speight will meet you here for dinner promptly at 7:30 P.M." He would. "Dinner will be brought to your room promptly at 7:45 P.M." And it was—with roses and champagne. Dorothy inhaled the aroma of exotic food concealed under dazzling white linen spread over glistening china and silver.

Elusively perfumed, she would be dressed the way he liked— elegantly in delicate exquisite soft pink and white flowing raiment. His gifts. He had greeted her calmly. Ready to dine. She more ready for what was to come afterwards. Kissing not too much, as if he knew her readiness, and teased her. A glimpse of his sensuous black body as he changed to his dressing jacket. She lowered her eyes. Eating casually, Jerome asking about her work, family, daughter, herself, as if there were nothing but time, and she had not come all the way to New York from North Carolina, and there was nothing else ahead. –And Dorothy conveying coy dispassion as if she did not have to meet that eight o'clock sophomore lit class Monday morning.

Finally, the lights appeared to lower themselves. They both knew there was lots ahead.

Had she remained married she would not have known this. Marriage had startled her, wakened her from charm, delight, and romance. Denied her charm, delight, and romance.

Jerome Speight came in a Rolls Royce equipped with a bar and telephone. Dignified, well-groomed, impressive. Visitors and hotel personnel stared. He was years her senior. Preferring older men, Dorothy never knew how much or cared. They found each other fascinating. She young and vivacious. He the essence of gentility. Ugly by her friends' standards, Jerome was tall, big, blacker than black. People conceded that he was not ugly because he was blacker than black. He was just unattractive. However, Dorothy liked what she saw. She liked the sound of his voice. She liked the way he touched her—and did not touch when she wanted him to–. She liked the way he made her feel about her self, the self that was *hers*: wanted, delightful, fragile, all his. She knew his divorce wasn't final, and didn't care. She certainly did not want to marry him or anyone. He and his wife had separated before Dorothy met him. Jerome's Don Juan escapades became so heartbreaking and embarrassing, his two older children had persuaded their mother to ask their father to leave and file for a divorce, at his expense. Jerome complied and moved out of their home, leaving everything except his personal items. He left his wife a car, and took care of expenses just as if they were together. However, he was cavalier about divorce proceedings. Lora said the delay was his protection. Jerome now lived in a spacious condominium in the outskirts of Stamford where he had freedom, not only from domestic life, but from alert community eyes. Dorothy knew the candle was burning at both ends and enjoyed its glorious light. She did not anticipate the inglorious night.

Jerome rarely mentioned his family, but Dorothy learned he left Mississippi and came to Connecticut years ago with his wife, two very young children, and one hundred dollars. With the same wife and four adult children, he was now founder and owner of Jerry's Real Estate Promotion and Sanitation Management, Inc. Upon arrival Jerome had observed Danielsville and surrounding small counties and had a vision that he believed would become reality. He began by purchasing and renovating a condemned house and dividing it into rooming house quarters. Performing much of the physical labor himself, he and his help often worked hours after their regular jobs and on weekends. Then another house and others. Unable to pay wages the men deserved, Jerome assured them decent living quarters at affordable rent rates, with living space for wives and children and their friends when each project was complete. Connecticut salaries were not bad for colored people in comparison, even domestic jobs for women, but unskilled colored workers, migrants from the South, had very few acceptable living accommodations. Nor did counties and cities pay much attention to their sanitation needs. With one overhauled truck and outdated equipment, Jerome began a sanitation business. He got contracts with selected cities and counties, rented, later purchased updated equipment from the selected cities and counties, and grew into Jerry's Sanitation Management.

Jerome became more than just Nigger rich. He was also a respected citizen in the middle-size town of Danielsville, Connecticut, a Great Church Worker and Philanthropist, fondly referred to as a Big Shot. Driving through scenic New England byways, Jerome told Dorothy that his wife had stuck by him when he was struggling in Mississippi, when he came to Danielsville struggling, and when he struggled to establish his businesses. He was generous with her now. She was a good person. Dorothy knew he had outgrown her. Besides, according to Lora, Mrs. Speight was not physically attractive, not even a little bit. All she had was her goodness, her "wholesomeness" that Jerome no longer needed. Dorothy remembered girls called "homespun," admired for it, but rarely selected, and if so, often later mistreated and rejected by "now successful" husbands.

Jerome said his children wouldn't go to college, and he suspected that they did it to annoy him. Their mother, soft spoken about everything, did little to persuade them. No matter how virtuous a person, there is frequently a hidden flaw that adulterates piety. Jerome felt her non-participation was revenge on him. He reminded his children of what he had done with no education, and what they could do with one. He wanted his older son and daughter to take over his business. The son would become owner, Manager. The daughter could be the accountant and bookkeeper—and Assistant Manager. They were too angry and rebelled. The older daughter, spoiled, defiant, and unfortunately for her, resembled him far too much physically, people commented. Education would have been an asset to her more than the boys. She went to college one year, but not to class and failed everything, even physical education. Along with the older son, furious with their father for the way he treated their mother, both older children tried to alienate the younger son and daughter. The son joined the army; the daughter went to New York and contacted her father for money only. "All I have is you, Dottie," Jerome had whispered.

Enraged after their mother had a heart attack, Jerome's older son and daughter hired a detective to trail their father. They found out what they needed. While Mrs. Speight lay in the hospital, her son and daughter threatened to demand a confrontation with that college professor and bring charges of alienation of affection. Jerome's telling them that his domestic woes began long before he met this present woman, and she had nothing whatsoever to do with his marriage, was ammunition for the son and daughter. This association was news. They would put in it the colored papers: *Afro-American, Journal and Guide, Pittsburgh Courier, Chicago Defender, Amsterdam News*: "WIFE OF CONNECTICUT BUSINESS MAN SUES COLLEGE PROFESSOR FOR ALIENATION OF AFFECTION. Daughter of prominent North Carolina lawyer." Jerome's son and daughter informed their father that a detective had taken photographs of him and the woman leaving a hotel and getting into his car that would be sent to the papers.

Not knowing if the detective was still trailing them, or if one ever did, but wanting to protect Dorothy, and himself, Jerome was cautious. After all, his children had information from some source. He confided in Lora and asked her to explain the situation to Dorothy and tell her that he would contact her soon as "it blew over." Dorothy and Jerome never saw each other again.

A few months later, Mrs. Speight had a fatal heart attack. Jerome married the next year. His marriage was immaterial to Dorothy, but she certainly did not want Mrs. Speight to die. Dorothy wondered if she had in any way contributed to Mrs. Speight's heart attack, and at intervals felt the weight of an albatross the rest of her life.

CHAPTER 8

Dorothy Vows to Banish Noisome Ghosts/ Jackie Discusses Her Marriage to Rev

Remembering her albatross, Dorothy chose *even this rather than Joe Cephus. Anything rather than Joe Cephus.* So great was Dorothy's fear of men like him, so terrified she was of being wanted by his likeness, knowing he wanted her as darning for his frayed garments, offering only the perverse side of being wanted as slave owners want their slaves! So warped was his need that he deluded himself into believing he offered gratifying plethora. Such added to the repugnance. To choose anything rather than Joe Cephus, Dorothy understood that her terror of matrimonial concupiscence and its serfdom raced past caution and became horror. She felt like a victim of rape and attempted murder, never feeling completely safe again, looking over her shoulders, peering behind bushes, fearing to walk down dark streets. Only this horror was worse, for looking over shoulders and behind bushes and fearing dark streets were in life's expressways. –And Dorothy Borden fought against revision and healing, fearing the lurking entrapment of havoc and diffusion in the disguise of forgiveness, or that which forgiveness can generate.

Dorothy longed to say all of this to someone–talk it over–and to find out if anyone else had similar thoughts. Jackie would listen, Dorothy knew, but would Jackie *hear*? Or was it the other way? Anyway, it took *both*.

"Jackie," Dorothy ventured, "do you –take inventory of your – self – your life –to see what's there – and what's missing? –Do you question *why* you did what you did or did not do, and *why* you feel the way you do about it?" Dorothy hoped she was saying what she wanted to say.

Jackie hesitated, "–Never thought about it much. Sometimes I think about things I did and did not do. Maybe I do take inventory–or evaluate–and just don't give it a name."

"Do you ever question how we were raised?" Dorothy asked.

"What do you mean?"

"I mean, I was raised to finish college, get a Master's degree, and marry. In that *order, Mama, Grandma, and my aunts told me* 'marry even if you don't stay. Every woman should marry.' And I did. Three times. I doubt if I'd honor their prescription today. Women are not under as much pressure. Marriage isn't for *every* woman. It's sad, pathetic–and unfair, especially to women, for people to be forced to *want* to do something they do not want to do. –Did your mother tell you the same thing about getting married?"

Jackie sighed. "She told me I should get a good husband. But it didn't bother me. Like Mama said, it was one way of not being alone. Both Mama and Daddy always told me what to do, and I did it. –What about your Daddy?"

"He didn't talk about getting a husband as much as he did about getting a Master's first. –He was the one who cautioned me about having children–not more than two. What did your parents say?"

"Mama said, don't marry a man who wants a house full of children," Jackie admitted.

Both women laughed.

"That reminds me of something else funny," Dorothy continued. "There is an air about me–or a personality trait that made both of my husbands think I loved them. Even though I had a disgusting feeling of possession, I could hardly stand them after a while. Whatever it is or was radiated to other men. Two others I considered platonic friends. The one that surprised me most was when I taught in a North Carolina high school and became friendly with one of the more sophisticated male members of the faculty who taught music. He was warm and courteous to me–a new faculty member. He even confided local scandal. It was one of those Big Shot High Schools where only the elite taught, whether they were good teachers or not. Most of the women really *dressed*. They were busy trying to out-dress each other and talking about their homes and having them remodeled or re-furnished, or refurbished–and, of course, they targeted young single women who were dating their husbands. –To my surprise, a female friend from another school in the next county said, 'Dottie, be careful. Henry [the music teacher] is very upset. He says you have a crush on him, and wants you to know he's happily married'."

"What did you say?" Jackie asked.

"I was shocked and disgusted and almost stopped speaking to Henry. He seemed relieved. He was not my type in the least–and had the worse halitosis."

As they cruised through Granston's streets, pleasant treasured apperceptions erased the Henry episode. There must be degrees of love, some sort of intensity, Dorothy analyzed, like shades, shadows, and silhouettes. The feeling she had for Mr. Asian must be a degree of love if love "guides the heart and mends the spirit." Dorothy liked fantasizing about things she could do for him and his pleasing responses if he were still on this plane of existence. She had a warm melting sensation that she felt physically and spiritually. Dorothy wanted to document her ability to love outside her family. There was a Dorothy Borden-self who felt huge drops of adoration for this glorious planet, its people, animals, vegetation, water, and sky with its beyond verbalization of sunrises and sunsets. There was enchantment when she walked on a college campus. She felt its presence in her classroom, while reading students' papers, during commencements, and in libraries. This Dorothy Borden-self—what was it? There were students who perceived it. Dorothy saw it in their eyes, heard it in their voices. Neither students nor teacher knew what it was, but knew it was present. And both were pleased.

Dorothy glanced at Jackie, seeming to be focused on driving, not trying to discover herself. "Jackie," Dorothy interrupted, "have you collected memories so delicious that you can taste them–and will in your next life?"

"Uu–mm–" Jackie was thinking of an answer.

"Your wedding, for example," Dottie prompted.

"My wedding picture hangs on the wall in the living room. I don't look at it often. When I do, I like to remember the songs they played and sang. 'I Love You Truly' 'Let Me Call You Sweetheart,' and 'Oh Promise Me'." At the reception one of Rev's friends sang 'When Your Hair Has Turned to Silver, I Will Love You Just the Same.' It was a popular song during the late thirties, I think."

"I remember that song. It was popular before we went to high school. Even Daddy liked it and got the sheet music hoping I'd learn to play it. I still remember the words: 'I will only call you sweetheart. That will always be your name–' And I believed all of those songs. And sometimes I still hear them. What about you?"

Jackie thought for a moment. "Maybe I do because I stand and think–and might be listening–."

Jackie drove slower as she approached a traffic light. Dorothy asked, "Did it happen? Does he love you just the same?"

Jackie unconsciously raised her left hand to touch her thin gray hair and replied reflectively, "People don't usually live for years without going through some change, but I can't think of any major change in the way we feel about each other."

"Does he still fit in your life's pattern–I mean, is he intrusive?"

Jackie shrugged. "Guess it's a matter of expectation–interpretation–or what you want. Dottie, I don't quite understand about fitting into my life's pattern. I know what you mean, but I don't know how it applies to me. You might think Rev is intrusive. I don't. I like his attention. He never gets in the way of what I want to do. He sort of helps me do it most of the time."

"What do you want to do?" Dorothy asked.

Jackie smiled. "Nothing that makes any difference to him."

You never wanted to do anything, Dorothy thought. Maybe that's why you were voted The Girl Most Likely to Succeed. Perhaps that was the secret of success–not wanting too much–getting whatever it is, accepting it, and being contented. Your classmates knew without knowing they knew.

Dorothy's classmates knew that she pursued dreams. She had caught up with some of them and had learned but not accepted that *realization* of a dream was quite different from the dream. The dream always eclipses reality.

Jackie was talking about her relationship as Dorothy had hoped. A brief break might be helpful. Dorothy suggested, "Let's stop at the next frozen custard drive-in." They did, parked and ate from cones as they would have as teen-agers. Only then they would not have been able to park and eat on the premises. Dorothy remembered seeing one or two small places that white people went to and that colored teenagers called "soft-ice cream places" and told each other they didn't want "none of that soft ice cream 'cause it melted too quick." They took their treasured and rare nickels and dimes to the colored drugstore and got little cups of mixed strawberry, vanilla, and chocolate hard ice cream or firm ice cream cones. They licked the cup covers and bit the bottom of the cones and sucked melted hard ice cream through the tiny opening. The colored drugstore was more fun because their boyfriends might be there, or girls who liked their boyfriends. And these teenagers would be able to see the other girls and find out it they had long hair, or good hair, or were light-skinned and nice looking, or just "wasted yellow," or black and ugly, or black and good-looking, and if they wore pretty clothes .

Dorothy returned to the present. "Was—is—your marriage—exciting?"

"I'm not sure I know what you mean—." Jackie wiped her mouth with a tiny napkin. "Dottie, nothing exciting ever happened to me, or if it did, I didn't know. But nothing ever happened that made me feel about marriage the way you say you feel."

"You have what is called a successful marriage. I wonder how many women feel the way I do and just don't talk about it—or even admit it to themselves. —A man gets services at home—housekeeper, cook, washer woman, and he takes on a girlfriend. He can afford one because his wife is contributing heavily to domestic upkeep, including vacations. And the *man* lives happily ever after."

Dorothy had almost finished her custard cone and wanted another one. Jackie still tasted hers slowly as if she were not certain that she should. Dottie watched her friend and continued, "Jackie, my marriages were domestic Bastilles."

Jackie didn't eat the custard cone as Dorothy had, but crushed it gently, wrapped it in another tiny napkin and placed it neatly in the garbage receptacle bought especially for her 2000 car.

"Jackie, do you remember what I said when women told me they were widows?"

"You said sympathetically, 'Some women have all the luck.'" Jackie had not forgotten.

"And the women laughed!"

Humor had been a great portion of Dorothy's and their survival. Dorothy smiled thinking how she fantasized becoming a widow. Perhaps it was a bit of shame or pity that prompted her to say, "Jackie, I'm going to be a far better person and do lots more in my next reincarnation after using this one for practice. I'll read and travel more. And write at least ten great books. I'll be a better person professionally, and enhance my inner self." Dorothy paused before beginning her monologue again. —" Jackie, I'll let that Phantom Man I thought I loved in college go much sooner. It took years to bid him farewell—to kick his arrogant BBB outta my life—."

"BBB?" Jackie interrupted.

"Big Black Butt– His friends said in college–and at the last Homecoming game– he didn't want to marry me because my hair was too short and nappy and I was too dark, and he had to consider how his daughter would look. It took so long for me to accept it. Guess what– he had one that looks just like him and that's what he didn't want. He doesn't even admit having a daughter if he can get around it. Just talks about the son his wife had before he married her. – Jackie, I wouldn't want a daughter that looked like him either. I like the way my reddish-black daughter looks with her wealth of good colored folks hair. She looks like an Ethiopian–Her father resembled one. Furthermore, this other man was an arrogant exploiter of women–financially. He would have been a liability. In spite of his intellect, he would have stifled my search for Shangri-La."

Jackie remained silent. Dorothy continued comfortably with her reflections.

This acceptance marked the launching of Dorothy Borden's letting go of meditative dilapidation she should have released years ago. She took a deep breath with relief, sensing the dawning of becoming unshackled. She closed her eyes and saw the birth of extricating herself from years of hating Joe Cephus and fantasizing negative acts she could and should have committed against him– and should and could commit now if he were alive. Perhaps later she would even have less delight in believing Johnnye Jamison made him pay a bigger price.

People should never permit others to take advantage of them. As with Joe Cephus and herself, it exacts mutual revulsion. Hating Joe Cephus was like hating the snake because it has fangs. Nature gave it rattlers also. Dorothy heard the rattlers before she even met Joe Cephus, but permitted herself to fall into his pit. Dorothy began to feel emancipation ease closer as she told herself she should not have permitted Joe Cephus to expose her worse self.

Instead of remaining with him approximately a year and three months that seemed like twenty-three years, detesting and insulting him, while he abused her, she should have left immediately. Failing to heed his rattlers before marriage is no excuse for remaining. She should have fled and kept her better self intact, instead of discovering the crypt that entombed decayed remnants of her lesser self.

CHAPTER 9

Joe Cephus Again

Jackie started the car. "Want to see our Mall?"

"Yeah. And make comparisons."

Jackie headed the car toward the Mall and asked suddenly, "Dottie, why did you marry Joe Cephus?"

"Jackie, I'm trying to analyze and understand what people want but do *not* want, and even dislike and do what they know they don't want to do. Right now all I can say is 'I know not why, where, or whence, but a change comes over me, and the task of common sense slips from me. I know not why, where, or whence that makes my world go hence.' I don't know the author or if I quoted correctly." Dorothy smiled. "Jackie, you never let the task of common sense slip from you. You don't know what a big fool you can be until you do."

Jackie looked straight ahead—unperturbed. –She had never been a fool.

Dottie continued seriously. "When I told the vet that my miniature poodle was trying to have sex with one of my cats, the vet said it was not sex, but power play. A show of who's in charge. Dominance. It reminded me so much of Joe Cephus. Jackie, there was no way even for a man like Joe Cephus to physically enjoy sex. He had an evil, wicked frown on his face. I wanted the lights out, shades drawn, and my eyes closed. Glad I had good times before and after him. He was enough to turn me against it. I wonder how he was with Johnnye Jamison."

The two women smiled and exchanged glances as if knowing something forbidden.

"How long did you stay with Joe Cephus? I've forgotten." Jackie asked as they reached the Mall.

"About fifteen months. Still feels like a portion of forever. The first summer I spent six weeks in New York attending summer school. Joe Cephus was scared to ask for a week or two off and go with me or come to visit. Time due him or it goes back to the City. I told him all the things we could do and see. Broadway plays, Statue of Liberty, Schomburg Library, U.N., Harlem and all. I was staying with close friends, Frankie's godparents in the Bronx. They called and welcomed him to join me. Joe Cephus said he 'didn't have no kin folks in New York and he had done enough traveling in the army.' His unit didn't even leave the States. The next summer I went to Europe to attend a special summer class. –He grumbled and humped like a fool after I returned from both trips. I can't believe we were married less than two years! Jackie, even if he had not been abusive and weren't so cheap, and stingy– and stupid– I don't want a man who says he can't go to a place because he 'didn't have no kinfolks there.' And one who looked sick when he's having sex. –A cross between looking like he was going to puke and straining to crap. How could he enjoy something or induce a woman to enjoy doing something that made him look so—sick—so—unhappy?"

They were walking around the Mall now. Jackie laughed quietly. "You shouldn't expect him to be like you. You don't mind going places–and by yourself. You won't even take planned tours. If I traveled, I'd want to go with a group and of course with Rev. As for the other thing–looking sick–maybe that's the way he lets you know–."

"–He likes it? His I-wanna-frig look?" Dorothy completed,

laughing also. "He didn't have that intensive-care expression in the beginning. Does Rev have a look like that?"

Jackie blushed. She had never discussed anything like this. Maybe it was time to do things she never did. Maybe she would visit Dorothy in Arizona. Jackie would talk it over with Rev. If they went to Las Vegas, he just might go to a Casino. Times have changed. She smiled, replying to Dorothy's last question, "Sometimes Rev looks at me kinda silly, and I tell him it's not a preacher-look. He says it is and can show it to me in the Bible. He never has."

They began inspecting the Mall and looked for anything interesting in the small Saks. Dorothy purchased souvenirs to take back to Arizona, really special ones for her daughter and son-in-law. The two women spent lots of time in the Health and Vitamin Center, where, Dorothy feeling guilty over treating herself with fast foods, got bags of health snacks, small drinks, and vitamins although she had a supply. The Book Store surprised Dorothy. It displayed many African American authors; however, Dorothy didn't see any books she wanted that she didn't already have and gave the store gold stars for having books by historian John Henrik Clarke and social historian V.P. Franklin. Jackie bought John Hope Franklin's *From Freedom to Slavery* that someone had borrowed from Rev and did not return. Dorothy selected texts by Clarke and V.P. Franklin and told Jackie to give them to Rev. Jackie asked if Dottie wanted to shop for something for herself–like clothes. Dorothy thanked her, but replied she wasn't in the mood for clothes shopping.

The two women had to search for their car. They both had not observed the parking lane and ID number. Dorothy was no help, saying "that looks like it" regardless of year, color, or model. Finally, Jackie by chance stumbled on her car. Feeling ridiculous and poking fun at themselves for being lost old ladies, they began to leave the Mall area. Dorothy held the books they purchased in her lap as if they were precious alive-things. They had life, she told herself, just were not alive on the same plane as people–fortunately. She looked at the titles again, opened one of the prized purchases, and looked at the Table of Contents.

"Jackie, did your mother or anybody in your family tell you stories they heard about slavery? Women usually told them."

"I don't remember hearing any. My family was in denial, like some light-skinned black people in our day. I am too. I never thought too much about slavery until the sixties."

"You'd remember if you heard those stories. You had Negro History in high school and college. Remember the text we used by Carter G. Woodson?"

"Dottie, I was not and am not affected as much by life as you are."

"I heard some horror stories. Trying to understand, I read any and everything people suggested. Had my students searching all over everywhere for copies of Michael Bradley's *The Iceman Inheritance.*"

"Never heard of it. What's it about?"

"It's an explanation of western man's racism, sexism, and aggression. You and Rev should read it. The last printing I know about was in 1980's, I think. Probably you'll have to get it from the library. White folks don't want to read it, and you know they don't want us to. Jackie, I read it–and was terrified.—That book exposes the root of slavery. I heard slave stories and was horrified. Hangings, beatings, torture, selling slave children, forced sex. My slave ancestors forced to murder—their own children, their masters, and kill themselves. But I'm not going to beat a dead horse as ex-slave owners would say. In spite of history and reading that book, I have dated interracially, made an interracial marriage and stayed with him longer than I did with Joe Cephus and preferred him to Joe Cephus. But not because he was white."

Dorothy felt perturbed, and sad, as she pictured and heard what the Black community may say about her confessions. Would they understand that Joe Cephus was a monstrosity in her land of rainbows, sun, and flowers?

"Maybe you have forgiven them—white people. Rev says he has." Jackie suggested.

"*No!* And never will. I don't even want to."

"Maybe you did it to get back at Joe Cephus."

"No! I had an interracial relationship before I met Joe Cephus. Resumed it after we divorced and I returned to New York. A male friend, Black, explained that women love conquerors. The female population even consort with occupiers during wars. And the white man is a conqueror. Even an adverse one. –Joe Cephus could have been a conqueror. 'The first colored hired' could have made him a dragon slayer. Jackie, why did I so willingly become a part of the white world that kicked my ancestors' asses–and still kicking mine–and Third World Countries–Grenada, Panama, Haiti? The White Majority in Charge fought a cold war with Russia forty years, and didn't give the non white countries forty weeks–or forty days– and will kick non white butts ad nauseam– No—quod umquam? How do you say forever in Latin?"

"I don't remember. –What explanation do you give yourself?"

"Adventure–curiosity–material for writing. Defiance. A social frontier. And, Jackie, I had a good time. The men treated me the way I wanted to be treated. –My life– my soul was not muzzled or shackled. *Freedom.* I don't know what love is or what a satisfactory relationship is built on, but it is not control–handcuffing a person's existence and by a man you got to help take care of and who can't even carry on a decent conversation–Mr. Asian wasn't white, but might as well have been since he wasn't a Brother. I learned about *caring* from Mr. Asian. I could unbridle my feelings and not be scared they would be misused. He never tried to hurt me, to make me jealous, or feel insecure. Maybe in all the years, we had two or three disagreements, nothing major. He would end it by saying 'no more talk' and the next day there would be a present, a gift, something special. We never 'rehashed.' I treated him the same way. Joe Cephus forced me to put *caring* in a straitjacket. There are people who do not know how to care or love, and if they do, they don't know how to let others know. Jackie, in that forbidden world, in those unforgivable relationships, I wasn't courted to become a sounding and pounding board and a future crutch or wheelchair.—Jackie, I began to learn that there were men who knew the difference between *her self* and *herself*—a hellava difference."

Back in what they once called Uptown Granston, both were silent until Dorothy continued. "What I told you complicates why I dated white men. I don't regret it–just want to know why. I'll include it in my story. Maybe during discussions on the Oprah Winfrey Show or Diane Rehm's Public Radio Program, or Tavis Smiley, somebody will have an explanation. Students in my African American Women Writers classes certainly would. I had many excellent students. –Jackie, do you think I'm looking for justification?"

"Maybe. Did Joe Cephus like white women, or try to date them when he was in the army?"

"No! Joe Cephus wanted somebody he could give the Three F's and ask to help support him. He was too scared of white people to treat a white woman the way he treated colored women. I never heard him or Luther talk about white women. People say most Black men want to date white women. Most I met did not."

Dorothy paused searching her memories and experiences. "Same thing with my Black girl friends. Only one I knew dated interracially. What do you think?"

"I don't know anyone personally, but heard there were some Black and White folks dating and marrying in Winston-Salem and other places in North Carolina–even South Carolina. I never did and still don't go around in interracial circles like you."

"Jackie, Black women are easy prey, even easier when young. They get little if any protection from the law. Black women are too loyal to talk negatively about their men. Except me. I really take Joe Cephus' name in vain. I went to different beauty parlors just to talk about him so it could get to his white colleagues. Now that is really disloyal and contemptible. That is why I did it. Joe Cephus brought out the worse in me. Joe Cephus and men like him make babies for women to support that they the fathers don't support and the men are pro-life. Colored women seldom went or go to court for child support and never for alimony. I didn't know any colored women who did. They were married to low-income men looking for support themselves. Middle-class women or up-to-date women *never* asked for or received anything. It was a disgrace to become involved in a court brawl and far from being worth it. The men had nothing and nothing to lose. The women had their profession and privileges that went with it and couldn't afford the publicity. Joe Cephus knew teachers really kept quiet. The worse thing colored people said about the male deserter and wife abuser was and is 'the mean old thing just walked off and left his wife and children . –But they got along all right. Her people help her.' Later the man surfaced married to somebody else's daughter. Just like Joe Cephus. Jackie, Daddy use to say 'that man, or boy, has nothing to lose and all to gain.' Honestly, it took years and years for me to realize that *I* was the man's gain."

So it wasn't revenge on Joe Cephus, Jackie thought. She was certain she could never "go with" a white man even though she had a white-looking family that only married light skinned colored people with hair like white folks. Unlike Dottie Borden, Jackie didn't try to understand why. She knew without saying or even thinking about it that she was satisfied with Rev, her children, herself, and all that was hers. There was no reason for her to even think about White people. Or even too much about Black people.

CHAPTER 10

He Was Not THE President—But—

During the silence, Dorothy eased into reminiscing about her Secret liaison.

"What are you smiling about?" Jackie asked.

"Thinking about something I haven't told anyone and wondering whether to include it in my story. It's soooo special." And Dorothy smiled again remembering the relationship that could become a mild, mild HarMonica episode if there were—well—a confidant she'd call Slipp in her life. She almost laughed aloud wondering how many readers would associate the words HarMonica and Slipp. He was not *the* president, but *A* president. Of what college? Or University ? What country? On what Continent? If she included it, Dorothy would be miserly with her pen. But she would tell that all he had to do was call and say two words, "I'm lonely," and she would board the Concorde, her heart beating rapidly anticipating seeing him waiting in the airport. Dorothy relaxed in the car seat for greater comfort savoring memories of his visits to New York City: horse carriage rides in Central Park, dinners at Tavern on the Green, Four Seasons, nights in Harlem's exotic spots, and stopping for the famous waffle breakfast at daybreak. She again was in quaint places on Manhattan's Middle East Side where there were soft lights and piano music that transported the two of them to their own Shangri-La. Then strolling arm-in-arm Downtown to Dance Land, jazz at The Village Blue Note, group singing at Your Father's Mustache in Greenwich Village. —And a colleague seeing them in The Village, stopping in shock and disbelief at her being arm-in- arm with a blond, handsome escort who resembled a Viking. This Relationship defies details. Memories so priceless are not to be shared. They were never-to-be-again-days in a forever-remembered time–.

CHAPTER 11

Dorothy Visits the House and Streets Where She Grew Up

"Wake up–see where we are," Jackie brought Dottie back to Now.

Dorothy heard it had happened. Now she saw it. Kyles Street Elementary School had been demolished, making way for integration. Her favorite elementary school teacher, Mrs. Cynthia Hobson, had taught her there. Dorothy felt the familiar peculiar twinge in and around her heart. *How could they? There was nothing wrong with that school. Mis' Hobson had taught her there–.*

"We're near where you used to live. Plum Street."

Dorothy braced herself for an avalanche of nostalgic twinges in and around her heart. – There it was. The same street, but different. The tennis court and baseball diamond were still there, along with phantom sounds of skate wheels on pavement as she whizzed past less adventurous girls, and ghostly sights of her brother George Jr., riding his bicycle at breakneck speed, racing with other fortunate colored boys. –The Borden home, the show place of the colored community at that time, demolished now. The spacious, once grassy, tree-lined yard sobbed from abandonment. Her doll house–even the spot where it had stood –seemed as if it had never been. Dorothy and George Jr.'s swings, seesaw, and sliding board—like their parents—*gone*. Colored people who would have lived in such a house were now Black or African American, and had built ranch style and split-level homes with basements called rumpus rooms equipped with bars dedicated to entertaining. Dottie remembered their basement, the envy of colored home owners then. It actually did not leak! And her mother had a washing machine in one compartment that was also the drying and ironing room. A large cemented portion proudly held George Jr.'s erector set and pool table. He was the only colored boy she knew who had an erector set. In one corner was a table tennis set. Dorothy heard the sound of cellophane balls hitting wooden paddles.

Dorothy had seen and visited people in homes that had replaced the Borden "old home place." Most of them were still void of libraries, the most important room, Dorothy thought. She knew the majority of houses her friends and adult children owned had built-in shelves in the family room and living room that displayed beautiful, expensive, delicate assortments of ornaments. If the occupants were doctors, lawyers, or up-to-date educated ministers, they had a small or medium size study with shelves for professional material. Teachers often exhibited copies of books recommended by the Board of Education, along with Alice Walker's *The Color Purple* and Alex Hayley's *Roots*. More recent additions were Terry McMillan's *Waiting to Exhale* and *How Stella Got Her Groove Back*. There were copies of Toni Morrison's *Beloved*, unread or read in selected segments, in addition to her *The Bluest Eye*. Children's books were in their rooms on transported shelves: school books, dictionaries, pulp fiction if teenagers, and the book "my godmother gave me for Christmas or on my birthday, or I got at school and forgot to take back."

Dorothy asked Jackie to open the window. Cars now had hidden controls, unlike windows in her father's cars that occupants simply rolled down using a door handle. Dorothy also suggested that Jackie turn the air conditioning off. Dorothy wanted to get as near as possible to Plum Street. She wanted open windows. Closed panes were barriers. She saw that Mr. Nathaniel Cohen Jones' grocery store had been replaced with a noisy happy-looking shop that sold records, cassettes, and video games. Sounds of a popular record Dorothy did not recognize came through the open windows. The sounds became fainter as the car slowly passed where Mrs. Gussie Mae Brown's house had stood. She used to have a kindergarten and also provided day care. There were no city or state regulations then. –Mrs. Hobson's house was still standing, remodeled and occupied by strange people. Thoughts of her treasured teacher reminded Dorothy that she had both learned much and failed to learn. Mrs. Hobson had diligently tried to teach her to spell. Dorothy never learned the way she should have. The knowledge of it made her insecure, forcing her to check even ordinary words. Dorothy saw herself, in the fourth grade, an extremely plain-looking child so unlike her light-skinned curly haired brother, her attractive mother and handsome father with a military bearing from army days that had a lifelong grip on him.

Dorothy had decided not to take the spelling lesson one day. It was no use. She would write a poem instead. Mrs. Hobson noticed that Dorothy did not write a word, look up and wait for the next one. She wrote continuously. Mrs. Hobson detained her after school for an explanation.

"Miz Hobson, spelling is ruining my tablets. I make 90's and 100's in everything else and 60's and 70's in spelling. Sometimes even 50's. I threw my spelling tablet away."

Mrs. Hobson had explained that was not the solution. She must study–every night—

"Yes'um. Daddy helps me every night, and I spell the words. Next day I can't."

"You must get another spelling tablet and start over." She looked at the red tablets Dorothy clutched to her breast. "Use one of those."

"I can't," Dorothy had explained. "This one's for hiss'try, this for 'rithmetic, this jar-graphy, and this for English."

"What about the other one?"

"It's for me."

"What is it for?"

"To write my poems and stories in."

"May I see it?" Mrs. Hobson had asked.

"No'am. I don't let nobody see it but Daddy."

"What do you write about?"

"My Daddy. My dolls. People I'm mad at. And pretty things."

"I like poems and stories, Dorothy, especially when little girls write them. Please let me see it."

"You do?" Dorothy had smiled and handed her the red narrow tablet.

Mrs. Hobson began to read:

MY DADDY
My Daddy is the best and smartest man in the world
I'm glad I'm his little girl

MISS RIVERS
Miss Rivers is mean.
Her teeth not clean.
She beats children too.
I don't like her, do you?

MISS HOBSON
Miss Hobson said a big ice sheet covered the land.
Must have been slippery, and people could not stand.

There were several others. Mrs. Hobson had asked, "Did you write them all by yourself?"

"Except for some of the commas Daddy told me to put in."

Dorothy remembered her mother had called her father to

tell him that Dorothy had not gotten home from school. He had bolted from his office, disobeying speed limits, and rushed into the principal's office, who escorted him to Mrs. Hobson's room. She apologized for delaying Dorothy and explained there was no really serious problem. However, Dorothy must concentrate more on spelling, especially since she liked to write. Her poems were interesting–and good.

After calming down, Mr. Borden had given Cynthia Hobson the smile that fascinated court rooms, and that evidently won him his reputation with the ladies. Dorothy observed her father's every move, and recalled his smile faded, his handsome face became grave. "Isn't it ironical that the very thing we need and want most is often that which we have least dexterity in mastering?" During later years, Dorothy knew that her father's words were for himself also. He had wrestled with the political, social, and psychological content of the day that denied him the opportunity to display his legal skill. He had tried to slay that dragon. How he wanted to be a dragon-slayer. And deserved to be. If only he could have lived to reap the benefits of the Civil Rights Movement. And George, Jr., had he survived World War II, might have been known like Thurgood Marshall, Johnnie Cochran, or Civil rights advocates William Kunstler and Conrad Lynn.

Dorothy remembered the conversation and the word dexterity, and they remained with her. They spoke of a little colored girl learning to spell, and of a colored father, an eloquent lawyer with one of the sharpest minds for litigation in the profession. As Dorothy matured, her parents confided that her father was and had been a "secret partner" with the respected Jewish lawyer Josiah Golden, who came to him for advice and consultation. Golden would tell him, "George, talking with you is like taking a five point graduate course in law. What a team we'd make in a court room on those tough cases." Golden never paid her husband what he was worth, Emma Borden criticized until she died. Dorothy also learned that her father called Mr. Golden Joe in privacy–at his insistence. How it must have pained the venerable George

Washington Borden to be George and even Georgie-Boy to white men, not in privacy, but *all* the time, even in court rooms, in the presence of clients, standing before judges. Down through the years, the insult to her father magnified. A man giving another man, his peer, superior to him in jurisprudence, permission to address him by his given name. It was worse than having to address the man as Mr. Golden at *all* times. It was a version of the master giving his slave permission to buy himself. Or at least a down payment on the purchase of *his self.* Dorothy began to know without knowing that throughout her lifetime, she would purchase bits of herself from former slave owners.

Mrs. Hobson's throaty voice echoed from the past. "You have an unusual little girl."

Her father's response, "I know. We parents think of children as the sovereign synthesis of ourselves."

Dorothy felt a break in her heart. She the sovereign synthesis of her father? There was so much she had put off until later. Now it was later. Too much later. She was trying to cram unrealized lifetime dreams into the too much later. Dreams she had for a lifetime and had not acted on. Dorothy remembered the time friends had taken her to visit a family she did not know and never forgetting how one female family member had stood looking out of a window most of the time. She confidently informed the group that years ago when she was young, a gypsy told her she would be famous some day. Years later, a matured woman, she was still looking out of the window.

"I still think my daddy was the smartest man in the world and far more handsome than Billy Dee Williams or Denzel Washington." Dorothy knew she sounded childish and didn't care. She would like to begin all over –or would she? *Do this all over again?*

"Jackie, if you could live your life again would you?—Before you answer, listen to the conditions: *You would not be able to change one thing. Everything, every minute detail, all errors, regrets, mistakes, and all successes and good times the first time around would happen again. Every damn thing. Would you give life another try?*

Jackie thought a moment, breathed deeply, "Yes..."

"You would not be able to change anything at all..."

"I'd still do it again. What about you?" Jackie asked.

"No. Not unless I could do and undo," Dorothy said softly and wondered about Thomasena, Lora, Johnnye–

Jackie frowned—Dorothy Borden who had written books, traveled, had exciting adventures—wouldn't want to do it again. – Maybe she, Jackie, should ask why—

The two women were silent until Jackie informed, "Better get some gas at the next filling station. I don't like self-service. Sometimes the pumps don't work and spill gas. It gets on my hands and clothes. Rev keeps the cars gassed. He takes care of everything about the cars. Insurance. Tune ups."

"Men like cars," Dorothy repeated what she had heard.

"He likes them for convenience. He takes care of everything else, too. All the bills. He shops for food. He does about everything. I'd be lost without him–."

Dorothy was silent, remembering her father was the same way. Doing every- thing. And they had been lost without him. Dorothy wondered if Jackie loved or depended on her husband more, and if he should die, would she mourn because of love or missing him. Dorothy thought of what her Frenchman—a relationship never shared with Jackie—told her once, "Don't analyze. Just enjoy." She did. A provocative and intriguing adventure it had been–.

Dorothy got out of the car to help Jackie. Dorothy could at least get gas on her hands. As she inhaled the not unpleasant odor, Jackie reminded her friend that she had not seen the new YW and YMCA. The YW and YM were adjoined when the women were YWCA members. After refusing to let her guest pay for gas, the two women headed for the new quarters.

As the new structure came into sight, Dorothy thought of how she and Thomasena use to go on "secret hunts" because she Dorothy believed Granston had lots of secrets. And it did. One of them was why Arthur Joeson* did not date colored girls, no matter how pretty, even if they were college girls or teachers. The two teenagers had gone to the Y to look at Arthur Joeson who was the basketball coach. He was so good looking. Dorothy and Thomasena had found out from Kate Crawford, the Dare-Devil Deb, who overheard while serving at a card party at a rich white lady's house *that Arthur was "going with" the wife of one of the white doctors.*** Dorothy wondered what happened to them. As small as it is, Granston has its secrets and she was still searching for the one surrounding Joe Cephus' death. She wouldn't mention Arthur Joeson's secret to Jackie. She would concentrate on Joe Cephus.

Now there was a parking area in the back. Dorothy was not impressed with the new building. Jackie told her that since integration, this branch did not have as many activities, nor as many members. Black people could go to the main branch now in downtown Granston.

Dorothy reminded Jackie what a good time they had in the old rustic building, especially the summer Dottie and Thomasena taught creative dance classes and presented a recital that people talked about for ages.** And did Jackie remember what a good time they had, even though dancing with boys wasn't allowed? They square danced, marched, had banquets on holidays, attended arts and crafts classes, and dressed in white dresses to have a candlelight ceremony that made them Girl Reserves.

"Jackie, I still remember some of the Pledge—'As a Girl Reserve, I will strive to be Gracious in manner, Impartial in judgment, Ready for service, Loyal to friends— it spelled out Girl Reserve."

"They are called Y Teens now. My daughter was one. Now she is a volunteer–teaching adult classes at night in Greensboro."

"And is Thad, Jr. still in Washington?" Dorothy asked.

"Yes. Still teaching in the medical college at Howard and also goes to the Y gym for some sort of special exercise. Our children did well. And your one and only is quite a political figure."

"Yes. And like your three, she made a stable marriage," Dorothy added, "but never got involved with the Y as I did."

*Character in *This Day's Madness*
** Episode in *This Day's Madness*

CHAPTER 12

The Two Ladies Exchange Experiences Teaching in an All-White Environment

"While we're not too far from the area, let me take you to the scene of the crime," Jackie joked, "the integrated high school I tolerated and that tolerated me."

Granston did look different Dorothy mentioned as they approached the campus of the once-all-white high school. Jackie entered the campus, drove around, pointed out where her classroom had been, and asked Dottie if she wanted to go inside. Custodians and maintenance people would be there, and maybe somebody in the principal's office. Dorothy said she could make comparisons with their old colored Frederick Douglass High. The two women inspected the building floor by floor, room by room, including lavatories and teachers' lounges. Just as Mr. Borden had said when the two women were teenagers, the white high school was a college compared with colored Frederick Douglass High. In spite of renovations, the basic superiority was evident. Dorothy became more introspective. Her mind leaped to the North East where she had spent the bulk of her college teaching days.

"Jackie, you said you tolerated and were tolerated in Granston during integration. Same thing happened in that haven New

York City. Some minorities just remain in a state of denial for the duration and don't talk about it. Some lived charmed lives, depending on how they are used. Then there are those who try 'to make things right' and really get in trouble. *All* are under the auspices of the WMIC."

"What's the WMIC?" Jackie asked.

"White Majority in Charge."

Dorothy continued as they left the building and returned to the car. "Jackie, unless the African American was stupid enough to be used, the WMIC had a 'Jesse can't swim' mentality toward them."

"What's that?"

"During a political debate, Jesse Jackson told a joke in an attempt to extinguish a fire between two politicians. He said some people had seen a boat capsize that he was in, and a man yelled, 'Look! Jesse Jackson is walking on the water!' Another man shrugged his shoulders and said, 'Yeah. Jesse can't swim.' This attitude was evident when a comment about an African American with a doctorate would be 'It's only an Ed. D.' More White professors had Ed. D's than Black ones . –And during full faculty meetings, no matter how important a Black person's remarks or how articulate the person, usually a Black male, you would hear a WMIC whisper, and not too low, 'He didn't make *many* grammatical errors, or *any* errors, or he *did*.' In these same meetings, WMIC's with titles of Associate and Full Professor regardless of degrees or publications would complain about their heavy teaching load of two or three point courses taught two or three days a week, class size no more than fifteen students, the women dressed like princesses or affluent hippies saying they 'felt like se-s-lay-ves'. It was an insult. Our ancestors were *their* slaves, and we know the slave-feeling through them. These WMIC's had an aura of intelligence gained by making comments from off-the-shelf books, and sounding as if their tongues and teeth were in somebody else's mouth."

"At least you had an integrated administration," Jackie offered.

"Down here all administrators were white. Most black principals were out. Their schools were closed. Those that survived did so in schools that were almost all Black."

"Jackie, where I worked, I faired better under white administrators. The Black Dean of Faculty was a real SOB who had it in for Black women. He had nothing to do with running the college and was scared of the consequences of being involved with white women in any way, no matter what they did or did not do, so he 'pulled his rank' on Black women. Joe Cephus-like, he defined his manhood by hounding and indicting Black women. He 'couldn't jump on women with anything' else according to reports, if you get what I mean. He attended functions in Harlem flanked by three or four Black women. People kidded the women about his having a multiple liaison. They laughed and said the dear Dean couldn't have a single liaison. He takes an entourage for protection. He tried to compensate for his–other inadequacies by showing his power over Black women professionally. One African American woman suggested we set him up with a white woman. I told her that would never happen. The dear Dean would not fall for that knowing she would find out he couldn't maintain the myth of the Black man's sexual prowess. Jackie, a Black man like him is lethal to Black women."

"I remember you said there were Black college presidents in New York in some community colleges, and your Branch had one for a while."

"Oh, yes! WMIC's didn't like him at all. In meetings, they asked silly questions, convoluted questions, and offered ridiculous proposals. They ignored even common courtesy. Dr. Black President was articulate, intelligent–too much for them. He knew verb and subject agreement, even with modifiers between the subject and verb. He pronounced final consonants. He even used possessives before gerunds and never split infinitives. He knew and used the subjunctive mood. How dare he! Off with his head! And off it went. WMIC's didn't want to manufacture anymore like him. They couldn't take *that* in a Black man!"

"How did the Black faculty take it?"

"Well, he was so dedicated to being fair and impartial that he catered to the white faculty. Blacks who wore WMIC bridles smirked with pomp and circumstance. Some of us talked with him and to college union representatives who were WMIC's."

Jackie responded, "There were no Black people in charge of anything where I was. Later on some Blacks were –well–promoted. I didn't hear about their problems. Dottie, there were things I did not want to know. I was there for the duration, did my job and honored my contract. That was it."

"Then you don't know, then, what they really thought about you–."

"Oh, yes I did. Nobody talked about it where I could hear with my ears, and I just didn't let it interfere with my –survival." Jackie said quietly.

"Well, where I was some WMIC's let it be known that they considered Black professors as mediocre as they considered Black students, to whom they gave inflated grades to prove WMIC's were not prejudiced and more concerned about them than Black teachers who are too hard on them. WMIC attitude was if Black students wanted to speak or write in substandard English, let them. Their dialect is legitimate as long as they understand each other. WMIC's rationale publicly was anyone with intelligence knows that 'I be' or 'I bees' means 'I am' and 'ax' means 'ask.' Job interviews? Don't worry about them. 'Come to my house for a sauna and relax. –Let me take you somewhere for a hot dog and a soda–' I bet teachers, even college teachers, didn't then and don't now have that type of relationship with students down here."

"I don't think so. I don't believe White or Black teachers down here related to students on that level. Now that you brought it to my attention, I also don't think either Black or White teachers stressed oral grammar. They corrected it on papers, and that was it. Black people had fought for integration and went along with it. Maybe now there are criticisms. Did hear through Rev that there was some whispering that integration didn't work out as it was supposed to."

"I read something about that, too. Some Black people want to go back to their own schools, especially in the lower and middle grades, even high school. Jackie, why are WMIC's so dedicated to mediocrity and sub-standards in Black folks! It's every where. On TV. They pick out the least articulate persons to interview as witnesses. If we criticize, WMIC's say we're paranoid. They seem to be obsessed with Black 'losers.' Jackie, there is so much Black potential, and I detect 'what's the use' in some Black teachers. To make things worse, Black students are satisfied with the double standard and proud of inflated grades—and some think they are earned grades."

"Maybe WMIC's are sincere, and just don't know any better," Jackie responded.

"WMIC's might be high grade morons, but they're geniuses in the art of survival. It's sabotage. They will never hire these students. They'll be sent back to minority communities to continue the cycle."

Dorothy and Jackie were still sitting in the car, the AC chilling them. Jackie turned it off and lowered the windows.

"Did your white colleagues make fun of Blacks?" Dorothy asked. "I know it's childish—puerile and stems from frustration, but it can be contemptible and vicious."

Nonchalantly, Jackie replied. "I suppose they did. We did. We laughed and talked about white teachers, always did, even before integration, the way they dressed and the way they talked—with a real southern nasal twang. We'd see them uptown on pay day, colored teachers togged down in I. Miller heels so high they looked like stilts, and clutching matching I. Miller bags. Even some wearing Italian imported shoes and carrying matching bags, costing more than they made in a month. White teachers would have on flat walking shoes, skirts and sweaters—good quality most times. And big leather bags that we said they used all their lives and even carried to church. I never considered laughing at them vicious. I didn't really laugh. Just smiled and listened. I dressed more the way you did–comfortable–better than white teachers–but better than you did," Jackie smiled.

"The ridicule where I worked wasn't about clothes. It was as degrading and insulting as Officials referring to Martin Luther King, Jr. as Martin Luther Coon, and men in Law Enforcement calling Black people Gorillas in the Mist."

"How do you know what White people said?" Jackie asked.

"Student Aides talk. Some became buddy-buddy with WMIC's. Some even pretended they didn't understand English. One, a relative of a Black faculty member, passed for white and got loads of information. I never questioned the students or made comments. The maintenance staff and disgruntled secretaries would sound off also. Some WMIC's were condescending toward secretaries. Too arrogant to accept that secretaries can be valuable and teachers main support. Even beyond the Chair at times–. A Black colleague told me student workers and maintenance personnel bugged offices and released recordings to a militant Black faculty member who was murdered."

"Was he killed because he had the recordings?" Jackie asked.

"Nobody knows. Black faculty who heard it was mute. Detectives never found out who murdered him, so they reported. This extremely competent man–who was also flawlessly articulate–was expendable."

Dorothy continued to use her friend as a listening post, adding how common it was in her Department to have meetings disguised as private social gatherings, a legitimate way to avoid inviting Black colleagues and questionable Whites. At these gatherings, WMIC's discussed secret and sinister plans. Via leaks provided by a Student Aide, it was reported to the Dean of Faculty that the Aide was paid from funds allotted by the school, her time entered as overtime day hours. She said many of these gatherings lasted all night, ending in drinking sessions in which jokes were told about absent ostracized members. Dorothy added that one Black colleague was labeled Miss Throw-up because her colleagues said her face resembled a perpetual puke. When their quiet Professor Sooty, labeled because she had extremely black skin, married and became pregnant, WMIC's in the Department showered her with gifts, hugged and kissed her, and predicted privately that she would be promoted to make ink for the Department. In another Department, two very black skinned instructors were called The Gold Dust Twins.

A favorite in her Department, Dorothy told Jackie, was Miss Stinker The Thinker, who WMIC's didn't want in the Department from the beginning. She earned her name on the basis of her offensive body order and mediocrity. She laughed loudest of all when she heard negative remarks coming from WMIC's about Black people. Miss Stinker The Thinker gave a party. WMIC's said her apartment had a colored smell as if she was forever frying chicken and making potato salad. They also commented that Miss Stinker The Thinker should buy her snaggle tooth mama some teeth instead of getting herself a BMW. One Aide said sometimes she'd call a cab to go home after serving parties because she didn't trust one of them driving while high, sometimes on something more than alcohol. When asked if she were afraid of the men taking her home so late at night, she laughed and said she was more afraid of the women. Neither ever made passes at her, the Aide admitted.

"I'm not the only Black person privy to inside information," Dorothy informed Jackie. "Others select to talk about it among themselves, and ignore it otherwise. After all, WMIC's and their cronies decide tenure and promotion."

"You said a student Aide told the Dean about the parties and how she was paid. What was done?"

"The Dean of Faculty is the same Dean I told you was scared of white women. He called a couple of the women and asked them to meet him for lunch as if it happened accidentally. No memos. No office visit. He smiled and advised them not to use student Aides again. He might not be able to protect them. He grinned and told them jokingly to invite him to their parties."

Jackie sighed. "And people go to New York to escape."

"There is no escape, Jackie. Shelters for some. Like the Three Little Pigs, depending on what your house is made of, WMIC's can huff and puff and blow your house down. I am not being pessimistic—just realistic."

Jackie had discussed the negative side of education for Blacks with Dorothy more than she had with anyone else—except Rev who was highly critical. Jackie mostly just listened to him. He was not in classrooms where students didn't read, did not bring in assignments, and who "acted up." Nor was he in classrooms where students read, brought in assignments, and did not "act up." So Jackie just listened—and survived.

They had been sitting in the car all that time. Jackie turned the ignition key, ready to continue their sight-seeing.

CHAPTER 13
Jackie Reveals More About Her Personal Life

"Would you like to see the new Police Department? It's quite a distance from here. Eventually we'll get there. You can compare it with what it was like when you were married to Joe Cephus."

"Yeah . –What have you heard lately about Johnnye Jamison?" Jackie never knew much juicy (as they called it in high school) gossip. Dorothy asked anyway. "Is it true she's a Lesbian or bisexual?"

"People said she came here and went straight to that group. I don't go out much, never did, as you know. Since I've retired, I go out and hear even less . –Dottie, two men who church members told Rev were 'like that' started coming to our church. They joined. Our membership is still small enough for Rev to extend the Hand of Fellowship to new members by inviting them to a special Sunday dinner at the parsonage. Some of our members suggested that Rev not invite them. I said we could take them to a Greensboro restaurant if the members were offended. The parsonage belongs to the church you know. Rev said it wouldn't be Christian. He accepted them as members, and they would be treated the same as other members. And if the members were offended, they could take the parsonage. Rev said we have our own home built the way we want it anyway. He invited them, and they came."

"Did you ever learn to cook?" Dorothy smiled, remembering the bland, boring meals Jackie could serve. Not caring much for food herself, she didn't care.

Jackie laughed. "Not as well as Rev. He still does most of the cooking. I remind him that before we married, I told him I couldn't cook. He laughs and says he didn't know it was *that* bad. He won't let me touch special company dinners. He likes to cook. I set the table with a centerpiece and proper silver, crystal, china –and wash dishes or put them in the dishwasher. After they're cleaned for the washer, I might as well wash them."

"How did the dinner with the two men turn out?"

"Dottie, they were two of the few guests who brought hostess gifts. One brought the most beautiful blooming plant. Tropical. I've never seen one like it. There were instructions how to take care of it, and I did. Just like it was a baby. The other one brought a gorgeous musical jewelry box. He must have ordered it from New York or Paris. I'll show them to you before you leave. Dottie, they held the chair when I sat down, and stood when I got up. They really know social graces–and talked on all subjects–."

"I know. Where do they work?" Dorothy wondered if Granston employed them usefully.

"Post Office and Veterans Administration. One teaches night classes at A. & T. University also. The one in the Post Office is applying for a teaching job at Winston-Salem State U. –They are so nice. It's hard not to like them. If they just weren't like that."

"What do you mean if they just weren't 'like that.' We're supposed to get rid of discrimination and that includes sexual orientation . –I always did like the men. I'm still working on myself to accept women on the same basis. Double standards. Society always did allow men more sexual freedom–and other social freedoms–than it does women. I never could bring myself to go to a bar alone, or ever wanted to. Always said it was a man's thing. Like sexual freedom is a man's thing. It's not fair. I know that intellectually. I always had a gay man as one of my best friends, especially after I stopped trying to be married. They are good friends, and you can have fun with them. And they give sound advice." Dorothy informed.

"That's what a girl who taught at Douglass High told me. She was from Philadelphia. I use to think she was—well—bad or wild until she told me some of the things they did together like going to the opera, plays, parties, even night clubs. I never went to places like that."

"What did you and your boyfriends do?" Dorothy asked.

"Rev was my only real boyfriend. Lots of Bennett College girls had boyfriends from A. & T., but none went steady with me. They came to see me once or twice and that was it."

"What did you and Rev do?"

Jackie smiled. "Nothing like the things you did. We went to drive-in movies a few times. Nice family movies–. We drove. *He* drove to Asheville, Mount Airy, and other places in the mountains. The scenery was beautiful every season. Sometimes I'd pack a lunch or he'd buy sandwiches and sodas, and we'd stop and eat. Once we spent all day at the beach. I didn't take a bathing suit. Wore slacks. On cold Sundays he'd come to my house and we'd sit in front of the fireplace and eat what we had for dessert. In summer, we'd sit on the front porch and eat ice cream he'd bring. We didn't date long before we married."

"I like doing things like that, Jackie. You did have a good time. As good as any I had. Good times are what people enjoy."

"I enjoyed dating Rev."

"Did you 'do it' before you married?" Using their high school term, Dorothy smiled.

Seventy-four-year-old Jackie blushed. Nobody had ever asked her that. Her mother had cautioned: "Don't think because he's a preacher, he won't take advantage of you. He's still a man."

"No." Jackie answered, wondering if she should tell Dottie the secret she hadn't told anyone. Even she and Rev never talked about it: *They almost did in the back seat of his car one night when*

Rev drove to a lonely unpaved road—before they remembered he was a preacher, and she was Dr. Sullivan's daughter. Suppose somebody saw them and called the police. People did that. "Following a telephone call lead, Granston's Finest were able to arrest – names here–for fornication. As it is with first offenders, their jail time was suspended." Police in those days were always looking for couples parked on back roads, *especially colored couples.* It would be published in the Granston paper under Public Records: Jacquelyn Sullivan, negro, 22, school teacher, Douglass High School, FORNICATION; Thadeus T. LeGrande, negro, 27, minister, Lutheran Branch Church of Granston, FORNICATION . –No! The paper would say PREACHER. Sounds more cul-lud . –And Jackie blushed and told Dottie what she had never told anyone–about that night on a lonely dirt road, adding, "We kissed a lot, too. At least a lot for me. We still kiss right smart to be old married Senior citizens."

Dottie blushed too, wondering what Jackie thought of her friend's having had two white lovers, a Black one and another Black one she did not know sexually, and an Asian. Jackie was one of the few people in Granston who knew that Dottie had had three husbands, one of them White. Dorothy wondered if Jackie fantasized. Dorothy thought of Ilka Chase's *In Bed We Cry*. Would critics and readers make comments about her similar to the ones they made about Chase years ago? If they did, hopefully book sales will soar and soar. Dorothy almost giggled aloud.

"Are you glad or sorry you married a preacher?" Dorothy asked.

"I don't think about being glad or sorry. If you mean am I sorry I can't do certain things because I'm a preacher's wife, no. Dottie, because Daddy was a doctor, Mama told me I couldn't do what other girls did. And, Dottie, there was something in our house that said light-skinned colored people are–well–better than darker ones. Mama and Daddy didn't come out and say it–" Jackie paused.

"But you heard it," Dorothy completed.

"Yes," Jackie replied softly.

Dorothy interrupted the brief silence. "I heard something like that when I was growing up. With Daddy dark and me not light-skinned, it had to do with status. They would say, 'Don't forget who you are–remember your background–don't let would-be-friends stand in the way of your becoming one of the Big B's–Brown, Bethume, Bourroughs-.'"*

Jackie Sullivan LeGrande had never talked so intimately about her family life, not even to her husband, and felt the need to tell more. And she did. "You asked how I felt about marrying a preacher—" Jackie breathed deeply, held it a moment. "There was nobody else I wanted. We married because he asked me, and he fitted the bill. We fitted each other: Young, but he ideally a few years older. Both of us had light skin and professional. All my life I knew I had to marry a light skin man. Remember, we're from that part of North Carolina where most colored folks looked white–or almost. Folks say we married cousins to keep it that way. Mama and Daddy, especially Mama, said brown skin grandchildren just wouldn't fit in. Because Daddy was a doctor, nobody in Granston knew we were color struck. Most of his patients were dark. Fair skin colored people usually went to white doctors. A status symbol. Dottie, I was a robot before we knew about them."

Jackie looked straight ahead. Dottie glanced at her, wondered what did this robot-like woman feel, and asked, "Did you love Rev–and do you still after all these years?"

Jackie hesitated briefly before replying. "I didn't think about it then and don't now. I don't think too much about things that are fixed: Civil Rights, prejudice, the atomic bomb or the new one they got, Star Wars, nuclear fall out, heaven and hell. People were concerned about Y2K. I wasn't–Did I love Rev? He was a new preacher in town, whom Mama invited to dinner because we attended his church. But mostly, as I told you, because he fitted the bill. I didn't go anywhere and he took me out for Sunday rides and to a few dull movies. Even to a Shriner's dance where we just stood around for a while talking, smiling, and sipping ginger ale. He kissed me one night. My second kiss. He asked me to marry him and then asked Mama and Daddy. They said it was up to me. I said it was up to them. It was kinda silly. Anyway, we had a big wedding. Remember, we wanted you to be maid–matron of honor, but you were in Africa or Europe. There was no other girl in Granston they wanted, so they sent for one of our insignificant, white-looking, country cousins. She never learned to march to the music and looked scared and stupid."

Both women laughed. Jackie continued: "Do I think Rev loved me? If he didn't he loved what he got. –And added to that, my life had been so dull nobody could gossip about me . –And other girls were brown skin or darker and straightened their hair– and had nappy edges and naps on the back of their necks. And some had led lives too interesting to be preachers' wives."

Dorothy had never known Jackie to talk so much at one time, and was delighted when she saw more-to-come in her face. "Do Rev and I still love each other if we ever did? I don't know. What difference does it make? Who else would we have married in Granston? Especially me. He could've gone somewhere else looking for a wife. I'm stuck here. There was absolutely no one in Granston for me. I didn't go anywhere, and had just a few friends who didn't include me in most things they did. Not even on church excursions. I really wanted to go with them to Myrtle Beach. Mama didn't let me go to parties. I was scared of parties, and never learned to dance well. Nobody ever asked me to dance. When we were in high school and Mama gave in and let me spend a couple of hours at our Deb party, nobody asked me to dance but your boyfriend Cap and Thomasena's boyfriend Bill Ware. Remember?"

Dorothy nodded. "I also remember that she didn't want you to be in the Debs after Thomasena came and joined."

"The only reason she let me join was because you were in it–and your Daddy was a lawyer and your Mama had light skin. Mama wanted us to be best friends–until you started going around with Thomasena.** Mama said your parents should be ashamed they didn't have control over you and kept reminding me that Thomasena had lived with a white man before Mrs. Hobson took her in, and that was why they sent her to the orphanage and then to the reformatory. And Mrs. Hobson must be out of her mind to take somebody like that in her home.*** Even before she came, I didn't flirt or do crazy things and go to the tennis court like you all did. Dottie, one time I really embarrassed Mama–and meant to."

"What did you do?"

"I told her Thomasena was light skinned and had real good hair–she was lighter than I was and her hair prettier, and I thought all light skinned people with good hair were nice."

"What did she say," Dorothy laughed.

"Girl, she got real mad, and said she was surprised and shocked that I would put that much emphasis on hair and color and wondered where I got such a thing from, and don't *ever* let anyone hear me say that."

Both women laughed. Dorothy felt proud of her friend.

Jackie continued, "Girl, my family could really embarrass me at times. Daddy took me to the Junior prom and came for me. I spent the time standing against the wall–a real wallflower. Mama and Daddy got a distant cousin to take me to the Senior prom.

How I prayed he would be dark so folks wouldn't think he was kinfolk. But there he was–yellow and countrified. After a while, I told him to call Daddy to come and get us. I swore I'd never go to another dance–Marrying a preacher was the right thing for me–insulation."

The two women sat reflecting until Dorothy broke the silence. "Jackie, do you ever want to–fly away–just soar–go looking for something–like your own personal frontier–?"

It didn't take long for Jackie Sullivan to reply. "I never had any real dreams. Just lived because I was born, and became what I became because it was the simplest thing to do. Do you know what I wrote when we had to list our ambition?"

"Thomasena sent me a copy of the school paper. I still have it. You wrote Undecided."

Jackie remembered, "And you had a list: writer, novelist, actress, and even aviatrix. Mama said maybe I wanted to be a nurse and help Daddy. I told her I want to help Daddy, but didn't want to be around sick people, and I was scared of dead people. But I could be his secretary or receptionist. They didn't think that was high enough on the scale to get them the kind of son-in-law they wanted."

"So they sent you to the most prestigious colored school in North Carolina at that time."

Jackie nodded. "I wanted to go to Hampton, but after you and Thomasena went, Mama said no. You were all right, but not Thomasena. If white colleges around here hadn't been segregated, she and Daddy would have sent me to one of them–to keep me away from undesirable Negroes. I realized later that they didn't consider that there were undesirable white people in white colleges. To them being Black and undesirable is worse than being white and undesirable. Mama and Daddy, especially Mama, selected Bennett because none of the debs went–and more expensive than a land grant College. When I graduated, a job was waiting. Daddy knew all the principals, and they all belonged to the Shriners, Masons, or the same fraternity."

Dorothy did not say what she was thinking: *You got the job they wanted you to have, the son-in-law they wanted and light skin grandchildren with good hair they wanted. You succeeded.*

Jackie might have picked up her friend's vibrations, because she said as if faraway and talking to someone not present. "I was voted The Girl Most Likely to Succeed in the Class of 1941 and I wonder if I did. If so, in what? And if I didn't, where did I not succeed?"

Dorothy assured her, "You succeeded, Jackie. You got what you wanted, and you are contented."

"What about you, Dottie? You traveled a lot. Met interesting people. Wrote and still writing books and articles. You succeeded, didn't you?"

"Not yet," Dorothy responded wistfully.

Jackie drove slowly and silently while Dorothy wondered if her friend's marriage was as flawless as it sounded. Dorothy encountered antagonism in every aspect of her marriage. She remembered her battle with birth control and wondered about this innocent robot-woman. Dorothy had no serious problem as a single woman. It was in marriage to Luther and Joe Cephus. They seemed to think that marriage was natural prevention. The use of condoms was unthinkable. Both of them would say something like "You married now." She never forgot how cooperative Magdar was—even more cautious at times than she was.

Dorothy decided to ask Jackie out right. After all, they had been talking so freely. "Jackie, how did you keep from having any more children?"

"Dottie, after the third baby, I got nerve enough to tell Rev that if he didn't consent for me to have my tubes tied, I'd have abortions. Bluffing. I didn't know anybody who would do that, but Rev thought I did through Daddy. He wouldn't have told me. Daddy was one of those old-fashioned doctors who made house calls until he died. I scared Rev one time. My period was late, and I took a whole bottle of castor oil with turpentine. I heard about that years ago, even when we were in high school, and Kate Crawford use to tell us things like that. I asked Mama why she had just one child, and she said it was God's will."

"A man has to consent! That is contemptible. An insult. A woman should have absolute sovereignty over her body and what grows in it!" –Dorothy snatched her mind away from the horrifying time when Thomasena was pregnant because of rape. "Absolute sovereignty," Dorothy repeated.

"Did you?—Have absolute sovereignty?" Jackie asked.

"Not when I was married to Luther or Joe Cephus when

it came to having sex." She did not mention that she did with Magdar. That marriage ended in divorce too. "Luther would be disgusting with 'you'll want to after we start', but I didn't. Joe Cephus would physically fight. Jackie, one night he actually acted the way I imagine a man does when he is raping a woman. I fought back and bit him–his chest. He got up, Jackie, the light was on, and he wiped blood from the bite with a handkerchief and had the most pleased expression on his face. It was sort of scary. As much as he fussed and fought, he never mentioned I bit him. The scar turned blue then black and was still there when we separated. I hoped it would become malignant. No, I did not have sovereignty over my body sexually while married, which is one of the main reasons I didn't like marriage. I did have control over child bearing. I never discussed it with either Luther or Joe Cephus after I found out they were anti-condoms. There was nothing to negotiate, and I did what was expedient for me."

Jackie pressed the gas pedal. The car accelerated as if verbalizing had given her spunk.

"Dottie, I married Mama and Daddy when I married Rev. Not much difference. I did what they wanted me to do, and if I didn't want to, they didn't know it. Same way with Rev. He never–acted in the bed the way you say Joe Cephus acted. If he did, I'd think he had gone crazy. It never occurred to me to ignore Mama and Daddy's opinion on important things. Same way with Rev. I discuss everything with Rev and tell him everything–just about. – Except unsavory things about you." Jackie smiled.

*African American female educators Charlotte Hawkins Brown, Mary McCleod Bethume, and Nannie Burroughs
**Character in *This Day's Madness*
*** Incidents in *This Day's Madness*

CHAPTER 14

Dorothy's First Interracial Relationship

Girl, you don't know the really unsavory stuff about me. A mischievous smile teased Dorothy's face, as she boarded her Time Machine. It was her first interracial liaison. The glorious free years after divorcing Luther, and before her marriage to Joe Cephus. She was young and sexy. Skin, especially on her legs, moist and golden brown. She was like a model in a bathing suit–measurements nearly perfect. It happened on Ball Island, Rhode Island, in the fifties when a colored woman's "going with" a white man was truly taboo. Dorothy went there to do summer stock after hearing in a New York University drama class that the Director was looking for amateur colored actors and actresses for roles in Broadway plays. An excellent actress but Dorothy could not sing or dance, and the summer stock plays were musicals. Since her plan did not materialize and rather than return home broke, Dorothy took a job as waitress and maid in the Island's summer resort hotel on the water front, part of and adjacent to the Theater. In addition to salary and tips, she received room and board. Besides, it was a new adventure, this Island. She heard the sea each night, and loved the way the moon lit it up and the way stars shone. People said the island was like Bermuda with its trade winds. Dorothy quickly learned to search for clams with her bare feet when the tide was right, and joined the colored couple who cooked for the resort hotel when they baked them on the beach at night after guests went to bed.

They have so much fun, these colored people, the Director thought and began to join them. He watched Dorothy when she walked alone along the beach at night. One night he asked what she was looking for. She told him "the Will-o-the Wisp, the phantom ship that I heard comes close to the shore at night, and marsh gas lights." He offered to help her look for them. They did the next night and the next. They began to know and like each other. He, the Manager and Director, French with a tantalizing accent, asked her to give up teaching and join the troupe. At least try it for a while. There would be roles for a colored girl. In the fall he was going to produce "The Little Foxes," "Deep Are The Roots," "Strange Fruit," and others. What would she do while waiting? He would take care of her–and her daughter. But he was married and had three children. His wife never came to the Island, he assured Dorothy, the children rarely. They almost never traveled with the troupe. They had their own lives. Dorothy did not find this sort of uncertainty attractive. His attempts to persuade her led to dinner and dancing on the Island and sailing to nearby Providence. At least twenty years her senior, which Dorothy liked, he became younger and began to play again.

Often after night sent sunbathers to bed, or to attend the local or off-island night spots, Dorothy and her Frenchman ran down to the sea, sometimes they strolled, continuing their vigil for the Phantom Ship. They listened for its ghostly horn. They searched for the will-o-the wisp. Monsieur Frenchman called it jack-o-lantern. They looked for marsh gases that made lights, and Northern Lights, and saw lights in their eyes. They had seen marsh marigolds and marsh elder plants in daylight. If these two looked with dream-filled eyes, they could find glimmers that special marigold and elder plants made at night. There was sparking everywhere–in their eyes, hair, and the sea.

One Thanksgiving, Dorothy met her Frenchman on the Island.

They swam and played in the frigid inky sea. Later Dorothy lay in his arms wrapped in a blanket, first in the sand, then before a fireplace sipping warm apple cider stirred with cinnamon sticks. She felt cozy and safe in the huge abandoned haunted-looking wooden building that housed the summer stock troupe and where rich and famous people hid away during summers. –And her Frenchman told her they would go to Paris, marry, live there and raise a family. And they made jokes they had become close enough to make, so Dorothy said their son would be Jean Henry. She enjoyed it immensely, knowing it was playtime, flattering make-believe. Suspending make-believe, she told him that she would go to Paris with him –or meet him there– during the summer, when school was over, and she did. They did things tourists do as well as things a girl can do who has a man in Paris who knows Paris and has no restraints. They saw things Dorothy read about in French classes, history books, and sights World War II soldiers talked about, and she had seen in movies. He took her to the Follies, to Josephine Baker's retreat and to Pigalle that American WWII soldiers had nicknamed Pig Alley. She saw things she had not heard about, but girls are privy to and enjoy when they know someone in Paris like her M. Frenchman.

Dorothy returned the next summer and the next and got the role of Addie in "The Little Foxes," he scheduled especially for her. He admired her acting. Adding to the adventure, she experienced her first hurricane, Dorothy's fears almost nil as she and M. Frenchman listened to its fury safe and cozy in her room. They saw the devastating results the next morning and marveled at the survival of the ancient hotel and theater.

Their friendship lasted until Dorothy married Joe Cephus, and rekindled after their separation and divorce when she returned to New York. Dorothy began teaching in a Manhattan college branch where colleagues (WMIC's) rejected early morning classes. Dorothy's transfer from Brooklyn to Manhattan brought her closer to her Greenwich Village apartment, a promotion, and the promise of a flexible schedule that would also allow her to be an adjunct at the Brooklyn branch if she chose. Dorothy loved "before dawn classes," as some instructors called them, and in exchange she asked to have classes scheduled on Tuesdays, Wednesdays, and Thursdays to satisfy the required number of hours and sessions. The chairman, anxious to please WMIC's, was glad to have someone willing to take "before sunrise classes." When Dorothy got wanderlust, or when Mr. Frenchman called seeking "someone exotic," she would fly to Paris Thursday after her last class, take papers to be corrected if necessary, and return Monday night.

Dorothy vowed to bring her daughter to Paris. They would get a hotel on the Left Bank because it was Bohemian. Dorothy would retain friendship with M. Frenchman, and they would show her daughter places and sights people see when they know someone in Paris like M. Frenchman. And they did.

Dorothy heard her Time Machine—and she was back in the present—. Call it Golden Years or Gray Panthers, she was still an old woman in her seventies, who, in spite of her intelligence and knowledge of biology, had not realized if she lived long enough she'd be past seventy wondering what happened to her life and where had the years gone. —Dorothy wondered as usual what Sisters and Brothers were going to say even though Brothers grabbed white flesh and Sisters did if they wanted to, but just didn't talk about it or advertise it like Brothers.

People could still drive leisurely in Granston, and Jackie, a slow driver, was poking along. The local term poking meaning moving very slowly made her smile. Dorothy liked the slow pace. She was thinking of her Great Escape—and her best friend Thomasena* who had not escaped and because she had not, their world was minus exuberant Thomasena, the talented scholastic marvel who could have written books all through the years, who could have become a brilliant teacher, a resplendent master teacher. The sparkling full-of-life Thomasena, for whom life was to be a great adventure, for whom the world beckoned to come live, had spent unfulfilled-dream years bearing children she did not want, yet remaining painfully and tragically devoted to them, with men she did not love, but would have won an Academy Award for her dedication, in employment she abhorred, but gave noble performances. Each time Dorothy saw Thomasena, she was more abandoned by the dead, more lost among the living, and her shoulders more stooped, and the more she would sit and stare at nothing in particular. Such is the way domestic bastilles had imprisoned her – Such is the way her own life could have been had she not escaped Joe Cephus–and Luther . –Dorothy had seen many Black women ending in quicksand–victims of wicked men like Joe Cephus or dreamless men like Luther. What happens to wicked and cruel people, Dorothy wondered, people who adversely alter the course of lives of others forever? Are they punished after death? Dorothy was grateful for interludes in her life that yanked her from the quicksand of perpetual regret. Her Frenchman had been such an interlude. Would she pay in another life?

Dorothy turned to her friend, "Jackie, do you believe you're going to heaven when you die?"

"Yes. Where else could I go? People who have had interesting seamy lives go to hell."

"You believe in hell–a place where people actually go and burn forever." Dorothy's statement was not a question.

"Of course. That's life's last chance to say 'I gotcha.'"

*Protagonist in *This Day's Madness*

CHAPTER 15
Jackie And Integration

"I'm going to make you a character in this story I'm writing."
Jackie laughed aloud.

"I'm serious. –So tell me what you think now and thought then about teaching white high school students in Granston at the beginning of integration. What about later on? Jackie, you were transferred from all colored Frederick Douglass to an all white high school named in honor of Wade Hampton and John Calhoun, who said 'Negroes couldn't absorb educative experience.' The Confederate flag waved on its roof and was draped on the auditorium stage." Questions Dorothy had wanted answered for nearly a half a century came like a cloud burst. "How did you feel? What happened to you inside–and outside? Were you scared? How did white students treat you? Did they respect you? Did you have disciplinary problems? How did you handle them? What about the white administration and your white colleagues? Did they talk to you? Eat with you in the cafeteria? And Black students– how did they act?–Above all–did you find White students more receptive to learning, as people say is based on test scores? Jackie, I can write about the experience on the college level as I saw it in New York–with its surface deceptive form of integration. I want to

242

hear first hand what happened in my Southern hometown. Wish I knew a white teacher willing to talk about it also."

Dorothy was almost certain Jackie made no White friends as she herself would have done–and retained the bond, but she asked anyway. "Do you know any White teacher who might talk to me–male or female? Doesn't have to be a teacher–can be a principal or counselor."

Jackie was silent before replying as if weary. "I'll have to think about how it really was." She smiled. "You made me use the work think–and I can't refer you to anyone white. I don't even remember their names now. I did for a while."

Dorothy closed her eyes visualizing material and information she would have collected and absorbed in the unique situation of integration Granston style. Perhaps Jackie had data she preferred not to believe–like other people in Granston. Dorothy would probe. She'd begin with a simple question that might draw out information. "Did you enjoy teaching?"

Jackie smiled. "Now you're making me laugh. People say I don't laugh much. Even Rev . –Did I enjoy teaching," she mused. "Not the way you did. I didn't have the –passion you had. Both my ratings at Douglass and Hamp-Cal were 'Highly Satisfactory.' Both Principals stated in Comments and on the Check List that they considered me 'calm and low-key, a welcomed balance.'–My classroom assignments were like anything else I had to do. I didn't–well– ponder over them. I did what was expected. Refusing would mean consequences. I don't like consequences. And–doing things I was expected to do didn't bother me. What would I be doing anyway, if not what was expected."

Dorothy began to chuckle. "Like– my tummy expects me to eat. If I don't, it'll make me wish I had . –My principal expects me to teach this class. If I don't, he'll expect me in his office to explain why and will write something in my chart that I expect will effect my rating.—Night: It's time to 'do it' with Rev." Again Dottie used their teenage term. "Rev expects me to and I expect myself to because he expects me to, and I do what people expect me to expect to do. Besides, if I don't, there will be consequence, and I don't like consequence. " Both women laughed.

"That's just about it," Jackie responded pleasantly.

"What do you think about when you're washing dishes or taking a bath–or lying in bed at night before going to sleep?"

"I don't remember thinking about anything in particular. My mind is absolutely blank if that is psychologically possible. Is it?"

"Suppose it is on a conscious level." Dorothy looked at this woman voted "Most Likely to Succeed." Her face held serene triumph. No provocative dream had been there, consequently there was no unrealized dream. And she had survived without mutilation. –Perhaps because there was so little exposed to vandalize.

Some Black teachers, however, were victims of integration. Dorothy asked Jackie if she knew anything about what happened to Flavella Thomas, who taught at Booker T. Washington Elementary during the beginning of bussing. On a visit to Granston, Dorothy heard that Flavella became so nervous and upset, she was forced to ask for early retirement. According to gossip, she wasn't considered a choice selection in colored schools, where her glory had been parading daring, expensive apparel, a different outfit every day, never the same in a month at least. The story goes, Flavella was ridiculed by white colleagues who sniggered or complimented her in an uncomplimentary manner. The grapevine said she feared white parents and administrators. And "down-right scared of white children." And they were elementary school children. She wasn't afraid they would attack her. She was intimidated about teaching them, terrified she would not come off as an authority figure as she had with colored children, or that she would make a mistake, or mispronounce a word. She is supposed to have confided that she overheard a student call her "Dressed-up Mammy." Tearfully, Flavella added that the child had to have heard an adult use the expression.

Dorothy asked about another very meek Black teacher who just left the system rather than face the scrutiny of "a harsh overbearing white principal." However, most of Granston's African American teachers survived to retirement. Dorothy also wanted to know if Black teachers modified their school dress code, "dressing down," and their use of language and diction around whites.

Jackie said she had not heard about Flavella Thomas, nor the other one who left the system. She did hear something about colored teachers dressing more like white ones and vice versa.

"Did you have any unique experiences?" Dorothy asked.

"Mmm-nn–some of the children–and parents–apparently had never seen or noticed light skin colored people–"

"White people don't see differences in colored people's *shades* of skin tones—unless they have extremely light skin."

"So Rev says. At the beginning of the first semester I was at Hamp-Cal, a mother brought her daughter to my class, looked at me and said, 'Mr. Mabley', the principal, 'told me Sue Anne would have a colored homeroom teacher name Mis' LeGrande. I came to meet her. He didn't tell me about the change.' I told her there had been no change. I was Mrs. LeGrande. Then checked my roster and told her Sue Anne's name was on it. The woman stared at me, and told Sue Ann, 'This is your new homeroom teacher. She'll also be your civics and vocation teacher. Now be good and learn. Good-bye.' Sue Anne looked at me and asked, 'you're not colored, are you?' I told her I was, and since she was the first one in class, would she please be one of my monitors."

"And you lived happily ever after," Dottie completed. Jackie nodded affirmatively.

"Jackie, is it true that Black teachers ate together in the cafeteria, and so did white teachers?" Dorothy began asking questions one by one while she had Jackie corralled and talking more than usual.

"I heard they did–at least most of the time. I was the only Black teacher at H. C. Senior High. One meant the school was integrated. Most Black high school teachers were sent to junior high schools, which became Middle Schools. Dottie, I think they sent me to Hampton-Calhoun because I had light skin and blended in."

"Why?"

"Rev and I both think so. I certainly wasn't one of the best teachers. Of course, I wasn't one of the worse either, but there were others who were rated excellent and superior. Some who even volunteered. I didn't have an outgoing personality. We filled out forms that had questions such as Do You Volunteer? I said *no*. Do You Want To Go? *No*. Will You Go If Assigned? I said yes, because I would–and I was *expected* to go." Both women smiled.

"How did you handle the cafeteria problem?"

"No real problem for me. I worked from the sixties until I retired in the eighties, and maybe ate in the cafeteria two or three times a year. At first I brought my lunch and ate in the lounge if nobody was there. Most time I sat at my desk, corrected papers, or made lesson plans while eating." –A driver honked a signal as Jackie made a wrong turn and kept going– "One day I forgot my lunch and didn't eat that day. Another time I was late getting to the cafeteria, and all the tables were just about filled, but there were empty chairs. I didn't eat that day either, and started keeping an apple, orange or a package of Nabs or peanuts in my bag. Another time I went to the cafeteria and sat at an empty table. After the other tables were filled, a white teacher asked if I minded if she sat down. I said no, and didn't mind. I was–kinda glad–and not glad. After we introduced ourselves, told what we taught, and where our rooms were, we couldn't find anything else to say. Two other women joined us. After introductions, they left me out of their conversation. I hurried and finished, wished them a pleasant day and went to my room. I avoided the cafeteria as much possible–and the lounge . –No man came near my table even when women were there. Two or three always sat with me after the first time. I knew from hearing them talk, they had meetings, parties, showers, visited, and went to the movies together, exchanged Christmas and birthday presents, but I was not included."

"Did you want to be?"

Jackie hesitated so long Dorothy thought Jackie had not heard the question. Finally, "I would have felt funny and made excuses not to attend. I felt funny also when they were making plans, and I was left out. You would have accepted, and you would have made friends. Dottie, I just did not know how. I had not learned in all these years, even years before my ancestors were born–How do I suddenly–assimilate?–Just the same, they had not even shown me common courtesy. I don't think they meant to be discourteous. It was as if I were not even there."

You weren't, not in their world, Dorothy said to herself, thinking how differently she herself would have responded.

Neither Dorothy nor Jackie noticed that they were driving aimlessly through Granston's streets. Jackie was letting her companion see whatever there was to see. Dorothy broke the silence. "People say White principals had meetings that did not include Black teachers. Years ago when I first started going to grad school, 'they' said instructors had secret lectures that did not include colored students."

Jackie responded, "Maybe principals called teachers in for private sessions, and we might have misinterpreted it. And maybe they did meet with white teachers. It was easy to do where I worked. Just tell the secretary not to put the notice in my box, or have someone take it out. It didn't bother me. Like you, I didn't like faculty meetings. The principal had a note placed in my box asking me to come to his office after school. Dottie, was I *scared*. He just wanted to know how I was getting along, and if there were any problems, suggestions, comments, etc. Of course I had none. Just wanted to hurry and get out of that–interrogation chamber."

"Was it that bad?" Dorothy asked.

"No. Actually the principal was nice. He had a real thick white southern drawl, and looked like a Red Neck, but he smiled a lot and was as decent as somebody like him can be under changing circumstances. He probably met with all his teachers, or called them in groups or by Departments. Principals have to do something. They don't teach. I was in Social Science. He met with us two or three times a year. I told you my classes were Freshman Vocations and Civics. Whoever made the assignments wouldn't trust me with history. And a visiting teacher who went around to various schools taught Negro History. Black folks say The Board of Ed selected teachers it could tell what to say and what not to say. Anyway, they didn't use any of our teachers for the course–I didn't care how many meetings they had and left me out. I didn't like them when I was in the all-colored school."

"I know what you mean. Most meetings were unnecessary. It was boring listening to folks trying to impress each other and the principal trying to justify his job. In college, it was the chairperson. But some of my colleagues loved meetings. Gave them a change to boast about how good they were and criticize others."

"Oh," Jackie remembered, "White people talk around colored janitors as if they are stupid or deaf like you said some of your white colleagues talked around student aides. Colored men were called janitors, white ones, custodians. Anyway, colored custodians said white teachers had lots of meetings when they found out schools really had to integrate. Some of the women said they were actually afraid of colored boys–and scared of girls too. Teachers brought up a case that happened in a colored high school in Leesburg. You probably remember it–a boy slapped a teacher. She hit him with a chair, and he ended up in the hospital. She was fired."

"Nowadays there would be two lawsuits." Dorothy reminded.

"She got a job in another city, and I didn't hear anymore about it–Oh, yes, white women teachers wanted to know what to do when colored students got out of hand. Not *if* they got out of hand, but *when.*"

"What were they told to do?"

"The janitor said they were told not to worry. The office had a direct emergency line to the Police Department. A special phone.

The janitors didn't find it. Said it was probably locked up in the vault."

"If Joe Cephus had known that, he would have found a way to brag about a special part he played."

Jackie responded, "From what I gather, it was for White policemen only. They registered in the school as students, teachers' assistants, and substitutes, especially in gym classes and athletics. If these janitors are still alive, you could really get some information." Jackie remembered, "Men teachers wanted to know what to do when colored boys tried to date white girls."

Dorothy had not expected news this spicy. "What was the remedy?"

"Let parents settle it. If they brought it to the school, the Principal would refer them to the Superintendent."

"Did anything ever happen?"

"No. It would have been Headline News. Things were smooth–after the protesting ended. A lot smoother than some of the places in the North East, according to Granston papers."

"Did anybody bring up what to do if White boys and Black girls began dating?" Dorothy asked.

"If anybody did, the custodians didn't hear. Rev said white folks weren't concerned. White boys and Black girls don't usually date. If they do, the law – police – don't get into it, and the Black community just calls the girl trash–her label is 'she ain't nothing.' Rev says the white community just calls it 'slumming' on the boy's part."

Dorothy wanted to take notes, but it might silence Jackie. It would be difficult writing in a car while riding anyway. She continued to take advantage of Jackie's avalanche of words and asked, "What were the White students like–overall?"

"There was some resentment that showed in body language. Most of them I think tried to show how different they were . –And superior to Black students who had a reputation for being scholastically inferior and having discipline problems. Black students for the most part had their best boot forward, too. They clustered together–in the cafeteria, classroom, on the campus, and walking home. Most integration I saw was in sports. And it ended on the basketball courts or football and baseball fields."

"Did you find White students superior scholastically?–And did Black students cause more disciplinary problems? One of the vices of segregation was that it denied Black and Whites equal opportunities for social and scholastic development."

Jackie sighed deeply. "If Black students would stop acting as if studying, wanting to learn, using correct or standard English are 'white things, acting white.' If they would stop ridiculing other Black students who refuse to be clowns and who are ambitious and apply themselves. That attitude is detrimental. It's as if there is something great at the bottom of the ditch, and they should get it–." Jackie stopped suddenly as if she had no right to these feelings–or to admit them.

Dorothy Borden stared at her friend. She had expressed Dorothy's precise feelings in some of the exact words. How many Black teachers felt the same way? What could they do about it? Black potential must be salvaged! Jackie had compared herself to a robot. Like a robot, she had been fed data and programmed. Pushing a button released what had been absorbed. There must be more inhumed in this usually silent woman.

"Jackie, I feel the same way. What can we do?"

Jackie sighed and fell into a relaxed speech pattern to lessen her feeling of invalidism. "What I didn't do in forty years in the classroom, I can't do now. Rev says—I– we Black teachers made a difference. According to the law of averages, he says we had to. Like his being a minister. A lot of people he didn't reach, but some he did. Rev says we're not failures."

They were both quiet. Dorothy decided against reminding her friend she had not responded to the major question: *Did she find white students basically scholastically superior to Black students?* That question would come later. For now another biggie: *"Based on your experience and observation, has integration helped Black students educationally–or their overall development?"*

Jacquelyn Julliana Sullivan LeGrande drove slowly, looking straight ahead. It seemed such a long time before she replied softly, "No."

"Do other Black teachers in the South feel the same way?"

"As far as I know. Remember there are exceptions, and I don't talk or discuss things too much with anybody but Rev. He and I attend NAACP meetings and civic gatherings like the Black Family. People say integration might have made a difference to the Black psyche. Rev says we should not expect overwhelming positive results in five or ten years or even thirty or forty years that would eradicate centuries of experiences."

Dorothy was grateful for the downpour from Jackie, a literal information storm, and decided not to push any harder. She would activate Jackie again later with an article reporting that the academic performance by middle class Black and Hispanic students was poor in comparison to White and Asian middle class students.

CHAPTER 16

Granston Unearths More Memories of Joe Cephus

Both women communicated inwardly. Dorothy, thinking of the other cynosure of her story, shifted the conversation and asked, "Does Johnnye live by herself–in the house where Joe Cephus died?" Dorothy had always felt strange about dead people, and the feeling magnified when she thought of Joe Cephus. She certainly wouldn't live in a house where he died.

Jackie nodded her head affirmatively. "Want to see it?"

"Yeah. He was so proud of the one he had when we were married. I'd like to see the house he gave it up for."

As Jackie turned the car toward the colored section, Dorothy felt a surge of pity for Joe Cephus, and tried to hold onto it since it could be a continuation of an effort to stop detesting him. Understanding him might also help eradicate hate. –Dorothy frowned–did she really want to cancel her hate? What feeling would replace it? Blankness? Not if she wanted to write about him. She'd try to understand him as a catalyst or an antagonist—understand his unique *him-ness*—and the image his mirror reflected.

Joe Cephus had been a victim just as he had victimized women.

His background with his sibling sisters had given him his Right of Passage. Society bellowed that the world belonged to men. *White men world over.* Black men had to create their world. Both Joe Cephus' awareness and unawareness had instilled that concept. Not knowing how to qualify and authenticate himself, Joe Cephus sought expression of maleness in his world with the only methods and materials he knew, sex, which defined and qualified him as a man, and power in the abuse of women in his world who would not strike back. These women were bound by a code of racial and class loyalty and silence, a Colored Domestic Wall of Silence. Dorothy knew she had been Silent in that she did not report his abuse—and above all for owning a gun without a permit and threatening her. He—a member of the Police Department.

Joe Cephus could have become a sadistic serial rapist, but was channeled into Civil law. He recycled himself by donning a policeman's uniform. His wickedness led him to trample and exploit female persons hallowed in his world, representing productive advanced society—its teachers, the molders of its children, its children's keepers. His scorn propelled him to pursue women with magnificent plumages, tearing and shredding them to grace his depraved abode and become a part of his evil pageantry of personal pomp, to adulterate and bandage his personal stigma.— His reward was a sense of power, of manhood—.

Planned and calculated, Joe Cephus embraced "provoke and engage in battles you are certain to win with the least loss." He saw vestiges in lawful and unlawful arrests. Each time he went to the IRS, the room was filled with poor black people. He might have perceived—even known—that they also filled jails, prisons, and execution chambers, but it did not penetrate his Joe Cephus Meness. Even powerful industrialized countries advocated "provoke and engage in battles you are certain to win with the least loss —or with expendable loss," *including the country he claimed as his and had fought for.* There lay in him memory of hearing Dorothy and her friends discussing a politician's proposal some years ago that "China be attacked while it was weak, while it was a Sleeping

Dragon." He had mentioned it in the Police Department as if it had been his idea and had been met with agreement, not only about China, but with people, local and national. Joe Cephus had held his head higher and thought of going home that night to further enhance his status by seeing how long he could screw his wife, a college per-fesser. Nobody on the police force, white or colored, could do that but him.

Joe Cephus got along with Black men, but kept a distance from them. This absence of camaraderie, male heterosexual love and devotion, prevented his having Black male peer models. They surrounded him as closely as his fellow officers. However, Joe Cephus cloned himself. The result was incestuous, and its decayed residuals. He did not clash, differ, or bicker with Black men or white people. Dorothy recalled that during debatable discussions, he would say, "I don't talk much. Just lissen." He continued to show mild offense toward the fellow white officer who had assaulted him. Forgiveness was speedy, after a barely audible "Captain and the Union told me to say I'm sorry." Not that he himself the offender was sorry; however it had been followed by a Joe Cephus grin and the extension of his hand suspended so long that the Captain, Union official, and fellow officers began to wonder if the white offending officer would give it that brief, weak touch of a shake he finally gave . –White officers sniggered. Black officers, colored then, were beyond being embarrassed and told their wives. Joe Cephus had come home that night shouting and having sex with his wife.

After going underground, Dorothy's psyche became aware, and she made connection with her subterranean thoughts. As they surfaced, she recalled that Joe Cephus never had a male friend whom he would grasp in an embrace. He never spoke fondly of a buddy whose friendship began in high school or the army. He never mentioned the man who brought him to Granston. He avoided him, and after a while forgot his name. Once Dorothy asked about him and received a hostile reply as if her inquiry had been personal. On another occasion, she asked about his partner, the officer who would save his life and vice versa, only to be told, "Why you so inter-rest-ted in him? He gotta young, yellow wife. Look better then you ever did or ever will. Smarter then you, too. You not the smartest person in the world. God or whoever made you didn't throw 'way the mol'–." Trying to provoke a physical fight that he would surely win, he went on and on until Dorothy left the room to escape, and joined his mother on the porch. Joe Cephus had followed. "Walkin' out when I'm tellin' the truth. Gittin' mad 'cause I'm tellin' the truth. Can't stand to hear nobody say you not the smartest person." Then to his mother, "Mama, she mad 'cause I told her she wasn't' the smartest person in the world. Think she better then us." Conversations were almost always in that vein. Dorothy began to say what was absolutely necessary, to which he would respond, "Think you too good to talk to me 'cause you teach in a college." –There were no friendly telephone calls with a male. No going out with the boys. His going out was a show of power over her. Dorothy suspected that he dressed, went out and drove around alone for a short time, parking to keep from using gas. He always returned demanding sex.

Dorothy had searched for spiritual separateness in Joe Cephus apart from his chemistry. She never glimpsed that hidden archangel that she felt in other men she had known and observed.

Joe Cephus had laughed at the disturbed child Rhoda in "The Bad Seed," his only outward reaction to the movie. At times Dorothy had shuddered down through the years thinking of his laughter in a protracted monologue about his meeting a girl when he was in the army who was a virgin. He proposed to her, and as he said "relieved her of her cherry which she was too old to have anyway. She was twenty-three sayin' she 'savin' herself' for her husband." Then he told her he was married, a lie to end the relationship. Joe Cephus laughed as he told Dorothy how the girl cried. Later, he met her accidentally and "that girl started cryin' again," Joe Cephus laughed. Dorothy lay beside him almost in tears herself. Joe Cephus crawled on top of her, not like an animal—no, they are noble, only like himself, laughing,

"If I hadn't done it, some other soldier woulda laid her." Dorothy felt a presence in her heart and throat that passing years failed to dissolve.

Dorothy had heard and read that there was no completely evil character, no matter how despicable. There must be something virtuous about Joe Cephus. She closed her eyes in an effort to see: He was a successful police officer in that he retained his job until retirement. He was independent financially, and purchased a home and a car. He permitted his mother to stay with him when he could have used his house as bachelor quarters instead of taking girls to the back driveway of his Cousin Daisy's house when using the back seat of his car, where they would be safe from raids by white members of the Department in which he was the "first cullud hired." Aren't those virtues? Where was his spiritual side? Can it be that he went to church almost every Sunday and gave a dollar almost every Sunday? Oh, yes, he said his prayers at the foot of his bed every night, the way southern colored Christians are taught from childhood. When he would forget, he would hurriedly get out of bed, kneel and pray. Dorothy would watch the agitated look on his face as he told God how to run His business. Doesn't that count? Dorothy smiled over becoming facetious.

She also heard and believed there were Black people who simply did not like Black people. Of course there are white people who did not like white people. But there was supposed to be something *different* about Black people not liking each other: It was motivated by racial contempt and self-hatred, whereas white disapproval of each other was personal, directed at specific persons, not racial disdain and contempt. One example of a Black person's contempt for other Blacks is a prominent judicial figure, who is said to have intense hatred for other Blacks and sees them as reflections of himself. According to his home town people, he is ashamed of his Negroid physical characteristics that he finds unattractive, and is angry because he's from "the wrong side of the tracks" and rejected by the "right side of the tracks" Blacks. Rumors are that he abused his ex-wife, a Black woman, unmercifully, but purchased her silence, the silence that prominent Women Right's groups are still trying to penetrate. This man is also said to have contempt for Blacks whose academic inadequacies parallel his. One of his former coworkers tells a story of when this Prominent Figure occupied a simple office, he used to wear tight trousers and sit on his desk in a manner that "revealed the outline of his genitals."

How much does this Figure resemble aspects of Joe Cephus? The Prominent Figure is said to adore white people, or pretend successfully. Joe Cephus gave no indication of having any feeling for them akin to adoration–or even liking them, but he feared and respected white people. Apparently other than providing him with a job, they had no place in his life. Whom did Joe Cephus care about other than himself?

Dorothy began to wish she were not so curious about dissecting Joe Cephus, about performing this psychological biopsy. –Could he have absorbed behavior slave owners instilled in slaves?— Dorothy recalled the experiment with mice—casting a shadow that caused an outward change of color that after generations became genetic. There is another theory. Dorothy spoke aloud after the long period of silence.

"Jackie, have you heard that undetected and untreated birth defects can cause lifelong brain damage? And so can inadequate, prenatal care and prolonged malnutrition? Did your father ever talk about it?"

"Yes, a lot when educators were talking about 'Why Johnny Can't Read' and Black children's low test scores. Daddy said it can and does happen. Why?"

"Still doing a psychological biopsy on Joe Cephus. His behavior was just too bizarre, even for him. There is so much I haven't told."

"Why not tell all–?"

"Jackie, some I don't know how to tell. Some I don't tell because it might negate what people can and will believe. Some folks will wonder and think there must be something wrong with me to stay with him fifteen months. I question it myself. And, Jackie, as I say over and over, I didn't want him. I know how to want a man and it was no way near that. And I certainly did not want him for a husband."

"There it is." Jackie slowed down and pointed to Johnnye's house.

"The scene of the real crime." Dorothy looked closely. Maybe she'd see Joe Cephus' ghost at the window.

Contrary to sites chosen by upwardly mobile, colored teachers, now African Americans, Joe Cephus' and Johnnye's house was in the middle of the Black community, on a street that once boasted of being the Mecca for the Black upper class before they began moving to once-off-limit areas. The house was quite ordinary, part frame, part brick, two stories. Six or seven rooms, Dorothy surmised. She was familiar with the "her day" houses: living room, dining room, kitchen and pantry, master bedroom and bathroom downstairs; two bedrooms, one bath, and utility or office or storage or junk room upstairs; and, of course, a basement with laundry room, half bath, and space for parties. Johnnye and Joe Cephus certainly had not joined the contest among many Granston Black educators to see who could occupy a home with the most grandeur, splendor, and originality.

The house was Johnnye's shelter, Dorothy decided. Johnnye did not need a showplace for that. She had cornered Joe Cephus and held him at bay. Shelters were now established for abused women. Johnnye had provided her own. She deserved a tribute. Planning to include Johnnye's pragmatism in her novel, Dorothy searched for a special word and thought about Paule Marshall's 1983 novel *Praisesong for the Widow*. Dorothy had attended Marshall's book signing at Schomburg Library and gotten an autographed copy. Dorothy liked the word Praisesong. Johnnye was a widow. Praisesong to Johnnye for providing her own shelter according to her specifications and on her terms. She had acted wisely.

Wiser than I, Dorothy mused, as Jackie circled the block, making a turn that put them on a one way street.

"Oops," Jackie noticed. "Looks like every other street is one way –."

Dorothy thought of how Joe Cephus could have led her into a one way street.

CHAPTER 17

Dorothy Remembers Her Father's Early Warnings

While Jackie painstakingly tried to find the correct turn that would take them back to Johnnye's house, Dorothy didn't even notice, remembering how her father had tried so fervently to guide her away from domestic sewage. In spite of his being a massive influence, she had not heeded that alarm. From him she had learned how to love, how not to love, sometimes called rejection; how to succeed, and how to react to the absence of success, accepting the inevitable; how to assort life's experiences, placing them in manageable perspectives, coping with life's multiplicities. Dorothy smiled and closed her eyes so that she would really see and hear her father as he gave one of his lectures on love. It was a Luther-Joe Cephus warning she discovered during her Luther-Joe Cephus years. What that adoring father had not told her was how limited her choices were. He advised relentlessly that in college she would find a worthy, educated, colored man. Mr. Borden rarely approved of her male friends, reminding her that her selection of girlfriends was superior to her choice boyfriends. The same was true about selections her female friends made, which was not a compliment to their brotherhood of male choices.

Dorothy was about fourteen or fifteen years old. She had fallen in love again. She did not know then as she began to know in later years and was well aware of now, just as there are seas one should not attempt for pleasure swimming, there are people who are also proscribed. Mr. Borden, the lawyer and philosopher, said there are consequences for disobeying a law of physics, and a person should conduct him or herself as if all life is based on physics, which indeed it is.

Dorothy sealed her ears to disquiet and heard her father's voice: "That boy has *nothing* to lose, and everything to gain. He is a zero Negro." Mr. Borden bellowed his favorite description of his daughter's latest choice.

"You always say that!" Dorothy had reminded him.

"Because it's always true. His father is zero, and his mother is zero. Two zeroes equal zero. Don't permit yourself to love somebody like that."

"*Permit* myself!"

"Yes. *Permit yourself!*"

"*You mean control who I love?*"

"*Whom* I love—Of course. If you don't, you're a damn fool."

"Did you–?"

"Of course: I married your mother. I only associated with women of her caliber."

Dorothy had not only permitted herself to associate *love* with her father's reification of zeros, she had done worse. She had permitted herself to *marry them*.

Dorothy held her breath as if the action reversed time and she could undo—untangle the done and tangled. She understood what her father meant and had for years, but was unable to put understanding in reading-words. Upon assorting and placing information in perspective, she could apply zero, a relative symbol, to the equation of her life. Luther was zero because he subtracted what she considered positive from her life and offered no acceptable addition. Unable to make a division of her self, Dorothy remained whole. Luther could not deal with entirety. Like Joe Cephus, but in a more tolerable way, Luther was also seeking a woman to be sparkling sequins in his discolored, tattered blankets.

As for Joe Cephus, in application to Dorothy's equation, mutation took place in arithmetic logic. Like fractions, the Human Equation can be reduced to its lowest terms —as it happened with Joe Cephus in relation to Dorothy Borden. She also knew that he would have reduced her to *her* lowest terms: a foul-mouthed, physically and mentally abused housekeeper, laundress, cook, and incubator for unwanted offspring; she would also be his main source of income who supplied fresh, pure butter and gourmet honey for the stale loaf of bread he begrudgingly doled out, with a frown etched so deep it must reach inside. She would be supplier of brick and marble, trees and fauna for a house and home for *him* because he had a minuscule plot of ground that she had successfully expanded after negotiating with white Real Estate Agents, asking them to please permit her to buy the adjoining plot, white men he refused to approach, but slapped and cursed her when she did, with accusations of screwing them to get the additional land that provided a place worthy of him. After work, he would come home, pick his nose, sit and read obituaries, his feet propped on the Ottoman she brought from Turkey that she dragged until a stranger helped her to the car, a man Joe Cephus said she had to be screwing. The Ottoman was too heavy for Joe Cephus—he didn't lift heavy things since it would break a man down, and he wouldn't able to function, and she'd have an excuse to continue screwing around. Joe Cephus would sit and rest and read about who drank homemade whiskey and died. He would then get up to criticize her performing her unpaid, thankless second job, the one at home, and demand to know in minutes when the food would be ready. "It oughta be soon because I don't want to eat so late and go to bed on a full stomach. It's bad for my stomach, and worse for doing what you married me for." He would smile at his crotch. Then snarl because he was tired of sitting and waiting while she set the table, etc., etc., etc.

Her second domestic job complete, he would belch, scratch

his crotch, look at it fondly, tell her to hurry and bathe and don't use too much water. Without a bath, he was a man, he would get into bed and wait for her to perform her third and greatest nightmare of all: going to bed with him, either a silent angry or raging Head of His House. –Above all, she would become so bogged down in the mire and muck of a Joe Cephus-life that she would cease the search for Shangri-La. –But would retain enough of her self to mourn that her ideas and creativity were also sinking into Joe Cephus created muck and mire. He would smile and be superbly happy because he did not need or want a woman with something he didn't know anything about, such as ideas and creativity. She would be no use to him. He would adjust his crotch with J.C. automation, contented that he would spend the rest of his life with a woman people would meet as Per-fesser Divine. He would let her know she was not Dorothy Borden and would never be again. He was the only man, colored or white, in all of Granston who had a wife like his. Thus Dorothy saw what would have been her life with Joe Cephus.

Dorothy also thought of life's being based on Laws of Physics in relation to Joe Cephus. He had attempted to defy a simple law. "No two bodies can occupy the same space at the same time." He had tried to occupy Dorothy–her life–and she had already occupied her self–and filled her life with dreams, plans, ambitions, fantasies, and her never-ending search.

Dorothy felt that she had surpassed compromising herself by not terminating the marriage to Joe Cephus the day he kicked her, and for not ending her marriage to Luther the night he threatened to put her manuscript on the dumbwaiter unless she came to bed immediately. But she had. Physically. And never went to bed with him again mentally. She had heard of married people staying together who did not want each other and in some cases hatred each other. These unions lasted sometimes for life. Dorothy had declared she could not understand such stupidity and vowed it would never happen to her. Yet it had. Twice. Five years of her life between the two men, five years of living in a gas chamber, or under a noose, or sitting in an electric chair. Floundering on Death Row.

Dorothy tried to explain it to herself. Maybe it was like making a purchase you wish you had not made, and you keep putting off returning it. It is too hideous to give away, and you are ashamed of having made such an obnoxious selection. You keep it because you *paid* for it. You don't want anyone to have it because it is *yours*. Perhaps you fear it might bring consolation to another owner. Something so repulsive must not comfort anyone. Instead of returning the merchandise, you keep it until the money-back period expires. You put it away. It is yours–in all its uselessness, ugliness, pain, its occupying needed space. It is a reminder of your disgust with yourself, a flagellation. As long as that detestable purchase occupies a space, you can never make another one.

She was finally back to the Now-Granston, for Dorothy heard a Now-voice. BACK. "Dottie, they had the front yard landscaped, and the back is fenced in so the dogs can't get out." Jackie was finally back to Johnnye's and Joe Cephus' house. "There's nothing else to see except the back yard with all the trees–and you can see where they had cookouts." BACK—

But Dorothy saw Joe Cephus' ghost.

CHAPTER 18
They Finally Reach the New Police Department

Jackie drove faster. "Our next stop is the new Police Headquarters." They headed for what was called Central Granston.

"I had forgotten you said we were going," Dorothy replied. "Since it's new, Joe Cephus' ghost won't be there. But I've heard that sometimes spirits haunt new places, too."

"Do you believe in ghosts?" Jackie asked.

"I'm not sure." Dorothy smiled. "I like mystery. I really had such a good time believing in Santa Claus, fairyland, the tooth fairy, magic—and little Irish specters. I replaced them with flying saucers, E T.'s, other Dimensions—and ghosts. Not the childhood 'spooks' and 'hants.' But real grown people's ghosts. Jackie, I still use the old southern word 'hant' for haunt. – Maybe a lot of things exist in other Dimensions. I had a dog that could see an unseen world. She communicated with a close family friend who had committed suicide. I'll tell you about it sometime—and about another dog who lay in bed with his terminally ill master and the pet's reaction the moment his master died."

After a brief pause, Jackie ventured cautiously, "Dottie, have you thought that trying to find out about Joe Cephus' death might not meet certain people's approval, and they might try to put a stop to it? You said yourself Granston can be ruthless."

"Yes. Somebody else mentioned it to me– when I told them my story plot was based on rumors."

"If – Johnnye did what people said she did to John Henry and Joe Cephus, she might–do the same to you. Or get one of her–women–to do something–"

"That is what somebody else said."

"Aren't you scared?" Jackie asked. "I am."

You were always scared of almost everything, Dorothy thought, but said, "I'll be cautious . –About eating at parties . –And I was paranoid enough to add a clause to my Living Will asking that an autopsy be performed–and listed persons to question if anything abnormal is found–and gave brief, but descriptive statements, as to the reasons the person is suspect. If anybody is guilty, the quieter they keep the better. I have no reason to indict anybody. I just want to write a novel that will sell. It might be therapeutic also. I've never been to a psychiatrist. Just used writing for therapy. My characters are composites–and as I stated, any resemblance is purely coincidence . –Besides, what about folks in Granston who told me things? Nobody has bothered them."

"Dee talks, but really just whispers. People don't take Dee seriously. You are *not* Dee and you are *not* whispering."

Dorothy remained determined to continue searching Granston's forbidden lacuna for glimpses of Granston's secrets.

"Here it is." Jackie sighed with relief when they reached the Police Headquarters. She felt safer. "I made some wrong turns. Rev says if I ever make correct turns, he'll know it's time for my Last Supper."

"Does he get angry?" Dottie thought how furious Joe Cephus became and slapped her when he tried to teach her to drive.

"No. He thinks it's funny. I believe he asks me to drive just to tease me. One time he told me to make a turn, and I did two blocks later. He laughed and said if I missed heaven like that I'd end up where he's trying to keep people from going."

The two women looked carefully where the car was parked so they wouldn't forget.

"Jackie, has Rev ever hit you or threatened to?"

Jackie stopped walking in surprise. "No. Why?"

"I was just wondering. Are you telling the truth?"

"Yes. I'd tell you if he did. If Rev ever hit me, I'd think he'd lost his mind. It doesn't have anything to with his being a preacher either. If he were a –well-anything–a gambler, he wouldn't."

"Does he or did he every make you have sex when you didn't want to?"

"No. He just acts quiet and pitiful– or gets up and reads, or tells me why we should. That ends up as a joke because I tell him why we shouldn't. We have a debate and a rebuttal. He's funny to be a preacher–when we're by ourselves."

"Do you every get angry with each other?" Dorothy asked.

"Not much. Maybe once or twice a year if that often. Come to think about it, we've never been really angry." Jackie smiled. "One time he stopped talking to me. I don't remember what it was about–might have been about my turning my back in bed –or maybe I almost had an accident. Or let a fast-talking salesman sell me a lemon. I still do. And buy something just because it's on sale . –Rev gets after me about that. We don't disagree too much. When we do, we just don't talk for a while."

"Who makes up–who starts talking again?"

Jackie thought for a while. "I'm not sure. He is the one who does most of the talking anyway. Dottie, we don't do things to make each other mad. I don't think we try not to. We just don't without trying. Remember that old song 'I want That Sunday Kind of Love?' That's what we both like."

Dottie wondered if a marriage to someone like Rev would have worked for her. But knew it wouldn't.

"You are lucky, Jackie," Dottie said sincerely.

They reached the Main Building. For Granston, a worthy structure Dorothy told Jackie, who suggested they go inside and take a tour. They did. White officers smiled and called them Miss. A black man seated at a computer looked up, smiled and continued to work. Another Black uniformed officer entered, bowed sternly,

267

filed papers, and left. One of the white officers joked, "Did ya'll come to turn yourself in or for us to arrest somebody?"

Dorothy responded pleasantly, "Neither. Granston is our hometown, and I lived here years ago before these Headquarters were built." She introduced Jackie, and the officers said they "knew that fine husband of hers, who was instrumental in trying to establish PAL." Dorothy introduced herself as Borden. If they read or heard she was a writer, they didn't say. The officers were young, but said they had heard some of the older officers speak of Lawyer Borden. She did not mention that she was once married to one of the first Black officers hired by the Department.

Two friendly, white officers introduced themselves, Sergeant Lucas Redmond and Lieutenant David Mack, and volunteered to be their personal tour guides. Dorothy immediately noticed large photographs of uniformed men lining walls of the corridor and the first was a Black officer. When she paused to read the inscription, Sergeant Redmond explained, "This part is our Hall of Honor. The first man to qualify was a Black officer, Sergeant Reece Greenwood, one of the first three hired when the Force integrated. Bob was awarded the Merit of Honor for his service beyond the call of duty. Unfortunately, he died of a heart attack a few years after he retired."

There was a picture of the first integrated Force. There he was–Officer Joe Cephus Devine. That same mustache she remembered in a face that people said was good-looking, but still to her resembled a Rhesus monkey.

"That guy there," Lieutenant Mack indicated another Black officer "is James Milford. We all loved Jim and cried like babies at his funeral. He was cited for community service with children and teenagers. That guy had all kinda mixed teams: Black and White, girls and boys. Baseball, basketball, football."

They continued, "William Hunt, the first Black Chief. He's still alive; and Frank Patterson, he died trying to save another Officer's life."

Pleased to see African American men represented, and wanting to find out what had been said about Joe Cephus, Dorothy asked if they had a written history of the Department. Officer Mack told the ladies that the historian was working on it, but there was some material available she could pick up on her way out. Dorothy hoped photos were included, and smiled over noticing at her age that policemen were usually good-looking and that she still admired men in uniform.

There was more to see: "That's the interrogation room," the Lieutenant pointed out. "Folks ask if we beat or torture suspects to get confessions or information. No."

Dorothy had heard too much and lived too long to believe him. "What is that big lamp used for?" She asked.

"Light."

"Do you need *that* much light?"

"It's the only light in here, and there are no windows."

Dorothy started to ask why, but the officers were so nice and she really knew the reason for the ultra bright light.

The women saw that the cells were clean and equipped with bunk beds and flushing commodes. There was a room filled with all kinds of guns. "No, they were not for swat units or riot control. This is *Granston*. We don't need all that. "Library?" They were informed this is a jail not prison, but there was a visitors' room with books detainees could read. The officers led Dorothy and Jackie to the back parking area. An African American officer got out of a squad car he was driving. A White officer got out and followed him into the building. –In reply to Dorothy's questions, no, they did not have dogs or horses. But with the rise in drug traffic, they were seriously considering adding a Canine Force . –Yes, indeed, they had female officers, a Black woman and two White women; in addition, two Black and two White women were attending the Training Academy.

Inside again, the officers offered Dorothy and Jackie coffee or tea from a new dispenser. They declined, stating there were lots of other places to visit. Still smiling and pleasant, the men assured the visitors they were welcome anytime and should come back to meet the Chief–and the female Officers.

Dorothy picked up a small thin brochure on their way out. There was a blurred picture of the first three African American officers to join the Force standing in front of the old building. Their names were listed. If she had not known Joe Cephus, she would not have recognized him. He was the only one with a mustache.

Dorothy envisioned how proud Joe Cephus would be. Not only that his picture was still around, but that Black policemen had the same rights now that White policemen had–at least they had been granted the right to have rights. –He could even *arrest* white suspects or perpetrators, instead of detaining them until white officers arrived. –She pictured Joe Cephus avoiding confrontation with white suspects and perpetrators whatever the cost, and never *never* approaching a white woman. To preserve his ego, he would "pull his rank" with brutal force on Black petty offenders, the ragged vagrant and the parking violator in a used and reused again and again car. The Black woman? In absence of witnesses or witnesses too scared to tell, or who didn't care, or who thought since he was a "po-leece" whatever he did was right, would he kick the ill-clothed, suspected cheap, almost hungry prostitute, or draw his gun on her or handcuff her–hands behind her back–never tight enough. Would he verbally abuse and "throw the book" at the Black unattractive female violator after finding out she wasn't married and worked in the mill or for unknown white people, this woman whom he had circled the block meticulously watching, fearing she would come back in time to put the next to her last dime in the parking meter? She was about two seconds too late. *I GOT YOU GODDAMMIT. Don't think you can break the law and get away with it because you cul-lud and I'm cul-lud.*

As they left the building, Dorothy looked up at the window. Joe Cephus' wraith was not there. She wondered what happened to the small gun he brandished and used to threaten her. Thinking again, she should have reported him, a policeman violating a gun law, but she and Joe Cephus both knew she was "too classy" for public exposure and embarrassment. She wasn't now. This is tell-all time. Joe Cephus' mother said that the gun had been pawned to him by a mill maintenance worker with a house full of children when Joe Cephus worked in the mill. She had begged him to return it, but he had increased the interest so that the man was never able to pay him. Did it become a part of his legacy to Johnnye Jamison? —Johnnye Jamison, the potter, the sculptor, whatever else she might be.

CHAPTER 19

Dorothy Borden's Early Teachers

Resuming their tour of Granston, Dorothy thought of her early molders, whatever else they might have been, who helped fix utopianism in her self so skillfully that its vestiges remained during her cycles of becoming and remained in her present cycle. Dorothy wondered how much of this deification was also a part of Johnnye Jamison, a part that only her students perceived and would at some date in the future utilize. Who said in essence "Men [and women] years after tell what manner of men [women] their school masters [mistresses] were"?

Dorothy remembered in colorful musical sequences her elementary school paragons and mentors, who appointed a different child to lead Devotions each morning before the first class session. Each student said a Bible verse and was proud to have learned a new one, the class sang a hymn and then stood and recited The Lord's Prayer in unison. Sometimes there would be a religious solo by one of the talented or not so talented children. They were all colored and Baptist, or Methodist, Holiness, Sanctified, or a derivative. It was the grade school teacher who reinforced standing when they heard the very first chord of "Lift Every Voice and Sing," and fixed in them that it was "The Negro National Anthem." These mentors told their classes a colored man named

James Weldon Johnson wrote the heart-rending words, and his brother Rosemond Johnson set them to music. Even to this day Dorothy Borden stood when she heard this anthem, sometimes the only African American or one of the very few standing, feeling betrayed and sad because the singer had "modernized" the "Negro National Anthem."

—And these classroom counselors had health inspections each morning to see if teeth had been brushed and fingernails and clothes were clean. Before innovations began casting away their devotions and morning inspections, these gurus taught their little disciples to recite "Little Brown Baby" and "In De Morning" by another colored man, Paul Lawrence Dunbar, preparing the little innocents to present assembly programs for the entire school to witness. Above all, programming them for life. Dorothy recalled she had learned a large portion of the poem "Imagination" by Phillis Wheatley, who Negroes at that time called the first Negro poet. Dorothy smiled remembering the praise she received from teachers and her parents who destined her for fame and greatness.

Those were the gone-now days when as children they had loved their elementary school teachers so that it caused a strange twinge in not-yet-ready hearts and saw with eyes not yet blinded by adult daylight that their teachers were so pretty and wore such pretty clothes and smelled so good and thought their mentors were perfect without knowing the semantics of the word perfect. Those were the days when no colored child Dorothy knew would dare say a "bad word" around a grown person. What if their teachers found out! It would be as bad as their mothers and fathers knowing. Even worse. Mothers and fathers whipped them and told them to shut up and made them eat what they didn't like, especially mamas who didn't dress up unless they were going to town or it was Sunday. They were not so unblemished, even though the children did not know the word, they understood it, as teachers who wore pretty clothes all the time and never did things that mamas and daddies did.

On cold days, children circled close to their favorite protectors to keep them warm when they had duty on the playground during recess, and fanned them on hot days and went to the cafeteria for ice water covered with paper towels to keep out germs. And these grown people who knew so much must have lots of money because they sent children to the cafeteria for their lunches and ate more than just vegetable soup. They watched them eat salmon salad and dessert. Teachers never ate pinto beans. Children did because beans filled them up. And while these pretty, sweet smelling ladies ate, their students told them family secrets and about plays they had seen in church like "Slab Town Convention" that was funny and "Ethiopia at the Bar" that was serious. These different grown people always listened to everything, especially to what the lady next door said about the preacher, unlike mothers and fathers who didn't always hear or understand, and warned them "not to talk about things like that" when children told mamas and daddies secrets classmates said were true–and bad–about other children's mamas and daddies.

When elementary school days ended and they graduated and became grownup, or almost, and went to Frederick Douglass High School, there was the thrill of seeing men with roll books standing behind desks. They didn't always call the roll, and you could cut class if you were bad or had the nerve, or if your parents didn't do anything about it if they found out. But only bad boys cut class. Often the only man in elementary school was the esteemed principal whom the children feared more than God or the "boogerman."

At Frederick Douglass there was brilliant Mr. Harriman, who taught with a style that solidified history classes in Dorothy's mind. He always had a story or anecdote about historical personages. Despite the passing of over sixty years, Dorothy still heard and smelled Hannibal's elephants as the mighty African General won acclaim leading the "most celebrated exploit in military history." Mr. Harriman etched psychological portraits of Haitian Generals Toussaint L'Ouverture and Dessalines, whose military strategy is practiced today. –Dorothy heard sounds of Demosthenes down by the sea his mouth filled with pebbles competing with its roar to overcome a speech impediment. Dorothy still held on to the image of Diogenes with a lantern at midday searching for an honest man . –And Mr. Harriman's lilting voice pleasantly haunted her, "After circumnavigating the globe, Vasco da Gama was rewarded with a glimpse of the Pacific." Mr. Harriman shocked his class also, especially the day a student announced that history was boring. The exciting Mr. Harriman told about Henry VIII, his wives and his having two of them, Anne Bolyn and Katherine Howard, beheaded, and about Marie Antoinette, the Russian Revolution, mesmerizing them with the story of Anastasia. –He adroitly wove a tapestry of Lucrezia Borgia that captivated eyes, ears, and imagination. The class had stared at him.

Alternate semesters Mr. Harriman fascinated classes with Ancient History and told of the Great Pyramids and Khufu or Cheops and King Tut. Dorothy told him and promised herself she would visit all of those places and more. She did.

Mr. Nesmith charmed classes with his physics lectures interlacing stories of a lost art, "the invention of a mirror that could snatch the sun's rays and focus them upon an approaching vessel and burn it up at sea." And Mr. Nesmith told of Archimedes and his words "Eureka! Eureka!" The words echoed when Dorothy made a discovery. Mr. Nesmith led them to Copernicus, Galileo, and Newton which led to experiments that led to students becoming fragments of physicists long gone and those to come–even for only minutes. Such is the essence of becoming.

Teachers had to be cautious about what they told students in classrooms, but Miss Browning, Dorothy's favorite, who taught English and science, discretely told them that "one day babies would be grown in bottles." Dorothy had pictured babies in bottles that a person could watch grow and then plant like flowers, only it would be a baby garden. Years later, Dorothy would associate Miss Browning's statement with test tube babies.

Both Miss Peterson and Mr. Carlyle taught required Negro

History during different semesters. Not yet accustomed to male gurus, even though only men taught math, just as only women taught French, Dorothy remembered girls hoped to be placed in Mr. C's, they called him, Negro History class. He was so handsome, almost as good-looking as shy Mr. Norman, who blushed as he taught algebra and geometry. Whether Mr. Carlyle or Miss Peterson, students learned about Timbuktu and that it was *not* a place to tell people to go to instead of hell. Timbuktu was once the seat of learning, the site of ancient and renowned Timbuktu University when Europe was a frozen hunk of ice. Students tasted the history of Africa and of American slavery and learned about Sojourner Truth, Harriet Tubman, Nat Turner, Denmark Vessey, Frederick Douglass, Booker T. Washington, W. E. B. Dubois, George Washington Carver, and so many Negroes who were inventors and everything else and more. Their text, Carter G. Woodson's *The Negro in Our History,* took its place as another one of Dorothy's favorites.

Sponsors, male and female, coached interested protégés in oratory, and they entered colored Statewide contests, orating speeches by men in their text: Washington, Dubois, and Douglass. There were debates, serious and humorous. And clubs, the two most popular were the Louise Beavers Dramatic Club and the Roland Hayes Singers. Yes, the renowned tenor Roland Hayes was colored. Miss Browning had been instrumental in naming the Dramatic Club in honor of a female instead of Richard B. Harrison. Harrison, who was the first to play the role of De Lawd in "The Green Pastures," also taught at A. & T. College where the auditorium was named in his honor. Students knew him also from Negro History classes. The Roland Hayes Singers featured songs by colored men whose names were also in Woodson's text: Harry T. Burleigh and Will Marion Cook. The choir Director, Mr. Stan Jefferson, would say "the next rendition was arranged by Noah F. Ryder," also colored. On Sunday afternoons the choir was allowed to broadcast over the local radio for fifteen magnificent minutes, for which Dorothy arranged or rearranged her activities in order not to miss. Mr. Jefferson recited between songs, poems like "If," "Invictus," and "The House by the Side of the Road," including poems by colored writers Langston Hughes, Countee Cullen, and many others in that great anthology *The Negro Caravan*. Dorothy turned the radio volume louder when Mr. Jefferson recited "I Want to Die While You Love Me" by a colored woman Georgia Douglas Johnson, and Dorothy wrote a love poem, or something like it, to a boy she would meet someday. Mr. Jefferson's voice would take on soul-form and melt into Dorothy's soul. She would never know an epiphany akin to the ones her teachers provided. –And she knew if only for a moment that it was all right to be colored.

That moment extended the first day of class when Dorothy became a college student. The professor looking at his roll sounded out *MISS BORDEN*. Dorothy looked up and realized it was her name. No one had ever called her *MISS*. She was Miss Borden now. She felt like Miss Borden and liked the feeling.

CHAPTER 20

Hubert Julian, the Black Eagle

Back to the present, Dorothy asked, "What teacher do you remember most in high school, Jackie?"

'Miss Browning. She was our Senior Advisor."

"Mine too, and my favorite. She helped Thomasena and me with stories and poems and advised us never go give up writing—and of course reading. She left Douglass for a college job in Virginia, and I lost contact. She would be in her nineties now. It's hard for me to think of some people dying, like Daddy, Mama, George, Jr., and Miss Browning. And even Joe Cephus. —Were you at the meeting when Miss Browning told the seniors about Hubert Julian, the Black Eagle, challenging Hitler to a duel? Thomasena said Miss Browning told the class the story during a senior class meeting."

"Yes. I never heard of Hubert Julian until then. He visited A. & T, while I was at Bennett—in 1943 or 44. I went to hear him, and felt so proud because I had heard about him before."

"I thought my Daddy and Miss Browning were the most informed people in the world. Smarter than Einstein," Dorothy laughed. "Later, I heard Colonel Julian lecture in New York three times. He talked about the duel and also his healthy lifestyle. He was so handsome. I immediately had a crush on him." Dorothy recalled Thomasena's version of Miss Browning's story:

The class artist, Victor Miller, wanted to be an airplane pilot. Waiting for Miss Browning so they could begin the meeting, Victor drew a picture of himself on the blackboard in the cockpit of an ultra modern airplane he designed. Victor printed USA across the fuselage.

Seniors, class of 1941, reminded him that America did not have colored pilots.

"I'll go where they do." Victor put finishing touches on his picture of himself in the future. He erased USA.

"Where is that?–Must be another world–" the boys told Victor.

"Maybe not." The group looked around. Miss Browning was standing in the doorway listening. She walked to the front of the class and began telling them about Hubert Fauntleroy Julian, known as The Black Eagle. He was a veteran of the United States Armed Forces, a former Colonel in the Ethiopian Air Force, and a former Captain in the Finish Air Forces.

"I can join up with him!" Victor had beamed.

Miss Browning smiled. "I can tell you how to contact him, and you can ask him where he got his training and experience."

"Tell us more about Hubert Julian," the seniors begged.

Miss Browning told them about Colonel Julian's hearing of insults Hitler hurled at Negroes and challenged him to a duel. Hitler was no pilot, so Julian challenged his Air Minister Hermann Goering in a cable from New York to Berlin, September 13, 1940.

"What were the insults?" The class asked.

"All Negroes were half apes and baboons and should be imprisoned in special camps," she told the now angry senior class.

"What did Colonel Julian say in the cable?" They asked.

Miss Browning had received a rare copy of Colonel Julian's proposed confrontation from the famous Schomburg Library in

Harlem, N.Y. The class sat transfixed as the Senior Advisor related the essence of his message.

"Colonel Julian, along with thousands of Black scientists and intellectuals, resented the dastardly insult from the Chancellor of the Reich. I remember Colonel Julian's words. 'I therefore challenge and defy you Herman Goering, head of the Nazi Air Force, to meet me, Hubert Fauntleroy Julian, at ten thousand feet above the English Channel to fight an aerial duel to avenge this cowardly insult to the honor of my race, thirty days from date with neutral correspondents as references.'"

They all heard the silence before the burst of, "What happened?"

"Did they fight?"

"Who won?"

"At a press conference," Miss Browning continued, "Julian said, 'I'll show that lousy nothing divided by nothing.'"

The class laughed, but more anxious to know the outcome.

Well, Miss Browning told them, "The following Saturday, Colonel Julian's frightened wife told him that he had received a call from a man in Washington who said, 'This is the military attaché of the German Embassy. Tell that black swine his challenge has been accepted and to be on the spot as promised. Never fear. I'll be there.'"

"Did they meet?" The seniors wanted to know.

"Colonel Julian set the date, October 15, 1940. However, the German Embassy denied Goering had accepted. In addition, British officials informed Colonel Julian 'they could not allow such a duel to take place, however noble. There was just too much dog-fighting between the Royal Air Force and the Luftwaffe.' Dog-fighting as you know is combat between airplanes."

"Ahh-hh," the class responded disappointed. They loved Joe Louis' winning over white men and knew Colonel Julian would win.

"Have you ever seen Colonel Julian?"

"How does he look?"

Miss Browning smiled. "Twice. At Schomburg in Harlem and the Harlem Y. He's very attractive, and looks years younger than he is–about thirty-three then."

Douglass High School Class of 1941 applauded Colonel Hubert Julian. Victor Miller saw himself bringing down enemy planes and returning to America as a transport pilot. Hitler had called them apes and baboons. Sometimes the class referred to themselves jokingly as spooks. In his next article in the "A Senior Speaks" column, Victor suggested that they refer to themselves as Colored or Negroes, and not as "spooks" or "Dee"–and never use the word "nigger," even in jokes among themselves. Colonel Hubert Julian would certainly agree.

Jackie interrupted Dorothy's reverie. "Victor Miller became an Architectural Engineer for a big company in California according to Douglass Alumni News. He's retired now, and has a son who's a Draftsman, the other an artist teaching in a college in California, and his daughter does scientific research in a laboratory in California. I'll show you the article if I still have it."

Dorothy knew Miss Browning would be proud. She had been Senior Advisor so many years, seeing all shades of Black, Brown, and Not-Black and Not-Brown faces glowing in anticipation of their glorious future. This class, these young boys were so self-assured in their Negro-hood, especially now that they heard about the Black Eagle. Dorothy knew what they wanted to be: a lawyer, a doctor, an engineer, a detective, a policeman, a judge.

And Dorothy saw the girls as Miss Browning had–with their 1941 It-Is-Great-To-Be-Colored aura. What would happen to it? Would their beautiful Colored confidence disintegrate in marriage to men with incomes so low that the aura would be buried? Girls who wanted to become beauticians would realize their goal; secretaries would scramble for jobs in colored public schools and insurance companies. Nurses would have jobs as long as there were colored hospitals. And some girls would attend land grant teachers colleges. Selected boys would attend land grant technical and agricultural colleges.

Former students also went in droves to New York, Chicago, and Detroit. Many of them contributed to the creation of more and larger ghettoes, promoting slums, and accepting low wages. –And many did not.

"That's the way it was." Dorothy said aloud as she released the gas pedal of her Back-in-Time-Machine, put on brakes, and parked again in the present.

CHAPTER 21

Black Middle-class Students and Test Results

"Let me take you to brunch, Jackie. Too late for brunch. Dinner. Aren't you hungry? You never use to be. I was always ready to eat, and still am. Let's go to one of the integrated restaurants."

"We'll have to. The best colored ones are closed. Nothing left but what we call greasy spoons that cater to colored people who won't go to white places." Jackie, like some older Black people, had never completely given up saying "colored." "Big Shot Blacks–I mean African Americans like you and me go to white places. A status symbol," Jackie joked.

Dorothy knew it was true and missed the colored atmosphere of her hometown. She recalled that "but we all colored" ambiance. In church, at parties, conventions, graduations, somebody would say, "Some of us got more money than others, more education, better houses, or even be better looking. Some got lighter skin and good hair. But we all colored." Everybody would laugh, look around, and laugh some more. How we loved each other, Dorothy thought. What happened to us?—

A greasy spoon would be different. Dorothy had traveled so much and lived in Greenwich Village so long, and associated with such a diversity of nationalities that she had saturated herself on varieties of strange and exotic foods and health fads. Eating real high-blood pressure, cholesterol-raising, old fashioned soul food would be like going to a party. Like occasional partying, it would not harm her health the short time she'd be in Granston and would certainly add to her soul and spirit. Besides, she had low blood pressure all her life and an amazing digestive system. "I don't mind going to a greasy spoon," Dorothy told Jackie.

"I do." Jackie was uncomfortable. "Rev would have a fit."

Even though Dorothy still preferred a colored place, she suggested, "Let's go to that sterile place where the Tillmans went–you know that white colored family. They went before integration. After they had eaten, Mr. Tillman asked to see the manager and told him, 'You have just served a Negro family,' and the manager shouted, 'GET OUT! I don't want Niggers in my restaurant, Black or White.'"

"I remember." Jackie smiled, paused, and became sober again. "I'll take you there if you really want to go, but I don't like going to eat where we're not wanted. Supposed they spit in our food. Lots of people have AIDS. Dottie, after all these years, they still don't want us around. They serve us, but it's just a law. Rev and I go where there is a cafeteria, and I can see what we're getting. Rev says I'm paranoid. Rather that than sorry. And I don't see that I'm missing anything–not eating where I'm not wanted. They have the same things we have at home, only ours tastes better. And cleaner. As for salads, Rev makes them–almost as good and pretty as the ones your Daddy use to make. I remember your Daddy made some for our Deb parties when each Deb had to bring something. And for birthday dinners you had."

Dorothy felt solemn as always when thinking of time then and when. They would go to a time-then-and-when-place. "Jackie, you turned me off. Let's go to a colored–I mean African American place in Greensboro. The one on Market Street. I read something about its history and survival in *Jet* magazine. People talked about that restaurant when we were growing up. It was small then, but all we had and we were proud of it even though we didn't go. Like Club 709 in Winston-Salem. I used to want to go there so badly.

When I got old enough, I was too old–and was disappointed. What's the name of the place in Greensboro? As well as I know, it slipped my mind. That ever happens to you?"

"All the time. Royal Oasis. A. and T. College students help keep it operating, Rev says. When I was a student at Bennett, we couldn't go to any public place. Neither could A. & T. girls. Rev says he's glad rules have changed that way. He's into promoting Black businesses. We go a lot for us. On Birthdays, Valentine's Day, after shopping together, and when neither one of us wants to cook." Jackie accelerated her driving a bit. "I'll call from there and let him know where we are and about how long we'll be out. Rev and I always call if one of us is away a long time." Jackie changed directions heading toward the highway. "Did you and Joe Cephus do that?"

"No. I doubt if such a courtesy entered his mind. Jackie, Joe Cephus was too bent on trying to make me think he was a ladies' man. And he was not polite and courteous –to me. Just to white people and colored men. He ignored colored women–unless she was somebody he wanted to flirt with." Dorothy continued. "My daughter and I have always called each other. Just like Daddy and Mama. –And Mr. Asian and I did, and we weren't married or living together. I used to call him from work, and tell him I'd be late, so if he called me at home, he'd know. He did the same for me. Even when he stayed at the restaurant playing cards with the employees. – I like to be courteous –I like genuine concern. I like being a nice person– Joe Cephus ridiculed it. Jackie, I want to know *why* so badly. Almost as badly as I want to know the reason he married the woman he had to know was guilty of the sex act he found so–so repulsive– and with the man he found equally as –as unacceptable."

Jackie remained silent until she asked softly, "Are you going to include it in the book you're writing?"

"Yes –and try to get it over to readers that it is more than Joe Cephus didn't approve and was angry. You and I grew up in the colored culture–and oral sex was taboo. In fact, no one we knew took it seriously. It was a joke. At school, children used to say if you want to insult a colored man and make him kill you and your mama, play the dozens, call him a bastard, or a cock sucker. That's what we called a woman's vagina. We'd laugh and say he'd be upset because what you said about his mama was probably true, more than likely he was a bastard, and the other thing meant he couldn't do it 'the right way' and had to resort to something nasty. –As many jam sessions we girls had in college, we talked about *everything*. I remember girls confessed a lot, but two things never came up: oral sex and interracial dating. I don't think anybody thought about either. Jackie, I've never seen anybody so irate as Joe Cephus was."

"Did he ever talk about it? Try to explain?" Jackie asked.

"*Never!* And never apologized. He acted as if it never happened. He did not respond when I mentioned it. But he got meaner."

"What would you say?" Jackie asked.

They were on the highway now. Dorothy calculated it would take Jackie at least two hours to reach the restaurant in Greensboro. It didn't matter. They could talk. "I talked about the kicking," Dorothy responded. "In subtle ways sometimes. I called him mule, and got the Mule Train record. I never let him forget that he kicked me and why he did it. Jackie, I hold on to things, negative as well as positive. Part of being a writer. Remembering. 'The pen is mightier than the sword.' Joe Cephus used the sword; I the pen."

"Since you stayed, you should have, as Rev would say, allowed healing to take place."

"There would have been no healing. Not with Joe Cephus. And my being the way I am. He inflicted wound after wound. None of them had time to get well. I made subtle remarks because I was good at it, and innocent of his accusations. I resent being accused when guilty. Accusation is unforgivable when I'm not."

Dorothy noticed the 'it's-going-to-get-dark-soon' warning and remembered Jackie's saying she did not like to drive at night. It would certainly be night when they got back to Granston. The signs along the highway were becoming shadowy. She should keep Jackie occupied. Not with talk about Joe Cephus. Enough was enough. Oh, yes, Dorothy had almost forgotten to ask about that article in the paper. She would like to find out what Jackie and Rev thought.

"Jackie, did you read the article in the *New York Times* last year–October–about the low academic performance of Middle Class Black students?"

"No. Rev doesn't get the *Times* every week. We let papers pile up. What did it say?"

"I let papers, magazines, and books pile up too, but my daughter and son-in-law told me not to miss this article. I made copies. According to the College Board, Black and Hispanic students perform far below White and Asian students of similar backgrounds. I brought copies with me and will give you one. Show it to Rev. According to the article, the information is significant since the number of middle-class Black families is increasing rapidly, and their children will expect to attend college. They'll have to compete with White and Asian students with far higher scores. Educators and their supporters make efforts to boost achievement of low-income Black and Hispanics. Middle-class students are neglected. And, Jackie, the gap is even greater between children of White and Black college educated parents than it is between children of parents who just finished high school."

A Jackie Sullivan pause, before she ventured cautiously. "We didn't see that article, but Rev and I discussed that there should be changes in African American attitudes about education–not just going to school–but books–reading at home. Even Rev and I–didn't have a library. Oh, we had a few books for the children. But nothing like we should have had–or like you had when we were growing up. You and Thomasena were the only girls I knew who had a book collection and used your own money to buy them and collected books libraries threw away in those days. –Rev had a set of theology volumes in his den. Dottie, we had no African

American books until after integration. *Crisis* magazines and colored papers made up our African American reading. Do you know we never even bought one colored doll. A church member gave a beautiful Black doll to the children one Christmas that they hardly played with, and was the first thing they gave to poor children whom Santa Claus might forget. –But Rev went and still goes to almost all Black meetings–and accepted and still accepts leadership roles in Black organizations."

Dottie was contented to let her friend talk, and Jackie continued. "You and Thomasena had a monopoly on Black books. I remember trying to read Jessie–what was her name?"

"Fauset."

"You and Thomasena just bragged about her and Nella Larson and Zora Neale Hurston. I forgot about them until Black Studies got popular. –Daddy had what I called doctor books and magazines in his study. I read about having babies and looked at the pictures. One day I got nerve enough to bring pictures of a baby inside a woman's uterus to one of the club meetings."

"I remember," Dorothy smiled. "That day I was supposed to tell what Daddy's law books said about rape, but didn't. We were too busy looking at those pictures."

"Your room was junky with books–stacked up on the floor. You and Thomasena lived in the library. You suggested that I go and told me what to read, not Mama and Daddy. I even went a few times. You read books by white authors, too. –Dottie, Rev got a set of Encyclopedias a man was selling. They stayed in the boxes for heaven knows how long, until I finally put them on Rev's shelves. One day I was dusting and looked through them. I stopped dusting and couldn't get back to it. To think all that information was in my house. Those books stayed on the shelves and still look almost new. –We don't stress reading and writing enough in our homes. My parents didn't when I was growing up, and we don't now–even though there is some improvement. We should put less importance on clothes, cars, and allowances and more on academics."

Dorothy agreed and added, "My daughter had a library in her room, but could use mine also. I got her Children's Encyclopedias and different sets as she grew older. I put books on her shelf, and she could add what she liked. I took her to Broadway plays. I didn't censor plays or books. She traveled out of the country with me. Met my NYU professors. She was the only middle class Black child we knew then who had that much exposure. And, Jackie, she succeeded–and so did all three of your children. And so did our friends' children in spite of what we did or didn't do. Of course, they had less competition with white students then."

Both women were silent, Dorothy wondering how African American children would cope in the Twentieth-First Century. Are middle class African American children, as one student told Dorothy years ago, spoiled?

"Jackie, the article stated that the problem is not discussed because of controversy."

Jackie asked, "Did the article give reasons for the low performance?"

"Yeah. It stated there might be hidden or elusive consequences of racial prejudice that are able to interrupt academic achievement. And that academic achievement among whites may be intergenerational and more ingrained. What causes me more concern is that researchers avoid the problem because of controversy. That is a disservice to African Americans. After you and Rev read the article, we'll hear what he has to say. It might be interesting to give copies to local people and have a session."

"Rev would like that. It'll give him a reason to use his new barbecue grill on the outside. He's only used it twice this year."

"Ask him, we can not only discuss the article, but Ebonics. And why just Ebonics and not Asiaonics or Hispanonics. —And discuss Marva Collins' philosophy of educating Black students. It'll be fun. Jackie, if it's O.K., I'd like to ask one or two people to join us. I'll make a financial contribution–."

"I know it'll be all right for you to bring somebody, but

Rev would be highly insulted if you even mention a financial contribution."

Dorothy laughed as she said, "Guess I'm thinking about Joe Cephus. –Tell Rev to set it up this week. I'm leaving next week."

Jackie pressed the gas pedal, as if rushing to begin the session.

Dorothy laughed and said that the Greensboro highway was a turnpike and Jackie should obey the speed limit.

CHAPTER 22

Dinner at the Royal Oasis

Less than the predicted two hours, the women were seated in the Royal Oasis Restaurant. Much more elaborate than Dorothy remembered, it was decorated with natural plants, small trees, shrubbery, and colorful flowers. However, it nostalgically resembled the Royal Oasis of her earlier years, just as Dorothy told herself that her grownup Christmases reminded her of childhood Christmases.

The seating area was much larger. Dorothy hoped the ladies' room was large and clean. They would order before going to do whatever and wash their hands. While Jackie called her husband from a telephone booth for customers now private and equipped with a seat, Dorothy discovered that the restroom facilities were larger, glistening white with gold framed mirrors. Really pretty, Dorothy smiled. There was an abundance of tissue paper, soap, towels, and hand lotion. A pleasing elusive aroma and soft music were unexpected additions.

Jackie told her that Rev asked if he should come and meet them. Knowing Jackie did not like to drive at night, she could trail him home. Jackie had told Rev no, but added "he'll come anyway."

To Dorothy's disgust, Rev's concern triggered thoughts of

the time her commuting car wouldn't start, and she had called Joe Cephus to come for them. His reply had been it was too cold, the highway was too slippery and dangerous. Her father had come. Dorothy refused to go to Joe Cephus' house that night and became angry now at herself for ever returning to his house. She was glad when Jackie interrupted with "Rev said try Creole shrimp."

Dorothy wanted to order lots of food, hoping Jackie ate more than she did when they were young. Dorothy usually ordered what she did not eat at home, something she was too busy to prepare. The menu surprised her. There were enticing headings, such as Continental, Foreign Dishes, Soul and Southern, Seafood, Vegetarian, and Unusual & Exotic. Along with Pastor LeGrande's suggestion, Dorothy ordered Southern fried chicken, peas and rice, and collard greens to take out—and of course, banana pudding. She'd have fun eating tonight in the hotel while assorting material. Enclosed in Reynolds wrap, it would stay warm or room temperature.

While waiting for the orders, Dorothy looked around the Royal Oasis. There were pictures and paintings on the wall of New York scenes Dorothy recognized and learned from the waitress were by local artists. Dorothy knew the improvements were to lure and retain Black customers integration might entice elsewhere. While they were eating, two White couples were seated. Jackie told Dorothy that White people came often to get Soul Food, and even had parties there, sometimes renting the place for the night.

Dorothy liked the Royal Oasis and wanted to return before leaving Granston. She had no idea she and Jackie occupied the same table that Joe Cephus and Johnnye did the night Johnnye walked out and left him with the enormous bill she had promised to pay. Dorothy and Jackie even ordered some of the same dishes. The restaurant retained most of its famous traditional specialties.

There were generous servings of everything. While Dorothy ate each course, including soup to pie a la mode, Jackie picked shrimps from her plate one by one and listened to Dorothy discuss another newspaper article about teachers cheating on an examination to boost students' grades. Dorothy told of a personal experience she had that might have been teachers "controlling" their evaluation: Second Language students wanted to know why she didn't tell them what column to mark when they were doing her evaluation since some of their "other teachers" told them what column to blacken with the Number Two pencil so they wouldn't mark the wrong answer. "I told them there was no right and wrong answers. I didn't want to do anything like that. It's not worth it. They would tell another teacher the same thing about me, and there was that Black Dean waiting to pounce on Black female Professors—'I gotcha.' The 'other teachers' were predominantly white females, and the Dean was scared of them."

Jackie said she had had no experience with teachers cheating. Sometimes they had students exchange papers and correct them if the answers were Multiple Choice or True and False.

While they waited for Dorothy's carry-out order, both women said they wouldn't mind being younger, they would like it in fact, but were glad they retired before schools became violent. Even colleges. It was frightening. They both hoped and prayed that Black students wouldn't mimic violent white students. People have a tendency to emulate vices instead of virtues . —Oh, teachers dating students? That was definitely a *no-no. Never below the college level no matter how much in love they are!* There had been occasional rumors in high school that girls had crushes on men teachers and men teachers "went with" female students. An intimate association was rare if it occurred. However, neither Dorothy nor Jackie had *ever* heard of a *female* teacher dating a student until recently. *—And never a colored female teacher.*

There was Rev standing in the doorway. "I told you not to come," Jackie smiled.

"I know how you feel about driving at night," and he gave Dottie a big hug, congratulated her again on her book, and asked her to please come to dinner, or breakfast, lunch, or all of them before leaving. Dorothy replied that Jackie would tell him about plans for a discussion. What about then? Fine. He would do the cooking. Not Jackie, he kidded . –His car was parked outside. Just follow him. And he would lead them safely back to Granston, and added with pretended pomp, "I have experience leading people, especially ladies, safely back to the fold."

Jackie trailing her husband, not letting him get too far ahead, his stopping for her to catch up if cars came between them, they headed back to Granston. Jackie driving carefully, peering as if she needed glasses, did not want to talk or be talked to, Dorothy perceived. It was fine because Dottie wondering when, if ever, she would return to Granston, fell into romanticizing it– but not really. For it had been the Land of her Youth. She knew it when rain water was pure, when she stood in Granston's rain showers, letting "the purest water there is," so her grandmother and mother said, fall into her open mouth as she held her head up and back. And she heard June bugs and saw butterflies and sun rays not yet frustrated by smoke and smog. And couldn't wait until night to see lightening bugs and hear frogs asking her to build toad frog houses. And in winter snow mixed with vanilla flavor and sugar became ice cream because snow melted into clean water. –Her life had grown like Granston, rain in her life no longer pure, June bugs and butterflies frightened away and exterminated by trucks that came in evenings spraying deadly gases. Sun rays in her life were frustrated by fog, smoke, and smog in her life. In winter she no longer made snow ice cream for snow left dirt and grime whenever it melted. –And Dorothy knew her seeking information was a further destruction of pure rain and sun rays, June bugs, butterflies, and lightening bugs.

"Jackie," Dorothy said quietly–with a bit of sadness, "I haven't danced enough."

After a moment, Jackie replied quietly, with texture Dorothy could not define, but knew it wasn't regret– and that it was Jackie's truth. "I have danced enough. I have waltzed, two-stepped, lindy-hopped, and even jitterbugged–my way. Dances that came later, I don't know anything about, so I don't know if I missed anything. I've danced enough." She looked ahead. There was Rev's car, slowing down, waiting, not too far ahead, but far enough to give space for safety if she had to make a sudden stop, but never completely out of reach or sight. "Like now," Jackie said, "I'm dancing."

CHAPTER 23
The Finale

Back at the hotel, Dorothy immediately began scribbling notes and assorting them. Since the best and most reliable source of information was beauty parlors and barber shops where men and women both relieved frustration and boasted, she would contact her former beautician for information about Joe Cephus and Johnnye. If Dorothy could not, she'd select a hairdresser for an emergency appointment even though she didn't need one. If necessary, she would even go to a barber for a hair cut–and find out who had been Joe Cephus' barber. Jackie had agreed to pick Dottie up at 8:30 A.M. the next morning. Dorothy reminded Jackie they would go to one of those forbidden drive-in places that served sausage or ham biscuits with eggs. It would be fun.

Dorothy covered the food container with a towel and began looking for her former beautician Carrie Lee Pickens in the telephone directory. –There she was–listed at her home address. Had to be the same person. It wasn't too late to call. Not even nine-thirty. People usually watched television until at least ten or eleven . – The party on the other end cleared her throat before saying "hello." After apologizing for calling so late, and explaining she was in Granston for just a short time, Dorothy identified herself and asked to speak with Mrs. Carrie Lee Pickens.

"This is Mis' Carrie Lee Pickens, and I certainly remember you, Mis' Borden. I seen in the paper you were here and would be at the li-berry talking about a book. I told a friend of mine I done your hair when you use to live here and taught in college. I don't do hair no more. Retired. But I want to see you and can recommend somebody for your hair. My husband died over five years ago, and I got plenty time. Still driving, except at night."

The same Mrs. Pickens, Dorothy thought, talking a mile a minute. Dorothy hoped she'd keep it up and run-off the way she did in the past. "My hair doesn't need doing. At least not now. Just want to see you. Trying to get around to my old friends–."

Flattered, Mrs. Pickens interrupted, "Where are you? I can pick you up tomorrow morning and bring you over here. We can have breakfast or go out. Colored–Black folks can eat anywhere. I don't go much. Specially since Mr. Pickens died. Not that he took me anywhere. I went out by myself when he was alive. Now I stay home. That's hind-parts-before, I know."

"I'd like to see you tomorrow morning. A friend and I are going to breakfast, and she'll bring me to your house afterwards. What time is convenient?"

"What about ten or eleven. We can eat lunch, relax, and talk."

Dorothy was pleased to hear they would talk and told Mrs. Pickens 10:30. Dorothy checked the address to be certain it was not different from the directory listing and gave Mrs. Pickens the hotel telephone and room number in event she needed it.

Dorothy got out a Native American sand painting and Dream Catcher to take as gifts to Mrs. Pickens. Better say Indian. That's what most people say. Dorothy brought Jackie a gorgeous handmade Native American bag and bracelet, and wished she had a bag for Mrs. Pickens. Dorothy examined her gifts to see if there was anything more impressive.

Time dashed by, the sausage and egg biscuits were delicious, and Jackie was now parked in front of Mrs. Pickens' house. "Don't worry about coming for me", Dorothy assured Jackie. If Mrs. Pickens couldn't take her back to the hotel, cabs were available. White and Black taxi companies had consolidated so it didn't make any difference. Jackie waited to be certain they were at the right place before slowly driving away.

Mrs. Pickens must have been waiting and watching. Just as Dorothy got out of the car, a tall heavyset lady with beautiful mixed gray hair appeared on the porch and met her in the cement walk. Dorothy's one hundred and four pounds were caught in an embrace.

"Miss Borden! I liked not to knowed you! You got so *small*. You never was no size to start wid. Guess you say you like not to knowed me–I got so *big*. Then I always was."

"I shriveled up, but you haven't changed much. –How many years has it been? –Twenty-five?

"About. Come on in and let me fix you something."

"No thanks. Remember I told you I'd eat breakfast with a friend before coming."

"Well drink something. Ice tea or lemonade."

"Water will be enough. Later on I'll take you to lunch."

"No," Mrs. Pickens protested, "you company now 'cause you been away so long. I'll take you out or fix something 'ere. Keep plenty food. Since I retired and Mr. Pickens died, I just eat and look at TV. Me and Joyful Noise."

"Joyful Noise?"

"My dog. I'll let 'im in after he finish his outside business. I remember 'ow much you like dogs, and you the only customer– and your daughter–who didn't laugh when I name my other dog Family. Y'all said it was all right because he was part of the family. Joyful Noise is name that 'cause I'm in this house by myself and when he bark, it's a joyful noise. Scares away robbers. He come when I call him J.N. too. Just like you told me years ago, I take 'im to his doctor to get shots and when he get sick. He eat what the doctor say. His doctor say not let him eat what I eat, but I give 'im a taste anyway. He want some so bad. Don't give 'im sweet stuff except a lil' ice cream." She went to the kitchen door and called, "J. N. Come on in if you finish."

In rushed a medium, shining black, pleasant looking mixed breed dog who barked friendly. "He knows you like dogs. I don't encourage nobody to come who don't. He with me at night. They not. Now go sit down," Mrs. Pickens told J.N. After Dorothy patted his head and caressed his soft shining fur, J.N. retired contentedly to a large fluffy doggie bed.

Mrs. Pickens smiled broadly over the gifts and could hardly wait to show her friends real Indian handmade presents Miss Borden brought her from Arizona and remind them she is the college teacher whose hair she did and who used to be married to that Joe Cephus Divine.—She must watch the way she said words, Mrs. Pickens reminded herself. Not that Miss Borden minded. She wasn't like some of them other teachers.

Dorothy wanted to start Mrs. Pickens talking. "You're here alone except for J.N. And scared of burglars. Maybe you should have married again. It's not too late."

"I'm not *that* scared. Me and J. N. do all right. A man's worse then a baby. Always got to wait on 'em. Wash. Iron. Cook. Clean up after 'em. Mr. Pickens got so he missed where he was supposed to go as big and white as it is and kept the bathroom smellin'. You know how clean I keep my house. After I house broke J. N., he never mess up. He go to that door and wait for me to open it."

Dorothy wanted to get her started on men and lead to Joe Cephus. "That's not like having a husband."

"That's why I like it," Mrs. Pickens laughed. "Besides, I'm not a fool. Nobody want me but somebody looking for a home. I ain't bragging, but this is a nice place, and I worked too hard to get it and keep it up. No man gonna come in at the last minute and get it and will it to his folks. No ma 'm. You marry again?"

Dorothy took this opportunity to take Mrs. Pickens as a confidant. Dorothy didn't care who knew it, she just had not announced it publicly in Granston, and it was customary to announce marriages in the paper. "I did marry again, Mrs. Pickens, but just didn't put it in the paper. He was white. Hungarian. That's not the reason I didn't announce it. People who visited me in New York knew and Mama did. Daddy died before I got around to telling him. He would not have liked it. I could tell. My marriage to the Hungarian lasted longer than the one to Joe Cephus." Now she had brought up his name.

"Well, white folks and black folks marrying these days, even 'round here.—Joe Cephus died. Guess you heard."

"Yes. What was wrong with him?" Dorothy asked.

Mrs. Pickens got two glasses and poured ice tea. "Who knows. He was sick a whole year 'fore doctors said it was high blood pressure . –Johnnye Jamison's–first husband died too. Doctor said he drunk too much. Johnnye seen to it that 'er husbands saw doctors *she* got for 'em. That first one was suppose to stop drinking after marrying her. Folks say he wasn't her first one to die. The first one was a man she married before she came to Granston. I don't know how folks find things out. Remember we use to say Dee kin find out anything about another Dee. Well, they said she poison her first one lil' by lil' 'til it built up and sent 'im to wherever he went."

"Why? Was he mean?"

"Folks say no. She got tired of 'im. He wouldn't divorce 'er. Just hung 'round. Got on 'er nerves. I can say this 'cause I know you won't repeat it–Folks say she had right smart insurance on 'im. And on John Henry Woodard–and a whole lot on Joe Cephus."

"How do people know?"

"Women come to get they hair did and talk. Johnnye might have told her women friends and they tell they women friends."

Dorothy didn't want to act too interested in the insurance. Too much concern might silence Mrs. Pickens. "How did Joe Cephus and Johnnye get along? I heard he treated her like she was a queen."

"He had to." Mrs. Pickens sipped tea. "The woman she went wid would help her beat 'im."

"What woman?" Dorothy feigned innocence.

"That's right, you wasn't here. Everybody know she was 'funny' but liked men, too. Joe Cephus Divine knew, but couldn't do nothing. She made 'im sell his house, he had no where to go, and had to stay wit her. Folks say he used to cry and started to move with his cousin, old lady name Daisy. Even policemen laugh at 'im. Made no difference 'cause Johnnye was a teacher. Folks say he was teacher-crazy and got worse after he married you and y'all got divorced. Folks say he even walked different. Thought he was too much a Big Shot to marry nobody but a teacher. All other women was below him. Well, folks say Johnnye sent him below."

"What's Johnnye doing now?"

"Goin' with Cora Lou Thomas same as she was when Joe Cephus was livin'. Johnnye got a man now, too, since she go both ways, folks say. She might have had 'im before Joe Cephus passed. She didn't pay a lotta 'tention to 'im when he got real sick. Folks started seeing her wit some man not long after Joe Cephus died. Didn't even give him time to get cold, as folks say about women who run around soon as they husband in the ground. Don't know if it's the same man, but Johnnye and a man eat at that white cafeteria where a lotta Black folks go. She and Cora Lou stay in Johnnye's house and sometimes in Cora Lou's house. One of my customers ax Johnnye if she scared to live in the house where Joe Cephus died. Johnnye said no. She wasn't scared of 'im when he was alive. She used to beat 'im every time he needed it. Even when he was sick. Folks say he got meaner and nastier then. Messed on hisself just to spite Johnnye. She stopped cleaning 'im. And he stopped messin'. He thought since he was sick he could get away with his meanness. Johnnye showed 'im. She wanted him to die in that hospital in Durham, but some folks down there who take care of patients when they dyin' put pressure on her to let 'im come home. Said he wanted to die with her holdin' his hands."

"Hospice?" Dorothy asked.

"No, but like Hospice, only they just take care of veterans. Folks said Johnnye cussed like a sailor and went off on a trip. Told the nurse what came to take care of 'im that she was just too upset to watch 'im die. He held on 'til she came back and passed few days later. Folks say his cousin stuck by 'im. He didn't leave her nothin'. Not even his dirty drawers, Johnnye told her hairdresser. His brothers and sisters came to stop Johnnye from having him cremated, but they left after they found out Joe Cephus signed the papers and left everything to Johnnye, 'his lovin' and devoted wife.' Folks say they told Johnnye to divide it. She did. Divided it with herself. Lord, did she talk about Joe Cephus. Said she deserved everything and more. She put up with 'im all those years. Pardon me, but I gonna tell you like it was told to me, she said she got tired of 'im wantin' her to sleep wit 'im. Too dumb to know he never could do much and now that he sick, he couldn't do nothin' at all ."

Dorothy smiled inwardly. "Was there a funeral?"

"Graveside. Buried his ashes. Folks say Johnnye say she just too upset to sit through a funeral. Johnnye so weak from grief they had to help her outta the car to get to the place where they buried his ashes. Folks say Johnnye say she didn't want to keep his burnt up ass. Pardon me for usin' that word, but that's what folks say Johnnye say. He didn't know what he was signin' when he sign to be cremated. I'm just tellin' you what folks say. Johnnye didn't want nobody runnin' they mouths so much that somebody might ax them to do what they do when they want to know why somebody died—"

"Perform an autopsy?"

"Yes. That's the word. Johnnye didn't want to spend money on a coffin. She'd been ashamed to get one too cheap. I heard they just put the urn in the ground. Somebody said it's a wonder Johnnye didn't have her first husband's grave open and put 'em in with him to save money. I don't think she want folks to remember her other husband died, too. Mostly the family was at Joe Cephus service. Not even the Police Department was invited. Some came anyway, and the Po-leece Department sent some real pretty flowers. Of course, Joe Cephus didn't have no friends, folks say.

They say Johnnye was dressed to kill at the ceremony. She always did dress up. 'Fore they married, Joe Cephus used to brag about how she dressed."

Mrs. Pickens continued after sipping tea. "I had a big funeral for Mr. Pickens. I looked nice, too. Wore navy blue instead of black. He didn't want me to wear black. Some folks might have talked about it. He went away in style. He had a lotta insurance, and I just used it the way he wanted me to. He had his faults, but he was all right in some ways. A good provider and I think he must have loved me–in his way. –Mis' Borden, some men, and I guess some women too but not as much as men, don't know how to let they wives and husbands know they love them. Mr. Pickens used to bring me ice cream and candy, and just say 'I put some cream in the freezer. Eat it,' or 'I brought some candy. You know I don't eat candy. Eat it.' I'd complain 'bout my weight, and he'd say 'I'm satisfied wit you. Look all right to me. –I got some extra money–here buy yourself another dress. You like to gota church. Wear the new dress, and I might go wit you.' Sometimes I'd catch 'im lookin' at me, and I saw somethin' like his kinda love."

"Did he die in here–in this house?" Dorothy asked.

"Right upstairs in our room. I moved to the one next to it where I could hear 'im. I thought about all the years we spent together and ice cream and candy–and that new dress. Folks told me I shoulda put him in a nursin' home, but I waited on him 'til he passed. God rest his soul."

Dorothy looked up the visible stairway and confessed. "Mrs. Pickens, I wouldn't live in a house where Joe Cephus died. Why didn't Johnnye sell it? To somebody who didn't know Joe Cephus."

Mrs. Pickens smiled. "Johnnye said he was scared of dogs except real little ones, and if he had the nerve to come back, her two big dogs'll send him right back to hell. She got two big ones in her back yard and a big and little one in the house. Joe Cephus was scared of big dogs. They better then alarm systems. Folks say Joe Cephus Divine ain't 'bout to come back. He was too glad to get away from Johnnye Jamison. Even hell is better–Mis' Borden, was he mean and crazy as some folks say?"

Dorothy breathed deeply, "Mrs. Pickens, being married to him was like being in hell without dying. Like living in Beelzebub's basement. I still say if I go to hell, I'll get time off for the time I spent married to him."

Mrs. Pickens laughed. "I'm not laughin' at you, Mis' Borden, but at the way you put it. One of my customers had a nephew who worked with Joe Cephus. That woman's nephew said Joe Cephus was so humble at the Police Department. Didn't talk much and looked so pitiful."

"He had an innocent look all right. Oh, but he was mean. An evil, wicked man, Mrs. Pickens. I wonder if he tried to beat Johnnye–in the beginning."

"I never heard about 'im fightin' her, but heard she could fight like a man and did if she had to. Joe Cephus was scared of her women friends. Folks said he knew about her bein' 'funny,' but scared to say anythin' and had no where to go after he sold the house he had when they married. Too stingy to get another place. His cousin moved to one of them senior places, and he couldn't live with her. Folks say he shoulda rented his cousin the house 'stead of sellin' it, and he'd had a place. Folks say Johnnye was Joe Cephus match. She was jes' as mean as he was. Maybe worse. He jes' beat colored women and scared of everybody else. Johnnye wasn't scared of nobody, even the superintendent, the law, insurance companies. I'm jes' repeatin' what folks say. Customers who come here say she was real nice to school children, and they was crazy 'bout her. And she was one of the best teachers in Granston, colored or white."

"Is Johnnye here now–in Granston?" Dorothy wanted to see the model for her creation.

"The lady what does her hair say Johnnye go away a lot. I saw her not too long ago in the Mall. Driving a Mercedes–2000. Vanity license. Got Y2K-ready on it."

"She must have money," Dorothy pushed her tea away.

"Don't you like tea?" Carrie Lee asked. "I read in health books that it's good for ya."

"Yes, but it makes me go to the bathroom too much."

"Go. Got one here. It's clean since Mr. Pickens gone. Always pay my water bill, so it flushes."

Dorothy smiled, retrieved the tea, and repeated, "Johnnye must have money." Not that Dorothy believed Johnnye had gotten rich, but she wanted to know if Johnnye were cunning enough to be comfortable for life.

"Folks say she have. They say she made 'im pay all the bills and sent her money to a cousin and aunt in Virginia or somewhere up that way. When they died, they will her her own money. She didn't have to pay no taxes on savin' it."

"What about insurance money?" Dorothy asked.

"Whatever it was, she got it all. Nobody knows how much. Not even her woman. Cora Lou told her she put up with her married to Joe Cephus all them years, and she ought get some of the money. Johnnye said Cora Lou can have her Watcha-Call-It, but not her money. One of her friends liked a woman I know. She said Johnnye used to go to a white accountant for income tax, but he axed too many questions, so she started going to a cul-lud –Black accountant. A woman. Give her big tips so she'll fix the reports."

"Why didn't Johnnye and Joe Cephus build–a better house? Black teachers in Granston have gorgeous homes."

"Folks say it was part of Johnnye Jamison's plan—makin' things look like she wasn't waitin' for 'im to die. Now she use the money takin' trips. Tours two and three times a year. She started 'fore he died while he was sick. Folks can't say she was waitin' for 'im to die before she start travelin'. She buy a new car almost every year. She always let the dealer be responsible for the car, and get a new one before she finish payin' for the last one and it's still under the warranty. Got lotta clothes and jewelry. The woman who Johnnye got to clean her house say it look like a palace inside. And Johnnye give her lotta clothes. They 'bout the same size."

"How does she look–Johnnye?" Dorothy asked.

"Good, everybody say. I don't know her that well, or see her often. What I see of her, she look all right. She taller and bigger then you. Her shape's not too hot, but not bad either. No waist line, but no pot-belly. Got nice skin and nice color. She and Joe Cephus 'bout the same color. Folks say he didn't like women, or nobody too black or too light."

"Did she care anything about him?" Dorothy wondered and asked.

"Some say she must have liked him some since he lived so long. Others say she let 'im live to keep down suspicion. There are them that say he was just hard to get rid of. One of her friends say Johnnye say he was too ornery to die sooner. Lived to get back at her."

Both women sipped tea silently until Mrs. Pickens asked hesitatingly, "Mis' Borden, bein' we talkin'–and bein' you and him divorced long time ago, I'm goin' to tell you something I heard from more then one woman–"

Dorothy felt heat come over her body. Was Mrs. Pickens going to tell her that Joe Cephus did what "colored men didn't do"–the forbidden thing that had him so irate he kicked her because a man she knew casually told him he knew a girl who liked to do "that." Dorothy did not ask what it was. She waited—

"–Mis' Borden, I heard that he was not good in the bed–that he couldn't do nothin'. Just thought he could. Johnnye not the only one who said so."

Oh, that–Dorothy sighed and smiled. She had heard it. Thus far Dorothy Borden had been truthful about Joe Cephus, and she didn't mind telling this truth. "Mrs. Pickens, I enjoyed him in bed until he kicked me and started mistreating me and forcing me to go to bed with him– and just–being abusive. I stopped wanting him. He was so cheap and stingy. He acted as if all he wanted me for was to pay bills and in the bed—and to be his housekeeper after his mother died. Mrs. Pickens, I stopped wanting him, lost respect for him, and actually hated him. And still do. I've heard women say, a man is mean and all but good in bed. I don't understand that. If a man mistreats me, the first thing that goes is my wanting him in bed."

Mrs. Pickens inhaled, paused. "Remember I told you about him going with a woman old enough to be his mother if she had 'im in her teens who he said tried to trick him into marrying her?"

"Yes." Dorothy also remembered that Joe Cephus had boasted about it to her during their marriage.

"She thought he was all right from what she said."

Dorothy paused, briefly wondering how she could include this conversation in her book. "Mrs. Pickens, I think sexual enjoyment is relative–I mean it depends on the people."

Mrs. Pickens sighed, "You might be right, but the man's got to be able to do enough to make it what you call relative."

Both women laughed aloud.

Mrs. Pickens looked at Dorothy carefully. "I wanna ax you something else. It's personal, too–"

"Go on." Dorothy didn't mind at all. She wanted to get as much information as possible and was willing to exchange. If it were too personal, she just wouldn't tell. To tell something you did not want people to know was sheer stupidity. Dorothy thought of people criticizing President Clinton for lying. If some arrogant Breaker-of-Treaties, In-The-Closet-Doing-the-Same-If-Not-Worse-Thing, or who-Can-No-Longer-Do-The-Same-If-Not-Worse-Thing, were to ask her would she lie under oath, she would tell the moron, I'd lie under *you*, Nut. My Ancestors did—

After the brief silence, Mrs. Pickens continued, "I don't know how to ax this–but you said you married a white man–"

"Yes."

"Can they–I mean, how're they in bed? I heard they not good as Black men."

Dorothy smiled. "I heard that, too. Mrs. Pickens, I certainly can't make an overall statement about White men anymore then I can make one about Black men. All I can say is my Hungarian husband was satisfactory. I have no complaints whatsoever of him in bed. I just don't like being married."

The former beautician mused. "Marriage's not what it's cracked up to be. Me and Mr. Pickens was together over fifty years. I married young. He was a lot older than me. He stopped 'carrying on' years ago. From what I heard other women say, he never did do much—and from the way they talked about they husbands, he weren't no size at all. I didn't know. He was the first and only real boyfriend I ever had. Guess that's why I stayed with 'im. I didn't know no better. Guess that's why he was so jealous. Didn't want me to do nothin' but work in this shop. Even would swell up sometimes when I dressed up and went to church. Said I was goin' to meet somebody or flirt wit the preacher." She sipped tea and stared into space. "Sometimes when I'm here eatin' too much and watchin' TV, I don't even know I'm eatin' and don't even know what I'm watchin'. I sneak a little Bourbon and wish I'd of left Granston and gone to New York or Chicago and had myself some fun. –Of course, I don't think I could've done what Johnnye Jamison did."

Both women smiled mischievously.

Dorothy seized the opportunity to get back to Johnnye and Joe Cephus. "Do you believe Johnnye was really responsible for Joe Cephus' death–and John Henry Woodard's?"

Mrs. Pickens, a contemplative look on her face, replied slowly, "Like the O. J. Simpson case, sometimes I do, and sometimes I don't. We Black folks don't kill like that. At least we didn't use to. Folks say we gettin' more and more like White folks, but in the wrong ways. —*How could Johnnye have did that and got away wit it?* How did she know what to do and cover it up and make it look like they just died from somethin' she had nothin' to do wit? She's not a doctor or nurse. When I was a child, people used to say nurses gave patients somethin' from a Black Bottle when they got tired of 'em. Ever hear that?"

"Yes," Dorothy admitted. "I used to hear people whispering

about a Black Bottle. A nurse lived not far from us, and I heard Mama and her friends whispering about her."

It's like a legend, Dorothy thought. It explains something people don't understand. Like a legend, some people accept it as fact and some take it as an interesting story. So the story of Johnnye Jamison became a legend among Black people in Granston. She became conversation material at parties, dinners, and impromptu social gatherings. Granstonians would take the intrigue with them on trips and vacations. They would point Johnnye out to visitors.

Time had passed quickly. "Let's eat lunch here. I always got plenty of somethin' good to eat," Mrs. Pickens enticed.

As the aroma of home baked ham, potato salad, hot rolls, and smells she couldn't decipher began to seep from the kitchen, instead of watching TV as Mrs. Pickens suggested, Dorothy began assorting mentally their conversation. –Dorothy suddenly had the idea that Johnnye and Joe Cephus had evoked literary illusions: Joe Cephus' marrying her had been his finest hour, his place in the sun. He had his Camelot, if only for one brief shining moment like the idealized city. —Like Ozymandias, Joe Cephus was reduced to "trunkless legs of stone" and "near them, on the sand half sunk," his "shattered visage lies."

Dorothy smiled at herself for thinking Joe Cephus suggested classic parallels. The thought began to take hold, and she saw paradigmatic allusions: She saw his resemblance to Tom Thumb, a minuscule man. Like Tom Thumb, Joe Cephus had escapades and escapes. Tom Thumb was swallowed by a cow as he lay asleep where she was grazing. Joe Cephus invaded Johnnye's turf as she "grazed"–while looking for a man who was looking for her. Asleep in that he was unaware of having made a foray, she devoured Joe Cephus. Tom Thumb crept up the sleeve of a giant and tickled him until he fell into the sea and was swallowed by a fish that was caught and taken to the King's palace. Tom Thumb met the King. The cow, giant, and fish symbolize Johnnye, and the house she occupied represents the palace. In the end Tom Thumb was poisoned by the breath of a spider. Joe Cephus had obeyed the invitation, "...walk into my parlor, said the spider to the fly."

Joe Cephus, like Icarus, flew too close to the sun, his wings of wax failed, and he fell into the sea. In a dual role, her bisexuality, Johnnye was also Daedalus, Icarus' father, who made the wings with feathers and wax and fitted them on his son. Johnnye fitted the wings on Joe Cephus.

As for Johnnye, like Biblical Delilah, she discovered the counterfeit Sampson Joe Cephus' vulnerable spot: his Narcissus quality. Joe Cephus loved himself unwisely. The best his world had to offer him, women of his choice, must love and want him for himself alone! That delusion was his Achilles' heel. –Johnnye was even like Fata Morgana in Italian folklore–a wraith in the guise of a beautiful woman who lured her pursuers into perilous places where they perished.

The sound of Mrs. Pickens bringing food into the dining room and the accompanying aroma signaled Dorothy that lunch was ready. And she was more than ready to return to her hotel room and record all that was churning around in her mind. She discretely, rapidly scribbled an ending to her account of Granston's secrets: While people point her out, Johnny Jamison Woodard Divine chews gum rapidly and at times carefully and slowly as she drives her 2000 Mercedes with Y2K Vanity license. Defiantly, she pops her chewing gum, its penetrating sound her trademark.

She has supplied the people of Granston with a story they know happened, but dare not believe.

END